D0446613

# The Dixie Widow

# THE DIXIE WIDOW

GILBERT MORRIS

BETHANY HOUSE PUBLISHERS
MINNEAPOLIS, MINNESOTA 55438

Cover illustration by Brett Longley,
Bethany House Publishers staff artist.

Copyright © 1991
Gilbert Morris
All Rights Reserved

Published by Bethany House Publishers
A Ministry of Bethany Fellowship, Inc.
6820 Auto Club Road, Minneapolis, Minnesota 55438

Printed in the United States of America

---

**Library of Congress Cataloging-in-Publication Data**

Morris, Gilbert.
The Dixie Widow / Gilbert Morris.
p. cm. — (The House of Winslow ; bk. 9)
1. United States—History—Civil War, 1861–1865—Fiction.
I. Title. II. Series: Morris, Gilbert. House of Winslow ; bk. 9.
PS3563.08742D59 1991
813′.54—dc20 90–23723
ISBN 1–55661–115–3 CIP

To Lynn

A man's firstborn<br>
is always a miracle—<br>
a gift from God.<br>
And you have always been,<br>
are now,<br>
and always shall be<br>
a treasure to me.

## THE HOUSE OF WINSLOW SERIES

★ ★ ★ ★

*The Honorable Imposter*
*The Captive Bride*
*The Indentured Heart*
*The Gentle Rebel*
*The Saintly Buccaneer*
*The Holy Warrior*
*The Reluctant Bridegroom*
*The Last Confederate*
*The Dixie Widow*

GILBERT MORRIS spent ten years as a pastor before becoming Professor of English at Ouachita Baptist University in Arkansas and earning a Ph.D. at the University of Arkansas. During the summers of 1984 and 1985 he did postgraduate work at the University of London and is presently the Chairman of General Education at a Christian college in Louisiana. A prolific writer, he has had over 25 scholarly articles and 200 poems published in various periodicals, and over the past years has had more than 20 novels published. His family includes three grown children, and he and his wife live in Baton Rouge, Louisiana.

# CONTENTS

PART ONE
## THE AGENT



PART TWO
## THE PRISONER



PART THREE
## THE MASQUERADE

PART FOUR
## THE PREACHER

# THE HOUSE OF WINSLOW

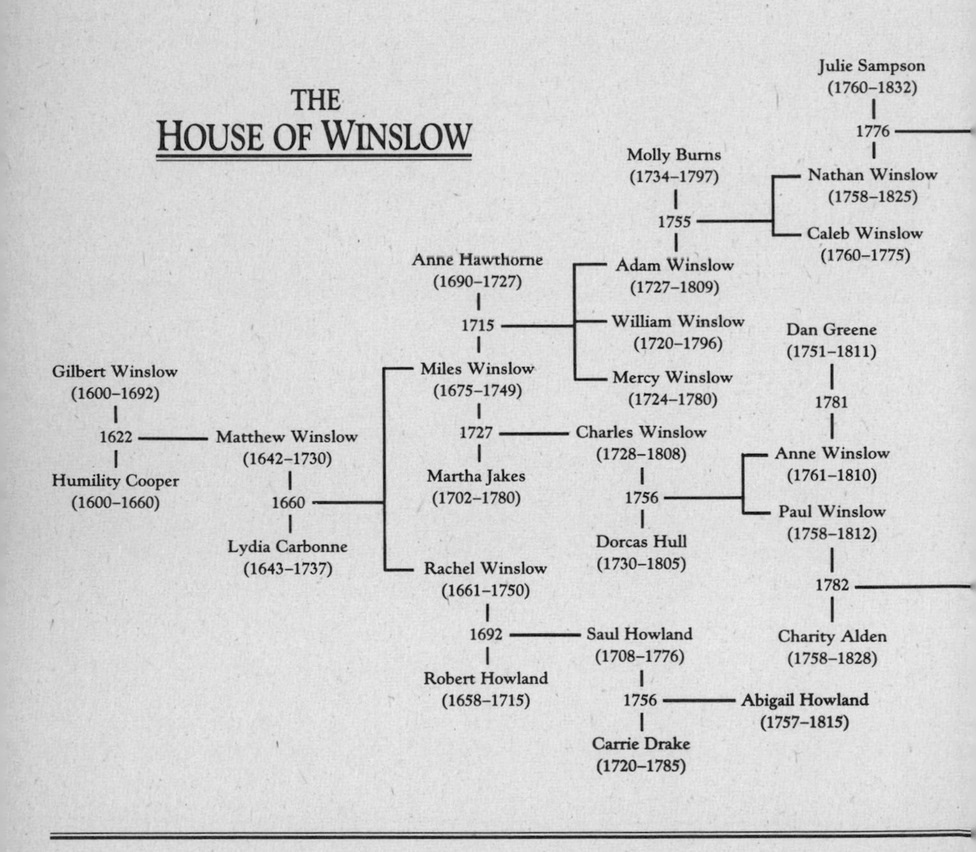

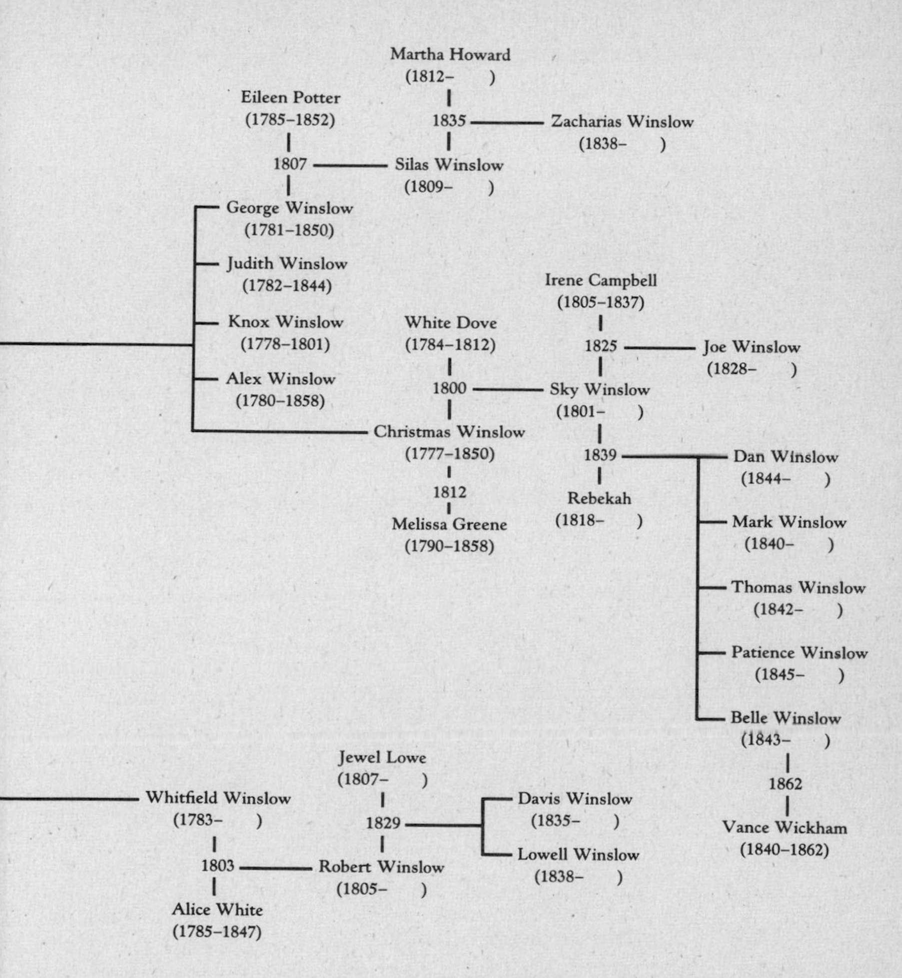

Martha Howard
(1812– )
Eileen Potter
(1785–1852)
1835
Zacharias Winslow
(1838– )
1807
Silas Winslow
(1809– )
George Winslow
(1781–1850)
Judith Winslow
(1782–1844)
Irene Campbell
(1805–1837)
Knox Winslow
(1778–1801)
White Dove
(1784–1812)
1825
Joe Winslow
(1828– )
Alex Winslow
(1780–1858)
1800
Sky Winslow
(1801– )
Christmas Winslow
(1777–1850)
1839
Dan Winslow
(1844– )
1812
Rebekah
(1818– )
Melissa Greene
(1790–1858)
Mark Winslow
(1840– )
Thomas Winslow
(1842– )
Patience Winslow
(1845– )
Belle Winslow
(1843– )
Jewel Lowe
(1807– )
1862
Whitfield Winslow
(1783– )
Davis Winslow
(1835– )
1829
Vance Wickham
(1840–1862)
1803
Robert Winslow
(1805– )
Lowell Winslow
(1838– )
Alice White
(1785–1847)

PART ONE

# THE AGENT

★ ★ ★ ★

## (October '62 – April '63)

## CHAPTER ONE

# A Cause to Die For

★ ★ ★ ★

Belle Wickham glanced quickly over her shoulder. The footsteps, faint but distinct, were coming closer. At first she thought it was the wind shuffling the crisp October leaves along the cobblestone street. Her heart raced as she peered into the darkness, but only the faint, bulky outline of the Confederate Chimborazo Hospital loomed behind her.

Belle had stopped to look at the bright yellow moon just perched above the First Congregational Church. The hour was late and she was on her way to the hotel where her father sometimes stayed. It had been midmorning when she had gone to help with the wounded, and the time had slipped away.

She hesitated, then remembered the warning her father had given that afternoon: "Better get back home before dark, Belle. Richmond's not as safe as it used to be—too many drunken soldiers and riff-raff roaming the streets."

Now, thinking of his words, she wheeled and walked rapidly down Cherry Street. The air seemed charged with danger as she hurried along the darkened sidewalk. Only the moonlight illuminated the center of the cobblestone street, casting deep shadows over the area. Because of the shortage of lamp oil—and everything else—in Richmond in 1862, street lights were reserved for special occasions.

Suddenly a man's bulky form appeared out of the darkness on the opposite side of the street. Belle stopped abruptly, frightened, then moved back into the shadows, her back pressing against the cold window of a shop. Fear gripped her as the man lurched across the street toward her. Her mind raced. What should she do? The police station! But that was five blocks down—on a side street! She could run or scream, but who would hear? Who would answer a cry for help?

The man moved unsteadily in her direction, mumbling in a rough, drunken voice. He stumbled, cursed loudly, then seemed to look straight at her. In the moonlight she could clearly see the outline of his heavy face. She remained motionless, thankful that she was wearing black. But even in that moment as fear washed through her, the thought of her widow's dress brought a bitter taste to her mouth.

A rising wind gave a keening note, and the drunk turned and lurched off, his muttering fading as he dissolved into the gloom. Belle sighed with relief and walked briskly, almost running, her shoes tapping a loud staccato on the sidewalk. As she reached Elm Street and moved across it, the town clock struck, sending its bass voice along the deserted streets.

She counted the brassy notes to herself until the eleventh sounded. In the silence that followed she heard the footsteps again. This time there was no mistake! It was *not* rustling leaves! It was the regular, crunching sound of heavy boots! She gave a gasp at the nearness of the sound and jerked her head around.

The tall outline of a man appeared not ten feet away! She began to run, but her heavy skirts and high-heeled shoes hindered her escape, and she stumbled, nearly falling. Catching herself, she heard the footsteps break into a run, and a voice called urgently, "Wait—!"

Belle's heart was beating wildly as she lifted her voice to scream, but before she could utter a sound he grabbed her and jerked her around to face him.

"Oh—help—!" she managed.

His hand clamped over her mouth, cutting off her words.

He was a large, powerful man, and pulled her into the recesses of a shop as easily as if she were a child. She tried to bite his hand, but his arms were like a vise. Stark fear clawed at her mind as he held her in the darkness. Her arms were pinned to her sides, and when she tried to kick him, he simply leaned against the wall, trapping her in an immobile position.

"Mrs. Wickham, please don't be afraid."

*Mrs. Wickham!* A flicker of hope raced along her nerves. *He knows me!*

The grip on her arms and the pressure on her mouth eased somewhat, and he said quietly, "If I release you, will you promise to hear what I have to say?"

She nodded quickly, and he slowly removed his hand from her mouth, pausing to see if she would scream. When she didn't, he dropped his arms and stepped back, saying, "Thank you."

She drew a deep, shuddering breath, and though she noted that he was dressed like a gentleman—not like a hoodlum—fear threaded her voice. "What do you want?"

"I must talk to you, Mrs. Wickham—but not here. Will you give me twenty minutes?"

His voice was soft, and even a few words revealed that he was educated. As she stood there regarding him, the fear turned to anger. "What is the meaning of this, sir!" she demanded. "If you want to talk to me, you can do so without attacking me on the street!"

"I can't argue with you here, Mrs. Wickham," he replied. "Give me the time, and I'll be out of your way—but I must speak with you now!"

"Where?"

"Anywhere you say—but we must not be seen together."

Belle stared at him, intrigued by his proposal. Now that she was fairly certain he would not attack her, she felt some assurance return, and said, "There is a place. Come with me."

As the man followed her, he noted with approval her swift recovery. She walked quickly, saying nothing as they covered two blocks, then turned off into a narrow side street. A single light threw out feeble rays in front of a two-story frame building with a sign PALACE HOTEL over the door.

"We'll be seen in there," he protested.

"There's no clerk on after ten," she answered, and without a pause entered the hotel. He followed, glancing around at the deserted lobby, then stepped beside her as she walked down a corridor dimly lit by a single lamp mounted on the wall. She stopped before a door near the end, fumbled in her small purse for a key, inserted it, and stepped in. "Light this candle from that lamp," she ordered.

With a slight grin at her bossy command, he entered the room and lit the lamp on the table while she shut the door. She removed her short cloak and stood waiting.

"My name is Ramsey Huger," he began, then paused. "I've been trying to see you for three days, Mrs. Wickham, but you're never alone."

Belle was examining him closely, noting his expensive attire. He wore a gray wool suit that accentuated his athletic figure, a pair of fine black boots, and a royal blue cloak, which he now removed, tossing it on a chair along with a rich-looking tan hat with a light brown band.

His face was square, and there was a bold look in his deep-set brown eyes. A small, thin moustache followed the contours of his lips, and when he smiled, as he did now, one side of his mouth rose higher than the other, giving him a sardonic look. His hair was carefully cut and brushed, and he had the air of a man secure in his good looks.

"Well, do I pass inspection?" he asked, noting her careful examination.

"Do *I*?" she shot back, her quick response bringing a slight flush to his broad cheeks.

He had seen her before, but always at a distance. Now he thought, *She's even better looking than they say.* She was somewhat taller than average, and her figure was perfect. Even the plain black dress could not conceal the slender waist and swelling curves, and her face was no less striking. Many women had one good feature and achieved the reputation of beauty by emphasizing it—but Belle Wickham's features were flawless, insofar as Ramsey Huger could tell. Her glossy black hair was coiled in a corona around her head, but would hang in a heavy weight if she let it down. Her skin was smooth and the coloring without cosmetics spectacular—cheeks that glowed with a rose tint, full red lips that curved softly, and large almond-shaped eyes. Her eyes were not black, as he had thought, but violet tinted and shaded by thick, inky black lashes that curved upward.

He smiled and said with some embarrassment, "Forgive me for staring, but—I suppose you're used to it. A beautiful woman like you must be."

She returned his gaze calmly, ignoring his compliment. "State your business, sir. Your twenty minutes are slipping away."

He was boldly handsome, accustomed to easy conquests, and her abrupt manner grated on him. He needed more time. He took out a thin cigar from a gold case, lit it from the lamp, and asked, "Whose room is this?"

"My father's."

"Ah, Mr. Sky Winslow." He puffed at the cigar thoughtfully, saying, "He's a man I admire greatly, though we've never met."

"Did you attack me on the street to tell me how much you like my family, Mr. Huger?"

He bit down on the cigar, took it out of his mouth and stared at her, still trying to find a way to gain her confidence. He knew this woman was almost as impulsive as he himself—that she might simply turn and walk out of the room. He was a gambler by choice, and now was the time for bold action. "I want you to be a spy for the Confederacy."

His blunt words had done exactly as he hoped—shocked Belle Wickham out of her self-assurance. Her eyes widened and her lips parted in an involuntary expression of surprise.

"Ah, you're not bored now, are you, Belle?" he said. "I had intended to give you a long speech, with patriotic references to our glorious Cause and a reverent tribute to your late husband, Captain Vance Wickham, the hero of Antietam. But with a woman like you, I think it's best to get right to the matter."

Belle was angry at her obvious reaction. She had always been able to control men, delighting at her ability to maneuver them. An impulse to whirl around and leave Huger rose in her. Instead, she squelched it and determined to drive that irritating gleam of self-confidence out of his eyes.

"That's a most interesting proposal, Huger." Belle half-smiled and commented, "I suppose we're on a first-name basis now?" She walked over to the chair and sat down. "How did you happen to choose me for this position?"

"You're a cool one!" Huger shook his head in admiration, then began to talk, at times pacing the floor, but coming several times to stand before her. "I know it sounds like something out of a bad French novel, but I'm being watched so closely that I had to come to you as I did tonight. If you do as I hope, you'll be marked immediately if you're ever seen with me." He gave her a direct look and added, "It could mean your life."

Belle stared at him. "Who's watching you?"

"Sloan—Jeremy Sloan. The top agent of Allan Pinkerton, head of Union Intelligence."

"I've heard of Pinkerton."

"He has a large organization. We've caught up with three double agents already."

"What's a double agent?"

"A spy who comes over from their side and makes his way into our intelligence system. They're deadly, of course, because we have to trust them with secret information." He paused, his face intent. "That's where *you'd* be most valuable."

"You're really serious about this thing?" She couldn't believe what she was hearing.

"I'm serious about winning the war," Huger replied, "and if you're as smart as I think, you'll realize we don't have much hope. The Yankees have all the cards—an unending supply of men, munitions factories, food supplies."

"But we're beating them!"

"No, we're only winning battles." He shook his head sadly. "But their strategy is to wear us out. Every time we lose a man, he leaves a gap in our ranks that can't be filled because we don't have the manpower. When a Yankee soldier dies, all the Union has to do is reach into the big cities for a replacement."

"I don't believe that!"

"No? Your father does."

"You're lying! You already said you didn't know him."

"I don't—but I know others who *do*. He's one of the most sensible men in the government—but there are so many fools that your father can't be heard."

She thought about the past months. Her father had said some of the same things. For two years the war had been played out, and only a fool could ignore the decline that was slowly drawing the South down. Intuitively Belle knew this man was telling the truth.

"I'm not a spy."

"Neither am I," Huger shrugged. "Not by profession. I'm a lawyer. But I want to help my country." He slapped his hands together angrily, adding, "Believe it or not, I'd rather be in the army! I get so sick of people staring at me with contempt because I'm not fighting!"

She was moved with compassion for him and said quietly, "It must be very difficult." She felt an urge to reach out to him. Instead, she curbed the impulse and asked, "Is this *your* idea—my being a spy for the Confederacy?"

"Yes. Other women have done the same thing. You've heard of Mrs. Greenhow and Belle Boyd?"

"Of course!" Belle responded. Both women had been apprehended as spies and were in Federal prisons. "I admire them, but—"

"But you don't believe you could do what they've done? Let me tell you what I think. Then you can make up your mind." She nodded, and he continued. "Everyone in Richmond knows two things about you. First, they know how hard you've taken your husband's death, and that you've sworn a vow to remain a widow until the Yankees are whipped."

"It's horrible to be on everyone's lips," Belle said bitterly. "They call me 'The Dixie Widow.' "

Huger nodded. "So they do. They say you claim the South as your husband now, and that you never think of anything but seeing the Yankees ejected from our country."

"That's true," Belle nodded. "When my husband was killed, I think I lost my mind for a little while."

"You had so little time together. I—I am sorry," he murmured kindly.

Belle looked up, tears in her eyes. She dashed them away and said quickly, "I usually save my tears until I'm alone. Now, what's the other thing everyone knows about me?"

"That you have relatives in the North who are strongly for the Union." He paused. "I think the court-martial of young Novak caught everybody's attention. It was very dramatic, wasn't it?"

Thad Novak had come from New York at the end of 1860 and had worked at Belle Maison, Belle's home. He had become a favorite with them all—especially Patience Winslow, Belle's sister. Belle thought of the young man and nodded. "He shocked us all when he joined the Confederate Army as a paid substitute—and used the money to buy a slave's freedom."

"That didn't do him any good, I suppose," Huger replied. "What did you think when he was charged with desertion and treason?"

Belle shook her head firmly. "We knew he didn't do it—but the evidence was so strong." A smile lit up her face. "My sister Pet rode into the Union lines to bring back the witness who saved Thad's life."

"I heard about that. A relative of yours—Captain Lowell Winslow. His grandfather is a retired naval officer, Captain Whitfield Winslow—who is now a frequent advisor for Gideon Welles, the Union Secretary of the Navy."

"And you want—"

"Whitfield Winslow has a son, Robert, in the House of Representatives—whose wife is very close to many key political figures—including Mrs. Lincoln."

He stopped, catching the guarded look in Belle's eyes.

"And you want me to—to *use* these people?"

"Yes," Huger admitted, putting his hand on her shoulder. "Belle, think of it! You could do something for your country that *nobody* else could. You'd be able to pick up information that gets batted around at parties where important people attend. Then, when you gained their confidence, you could give them information that would help us. You could say, 'Oh, I've just heard from my cousin that General Lee's army has built up to a hundred thousand men!' When McClellan hears *that*, he'll stop dead in his tracks!"

"But everyone in Richmond *knows* how I hate the Yankees. Surely that agent—what's his name, Sloan?—he'll know it as well. He'd report it, wouldn't he?"

"He certainly would," Huger nodded. "So you must change your story."

"What?"

"You'd have to make an about-face," he said evenly. "You'd have to convince everyone that you've changed your mind. You're angry at the South for starting this war that killed your husband. You'd say that we're doomed to lose, and the quicker we give up, the better off we'll be."

"But—nobody would believe me!" Belle exclaimed.

She expected Huger to argue, but he didn't. He stood there staring at her carefully. Finally he said, "Then it's a washout." He studied her a moment and added, "Belle, it's asking a lot. I think you could do it—convince everyone that you've changed. But if you did," he warned her, "your own people would hate you."

Belle nodded slowly. "Yes. I know how we all talk about traitors, people who turn from the Cause."

"I couldn't help you with that," he said quietly. "Nobody could. You'd have to bear it alone. I can't even urge you to do it—because I'm not sure *I* could go through with it. It's a thing you'll have to decide."

Ramsey Huger was a good lawyer. He knew the danger of saying too much. He'd seen juries ready to vote *not guilty,* but when he'd said just a little too much, they'd been talked out of doing just what he wanted. So he stood quietly, admiring her face, but convinced she would refuse the proposition.

Belle sat silently, confused and afraid. One moment she was ready to rise and leave the room—for she knew what anger and bitterness would fall upon her if she agreed to Huger's plan. But she was also forced to think of her duty. *I've been nothing but a party girl all my life,* she mused. *How can I do this thing?* She thought of Vance, her husband, and of the few precious days they'd had before he marched off to die at Antietam. Thad Novak had been with him when he drew his final breath, and she recalled his last words as Thad reported them: *You're the best thing that ever happened to me!* She rose and walked to the window.

Staring into the murky night, Belle *knew* what she must do. She turned slowly and came to stand in front of Ramsey Huger, her eyes large and a tremor on her lips.

"My husband died for the Confederacy. If it comes to that, I can do the same. Tell me what I have to do!"

## CHAPTER TWO

# JUST ANOTHER SOLDIER

★ ★ ★ ★

The three officers dismounted in front of the large white two-story mansion, handing their horses over to a tall, massively built black man who grinned broadly, saying, "Sho' is good to see you gentlemen back to Belle Maison! Miz Winslow done say she gonna stuff you lak Thanksgiving turkeys!"

He spoke to all three, but his eyes were on the youngest, Third Lieutenant Thad Novak—for the young man had bought the black man's freedom by joining the Confederate Army as a substitute for a rich man's son. "Miss Pet—she say fo' you to come ovah to de barn, Mistuh Thad. Dat new sow is havin' her fust litter of pigs—and she say you gotta help."

Mark Winslow, first lieutenant of the Richmond Blades, laughed at the look on Thad's face. "Now, there's romance for you, Beau! No moonlight and roses for this lover!" At twenty-two, Mark was the oldest of the Winslow boys, and the darkest.

Captain Beau Beauchamp was by far the largest of the three. He was a handsome twenty-one, six feet tall, and powerfully built. He gave young Novak a smile, his light mustache twitching. "I guess nobody will call you a Yankee now, Thad. No real Yankee would do his courting in a barnyard over a pregnant sow."

Thad glared at the two out of an angular wedge-shaped face.

His black eyes were set between high slavic cheekbones. "You gentlemen treat your women in your own way," he said with a flare of humor. "Pet and I will take care of our own courtin'!"

He turned and walked away, and Beauchamp laughed. "I never thought I'd grow fond of that young fellow—but I have." He thought of the early days of the war when he had been highly suspicious of Thad Novak, and had done all he could to get Sky Winslow to put the Northern boy off Belle Maison. He added as they went up the steps to the house, "He's going to be a good officer, Mark—after he gets over the shock of his promotion."

"Not many men are breveted from a corporal to third lieutenant by Robert E. Lee," Mark remarked thoughtfully. "He earned it though, the way he saved the major at Antietam." Thad had gone in under heavy fire and pulled Major Shelby Lee, a nephew of General Lee, to safety. That terrible day more men died than on any other single day of battle in American history.

As they entered the house, Beauchamp commented, "Too bad we couldn't have saved Vance as well."

The still form of Captain Vance Wickham as Mark had last seen him, slain by a sharpshooter's ball at Antietam Creek, was ever in Mark's thoughts. Not only had Wickham been his sister Belle's husband, but he was much more than that. "I still can't accept it, Beau," he said as they took off their cloaks and handed them to Lucy, the housemaid. "I keep looking around expecting to see him."

"And I'm supposed to take his place as captain," Beauchamp frowned, and shook his head as a gloomy look swept across his face. "It just about wiped me out when Belle chose Vance instead of me," he murmured. "But I never hated him—as I would have just about anybody—"

"Mark! Beau!" Rebekah Winslow ran excitedly down the stairway. She hugged Mark, and smiled at Beau. "Come now, Captain, don't you have a kiss for an old woman?" At forty-four, Mark's mother was an attractive woman. Her figure was still shapely, and her auburn hair had lost none of its curl over the years.

"No—but I've got one for you," Beau grinned, and kissed her on the cheek and stepped back. "I've wanted to do that for a long time—but that jealous husband of yours is always around."

"I still am!"

Sky Winslow had entered unnoticed, and grinned broadly at the two men. "With all the other jealous men in the county, I'd have to get in line, Captain Beauchamp." At sixty-one, Sky Winslow's hair showed only a sprinkle of silver at the temples. His blue eyes still held that electrifying quality in his dark face. Being half Sioux, he had been named after the unusual color of his eyes. He shook hands with both men and asked, "Where's Thad?"

"Oh, he and Pet are having pigs in the barn," Mark grinned.

They all laughed. "It's a good thing someone in this family has a little practical knowledge," Sky commented. "Come sit down. I want to hear how you've been winning the war."

They filed into the parlor and for the next hour, Rebekah scurried in and out, preparing supper while listening to the news from the front.

"We got cut up so bad at Sharpsburg," Mark said sadly, "that we've been hard put to fill the gaps. It's not as easy to recruit as it was in the beginning."

"But we're almost up to full strength, sir," Beau added enthusiastically. "We'll be ready to meet whoever Lincoln gives the army to."

Sky Winslow listened intently, his face in repose, but he knew much more than the young officers were aware of. As a special assistant to President Davis, he was privileged to sit in many high-level meetings, often with General Lee and others. "I don't want to be a prophet of gloom," he said slowly. "But we're going to be hit harder than ever in the next few months."

"I suppose so," Beau shrugged, "but we'll be ready."

"We gave it all we had the last few months—and it wasn't enough." There was a strain in Sky's face as he spoke. "The plan was to launch a threefold offensive—invade Maryland, hit Kentucky, and roll up Grant's army." He held up his fingers and slowly ticked them off, saying, "The invasion of Maryland stopped at Sharpsburg, Bragg lost at Perryville on the eighth and had to pull out of Kentucky, and Rosecrans whipped us at Corinth."

"But we hurt them, sir!" Mark interjected. "They say that Lincoln is trying desperately to find himself a general like Lee or Jackson."

Sky smiled as Rebekah came back and sat beside him. "I'm too gloomy," he admitted. "Let's have a good supper and forget the war."

"How's Belle doing?" Mark asked.

Sky and Rebekah exchanged a look that both men caught.

Beau asked hesitantly, "She's still taking it hard?"

"I—we've been dreading your return, Mark—and you, too, Beau," Rebekah said sadly. "You know how we long to have you home, but—" Rebekah broke off in agitation and walked to the window.

"What's wrong?" Mark asked in bewilderment. "Has she been sick?"

"No, not that," Sky said. "But she's broken mentally, Mark."

Both men stared at him, and Beau asked incredulously, "She's lost her mind? I can't believe that!"

"Neither could any of us," Sky answered. "But you know how she almost died over Vance's death? Never smiled, and began saying she'd never rest until all the Yankees were either driven from the South or dead?"

"She *was* frantic," Mark admitted. "I was worried about her."

"So were we all." Rebekah came back and sat down beside Sky, taking his hand. "But she wouldn't listen to any of us. Everybody knew how she was. They called her 'The Dixie Widow.' "

"We thought she'd get over it," Sky spoke up. "But about two weeks ago she began to change." He frowned at the memory, adding, "If anything, she's worse off than she was hating the Yankees."

"For goodness' sake!" Mark burst out. "What's the matter with her? Tell us!"

"She says now that the South is all wrong," Rebekah replied. "She blames the government for starting the war that killed Vance." Fighting back the tears, she whispered, "It started with a few complaints—but it's gone far beyond that now!"

"We had to tell you—so that you wouldn't be caught off guard," Sky said painfully. "And Pet will tell Thad."

"Maybe shes had—some kind of a nervous breakdown," Mark muttered. "Has she seen a doctor?"

"No. She says there's nothing wrong with her," Sky answered

stonily. "You'll hear it soon enough if she comes in to dinner. Try to be patient with her. I—I'm more afraid for her than I am for you boys."

He got up abruptly and left, with Rebekah following. "I'd better go with him," she whispered. "He's taking it very hard."

"I still can't believe it, Mark!" Beau got to his feet, his blue eyes reflecting helplessness. "Belle's not that weak!"

"You have to remember," Mark returned, "Belle never had to face anything difficult before. She's always had everything she wanted. This is the first time she's ever had to face hardship. And we've seen some pretty steady women collapse under this kind of grief."

They sat silently, thinking of the vivacious girl who had reigned over Belle Maison since she was sixteen years old. Finally the men went to their rooms until Lucy's call to dinner. As they came down the stairs, their hearts were filled with apprehension.

The table in the small dining room was set with silver, and the gleam of old china reflected the hundred candles burning in the chandelier overhead. Both men immediately looked for Belle, but she was not there.

"Hello, Pet," Mark said, going to kiss her. "Did your pigs make it?"

"Oh yes!" she smiled happily. "Fifteen of them—and all little darlings!"

At seventeen, Pet Winslow would never be the beauty her sister was, but she didn't mind in the least. She was a wholesome girl with a nice figure, and a face that was strong rather than pretty. A pair of large gray eyes, a small nose, together with a prominent dimple and a widow's peak gave her a piquant look. She had fallen head-over-heels in love with Thad Novak and now took hold of his arm, saying, "It's so exciting being engaged to an officer in the Richmond Blades!"

"More exciting than birthing pigs?" Thad grinned.

"Just slightly," she teased. Then a shadow swept her face as she saw her sister enter. "Why, Belle, I thought I'd have to go and get you."

Beau hurried forward to greet her, holding out his hand. "Belle! It's so good to see you!"

The hand she offered him was limp, and her eyes dull, not

alive and shining as he remembered. "Hello, Beau—Mark." She allowed Mark's awkward embrace, then went to her chair.

A silence fell over the room. "Well, I guess you young men are starved for some good home cooking!" Rebekah said nervously, trying to lighten the heaviness. "Sky, will you ask the blessing?"

They bowed their heads and Sky prayed, "Lord, we thank you for the good food, but we are more grateful for the safe return of our young men. Thank you for that in the name of Jesus Christ."

When they raised their heads, Sky warned, "Don't get your hand too close to Thad's plate, Mark. It's a good way to lose it!"

Thad blushed and the others laughed at his embarrassment. The meal went on as Lucy brought in platter after platter of food—chicken, chops, roast, followed by late vegetables, all eaten with gusto by the three officers.

While Pet kept them entertained with her plans for Thad during the brief furlough, Beau studied Belle covertly. She was as beautiful as ever. Even the harsh black dress could not hide that, but she seemed somehow harder. Before, she had always been happy and bubbly. Now she sat there eating only a few bites, her head bowed, except for an occasional glance around. When she did look at Beau, there was no warmth in her dark eyes. Instead, her expression was enigmatic and she seemed to be studying him as she would a stranger. It unnerved him, and he began to see what the Winslows had tried to explain.

As they finished the main courses and began enjoying the blackberry cobbler swimming in thick cream, the conversation turned to the war. It was inevitable, for their world was surrounded and formed by it, but even as Mark and Sky talked of battles and strategy, Beauchamp saw Belle's face assume a cast of distaste. Her lips thinned and she stared at her plate in silence.

"Well, Beau, where do you think the next campaign will take place?" Sky asked.

"Most of the officers say the Yankees will mount some sort of drive on Richmond again," he replied. "They've lost so many men, though, that the Northern newspapers are calling their generals 'butchers.' I guess most of them are, the way they feed their troops into deathtraps—"

"Well, aren't all generals 'butchers'?" Belle broke in bitterly, her lips twisted with anger. "How many of our Southern men have died needlessly?"

A thick silence invaded the room. Finally, Mark spoke. "Nobody likes war, Belle. But we've got to fight—and some of us will have to die for our Cause."

"And what good does the *Cause* do Vance now?" Belle demanded sharply as her eyes swept the room. "We'll never win this war. And who's dying in it? The *best* men! They rush to join the fight, while the cowards lag behind. I've heard you say so yourself, Father. And after all of our best are killed and our worst are left, what will remain to build on?"

"Belle!" Sky protested.

But she brushed his words aside and went on. "Richmond is doomed. Every day the ring draws a little tighter. They're digging up old outhouses now to get nitre to make gunpowder! We're out of weapons, and can't get any from overseas because the blockade is strangling us!" She jumped to her feet, and in a voice edged with hysteria she cried, "My God! The South is dying, and you all sit here and talk about going to fight as if it were a picnic!"

She whirled and ran to the door, stopping to turn and face them, her eyes wild as she whispered, "Well, I lost my husband to this war—but I'll not lift a finger for your precious *Cause*! Never!"

She fled up the stairs, leaving them white-faced and ashamed, as though they had observed something obscene.

"Now you know," Sky said heavily. Then he got up and left the room, and the rest followed as quickly as they could.

"She's—she's lost her mind," Mark groaned as he walked out of the house with Beauchamp. "My poor parents!"

Beau stopped short, feeling as if someone had punched him in the stomach. "I'm going back to town, Mark. I can't stand this."

Beau departed immediately and Mark returned to the house, where he found Rebekah standing at the window looking out.

"Mama, do people know about Belle?"

"Yes, they do," Rebekah answered and came to stand beside him, reaching out her hand for support. "She's made her views known all over Richmond. Not only that, there was a journalist who took it all down. He did a story in the Richmond paper—all about how one of our greatest heroes has been disgraced by his widow's behavior."

"Mama, no!"

"She's leaving, Mark."

"Leaving! To go where?"

Rebekah's gentle eyes showed the pain she felt. "She says she'll not live in a country that's bent on suicide. She's going to the North."

Mark stared, incredulous. "She's insane, isn't she?" A wave of bitterness swept over him. "She'd be better off dead!"

"Mark! Don't say that!" Rebekah clung to him, and finally regained control of her voice. "We must pray, Mark! God will have to help her!"

★ ★ ★ ★

Belle had met Ramsey Huger only twice since she had agreed to become an agent—once at a deserted house just outside of Richmond on a dirt road and once on the platform of the railroad station at dusk. Each time he had been impressed with her determination, telling his superior, a short man named Les Butler, of the girl's progress. "She's a natural actress, Les," he had said. "And with the story in the paper about her Union sympathies, word will seep into the North right away!"

"I take credit for that, Ramsey," Butler smiled. "The writer was my man!" Then he had said, "Get her in place as soon as you can—but it'll have to be done right. The Yankees are a little harder to fool now than when Mrs. Greenhow and Belle Boyd first got to them."

The still morning air hung over the city as Huger rode along a deserted country road. He was not surprised to see a carriage waiting in front of a burned-down house, for it was the spot he and Belle had agreed on the last time they met. He rode up, dismounted and quickly tied his horse to the rear of the buggy. As he got inside, she gave him a quick smile, and he almost kissed her—but not quite.

"Ramsey, I've got it—a letter from Captain Winslow!"

He took the envelope but kept his eyes fixed on her face.

"Belle, I've been worried about you," he said, putting his hand on hers. "It's been hell on you—and I've been unable to do anything."

She blinked at his obvious concern, gave a short laugh, and said, "Never mind. It was something that had to be done."

"Your people—they all hate you, I suppose?"

"No. It'd be easier if they did." She faltered, then pleaded, "Ramsey, let me tell them! Please!"

"You mustn't, Belle!" he insisted. "They're not actors, you know. And they're being watched—carefully watched! If just one of them failed to keep up the deception, it'd bring great harm!"

She dropped her head, whispering, "I suppose—but they just—keep on loving me—and being so kind . . ."

He put his arm around her and tipped her face up. "Who could help that, Belle?" Impulsively he lowered his head and kissed her.

Belle knew it was wrong, but she had been alone for so long, cut off from her family and ostracized by almost the entire population. His caress was unexpected, and she let his lips rest on hers, savoring the moment of tenderness . . .

"Don't do that again, please," she said quietly, drawing back. "I'm lonely and you're an attractive man. I have no doubt many women have found you so—but I didn't agree to give up my life for a flirtation."

He was wise enough to say at once, "I apologize—but at the same time, Belle, I promise you it was not that kind of kiss."

"Oh, never mind, Ramsey," she said wearily, adding, "The letter is from Captain Whitfield Winslow. It's an invitation to visit him in Washington."

"Great!" Huger cried excitedly as he removed the letter and scanned the contents.

Mrs. Belle Wickham
Richmond, Virginia
November 20, 1862

My dear Mrs. Wickham:

Of course I remember you! My grandson Davis and I have spoken often of you since our visit to Richmond, and my other grandson, Captain Lowell Winslow, has mentioned you in his letters more than once.

I grieve over the loss of your husband. I remember him very well, though I met him only once, I believe. I am an old man, Mrs. Wickham, and have seen much death, but have never grown callous, I trust. When I say that I grieve with you, it is not an idle remark.

As to your present views on this terrible war, I can only say that you are not alone in being confused. Many of our people have great sympathy for the Confederacy, and now you seem to have changed your own view. I realize how uncomfortable it must be for you, holding such views, and I would like to help you.

If you feel that moving to the North would be better for you, I offer my help; however, you must understand that many will be suspicious of your motives. If that is clear, and if you feel that you must leave the South, I will do all in my power to help you—and my son Robert and his wife will, no doubt, feel the same way.

Come when you will. I am somewhat indisposed, but Davis is here and will be available to meet you and see you settled.

Sincerely,
Captain Whitfield Winslow

"What an opportunity!" Ramsey exclaimed with a broad smile as he gave it back to her. "When do you leave?"

"As soon as possible," Belle replied. She held the envelope, hesitated, then gave him a strange look. "I am going to betray this old man's confidence. How can I find it in my heart to do that?"

He knew she wanted assurance, but he was careful to say, "Belle, don't you think I've had to do the same? All of us do in this work. It's not a thing we'd do in peace time—but in a war a different set of morals come into play. Every soldier in the line tries to shoot the enemy—a thing most of them wouldn't think of if they weren't caught up in a war."

She nodded, sadness in her voice. "You're always saying we have to do a lot of wrong things in order to get one right thing."

"That's what war is, Belle—and you're no different from any

other soldier. If you're caught, I guarantee they'll execute you."

"I'm not afraid of that," she said, lifting her head proudly. "But I don't want to become callous, Ramsey! I believe in our Cause, and I'll do this job—but I'm afraid of what it will do to me."

Thinking quickly, he knew it was time to give her the full story. "Belle, we've talked about what you'll do when you get the confidence of the people there—but I don't think you really understand it."

"Why. . . ?"

"Belle, listen to me. You remember we've talked a lot about Colonel Henry Wilder?"

"Yes, of course. He's the officer who's known to be talkative about what he hears in meetings."

"Yes, but do you understand that in order to get information from him, you may have to . . . do things that will seem wrong to you?"

She stared at him as the impact of his words sank in. A strong feeling of revulsion swept over her face. "Nothing was said about—about *that*!"

"Belle, I thought you understood." The anger and distaste on her face was so strong, he knew she was on the verge of refusing the assignment. "Let's not worry about that now," he said hurriedly. "Just go to Washington and keep your ears open. You'll be a help to us—you'll see."

The morning light coming through the window fell across the young woman, wrapping itself around her like a cocoon. Not a muscle moved as she watched the horizon turn pink. She was stirred in her heart, fearful of the consequences of this mad adventure she had agreed to. Finally she nodded slowly, "I'll leave as soon as possible, Ramsey."

"Fine! Fine!" he responded, and then they carefully went over the procedures she would use when she was in Washington. Finally he walked her to the buggy and paused, his eyes thoughtful. "Be careful, Belle," he warned. "I don't want anything to happen to you."

She flashed a smile. "I'm just another soldier, Ramsey!"

## CHAPTER THREE

# AGENT IN PLACE

★ ★ ★ ★

"If you'd only *ask* before you go off on these wild tangents!"

Robert Winslow stood over the elderly man on the couch, glaring at him with intense irritation. Robert had been an officer in the United States Navy, the leading criminal lawyer in the state of New York, and was presently a powerful member of the United States House of Representatives. All of his life he had, by the force of his personality, been able to overwhelm juries, legislatures, and even one president—but he had absolutely no power to sway the frail white-haired man who lay back looking at him with amusement.

"Why, Robert," Captain Whitfield Winslow said, "I never thought of mentioning it to you." He considered his son with a glint of humor. "You're so busy running the House, I didn't want to bother you with such a small thing."

The "small thing" that had touched off the younger Winslow's anger had been the captain's announcement: "Oh, by the way, I've got a new housekeeper coming." Robert had been agreeably surprised, for since his father's accident, which resulted in a broken ankle, he had been trying to get him to hire a full-time housekeeper. But the elderly man had stubbornly insisted on getting along with the help of his grandson Davis and a cleaning woman who came to the small house close to the Capitol three times a week.

Davis, who had been listening to the lively exchange, spoke up, a covert grin on his face. "I'm sure you'll *like* Mrs. Wickham. And, Mother, you'll be able to embellish your parties with a most interesting guest—a fire-eating Southern belle from the heart of Richmond."

Both Robert and his wife, Jewel, exploded simultaneously, "What! In *no* way and on *no* occasion will we have a Rebel working in *any* capacity!"

Davis winked at his grandfather, and they let the two protest vociferously. Robert based his outraged arguments on the ground that as a political leader, he could not *allow* his father to have such a woman in his house. Ever since the beginning of the rebellion, Robert had been an outspoken proponent of the hardline policy against the South, and the very suggestion that one of *those* people be allowed to contaminate his father's house was more than Robert could bear.

After his overflow of invective rhetoric slowed somewhat, Jewel took up the refrain. Jewel Winslow had been a Stanton before her marriage to Robert, and seldom terminated a conversation without a reference to the fact that Edwin M. Stanton, secretary of war and the most powerful man in government next to Lincoln, was her relative. She was, at fifty-five, still an attractive woman, though somewhat overweight. Inclined in some degree to hypochondria, she was actually in excellent health. She sat back in her chair, fanned herself rapidly, and protested, "Captain, surely you can't be serious! After all, we must think of our *position*!"

Both Davis and his grandfather knew that Jewel rarely thought of anything else, but the old man said reasonably, "Why, my dear, I think Robert has put this thing in the wrong perspective." He explained quietly that the young woman was a widow whose husband had been killed at Antietam, and added that his death had caused a change in her sympathies. "And since the poor girl is miserable in the South, I simply asked her to come and be my housekeeper. And, after all," he said with a straight face, "the woman *is* a relative."

Robert snorted and paced the floor. "That may be all *you* need to know, Father, but some of us will require a *little* more information."

"I don't feel at all well, Robert," Jewel complained petulantly, and rose to her feet, saying, "Captain, I trust that you will not ask me to have this woman as a guest. Surely even *you* wouldn't expect me to go through that with *my* nerves!"

"Father," Robert pleaded in a plaintive voice, "can I say *nothing* that will change your mind?"

"I'm afraid so, Robert," the captain replied without a trace of remorse. "Davis is picking her up this afternoon at two."

Davis left the house with his parents, trying to soothe their ruffled feathers. "It's not all that bad," he said cheerfully as he helped his mother into the carriage. "She's a very vivacious, attractive woman. I expect she'll find a nice officer and marry now that she's changed sides."

His father stared at him, offended by the remark. His older son's refusal to join in the war fever that gripped Washington was, to his mind, a mark of weakness. He had even less respect for Davis's choice of a literary career—which to Robert Winslow seemed fit only for women and effeminate men!

"I'm sure *you* did nothing to talk him out of this madness!" he snapped. "If Lowell had been here, *he* might have been able to do something."

Davis's face fell. He was tired of having his younger brother's virtues thrown at him. He could have hated Lowell, but he didn't. He carried only genuine affection for Lowell, whose military career was a source of pride to Davis. However, he himself had no temperament for the life of an army officer. His only desire was to get back to England where a promising academic career at Oxford had been interrupted by the war.

He stepped back, ignoring his father's barbed remark, saying evenly, "Perhaps, Father. I'll see you tomorrow."

When he returned to the house, Davis's sober expression caught the old man's eye. Nearly eighty, Whitfield had lost none of his astute intelligence, and he had observed, with regret, that Robert frequently used the hard side of his tongue on Davis.

"Didn't like my surprise, did they, Davis?"

"Did you expect them to?"

"No. I expected them to act just like they did—like a pair of fools."

Davis looked up sharply, for he had never heard his grandfather speak so harshly about them. "That's pretty hard, sir."

Whitfield scowled. "Why, so it is." He glared at the cast that encased his ankle, adding, "I'll be snapping at the archangel Gabriel if that sorry excuse for a doctor doesn't get me on my feet pretty soon."

Davis glanced at the clock on the mantel. "It's almost time to meet our new housekeeper. I'll fix us something to eat."

"I hope she can cook," the captain grunted. "If we eat much more of that cold chicken, we'll be sprouting pin feathers!"

They nibbled at the lunch, both lost in thought. Before leaving for the train, Davis assisted his grandfather to his room. When the old man was comfortable, Davis said, "I'll bring her in when we get back."

His grandfather kept a buggy at a livery stable only a block away, and by the time the stable hand brought the horse and buggy, it was almost half past one, and Davis rushed to the station. On the way he passed the still-unfinished Capitol, which rested on a small hill. The building did not dazzle the eye, and Capitol Hill itself was muddy, dreary, and desolate most of the time—like the rest of the city.

Davis hated Washington. He despised the raw buildings, many still unpainted. The devastation of the war was apparent by the numerous public buildings renovated into hospitals, and long ambulance trains were commonplace. He longed for the dignified structures of Oxford with the moss of centuries and the air of antiquity.

Guiding his way through the busy streets, Davis felt the rough vitality that pervaded everything. Washington was the funnel through which troops poured toward the Virginia fighting front. He had to pull over more than once to let freshly equipped regiments from Pennsylvania pass.

Passing by the Old Capitol, now a huge war prison, Davis recalled the time he had accompanied his grandfather on a visit to see Thad Novak. They had arranged for the young man to be exchanged, and the thought struck Davis that the same young man might well fire a musket ball that could take Lowell's life! The bitter thought, to Davis, was a sample of the insanity of the war, and he tried to shake it from his mind as he drove toward the station.

The train was late, as he could have guessed. Timetables for trains were flexible, and when someone arrived on the same day scheduled, that was about the best a person could hope for. While he waited he talked with a wounded soldier on crutches who was waiting nearby. The boy's name was Fred Hotchkins, from Maine. He was eighteen years old, and had just been released from the hospital. He was sick of war and longed to get home.

"Where were you wounded?" Davis asked.

"There was a hill we had to take—and we nearly did. We got our fill and we bled all the way up and down; then we broke and ran away." He shook his head, vowing grimly, "No more for me!"

"What did you do before the war?" Davis asked.

"Lobster fishing—and lordy, will I be glad to get back at it!" For twenty minutes Hotchkins extolled the joys of catching lobsters. "There's no place like the state of Maine—fishing and everything else." According to his testimony, Maine put Eden to shame.

"You'll be coming back to fight when you get well?"

Hotchkins stared at Davis as if he were crazy.

"Comin' *back*!" he exclaimed. "Not likely, mister!" When Davis gently pressed the point, he was given a list of the mistakes of the Union leadership—all the way from Lincoln down to his corporal. "I jined up 'cause it ain't right for one man to own another—but we ain't goin' to win this war, no, sir!"

Davis bought the boy a sack lunch when his train came in. They had talked for about two hours, and time had gone fast. After Hotchkins left, Davis let his mind wander, thinking how wonderful it would be to sit beside the quiet pool near Oxford—at a pub called the Trout Inn at Godstow. It was a place by a weir pool, a very old gray stone house beside a little bridge. There was a continuous sound of running water, fish swimming in the clear pool, and flowers everywhere. He leaned back and closed his eyes, wishing he could soon leave the maelstrom of war and return to London.

He dozed off and awoke with a start when the noisy coal-burning engine arrived with a piercing whistle blast. The passengers streamed out of the cars, most of them soldiers, but here and there a few women and children. Twice he walked up and down the length of the train, and was beginning to think their guest had missed it when a voice at his elbow said, "Here I am, Davis."

He whirled around and found her standing beside him. "Belle—I was afraid you'd changed your mind." Actually he hadn't recognized her, for he was subconsciously expecting a pretty young girl in bright clothing, not a grave woman in widow's black.

"No," she smiled. "Have you or the captain changed yours?"

"Of course not." He felt embarrassed by the question, for he *had* tried to dissuade his grandfather, though he hadn't said as much to his parents. "Let me help you into the buggy, and I'll get your luggage."

She had a trunk and three bags, and after the porter loaded them into the buggy, Davis climbed into the seat, asking Belle, "Is that all?"

"Yes. As you can see, I've come for a long stay." The enigmatic remark matched the expression in her eyes, and she added, "I'm not sure it's wise for me to stay at your grandfather's house. I'll be quite a problem for him."

Davis grinned and spoke to the horse sharply, and they moved down the street. "As far as I know, an enemy fleet of warships didn't bother my grandfather," he said. "I doubt one small woman will cause him to lose any sleep."

She said nothing, but looked out at the humming streets and the scurrying crowds along the way.

Finally he spoke up. "You'll be a help to my grandfather. He's not well."

"He said he was somewhat indisposed."

"Slipped on the sidewalk and broke his ankle—and then got the flu. He's always been so active that it's been difficult to keep him still."

She glanced at him curiously. "You said at Richmond that you'd be going back to England."

"Well, I was all packed—before grandfather got hurt. He wouldn't stay in a hospital, and he would've driven my parents crazy in a week. So I moved into his house to take care of him."

"You still won't get involved with the war?"

He gave her a sharp look, and shook his head. "I'll be leaving as soon as you are able to take care of Grandfather. There'll be a servant to help him, too, of course, but I hated to leave him without someone to talk with." He pointed ahead, "There's the house."

The little cottage was set back from the street, with two large trees in the front and a garden in the back. He helped her out, saying, "Let's go in. I'll get your bags while you and Grandfather talk."

They entered the house and he led her through a small foyer into a hall that turned off to the right. He opened the first door on the left. "This will be your room, Belle."

She stepped in, noting the yellow wallpaper, the walnut bed with the ornate wardrobe and the small desk beside it. She walked to the large window overlooking the garden. "This is lovely, Davis," she smiled. "Let's go see your grandfather."

He escorted her to the master bedroom off to the left, opened the door and said, "Grandfather—Belle is here."

"Well, bring her in!"

Captain Whitfield was sitting up in bed, reading. He smiled as she approached. "My dear, how good to have you here, but I'm afraid I'm going to be a great bother to you."

She knew his words were meant to alleviate the strangeness she felt, and it touched her heart. "We'll be trouble to each other, Captain," she returned. "Both of us have been spoiled, I think."

"Nonsense!" he responded. "Davis and I are heartily sick of each other's company. We'll be much better by your presence! Now sit down and tell me all about our family. Davis, go bring Belle's baggage in!" She sat down, and as soon as Davis left, Whitfield nodded toward the door. "Belle, no matter what anyone says about that boy and his attitude—he's been a godsend to me! If I had gone home with Robert, one of us would have shot the other by now!"

They talked about her trip for a time, and then Davis came back and announced that her luggage was in her room, adding, "It's too late to fix a meal. Suppose you and I go out to a restaurant, Belle? We can bring something back for Grandfather."

"Oh no," she said promptly. "I'd rather stay in tonight. Let me try my cooking on you." They protested, but she insisted, and soon Davis was sitting on a high stool in the kitchen as she put together a quick meal, the main course being a cheese and mushroom omelet. He set the table when she announced that the meal was ready, and he went to get the captain.

"Well, now! This is something I like!" The captain wolfed down the omelet and waved a thick fluffy biscuit in the air. "A few days of this and I'll be ready to take command again."

"Don't speak too soon," she warned. "This is my easiest dish—Mama's recipe. It's a sure success, too." A smile broke across her face. "I've just put my best foot forward for the first meal."

Davis laughed and poured himself another cup of tea. "Whatever you cook will be better than my efforts." He gave a few humorous anecdotes of his abortive attempts at cooking.

"That reminds me . . ." and the captain related a story of the time his cook died at sea.

When he finished, an awkward silence fell across the table. Belle looked at the men. "You've been good to invite me here—but I want to make one thing clear," she told them. "I don't want to cause you any problems. I can find a room at any time if I become troublesome."

Whitfield Winslow gave her a steady look. "Most things in this life are trouble, Belle—most worthwhile things, that is. You're a smart girl, and you know that some people are going to doubt your motives. Nothing to be done about that, my dear. But this is your home as long as you choose to make it so."

The simplicity of his reply brought a swift reaction from Belle. She had seemed stiff and somewhat artificial in her manner. Now for the first time since entering the house, the set expression on her face broke, and the softness they remembered returned. Her eyes glistened and she said in a husky voice, "Thank you, Captain."

Davis saw that she was on the verge of tears, so he changed the subject. "How is Thad, Belle? And the rest of the family?"

Swiftly Belle brushed her handkerchief across her eyes, smiled, and began to report on her family. They talked for an hour, and finally she said, "I'm a little tired. If you don't mind, I think I'll go to bed early tonight."

"I'll do the dishes," Davis offered.

After Belle left, he asked quietly, "What do you think?"

"She's troubled, Davis. She's lost her husband, and now she's really losing her family—and she's not too sure about anything." Whitfield took out his pipe, lit it from a candle, and with a sad look in his wise old eyes concluded, "It'll depend on how our people respond. Some fools will hate anyone who's ever had a thing to do with the South."

"If Father and Mother accept her, it would help a lot. Mother, especially. Why don't you ask her to invite us all to the big party she's giving next Wednesday, Grandfather?"

"That's not a bad idea!" A wicked gleam shone in his eyes, and the edges of his lips curled in a smile. "They'll *have* to let me bring her, won't they? I mean, as an invalid I've got *some* rights!" He slapped the table with glee. "If they ask her to that party, it'll mean they're endorsing her—and I'm going to make them do it!"

As he lay in bed chortling over his plans to maneuver Robert and Jewel to invite them to the party, Belle was in her room, seated at the small desk, musing over the events of the last few days.

Everything had been theoretical—until she had gotten off the train. She had spent the long train ride planning ways to subvert and destroy all she could of the Union cause. When struck by the fact that she might be responsible for the death of federal soldiers, she had thought bitterly, *They started this war—they killed my husband. Now let them suffer!*

But Davis's cheerful face and the captain's warm welcome had made her plan difficult. She sat for a long time, her mind in turmoil. Finally she raised her head, and her lips drew into a tight line as she whispered, "I've *got* to do it!"

She got up and walked swiftly to the luggage on the floor, picked up a small blue case and placed it on the bed. Opening it, she removed the cosmetics and feminine personal items. Then she pressed one of the rivets that held the handle, and with the other hand reached down inside, pressing firmly on a small pencil mark near the bottom. A faint *click* sounded and the bottom swung up on one side, held on the other by an invisible hinge. Taking out a single slip of paper that lay in the false compartment beneath, she remembered Huger's instructions when he had given it to her: *Keep any messages for your contact in this compartment. When you have something to give him, put it in here. Then go for a walk to a place he designates, and leave the case on a bench—as if you've forgotten it. Later, go back for it. You'll find your message gone and new instructions in its place.*

Belle took a pen and a sheet of stationery from the desk and wrote "Agent in place" and her message. When she had finished, she folded the sheet and sealed it; then from a slip of paper in her hand she copied a name and address on the front of the letter. Inserting her note, she closed the compartment and replaced the contents.

It had been a long day, so she undressed and lay on the bed; but despite her fatigue, she could not sleep. About midnight it began to snow, and she watched the flakes softly falling to the earth. How she wished she could feel as clean and fresh as the bright silver mantle that would soon blanket the brown soil!

# CHAPTER FOUR

# Belle Meets Stanton

★ ★ ★ ★

For most people a seasonal party was only an opportunity to gather with a few friends and enjoy a time of fellowship and laughter. But not for Mrs. Jewel Winslow. To her, a Christmas party was like every other social function—a means of increasing her standing in Washington circles. Her husband's goal was no less secular, for he saw everything through a politician's jaundiced eye, and was quick to turn any meeting into a useful platform to promote his politics.

Their home had been built to stage such spectacles, with most of the lower floor comprising a huge ballroom, and on the night of December 23 it was nearly filled to capacity.

"Good lord, Jewel!" Robert complained as the pair descended the curving staircase leading down from the sleeping quarters, "did you invite *everybody* in Washington?"

"I don't think you appreciate how hard I work for you, Robert," Jewel said reproachfully. "It's gotten to be quite an honor to be at our Christmas Ball. Anybody who isn't asked—isn't *anybody*."

He grinned, knowing that to a large extent she was right. Many major policy decisions of the United States had their origin in the cliques that met at such parties. "Is Stanton going to be here?"

"He promised he would—if I could guarantee that the President *wouldn't*." Jewel frowned, and added as they reached the foyer and turned into the ballroom, "Edwin is much more gifted than Lincoln! It's a shame he's not the president!"

"Stanton's feelings are pretty plain—that Abe is Edwin's assistant." Robert grinned sardonically. It was common knowledge that the secretary of war treated the President as if he were slightly retarded. Stanton had even been heard to say on several occasions that the only salvation of the Union lay in *his* hands, not those of a country rail-splitter.

"I hope you seated Mrs. Wickham as far away from Stanton as possible," he remarked. "He's liable to have her arrested for no other reason than that she was in Richmond a few days ago."

"Edwin *has* to be hard on the Rebels!" Jewel snapped. "The President is far too lax."

Half the ballroom was occupied with banquet tables, with guests already seated, while the other half was left for the dancing that would follow. The walls and ceiling were decorated with holly and mistletoe, and the great clusters of candles from the chandeliers reflected their golden light in the brass buttons and insignia of the Union officers who sat at the long tables. Their dark blue uniforms served as a counterpoint to the reds, blues, and whites of the women's dresses, and Jewel was pleased.

"There's Edwin," she whispered, scurrying off to greet the secretary of war, as Robert followed dutifully.

"Edwin! I'm so glad you could come!" she exclaimed.

Stanton was short of stature with a bristling beard and a pugnacious look in his eyes. His temper was mercurial, the dread of the rest of the Cabinet—and everyone else. However, tonight he was in a cheerful mood, and gave Jewel a peck on the cheek. "Jewel, you look downright beautiful!"

Salmon Chase, secretary of the treasury, came forward and greeted Jewel with a simple "Good evening," then was shouldered aside by William Seward, secretary of state. Robert Winslow's eyes gleamed at the obvious thrust, for he recalled a comment the President had made once about the two men. Each was convinced he was better qualified to be President than Abe Lincoln. Winslow's mind flashed back to the early, dark days of the war. He had been in Lincoln's office, and had complained to the

President that Chase and Seward showed no respect for the Chief of State. Lincoln leaned back in his chair, and with a light of humor in his deep-set eyes said, "Winslow, when I was a boy, I used to carry pumpkins to town in a sack. I figured out that if I had just one pumpkin in a sack, it was hard to carry, but once you could get two pumpkins in, one at each end of a sack, it balanced things up. Seward and Chase'll do for my pair of pumpkins."

Now they all moved toward the heavy-laden tables and sat down. Jewel had made sure she was seated in the midst of the important guests so as not to miss a word that was said about the war. Chase began by needling Stanton about the tragic losses at Fredericksburg.

"Well, Mr. Stanton, I suppose you will be ready to go back to General McClellan—now that your last selection proved so inept."

"I think you can trust me with the selection of our military leaders, Mr. Chase!" he shot back angrily, his face flushed. It was a sensitive subject, for General Burnside, who was practically forced to take command of the army after Lincoln had relieved McClellan from his post, had led the army into a tragic blunder at Marye's Heights outside the small town of Fredericksburg. Burnside had allowed Lee to get his army on a hill across the Rappahannock, where he commanded a charge against the impregnable lines of Confederates. Wave after wave of Union troops had rushed forward, jumping over the bodies of their dead comrades—straight into a murderous fire, six charges in all. The dead had been piled up three deep in that violent and useless attack. Over 12,000 Union soldiers were killed or wounded for no gain.

Chase lit his cigar and countered daringly, "But, Mr. Stanton, how is it that the Army of the Potomac, the nation's best trained fighting force, can be routed by an army of poorly armed barefoot beggars?"

Stanton almost rose out of his seat, and his voice carried over the ballroom, causing every head to turn. "I'll hear no such talk, especially from a member of the Cabinet, Mr. Chase!" He railed on, blaming McClellan and the other members of the Cabinet.

Jewel shot an agonizing glance at Robert, whispering, "Robert! Say something!"

Robert waited until Stanton paused in his diatribe, then stood to his feet and called, "I propose a toast—to the gallant men who wear the uniform of the United States. They may lose a battle, but they will emerge victorious over the foe!"

Everyone rose, and Stanton was forced to join in the toast. When they were seated again, Jewel steered the conversation around to less explosive issues. She was congratulating herself on handling the volatile situation so well when Colonel Henry Wilder, Stanton's military advisor sitting to her left, asked suddenly, "By Jove—who is *that*?"

Jewel looked up to see Davis enter the double doors, pushing Captain Winslow in his wheelchair—but it was Belle Wickham, Jewel noted with displeasure, who had seized Colonel Wilder's attention, along with that of every other man in the room.

Belle was wearing a black dress as usual, but it was no ordinary widow's garment. The gown was made of black silk and shimmered with shifting radiance, reflecting the thousands of lights from the candles. It was not low cut, as were many of the dresses in the room, but it clung to her so snugly that the curves of her body were apparent. A single pearl hung from a golden chain around her neck—and the simplicity of that one piece of jewelry made every other woman in the room look over-adorned. Her glossy black hair fell down her back like a shining waterfall, enhancing the queenly air she bore as she walked lightly across the room with one hand on Davis's arm.

Davis wheeled his grandfather's chair to the left, and the men at the table most distant from where Robert and Jewel sat rose at once. As Davis assisted his grandfather to a chair, three officers moved quickly, almost falling over one another to help him.

Edwin Stanton had been watching the entrance, and now echoed Colonel Wilder's question, "Who is that with your family, Jewel?"

For once Mrs. Winslow was speechless, and Robert was forced to explain. "That young lady, Mr. Stanton, is Mrs. Belle Wickham, a relative of mine. She's—come to help my father since my son is leaving for England."

It was the best he could do, and both he and Jewel fervently hoped the trio would be forgotten, but Stanton persisted. "Where is she from, Winslow?"

Robert gave up all hope of anonymity for Belle, and plunged in boldly. "Why, sir, she's from Richmond." He got the hum of surprise he expected, and went on smoothly, "You'll be interested in her story, I think. You don't have many opportunities to meet converted Rebels—especially one as beautiful as Mrs. Wickham."

His words startled everyone, and Stanton exclaimed, "What in the world do you mean—'converted Rebel'?"

"The lady is a daughter of one of my family, Mr. Sky Winslow, who is a special advisor to Jefferson Davis," Robert said. "She was married to Captain Vance Wickham, of the Third Virginia Infantry." It had grown very quiet at the table, for everyone was hanging on Robert's words and staring across the room at Belle, who sat between the captain and Davis.

"She's a widow, then?" Colonel Wilder asked.

"Yes. Her husband was killed at Antietam."

Stanton was intrigued. "You've got courage, Winslow, bringing the enemy to this ball. I'd like to speak with her; come along and introduce me."

He rose and Colonel Wilder promptly joined him as Robert led the way across the room. "Mrs. Wickham, may I present Mr. Stanton, the secretary of war—and his aide, Colonel Wilder?"

Belle nodded. "How do you do, Mr. Stanton—Colonel Wilder."

"May we join you?" Stanton asked, which was a broad hint to the three officers seated at the table to leave. They rose hurriedly and scurried away with disappointment on their faces. Stanton took a seat directly across from Belle, leaving the places beside him for Robert and Wilder.

Belle asked immediately, "Have you come to arrest a poor Rebel, Mr. Stanton?"

Stanton was taken off guard by her piquant smile, and her beauty rendered him speechless for an instant. She had the most enormous eyes he had ever seen, almond-shaped, violet in color, and shaded by long, thick eyelashes. Stanton was no ladies' man, but the creamy complexion, the curving red lips, and the smooth white neck formed a combination he had never observed in any woman.

Besides this, her direct teasing question pleased him. He was not a man anyone ever joked with, and he realized she was doing exactly that. He well knew that he was the most feared man in Washington—indeed, he had sought to be exactly that—and now this beautiful young woman sat there, smiling at him, daring him to answer.

When he said, "Why, certainly not, Mrs. Wickham!" Robert breathed a sigh of relief, for he knew an arrest could have been possible.

"Captain Winslow," Stanton continued, "you are fortunate to have such help."

The captain nodded. "You are correct, sir. I met Belle when I was in Richmond some time ago—working on our family tree."

Stanton gazed at Belle searchingly, desiring to know more about her, yet cautious. Finally he said, "I understand you lost your husband at Antietam, Mrs. Wickham. My condolences." When she nodded, he added with a casual air that fooled nobody at the table, "It must be very difficult for you to be here—among your enemies."

Belle recognized her opportunity and responded quietly, "I would have thought that not so long ago, Mr. Secretary. If you had asked me to come to this place right after my husband's death—I would have died first, I think." She paused, her face serene but marked with pain. Then she continued. "I was filled with hatred for the North—especially Abraham Lincoln and his Cabinet."

Stanton blinked at the unexpected statement. "I suppose such hatred is widespread in the South."

Belle nodded. "Yes, and it will destroy her—as it almost destroyed me. I found myself consumed with hate. I lived for nothing but revenge, and found myself gloating over every Union soldier who died."

She dropped her head and sat silently. After a moment she lifted her eyes and went on. "One day I was at the hospital caring for our men, and for some reason they brought in several captured Union soldiers. I was bathing the face of one of them—not knowing he was a Yankee. Then someone whispered that he was a Union soldier—and I . . ." She brushed her hand across her eyes and murmured, "I spit in his face!"

A shock of revulsion swept over the table. "That sickens you, doesn't it?" Belle said. "It should! I stood looking at him, and for the first time I saw that the poor Northerner was no different from the Southern boy in the next bed. I . . . wiped his face and begged him to forgive me. And he did. But I couldn't get away from it—what the war had done to me. That was the turning point, Mr. Stanton."

"The turning point?" Stanton asked, moved by her story.

"Yes. I began to see that every soldier who died or was wounded was the result of one thing." She lifted her eyes to meet those of the secretary and said quietly, "The South's mindless refusal to get rid of slavery. You must understand that this was not the first time I'd thought of it. My father is one of many who hates slavery—as Captain Winslow will tell you. But those of us who felt that way were weak, and went along with secession, losing our sons and husbands in the process. It took the death of my husband, and almost losing my mind with hate, to bring me to the realization that all of it was wrong."

"Did you tell anyone how you felt?" Colonel Wilder asked.

She gave him a sad look, her lips trembling as she replied, "Why else would I be here, Colonel? Yes, I told them—and they turned on me. My family loves me, but they think I've gone crazy. The rest of Richmond who so loved me when I was faithful to the Cause rejected me as if I were a leper."

"And that's why you came to Washington?" Stanton prodded.

"I'm a woman without a country, Mr. Secretary," Belle sighed. "I've been cast out by my own people—and I can expect little from you, since I have been your enemy and hated you so bitterly."

Stanton had come to the table merely curious, but Belle Wickham was not just an object of curiosity. Though he was not swayed by her beauty, there was something in her youthful tragedy that moved him. He found his compassion reaching out to the girl, seeing her dilemma clearly. This woman was different from the large number of Southerners who came North, proclaiming they had seen the error of their ways.

He spoke to her gently. "I am sorry for your troubles, Mrs. Wickham—and I welcome you to Washington. If I can help you, please let me know."

He rose, bowed, then returned to his table, with Robert and the colonel following.

Davis gave Belle an astonished look. "I don't think you know what a conquest you've just made, Belle."

The captain agreed. "Never saw the old lion so tamed!" He looked across the room at Jewel, who was listening intently to Stanton. "You've just been given the key to the city, my dear. Even my daughter-in-law won't be able to turn her nose up at you now."

He was correct, for as soon as the music began, Colonel Wilder was across the room immediately. "Mr. Stanton commands me to ask you for the first dance, Mrs. Wickham, as a welcome to our society." He smiled broadly, adding, "And I must say, it was the most welcome command he ever gave this poor soldier!"

Belle rose and as they moved across the floor she said, "You are a brave man, sir, to dance with one so lately under the banner of your enemy."

He answered her in the same light vein, and she studied him as the dance went on. He was a good-looking man, tall and on the slender side. Not over thirty, she guessed, and carefully groomed. His large brown eyes were bold, and she would have known, had she not already been informed, that he was fond of women. His thin face was highly intelligent, and she was well aware that he was not only pursuing her as a woman, but was studying her as a political being.

At the end of the dance, Davis was waiting, and she deftly changed partners. He was not as good a dancer as Wilder, nor as good looking. Belle's first recollection of him in Richmond had been: *He'd be nice looking if he weren't so fat.* But she brushed the thought aside and commented, "I hope this isn't too much for the captain."

"I can't think of anything that would be too much for him," he grinned. Then he remarked, "You're a smashing success, Belle. Edwin Stanton is the weather vane of society in Washington, and he's given you his approval."

"I expect he's not quite sure of me, Davis," she replied. "Nor is Colonel Wilder."

"Better watch him, Belle," he returned quickly, adding with some hesitation, "He's known to be quite a womanizer."

"Are you worried about me?"

"In a way, I guess. I'll be leaving next week, and I wouldn't want anything to happen to you—for Grandfather's sake, I mean."

"I see." She let her eyes rest on him a moment, considering his comment. "Don't worry about me, Davis. I'll not succumb to the colonel's charm."

But as the evening wore on, Davis noticed that Belle danced with the tall soldier several times, and from what he could tell there was more than casual interest in her face as she laughed in response to her partner.

"Better watch out for Belle after I leave," he said to his grandfather. "I think Wilder's got his eye on her."

"So does every other man in the room," the captain grunted. "They're already calling her 'The Dixie Widow,' did you know? I think my foolish son let it slip—but Pinkerton will find that out anyway."

"You think Stanton will have her investigated?"

"That fox? You can bet on it!"

The dance ended, and as Stanton left, he said to his aide, "I see you're quite taken by the Dixie Widow."

"Who wouldn't be?" Wilder responded. "She's beautiful, isn't she?"

"Have Allan check on her, Henry. Her story sounds good—maybe too good. I don't trust anybody from Richmond these days."

★ ★ ★ ★

When Belle undressed that night, her nerves still tingled from the excitement of the evening. But before retiring she removed the false bottom of the blue case and began to write a report: *There is much talk that General Hooker will replace Burnside as commander . . . and a possibility that Grant will begin an assault on Vicksburg. . . .* She wrote rapidly, put the sheet in the false compartment, turned off the light and crawled into bed.

The next morning, she went for a short walk down the snowy streets, entered a cafe and sat on a bench just inside the door. After a time she left, leaving the case behind. Twenty minutes later, she returned and picked up the bag.

When she was in her room, she opened the compartment and eagerly read the note inside: *Fine work! Your information will reach Richmond in two days. Next meeting at railroad station. Leave case beside front door. In emergency, contact Lillian at 405 Birch St. Do not use this contact except in extreme emergency!*

She lay awake for a long time, unable to sleep, for the previous evening had been nerve-racking. It had been a struggle to keep up the facade, but she knew now that she could do it. She knew also that Colonel Wilder would be pursuing her as well as watching for any hint of disloyalty. As she drifted off, she thought, *Oh, Vance, I miss you so much!*

CHAPTER FIVE

# AN ENCOUNTER AT CHURCH

★ ★ ★ ★

By the middle of March, the bitter cold of winter retreated from Washington, leaving dirty patches of snow in the corners of fences. The war had grown stale, and although it was only a month away from the end of the second year, the old days of peace seemed lost in a blurred past. The armies had fought themselves into a stalemate, and after the massacre at Fredericksburg, the morale of the Army of the Potomac was shattered. Lincoln chose Major General Hooker, nicknamed "Fighting Joe," the former commander of Burnside's Center Grand Division, as the new commander. While Hooker rebuilt his army, the Confederate General Bragg met General Rosecrans and his army at Murfreesboro in the battle of Stone's River, in the North. The Confederates almost crushed the Union troops in the first stage, but then faltered. The two armies fell back, neither side claiming a victory.

Davis had left for England a week after the Christmas party, so Belle had spent many hours with the captain. His kindness was a constant reminder of her deceit, and she subconsciously attempted to make up for it by giving him special care. He was off his crutches now, limping heavily; but with the use of a cane, he was able to make short trips around town, usually to a restaurant, so the pair became well known.

The first warm Sunday morning Whitfield took Belle to

church. Though the service did not begin until ten, they left early and drove to the outskirts of town. As they passed beneath the spreading oaks sprouting with tiny emerald leaves, he took a deep breath of the fresh air and exclaimed, "What a wonderful change! This feels good, Belle! I'm sick of the house."

"It *is* nice," she smiled. "But you'd better keep covered up," she admonished, adjusting the blanket over his knees. "I thought you'd never get over that last cold."

"You treat me like a baby!" he complained, "but I like it!"

"You're due for a little spoiling," she answered, then asked, "You miss Davis, don't you?"

"Yes, I do. He's a pest with all his literary talk, but he's got sense." Then he added defensively, "I'm enjoying Lowell, of course, but he's too busy fighting off these Washington gals to pay any attention to me."

Lowell had been in the city on leave for a week and had paid two visits to his grandfather. He loved the old man, but the officer was caught up, as Whitfield said, in parties and balls hungry mothers arranged almost daily for their maiden daughters. Lowell had been very kind to Belle, but she was aware that his older brother had a special place in the captain's heart.

"I wish his parents wouldn't show such partiality for Lowell," Belle said hesitantly. She would not have dared make such a remark when she first arrived, but she had become at ease with Whitfield, knowing that he never broke a confidence. "I'm sure they're disappointed in Davis's decision to become a writer, but they make him feel rejected."

"That's true, though the boy never complains." The captain looked at her, then shrugged. "Can't do anything about it, Belle. Robert and Jewel have always favored Lowell—even before the war. Just like I've always favored Davis. I don't know what it would do to them if Lowell were killed."

"They'd have nothing at all, would they? They haven't tried to build any kind of loving relationship with Davis."

He nodded, then dropped the subject, saying, "Let's have no gloom on a day like this! Tell me about the list of officers who are ready to marry you, Belle!" He laughed at her expression. "It's become quite a feather in their cap to take the Dixie Widow out for an evening."

"Now, Captain," she countered crossly, "you're exaggerating. I've been out only four or five times since I've been here—that is, alone with an officer."

"I think they're scared off by Colonel Wilder," he said. "You know what happened to Lieutenant Hicks." He referred to a young officer whom Belle had liked, and whom the captain always insisted had been abruptly transferred to the front by Colonel Wilder out of jealousy.

"That is just a fanciful idea of yours."

"Think so? You don't know the colonel." He gave her a sharp look. "Or do you? You've been seeing him quite often."

"Why, I can't help it!" Belle protested. "He's at every gathering in Washington. I wonder when he has time to do his job. And just to keep you from saying 'I told you so,' I'll tell you now that I am going out with him tomorrow tonight." She stared defiantly at the old man, adding, "He's got two tickets to that Italian opera everyone's dying to see."

"Never been to one—nor want to," Winslow snorted. "Bad enough to pretend there's some kind of world where everyone sings everything they say—even *pass the butter*—but to sing it in Italian, why it's against nature, woman!"

He slapped the reins across the horses, and the team broke into a brisk trot. "We better get to church."

The Presbyterian church he attended was a white structure with an imposing steeple, located not far from the Capitol. As they pulled up, he stepped out of the buggy, moving very carefully, and handed the lines to a young black man. Belle stayed where she was, allowing him to come around and help her step down. Then she took his arm and matched her pace to his as they walked down the brick sidewalk. He had some difficulty ascending the steps, but with the aid of his cane and her arm he made it.

"Service started yet?" he asked the one-armed attendant who met them in the foyer.

"No, Captain, you're just in time," he smiled. "I have two seats in the section you like best."

Belle felt uncomfortable as she walked down the hardwood aisle, sensing she was the target of many eyes. She kept her head high, but was relieved when she took her seat beside the captain in a pew close to the front. Fortunately she was seated at the end of the bench and wouldn't have to converse with anyone. She glanced across the aisle and saw Mr. and Mrs. Seward. Both of them nodded, and she smiled back.

She let her eyes sweep over the audience, looking for someone else she might recognize when the captain nudged her. "There he is!" he whispered.

She turned her head, and a shock ran through her as she saw Abraham Lincoln, the President! His wife held his arm, and a young boy walked by his side.

*So this is the man the people in Richmond call "The Gorilla"—and much worse.* She had, of course, seen pictures of him, but mostly caricatures in the newspapers. He moved slowly past her, and turned to let his wife and son enter the pew two rows down and across the aisle.

Belle studied him closely. He seemed even taller than his actual height, which she had read was six feet four. The black suit he wore emphasized his lanky body, his narrow shoulders and lean chest. In spite of that, there was an air of strength about him, Belle thought. Much had been made in the Southern press and in the London *Times* of his awkward height, his too prominent ears, his shambling gait, his huge feet and hands, his too large mouth and too heavy lower lip.

*Some of those characteristics seem true,* Belle thought, *but I'm sure there is more to the man than that.* Despite her preconceived notion to hate him, she saw that his gray eyes were full, deep, penetrating and ineffably tender. Instantly she knew he was not the monster portrayed in the press. He had such infinite wisdom in his face that it would be impossible for the most indifferent observer to pass him on the street unnoticed.

"He's got a mighty heavy load to carry," the captain whispered, interrupting her thoughts. "And not much help at home, if truth be told."

Mary Lincoln's reputation as a shrew in Washington was often documented by her public display of jealousy, but in appearance, she did not seem so. Belle had noticed in the quick glance she had that Mrs. Lincoln was less than medium height, and inclined to plumpness. She had fair skin and masses of brown hair braided about her well-shaped head. When she turned to whisper something to her husband, Belle noted that the lady's forehead was full and high, her eyes large, and her mouth somewhat thin.

When the service began it was not what Belle expected. She had grown up in the Methodist church in the fires of revival. The religion of the slaves was embodied in an emotional release, and some of their spirited singing and loud "exhorting" had crept into the white church. Belle may also have been influenced by George Whitfield and John Wesley, who were better suited to the warm country than to the North.

In any case, Belle had a typical Methodist disdain for Presbyterian churches, having heard others dismiss them as "high church." She joined in the singing, which, to her, seemed dull and listless after the lively worship she was used to at camp meetings. And when the pastor got up to preach, dressed in a robe and speaking in well-modulated tones, she felt that the reputation of the Presbyterians was well earned.

The pastor was not a large man, and he spoke quietly at first. He welcomed the guests to the services, not mentioning the President at all, then began his sermon by announcing his text.

"This morning, we will consider the words of Hagar in Genesis sixteen and focus on the thirteenth verse, which says, 'Thou God seest me.' "

Belle followed the story in the Bible the captain shared with her, remembering more of the story as the preacher gave a brief summary. "You will recall," he continued, "that Abraham and Sarah had been promised a child, though they were both old. Somehow they lost sight of God's promise and Sarah proposed that Abraham have a child by Hagar, her handmaid. Abraham consented, and the child was born. But as we have read, Sarah grew to hate the young girl Hagar, and Abraham finally told her, 'Behold, thy maid is in thy hand; do to her as it pleaseth thee. And when Sarai dealt hardly with her, she fled from her face. And the angel of the Lord found her by a fountain of water . . . in the way to Shur.' "

Belle lifted her eyes to the preacher, wondering what sort of a sermon he could get from that. He seemed to look directly at her as he said, "God gave Hagar a promise, and when He did, she gave God a name, a very strange name—Thou God seest me. It is this name and this truth that I would like us to receive today. For each of us has this God that Hagar saw, and we may all say with her in fear and in love, 'Thou God seest me.' "

He began to speak of the omnipresence of God, and although it was a truth that Belle had rarely considered, she began to grow restive as the pastor drew illustrations both from the Bible and from life. "When Adam and Eve were in the garden, God saw them . . . When Moses struck the Egyptian, God was watching . . . Though Daniel may have felt alone when he prayed at the risk of his life, God's eye was on him."

Then he began to speak of evil-doers in this same manner. "When Cain slew his brother, did he not realize that God saw him? Did David think the Lord God of Israel was asleep when the act of adultery was committed with Bathsheba? Why did Peter not cry out 'thou God seest me' when he denied the Lord Jesus Christ?"

The minister paused from time to time, solemnly quoting the text: "Thou God seest me." As the sermon went on, Belle began to dread that quote, for she had begun to feel very uncomfortable. For three months she had been in the home of Captain Whitfield Winslow, and had passed only five messages to her unseen contact, none that seemed very important. Many times she had despaired, asking herself, *What am I doing here?* and more than once determined to return home.

But always she had stayed, justifying herself by saying that she was a soldier and must stand whatever hardship came, even as her people in Richmond and the soldiers in the field. But she had lost the keen pangs of guilt, for though she knew it was a breach of confidence and a violation of hospitality to carry on such activities while a guest in Captain Winslow's home, still—it seemed that what little she did had no serious consequence.

Now as the words "thou God seest me" reverberated against her mind, the guilt rose like a specter, and she realized the enormity of her deeds. She tried to shut out the words, but they seeped into her spirit.

When the pastor began his final point, Belle squirmed, knowing she must endure it, but wishing she could escape.

"So Hagar discovered there was a God, that He was a God who *cared.* But in chapter twenty-one of Genesis, she learned even more about this God who watches us. Isaac was born, and Sarah once again drove the girl out, this time with her son who was only a youngster. We read the sad story beginning in verse fourteen: 'And Abraham rose up early in the morning, and took bread, and a bottle of water, and gave it unto Hagar, putting it on her shoulder, and the child, and sent her away: and she departed, and wandered in the wilderness of Beer-sheba. And the water was spent in the bottle, and she cast the child under one of the shrubs. And she went, and sat her down over against him, as it were a bowshot: for she said, Let me not see the death of the child. And she sat over against him and lifted up her voice, and wept.' "

He looked over the congregation and asked pointedly, "Are there any here in Hagar's condition? Have you been put in a desert of some sort and left to die of thirst?" He raised his voice and for the first time cried, "God knows your thirst! He knows your need! And if you will look to Him and to His power, you will not die!"

He lifted his Bible high. "In verse nineteen we read: 'And God opened her eyes, and she saw a well of water; and she went, and filled the bottle with water, and gave the lad drink.' " Then he lowered his voice, and swept the congregation with his eyes, now damp with tears, asking, "Where did that well of water come from? It was there all the time—but Hagar couldn't see it! God had to open her eyes to the provision she needed so desperately. And that is my message—to all of us. God sees us, and there is a fountain He has prepared for our thirst. We may not have seen it, but it is there. Jesus Christ is that fountain, and though men may pass by, ignoring Him in their lust for other things, still, we long for the day when God will open their eyes—and we may all see that blessed spring that flows from His only begotten Son!"

As he finished, Belle sat transfixed, then somehow got to her feet and blindly turned to go.

"Well, this must be our friend from Richmond!"

Startled, Belle looked up into the kind eyes of Abraham Lincoln. He extended his hand, and when she did the same, he enveloped it, holding it gently, saying, "My friend Stanton has told me about you, Mrs. Wickham," he said softly. "I grieve over your loss."

"Thank you, Mr. President!" Belle gasped. The guilt that had built up during the sermon now caught in her throat, and she could only stare at him as the tears welled up in her eyes.

"Mary, this is the young lady from Richmond that Edwin was telling you about. I think it would be fitting if you had her in to one of your teas someday."

Mary Lincoln was neurotically jealous of her husband, having been known to physically pull at least one woman away while screaming at her. But she apparently saw no threat in the young woman who stood beside the captain. She noted the quivering lips, the tears ready to spill over, and impulsively stepped forward and touched Belle's arm. "Why, I was talking with the captain's daughter-in-law yesterday," she said. "She'll be bringing you to our home next Wednesday."

"Now, that's fine!" Lincoln nodded, breaking into a smile, making his homely face almost beautiful. "Be sure she feeds you well, Mrs. Wickham," he said, moving down the aisle.

The drive home was somber. Not until they were halfway to their destination did Belle speak. "He's not at all as they say—the newspapers."

"No, he's not," Captain Winslow agreed. "He's not like *anybody* else, Belle, and that's God's truth."

He considered her quietly. "He's the only thing that's held the Union together, Belle. He's been insulted by everyone, but if he goes down, so does the country. I went to a party once with Robert, and Lincoln was there. Somehow we got left alone, and I told the President how much I appreciated him. He grinned at me in the way he has, and he told me this story:

" 'There was a man I knew who kept a kennel full of hunting dogs—young and old. He'd sell the young ones every now and then, smart as they were and slick as they could be. But the one dog he'd never sell or lend was an old half-deaf foolish looking hound you wouldn't think was worth five dollars. That old hound would just lie around and scratch fleas, and I used to plague the man, ask him why he kept such a dog. "Well," the man said, "he ain't much on looks or speed. A young dog can outrun him anytime. But, Abe, that dog's hell-bent on a cold scent, and once he gets his teeth into what he's after, he don't let go until he knows it's dead." ' "

The captain thought for a moment before going on. "You know what he said then, Belle? 'I'm that old dog, Winslow. There are lots of smarter and faster dogs, but I won't quit!'

"I guess that's why I love him, Belle." The captain seemed sad, and they made the rest of the trip in silence.

Belle wished she'd never met the man she'd been taught to hate—for she knew she could never hate him again.

# CHAPTER SIX

# "SHE'S PAID TOO MUCH!"

★ ★ ★ ★

Monday morning Belle received a letter from her mother, and the captain saw that it depressed her. He never asked about Richmond, but was always interested in the family. When Belle came in that evening dressed for the opera, she sat down beside him and began to talk. "The family is well, but the boys are all gone, and Mama worries about them a great deal—especially Dan."

"He's in the army, too? How old is he?"

"Eighteen."

"So young—all of them seem so young!" the captain said softly. "But I was only eighteen the first time I saw action. Seems like a millennium ago! How about young Novak and your sister? They married yet?"

"Oh no. Pet wants to but Thad says they've got to wait. I'm glad." A sudden spasm of grief swept over Belle's face, and she whispered, "I wouldn't want her to go through this!"

Whitfield looked at her searchingly. "Remember what the preacher said? 'Thou God seest me.' I reckon that's what all of us have got to hang on to."

Belle looked at him, her eyes filled with doubt, even fear. "You're so sure of that, Captain—and so are my parents and Pet. All of you must have something I don't."

"Aren't you a Christian, my dear?"

"Why, I've thought so for a long time. I was converted when I was twelve, and baptized. But . . . sometimes I wonder if there's not something more!" A knock at the door interrupted any further words, and she rose. "I'll let the colonel in."

When Colonel Wilder stepped inside, he exclaimed, "You look beautiful, Belle!"

"Same old dress, Henry," she smiled. "Come and speak to Captain Winslow."

The old man stood up as the two entered the room. "Better stay and play a game of chess with me, Colonel," he suggested. "Be more fun than taking this woman to hear a bunch of screeching I-talians!"

"Duty first, Captain Winslow," Wilder grinned. "Besides, I hear you're unbeatable at chess."

"So I am," Winslow nodded without modesty. "But you need to lose at something. Be good for your humility."

"I'll come another time, Captain, but I paid too much for the tickets to this performance to waste them. Are you ready, Belle?"

"I'll get my coat."

While the colonel helped her on with her wrap, she said to the captain, "You'd better get to bed early, and if you want something to eat, I put some cookies on the table."

"Humph!" he grunted and went back to his easy chair.

When they were outside, Wilder commented, "Wonderful old man! Wish we had his kind around today."

"He *is* wonderful, isn't he? He's been so good to me."

"I don't think he deserves any credit for *that*! From what I hear, you've waited on him as if you were his slave. Besides, he's just like the rest of us."

"In what way?"

"For a beautiful woman, the world will not only wait, it will roll over and play dead if that's what she wants." His white teeth gleamed as he smiled. "Even Mrs. Lincoln admires you—which is a miracle!"

As they made their way to the performance, Wilder related happenings around the War Office. The news didn't seem important, but even from this, Belle found herself gleaning things that might be of interest to Richmond.

The opera was held at Ford's Theatre, and when they were seated, Wilder pointed out Lincoln's box to their left. "He comes here a lot—mostly to light comedies, though." He let his arm drop on Belle's shoulder and added, "He's a brooding man—but he likes Joe Miller's jokes and the comedies. Guess they take his mind off his problems."

Belle was acutely aware of the pressure of his arm, but could do nothing but endure it. He had tried to kiss her once, but she had deftly avoided the caress, thinking he might be put off. But she realized now that love was a game to Henry Wilder. If he lost, he didn't brood, but planned other means to capture his prey. He had been successful with women, she knew, and was sure he would never be satisfied until he had conquered her.

She thought, *Why, I'm no better than he is! He's trying anything he can to get what he wants from me—and I'm doing the same to him!*

Finally the curtain rang down, and they left.

"It's early yet, Belle. Let's get something to eat."

"Well . . ."

"Or we could stop by my place," he offered without looking at her. "I've got some of that caviar the Russian ambassador gave Stanton. Edwin can't stand the taste of it."

"I'm not sure I should, Henry."

"Because you're a widow? Nonsense! We'll pop in, have some of the fish eggs and a glass of wine; then I'll rush you home."

He suited his actions to his words, and soon was showing her inside his house—a Cape Cod made of red brick. "This is my little castle," he said. "Let me take your coat and I'll show you around before we eat."

The first floor held the parlor, a large study with a huge desk, the dining room, and the master bedroom. Upstairs were two small bedrooms. As the colonel brought her down, he waved his hand, saying proudly, "It's too much for a single man, of course, but a soldier's life is so insecure that I don't feel guilty about indulging myself. Now, let's see about that caviar."

She ate some of the strange food, grimaced and said, "I rather agree with Mr. Stanton!"

He laughed. "Well, there's plenty of cold chicken and potato salad—and I think there's some cake."

He made the coffee and while they ate the pastry, he rattled on about improvements he planned on the house. As he talked, she was thinking of the desk in the study. How she longed to have access to it for half an hour! He was, she understood, a careful man in all things, and it would be strange if he didn't keep written records. He had mentioned several times that he did more work in his study than he ever did at the War Office. It was in that desk, she decided, that she would find any worthwhile information for Richmond.

She rose to go, but he guided her smoothly into the parlor, insisting that she had to see the latest photographs from the war zone. She allowed herself to be led into the room, and he pulled a large box from a shelf, and soon she was staring with fascination at an incredible array of pictures.

"Matthew Brady made all these, Belle," he said. "Those photographers go right to the battlefield with their closed wagons—some of them have actually been killed because they got so close to the action."

Belle stared at a picture so clear in detail that she could see individual blades of grass. A young soldier was lying dead on his back. His musket lay over his head and one arm was flung up in a strange position. His coat was unbuttoned and his mouth gaped in a voiceless cry.

"Pretty grim, isn't it?" Henry remarked, and took the picture from her. "This is a Rebel, but you can't hate them when they're like this, can you?"

"No." Belle was sickened by the picture and said faintly, "I—I don't want to see any more, Henry."

"Of course not!" He tossed the pictures to one side, then suddenly put his arms around her, saying, "Belle, I've been trying to get you alone for weeks—and then I act the fool and show you ugly pictures."

Belle felt his arms drawing her closer, and was terrified. If she turned him away coldly, she knew there was no chance for her to exploit the contents of his desk. Yet she hated the touch of his arm, and as he lowered his head to kiss her, she felt nauseated. There was no time to think, however, for he bent his head and his lips met hers. He was an accomplished lover, but that did not concern her. She endured his kiss, then pulled back and said quickly, "Henry—I shouldn't be here."

"Yes, you should," he answered swiftly, and did not release her. Instead, he pulled her tighter, the hard buttons of his uniform pressing against her. He slowly kissed her again, and when he raised his head, she saw the hunger in his eyes.

"Henry—no!" she said weakly and pushed him away.

Wilder grabbed her again, his eyes boring into hers. "Belle—I've *got* to have you! You're the most beautiful woman I've ever seen!"

She twisted around, but his arms pinned her to him. He kissed the side of her neck and murmured, "Belle," his arms growing ever tighter. Then, just as she was about to struggle free, there was a loud knock at the door.

"Blast!" he snapped. "I'll be right back, Belle."

He left the parlor and she went to the window and peered out. By the light of the lantern over the door, she saw the outline of a soldier. The door opened, and the man began talking urgently. She could not see Henry, but she heard the sound of his voice. He was angry. Finally the door slammed, and he came in, saying, "Belle, I've got to go to the office. I'll drop you off on the way."

"Of course, Henry," she responded, relieved that the personal crisis had been averted.

"I have to get a few papers from the study before we go," he said. He was gone for a short time and returned with a brown leather briefcase in his hand. "Ready?" he asked.

"Yes."

They drove rapidly through the dark streets. She remained quiet but felt he would speak of the emergency, which he did. "I spend all day long at the office," he complained, "but that's not enough for Stanton! He can't keep track of anything himself, and every time he wants to know something, he sends for me."

"You must get awfully tired, Henry," Belle replied, placing a hand on his arm. "I don't see how you ever keep up with all the things you have to know. I'd forget half of them."

"Well, I do have a good memory," he admitted with satisfaction, "but I have to keep things on paper, too." He nodded at the briefcase beside them. "I could tell Stanton what's happening down at Vicksburg, but that wouldn't be good enough. He wants it written down, or he won't believe it."

Belle picked up on the name, and said innocently, "I was in Vicksburg with my family three years ago. It was the best summer I ever had, Henry—such a nice town!"

He grinned. "Wouldn't be a good spot for a vacation now, Belle. When U.S. Grant and Sherman move into a place, it sort of brings the real estate value down." He stopped abruptly as if he had said too much, but she gave no sign of interest.

When he took her to the door, she turned and said, "I had a wonderful evening, Henry. Thank you so much."

She lifted her face to his, and he kissed her as though he were famished. She forced herself to respond, then pulled back and whispered, "You—you frighten me, Henry!" Then she slipped inside and closed the door gently.

He walked back to the buggy, leaped into the seat, and slapped the lines, grinning from ear to ear. "Henry, old boy—you'll get her the next time!"

★ ★ ★ ★

The next day Belle gave a humorous account of the opera to the captain and Lowell, who came to spend the afternoon with his grandfather. They both laughed at her account, and Lowell said, "I'm taking Grandfather down to the dock to see the newest warship, Belle. Would you like to join us?"

"No, thank you, Lowell. I have some shopping to do. But you can tell me about it when you come back."

As soon as the two men left for the harbor, Belle went to her room and opened the blue case. She read the slip of paper retrieved from the compartment: "In case of emergency, you can contact Lillian at 405 Birch Street." She replaced the note, closed the case, and left the house.

Her next meeting with her contact was not for four days, but she felt someone should be told about Vicksburg and about Colonel Wilder's brown briefcase. She had no idea where Birch Street was, so she asked a cabbie if he could take her.

"Birch Street?" He seemed to be taken aback by the address, and said rather grudgingly, "Why, yes, ma'am, I can take 'e there. Wot's the number?"

"405."

He peered at her, puzzled, asking again, "That's 405 Birch Street, is it now?"

"Yes. And hurry please."

She stepped into the cab, and he slapped the reins across the horse. Soon she was quite lost, for he had turned into a section of town she had never seen, mostly comprised of decaying old mansions and a smattering of small shops, none looking very prosperous. There seemed to be a great many idle people, and more saloons than one would expect.

"This is it, ma'am." The driver did not get down at once, but twisted his head and asked, "Is this where you be wantin' to go?"

Belle stared at the dilapidated brownstone house and almost told the cabbie to drive on. The house sat next to a saloon, with several men in rough dress lounging along the front, obviously already started on their day's drinking. In one of the windows of the brownstone house, a woman with a brightly colored face leaned out and called loudly, "Bill—you there—Bill! Bring up a quart of beer for me and me gentleman friend!"

One of the loafers grinned, said something to the other men that brought forth a coarse laugh, then disappeared into the saloon.

Belle took a deep breath. "This is the place. How much?"

After taking the money he asked, "Want me to wait, ma'am?"

"No."

Belle got down, feeling a sudden wave of fear at being so vulnerable. As she walked up the steps, one of the men called out, "Hey, sweetie, let's you and me have a drink, okay?"

She did not turn, but knocked firmly on the door. When it opened, a hard-looking woman of indeterminate age stood before her. She might have been twenty-five, but hard use and abuse had erased the soft lines of youth, and beneath the heavy coat of rouge, there was a cynical look.

"I'm looking for Lillian," Belle said.

"There ain't no Lillian here!" the woman snapped, and almost slammed the door, but Belle spoke out quickly.

"Please—!"

Belle hesitated, not knowing how to explain. Finally she spoke up. "I was told I could come here—in case of emergency!"

The woman studied Belle for a moment, shrugged, and barked, "All right! Come in!"

Belle followed her into a parlor to the right of a narrow hall. There was an acrid smell in the air that Belle did not recognize, and fear tingled along her nerves.

"I'm Lillian," the woman said brusquely. "Who are you and what do you want?" Her eyes swept over Belle's expensive attire. "This ain't the kind of place for you."

"I'm Belle Wickham."

The name meant something to the woman, for her eyes narrowed and she gave a slight nod. But she was not swayed enough to give anything away. "Well, what do you want?"

Belle stood there, uncertainly, and finally said, "I have—some news. Important news, but I don't have an appointment with—my friend—until later this week."

"And who is this 'friend'?"

"I don't know his name—but I usually meet him by leaving a blue case with a message in it."

Lillian eyed her for a minute. "I guess you're all right. But your 'friend' isn't here."

"Can you tell me where to find him?"

Lillian shrugged. "I can send for him—if you want to wait."

"Oh yes—I'll wait! Thank you."

"But you can't stay here. Come to my room."

Belle followed her out of the parlor and up to the second floor. A burly man was weaving his way down the stairs, obviously drunk. As the two women passed, he grabbed Belle's arm, saying, "Hey, Lillian, I ain't never seen this one."

"You're drunk, Harry!" Lillian snapped, knocking his hand aside and putting herself between the pair. "Leave her alone, but you come back quick, you hear?" she ordered.

The drunk stumbled down the stairs, and with a beating heart and trembling knees, Belle followed the woman into a room at the top of the stairs. It was a large room, with a bed on one side, a couch on the other and several nice pieces of walnut furniture along the wall.

"Sit down and I'll fix some coffee," Lillian said, indicating a chair. She hurriedly fixed the coffee and set it in front of Belle before speaking. "I'll have to send a message. Help yourself to the pie if you want."

After the woman left, Belle rushed to the window. Lillian appeared on the steps and called to one of the men beside the saloon. She spoke to him briefly and slipped something into his hand. As the man took off down the street, Lillian turned back into the house.

Belle was on the couch when Lillian returned and took a cup from the cupboard. Sitting opposite Belle, she said, "He'll be here pretty soon, I guess."

"I appreciate your help." Belle sipped at the coffee, trying to find something to say.

"I thought you'd be older," Lillian commented. "You're just a kid."

Belle reddened and lifted her head. "I'm not! I've been married and I can look after myself."

"Can you?" the woman laughed. She waved toward the street. "If you tried to make it through that street, I doubt you'd get a block. This ain't your world, honey!"

Belle dropped her head and replied quietly, "No, it's not—but I had to come."

The woman's hard face softened. "Well, take your coat off. It'll be a while. I've got to go, but you'll be safe here."

She got up and left the room, and Belle began to pace the floor. The clock on the wall seemed frozen, and she went to the window again and again. She didn't have the vaguest idea who her contact was.

The woman came back once, took something out of a drawer, and left, saying only, "He may not be at home. I'll get a cab for you if you like."

"No—I'll wait."

"All right."

She was sitting on the chair, drinking a cup of cold coffee when the door opened. The woman entered and asked the man behind her, "This the woman?"

"Yes."

Belle couldn't believe her eyes. *Ramsey Huger*!

He shook his head in warning as she started to speak his name, and said, "Thank you, Lillian."

She recognized her dismissal, so turned and closed the door behind her.

"Belle!" he whispered, coming to sit near her. "We must speak softly. Someone may hear us. But it's so good to see you!"

"Ramsey!" Belle grabbed his hands, her voice quivering with joy. "I thought you were in Virginia."

"I have been," he smiled, his voice low. "I got in two days ago. I was going to meet you—but you've beaten me to it."

He was dressed well—as she last saw him, and he still carried a self-assured air. He reached over and hugged her. "I've begged them to let me come and work with you, Belle. I guess they finally got sick of my persistence and here I am."

She laughed. "I can't believe it!"

"Well, it's true. Now, what's so important that you risked our cover?" He shook his head. "Lillian is well paid, but she's no patriot. We'd better change your instructions. I don't want either of us to come here again now that's she's seen us together."

"All right—but listen to what I have . . ." He listened intently as she talked, and his eyes narrowed when she mentioned the papers in Wilder's briefcase. Finally she said, "Ramsey, you must have someone who can get into his house. The papers are right there in the desk."

He moved away and began to walk to and fro. Finally he shook his head. "We've known about Wilder's habits for some time. And we've tried to get a man in to get at that desk—but it's impossible."

"But—!"

"You see, the only time Wilder lets that case leave his hand is when he's asleep, or so it seems. He carries it with him when he goes to the office, and carries it home when he leaves."

"But when he goes out at night, what about then?"

"Didn't you know? He has a private guard, a soldier. It's his job to watch the house when Wilder leaves."

"Yes, he was there last night."

"Belle, this is the best chance we've ever had!" Huger's eyes gleamed with excitement, and he began to tell her the importance of the papers. "They contain troop movements—that much we know."

"Is the information so important?"

"Think about it, Belle," he persisted. "Lee's armies are outnumbered three to one—sometimes much more. He has to shift his men around on short notice, trying to plug the gaps. If Lee could know for a certainty that the Union had moved a mass of troops from one place to another, he could ignore the place left thinly manned, and rush his men to meet the biggest danger."

"I see, but. . . ?"

"Did you know that McClellan knew every move Lee was going to make at Antietam?"

"Impossible!"

"No, it happened! Lee's Special Order No. 191 outlined the entire plan—and it fell into McClellan's hands. What a golden opportunity for the North, Belle! If any other general had been in McClellan's place, the North would have ended the war."

"If that order hadn't been in the hands of McClellan, my husband might not have died."

"Entirely possible, Belle," Huger nodded soberly. "A great many of our men died because of that." He took her arms firmly and with more intensity than she had ever seen, said, "Now do you see why you *must* get that information!"

"But, Ramsey, if your agents can't get it, how can I?"

He looked at her searchingly. "My agents aren't beautiful women, Belle."

With horror she grasped the implication, and whispered, "You warned me once it might come to that—but I—I just can't do it, Ramsey!"

He nodded. "No one is going to force you. Nobody *could*. But give it some thought before you refuse. If we don't get this information, it may mean the end, Belle, and I'm not being melodramatic. You've seen how strong the North is—and you know how we're down to almost nothing at home. What we need is one good, solid victory, and England will recognize us. That'll change everything."

"Can that happen?"

"Yes. I have it on good authority that if we can hold out—just hold out, Belle—and win one solid battle, the Queen will favor our Cause. But we don't have the men or the guns. We need something else—and I think you're the only one who can get it for us."

She sat transfixed, her eyes large, and a vulnerable look on her face. She could not doubt that he believed every word he was saying. She longed to see the South win the war. Everything in her wanted that. She thought of her brothers lying dead if the war continued on its interminable course.

Then she considered what he was asking, and was repelled by the very thought. "I—I can't decide, Ramsey!"

She rose and walked to the window. The evening shadows were beginning to creep in. Her heart felt like ice. Finally she turned and asked, "What would you think of me—if I did such a thing? What would *any* man think?"

"I would never think of it at all, Belle," he answered instantly. "Would you hold it against your brothers that they have killed men in this war? No. I can answer for you. You wouldn't, for they do what they *must* do. What I am asking you to do is no different. Help your country, Belle! No man will think less of you."

She answered slowly, her lips numb, "But *I* will think less of myself, Ramsey."

He stood near her, a strong figure in the lamplight. "I can't help you, Belle," he said gently. "The decision must be yours." Then he took a small box out of his pocket and opened it, revealing a small bottle. "This may help, Belle. If you put three drops in a drink, it'll put a man to sleep in less than ten minutes." He gave it to her, urging, "Use it, Belle! Get him drinking, then slip him this. He'll be out, and then you can copy the papers. The next time you see him, tell him he passed out."

She took the vial and said quietly, "I want to go home, Ramsey."

"Of course."

He led her down the stairs and out of the house, then got into a cab with her. No one seemed to notice them in the darkness. They said little on the way, and when he got out a few blocks from her house, he gave her a card. "If you need me, Belle, I'll be at this address. Come alone and after dark."

He stepped back, and spoke to the cabby, who lifted the reins and urged the horse on. After the cab had disappeared, Huger went back to the east side of town where he met a man in a shabby room. He told the story, and the agent had one question: "Will she do it?"

Huger replied slowly, "I don't think she will, Jake. She's too good a woman for this kind of work."

But he was mistaken.

Three nights later, a knock sounded at his door, and he opened it to find Belle standing there, her face pale as paper.

"Belle! Come in!"

"No." She pulled a sheaf of papers from her bag and handed them to Huger. "This was the best I could do," she said wearily. "I copied those that seemed most important to me."

He shuffled through them, then cried out, "Belle, you've done it! This is what we needed!" He took her arm, but she pulled back. He leaned forward and peered into her face, and was shocked at the emptiness in her eyes. She looked like a dead woman. "Belle, what's wrong?"

Her eyes were blank. "Your drops—the ones you gave me?" she said in a hollow voice.

"Yes?"

"They didn't work, Ramsey." She looked at him emptily and said, "I got what we had to have—but it—"

Then she gave a small cry, and wheeling, turned and raced away.

"Belle!" he cried, and moved to go after her, but caught himself. He stared into the darkness, his handsome face lined with pain. As he peered into the night, he whispered, "She's paid too much—too much!"

## CHAPTER SEVEN

# ARRESTED!

★ ★ ★ ★

For Captain Whitfield Winslow, April 3, 1863, began as usual. He rose at six, read his Bible for thirty minutes, then limped down the hall for a breakfast of battered eggs, ham, biscuits and plum jelly. All through the meal he kept up the conversation—with little response from Belle. She had been quiet and subdued for two weeks, but insisted nothing was wrong. Now he looked at her pale face and wanted to suggest she see Dr. Mattox, but he knew she would refuse.

After breakfast he hobbled out to poke around in the flowers springing up through the warm earth. He had nearly recovered from his accident, but knew the doctor was right when he said, "You'll always favor that leg." He grinned as he moved across the lawn to check his roses, thinking, *At eighty, I'm glad to be as spry as I am!*

He enjoyed the morning, taking time out twice to drink the hot coffee Belle brought him. There was no portent in the bright sunshine, nor hint of evil tidings in the scarlet buds that peeped out of their tidy green cloaks. Later he would wonder at it, thinking how that which we fear does not always come when the clouds are cloaked with black, but often when the heavens are a delicate blue and the air cheerful with the songs of birds.

Even when his good friend Colonel Charles Taylor rode up

and dismounted at Whitfield's gate, there was no premonition. He had served with Taylor's father aboard the *Ranger* in the War of 1812, and for several years had followed the career of his old friend's son with pride. Colonel Taylor and Whitfield served under Sherman, which gave the colonel and the captain a common bond in the person of Lowell Winslow, who was part of Taylor's Cavalry Troop.

Whitfield walked to the gate and smiled. "Get down, Charles, and come in!" Winslow looked at his soiled hands, saying, "Can't shake hands now—but come in and have some coffee—and I'll beat you at chess again."

Taylor was a thin man of forty-six with a pair of steady gray eyes and a firm mouth. He was an inveterate chess player, but had beaten the captain only three times in their many games. He had a strong affection for the elderly man, and the two had had many pleasant evenings together over the past few years.

"How's your leg?" Taylor asked as they went into the kitchen, where he pumped water while Winslow scrubbed his hands with a bar of strong yellow soap. "You seem to navigate pretty well."

"Oh, fine—fine!" He wiped his hands on a rough towel, turned and said, "Well, let's set up the board."

At that moment Belle entered, saw the visitor, and would have turned to leave, but the captain spoke up. "Now, Charles, I have someone for you to meet. This is one of my relatives from Virginia—Mrs. Belle Wickham. Belle, one of my best friends—Colonel Charles Taylor."

Taylor bowed slightly. "We met once, Mrs. Wickham—at the party for the Satterfields. But in that crowd, I doubt you remember me."

She smiled. "Oh, but I do, Colonel." She shook his hand and would have left the two men had not the officer spoken. The sober look on his face made her uneasy, though she didn't know why.

"Mrs. Wickham—would you please stay a moment." He shot a glance at Winslow. "I have something to tell you, Captain. Could we go into the parlor?"

Winslow stared at him hard, then nodded. "Come this way, Charles." He led the way to the room, gestured toward a chair, and when they were all seated, said, "Let's have it then—whatever bad news you've brought. I can see it in your face."

Taylor bit his lip. "It *is* bad news, sir—very bad."

Captain Winslow stared at him. "Is it Lowell?"

Taylor swallowed. "Yes, it is." He dropped his eyes, unable to look at the pain in his friend's face.

"Is he wounded . . . or is it worse?"

"He's . . . he's gone, sir. Killed in action in Georgia."

Belle's eyes filled with tears. She had not been close to Lowell, but she had grown to love his grandfather. The captain sat with his eyes closed, rocking slowly. She knelt beside him, holding him tight, feeling the grief that shook him. How she wished she could take away the pain that racked him!

Taylor's face was fixed in a stony expression. He had known Lowell Winslow as one of his junior officers, and felt the loss personally, though he realized it couldn't compare with that of the grandfather's, but he had to bite his lip to control his emotions.

Finally, the captain pulled away from Belle and wiped his eyes. "Tell me about it, Charles."

"That's why I came, Whitfield," Taylor replied. He spoke slowly and gave the details so clearly that even Belle, who knew little of battle, understood. "We were sent on a raid to Georgia. Mosby had brought his cavalry behind our lines at Fairfax, Virginia, and nearly wiped us out! He captured a brigadier general, several other officers, and a bunch of horses." Taylor smiled grimly and added, "Lincoln hated the loss of the horses more than the general—said he could always promote somebody to general. But the defeat hurt our morale, so I took the troop down at the command of Stanton. We were to retaliate, but we failed."

Winslow noted the anger in Taylor's face. "What happened, Charles?"

"We were *ambushed*!" Taylor exploded, shaking his fist angrily. "They *knew* we were coming, and we walked right into their trap. Earlier I had become a little suspicious because we were making no contact with the Rebels. I almost turned back, but Stanton had said we had to have the victory to counter what Mosby had done, so I went ahead. And when we rode into a valley with hills on both sides, the Rebel troops closed in! It was hell, sir! They had field pieces on either side of the valley already set up, and a whole brigade of infantry jumped into the gap in front of us."

"I suppose you tried to retreat?" Winslow asked.

"We tried—but they were waiting for us," Taylor replied, his face twisting with grief as he relived the moment. "Forrest and his cavalry held us in like a box. They cut us to shreds. I could see no other way out than to hit Forrest full force, so I called for a charge. Those of us who were able carried the wounded behind us—and that's what Lowell did. He saw Major Whitlow fall, and he jumped down to help him. They were right beside me most of the way, both on Lowell's horse; and when we hit the Rebels, I saw Lowell pull his pistol and fight his way through the first line. It was horrible, sir! Many of our men fell, but there was no way to stop and get them. None!"

"What happened to Lowell?" Winslow asked quietly.

"The horse he was riding was hit and fell. Both Lowell and Whitlow went down hard, but Lowell was up in a flash. He shot a Rebel off his horse and got Major Whitlow in the saddle. He was just getting ready to mount behind him when he took a bullet right in the heart."

"You're sure?"

"Yes. I stopped long enough to make certain," Taylor said. He made it sound easy, but in fact Taylor had thought he would never escape the hail of bullets that whipped around him as he knelt to examine Lowell. "He died instantly, Whitfield, in the act of saving one of his fellow officers. A hero indeed! I am recommending him for the highest award our country offers."

"That was like Lowell," Whitfield said proudly. Then he cocked his head. "They knew you were coming?"

"Yes, we know that for sure," Taylor nodded. "We captured only two prisoners—but one of them was a lieutenant. After we fought our way clear and got back to our lines, we questioned him. He laughed at us and said they'd had exact information of the route we'd take and the time we'd be there. When I asked him how they had scouted us so well, he said that Forrest had gotten hold of a Federal War Order. It had all the details of our movements—everything."

"Dear God!" Winslow whispered. "How could it happen? How?"

"I don't know, sir," Taylor replied. "We all rejoiced when McClellan acquired Lee's Special Order 191 with all the Confederate movements at Antietam—now we see how painful it can be when it happens to us!"

"Have you told the boy's parents, Charles?"

"Yes. They took it badly, sir. His mother is distraught. Your son asked the doctor to give her a sedative to calm her. Robert asked me to break the news to you."

"Thank you, Charles," Winslow said, and got to his feet. He straightened his shoulders and stood erect. "You loved the boy, too, I know."

"I did!" Taylor's face reflected his own grief as he spoke. "I'll miss him as if he were my own, Whitfield! He would have gone to the very top in the army. He was a good soldier." He turned to go. "I'll be back very soon, sir. I wish . . ." He hesitated, then said, "All I can do now is try to find out who leaked that order to Forrest. It won't bring Lowell back, but it'll make me feel as if I've done what I could for him."

Belle accompanied him to the door. As she opened it, Taylor paused, looked down at her, and said sincerely, "I wanted you to hear this, Mrs. Wickham, because I know it's a hard blow for Captain Winslow. He needs all the support he can get. His son told me how much you've done for him—and how much you mean to him. God bless you."

Belle's face was fixed, and she nodded numbly as he took his leave. She closed the door, then leaned back against it, pressing her hands to her mouth to hold back the sobs that rose uncontrollably. *Georgia!* her mind screamed. For the instant Colonel Taylor had related the story of the special order that had gotten into Confederate hands, she knew! *The cavalry raid—that was part of the orders I copied and gave to Ramsey!* She recalled them clearly, almost word for word. Sick at heart, she knew there was no room for doubt, no matter how she sought for it.

She recalled the night she left the house of Henry Wilder, running through the streets with a copy of the secret orders. The night had been dark, but not so black as the sense of guilt and the foreboding of doom that had gripped her heart—and never left! She had fled like a guilty murderer fleeing the law, and she remembered how the preacher's words had thundered in her breast: *Thou God seest me!*

Since then she had no peace, and now, leaning against the door with great sobs rising to her throat, Belle knew she would never feel clean again. She hadn't thought of the implications of her work with Huger; always it had been some pins on a map, or a newspaper headline that mentioned troop movements.

But Lowell Winslow was not a theory. A vision of his cheerful face at the ball in Richmond flashed before her. How handsome and full of life and hope! How generous and kind to ride to the heartland of his enemies to save the life of another! She pictured him as he had been the last time she saw him alive—in the parlor where his grandfather now grieved. The colonel had taken her hand and wished her a good time at the opera, saying, *"You've been a godsend to us, Belle!"*

Then she thought of his body lying in the dirt, bleeding his life away, far from home and kin—*and it was her fault!* Though others had died, her mind was consumed with only one. If she lived to be a hundred years old, she would never be able to blot out the memory of Lowell Winslow's death.

Slowly she forced herself to stop weeping. Wiping her tears, she moved toward the parlor, hating the thought of facing the old man who sat there with a precious part of his life cut away. She moved stiffly, her limbs not coordinated, and when she saw him bent over with his face in his hands, she almost wheeled and fled. But she forced herself to enter, and went over to sit beside him.

They said very little, but several times he patted her hand and said, "I'm glad you're here, Belle."

★ ★ ★ ★

The interrogation room was located on the third floor of the Capitol building, at the end of a dim hall. The room itself was a windowless space ten feet wide and fifteen feet long. It contained one table with four places for seating around it, and one straight-backed, armless chair at one end of the room, faced by a series of lamps with mirrors behind them. These lamps, when lit, cast a harsh light directly in the face of anyone sitting in the single hard chair.

Colonel Henry Wilder had been present at the questioning of several men, but always seated on the dark side of the room.

Now he sat in the single chair with his eyes half-blinded by the lamps. The rest of the room was dark, and he was unable to see how many men were present.

He had been arrested at his home by two men in civilian clothes. These he had recognized immediately as members of Allan Pinkerton's force—the Secret Service. He was not allowed to speak to anyone, but was locked in a room in the Capitol for twenty-four hours. They had not mistreated him, but by the time two privates came to get him at nine o'clock in the morning, his nerves were completely unstrung and his legs so weak from fright that he stumbled on the steps leading to the third floor. "Careful, Colonel," one of the privates said, steadying him, "you'd break your neck if you fell down these stairs!"

He had recognized the room, and the terror that had gnawed at him ever since his arrest overwhelmed him as he was seated in the single chair. One of the men lit the lamps, then blew out the overhead light so Wilder could see nothing but the glare of the mirrored lamps. He sat in the thick silence, so frightened he thought he'd lose his breakfast. Finally the door opened, admitting a shaft of light, and he heard a voice say, "Wait outside."

Wilder recognized the sound of soldiers' boots, then the door closed. He peered into the light, shading his eyes with his hands, and said in an unsteady voice, "I demand to know what this means! I am an officer of the United States Army, and I have the right—!"

"Colonel Wilder—you are in a very critical position," a voice said, and Wilder recognized the voice of Allan Pinkerton, the head of military intelligence. "You have only a minute chance of extricating yourself from the charges lodged against you—and none at all unless you cooperate fully with our investigation."

"But, sir!" Wilder gasped, "I haven't even been told what the charges are!"

"Just answer my questions, Colonel," Pinkerton said. "There is, as I say, one small chance that you may be able to clear yourself. My associates are convinced that you are guilty. They have pressed me to bring you before a court-martial immediately. However, I have taken it on myself to give you one opportunity to avoid the disgrace of being dishonorably discharged—and the prison sentence that will follow."

"Sir! I'll do *anything* to clear myself!" Wilder cried out, panicking. "Ask me anything!"

"Very well. You drew up War Order Number 204 for the secretary of war, did you not?"

In spite of his fright, Wilder's remarkable memory did not fail. "Yes, sir, I did."

"Can you repeat the general nature of the content of that particular order?"

Wilder rattled it off, not in general, but in concrete specifics, going into great detail about the movement of Grant toward Vicksburg, the shifting of Rosecran's army, and the cavalry raid planned for Georgia.

"Very good, Colonel," Pinkerton said, admiration shading his voice. "Now, think before you answer this question. Take your time, and consider that your career may rest on your answer." He paused and then asked slowly, "Who, besides you, had access to that order before it was given to the officers in charge of the operation? Think carefully."

Wilder sat still as a stone, his mind racing back to that time. He thought of the conferences he had with Edwin Stanton and others as the plan was put together. He thought of how he had taken the notes made from those meetings home and worked on them several nights. He had an extraordinary ability to remember dates as well as figures and words, and suddenly a thought exploded in his mind that was reflected on his face.

"Ah? You've thought of something?"

Perspiration burst out on Wilder's forehead, and he passed a trembling hand over his face. Twice he tried to speak, and finally he managed to say, "Sir, there is one person who might have seen those orders—but I—I can't possibly give you the name."

"That's your choice, Colonel," Pinkerton said coldly. "I take it, then, that we must go the route of the court-martial?"

"No!" Wilder burst out. "I—I'll tell you about it—but I beg you, don't let this get into your report."

"Give me the facts, Colonel. You have no bargaining power. However, I will say this: If you have been victimized, we have no interest in destroying you. You are a valuable man to the secretary. But we must have the guilty party."

Again Wilder passed his hand over his brow; then his lips

tightened and he burst out, "It was that Wickham woman—the Dixie Widow!"

Pinkerton whispered something that Wilder couldn't hear. He went on. "But how could the woman have gotten to the papers if you didn't give them to her?"

"I—she was a guest in my house," Wilder gulped. Finally he said, "I may as well tell you, sir—she's a woman of no morals. She'd been chasing me for some time, and I finally asked her out a few times. Then, one night, she asked if we could stop by my house for a drink. Well, frankly, I was suspicious of her from the beginning, so I thought it might be possible to find out what she was like. So we went to the house and I tried to get something out of her."

"You didn't believe her story about being a converted Rebel?"

"Of course not!" Wilder shook his head emphatically, allowing a downcast expression to show. "But she's clever! Oh yes, I'll give her that."

"How so?"

"Well, sir, we were having a drink, and she asked for a glass of water. I went to get it, and she drugged my drink!"

"Did you taste the drug?"

"Why, no, sir, but it had to be that way . . ." Wilder hesitated. "I was out in no time—I mean just passed out!"

"You'd been drinking. You were just drunk."

"No! I'd only had a couple of drinks, I swear it! And I have a good head for liquor—ask any of my friends!"

"We have," Pinkerton spoke up dryly. "And they agree with what you say. So you were drugged. When you woke up, was the woman there?"

"No, sir!"

"Did you check your papers?"

Wilder hesitated. "Yes, sir," he answered. "They were all there—but I know now that she must have copied them and passed them on to the Rebels."

"Why didn't she take the papers themselves?"

"Why, then I'd know that she had done it. I suspect she wanted to get more information out of me."

Abruptly the bright lights dimmed, and with a shock Wilder saw the secretary of war standing beside Pinkerton. He was glaring at Wilder with an angry look. "What a fool you are, Wilder!"

"Sir, I—"

"Pick up the woman at once," Stanton commanded.

"What about the colonel?" Pinkerton asked.

"He'll have to testify against the Wickham woman."

"Yes, sir, I'll do that with great pleasure," Wilder agreed, relief flooding him. "I'll nail her for you, sir!"

"And after the trial, you can have what you're always complaining you never get!"

"Sir?"

"I'm having you assigned to active duty under Grant," Stanton stated with a hard look in his eye. "The average life of his company officers is about two months. Sorry there won't be any women down there in the lines at Vicksburg for you to dally with." He turned on his heel, ordering, "Keep him under house arrest until after the trial, Pinkerton. *And get that woman!*"

★ ★ ★ ★

Less than an hour after Pinkerton left Colonel Wilder, who was reduced to a fit of hysterical pleading, he walked up to the home of Captain Whitfield Winslow and rapped on the door. Soon a woman dressed in black appeared. "Yes? Did you wish to see Captain Winslow?"

"Are you Mrs. Belle Wickham?"

"Why, yes, I am."

Pinkerton pulled a paper from his inner coat pocket, handed it to Belle, who stared at it uncomprehendingly. "What is this?" she asked.

"It's a warrant," he said, keeping his narrow eyes on her face. "I arrest you, Belle Wickham, on the charge of treason. And I warn you that anything you say may be held against you!"

CHAPTER EIGHT

# HOME TO RICHMOND

★ ★ ★ ★

The *Calcutta* docked at New York at dawn, and Davis Winslow was the first passenger to step off the gangplank. He shouldered his way through the crowd waiting to meet the ship, tossing his bag into the first cab he saw. As they drove through the city, he paid no heed to the cherry blossoms filling the air with its fragrance. He had left England the day he got the news of Lowell's death, and had made record time on the fastest ship making the New York run. Now arriving at his destination, he was reluctant to enter the house. He went up the walk with a heavy heart and gave the brass knocker a solid rap.

The door opened, and his mother cried, "Davis!" He dropped his bag and held her, shocked at how thin she was and at the ravages that had destroyed the smooth lines of her face since he had last seen her. She clung to him as never before. Finally she lifted her face and kissed him. "Come in, dear!" she whispered.

His father came down the stairs at that moment, pulling on his coat. The jaunty assurance in his manner was gone. Robert had always greeted his sons with a firm handshake, but this time he put his arms around Davis and held him close. "My boy—I'm glad you're home!" His voice was husky.

*It's just about destroyed them both!* Davis thought. He tried to break the emotional atmosphere by saying, "It's good to be home. How about a little food for a hungry traveler? Then we'll talk." He didn't feel like eating, but they needed activity to get over the awkwardness of the moment. They moved to the kitchen, where Davis told them about his trip as his mother bustled around getting the food ready.

"The Prime Minister came to Oxford, Father—Mr. Gladstone. I got to speak to him."

"You did? What did you say?" Robert asked intently.

"Well, I was the only Yankee in the party, and he wanted to know my views on the rebellion. I turned it around and asked him if the British government would recognize the Confederacy as an independent nation."

"And?"

"He said no!" Davis shrugged. "Oh, he weaved it in with all kinds of political language, but that's what he meant."

Robert fired questions at him about the event, while Jewel was more interested in what the man wore. She set the food on the table, and they ate, mostly picking at the light lunch.

Finally Davis put down his coffee cup and said simply, "I grieve over Lowell—more than I ever thought I would. I didn't realize how I loved him—until he was gone."

That brought tears to their eyes, and they began discussing the tragedy. As his parents spoke of their loss, Davis knew he had been right about coming home. Lowell had been their favorite, but Davis had never resented that. Now they needed him as never before.

"How's Grandfather?" he asked.

"Better than your mother and I," Robert replied. "He's tougher than we are. Always has been. The hardest thing, of course, was *that* woman."

Davis had wondered at the rumors. "Is it true? Was she a spy?"

"Of course she was!" Robert snapped bitterly. "The trial's still going on, but she's guilty as Judas Iscariot!"

Davis looked down, then lifted his eyes. "Does Grandfather believe she's guilty?"

"Oh yes. He's accepted that," Robert answered. "He *had* to, Davis. She told him she was."

"She did?"

"Yes. She's admitted it all. You must not have read the reports of the trial. But I guess you couldn't on the ship. The trial's gone on for two weeks, and from the first the woman has confessed her guilt."

"It's dragged on because Stanton wants to make an example of her," Jewel added. Her mouth moved in agitation. "How I *hate* that woman!"

"Nobody loves a traitor," Davis said.

Robert frowned, puzzled. "You don't know what she did, Davis. She was *directly* responsible for Lowell's death."

His words sent shock waves through Davis. He stared at his father, incredulous. Robert gave him the full account, and when he was through, he said, "I've been a hard man at times, Davis. Politics and law—it's difficult to be gentle when you're in those things. And I've done some things I wish I could change—but this woman!" His face flushed with rage as he got up and walked to the window, staring blindly out until he could control himself.

Davis was stunned, and for the first time he hated Belle—so intensely that his hands began to tremble. His parents had never seen such fury in him before. After what seemed an eternity, Davis raised his head, and for the first time in their lives, they heard him curse—he cursed Belle Wickham, and he cursed the Confederacy.

He spewed out his invectives for several minutes, gradually quieting down. "I shouldn't have spoken like that," he said, getting to his feet. But there was a hard light in his eye that disturbed them. Neither had ever felt close to Davis, partly because he seemed to have so little drive. Unlike Lowell, Davis had been easygoing; and for two ambitious people such as Robert and Jewel Winslow, that was a serious character flaw. They had despaired of his ever making anything of himself, blaming that gentle side of his nature.

But now the deep rage in his brown eyes frightened them. Robert said quickly, "I know you're upset. Your mother and I—we've had time to adjust. I hate the woman, but we can't let our feelings get out of hand."

"Your father's right, dear," Jewel added, patting his arm. A thought flashed through her mind. *This is the only son, the only child I'll ever have. Will I lose him, too? Will this bitterness destroy him?* She spoke gently to him. "We must put this behind us, Davis. We can't let our feelings for that woman ruin our lives."

"I need to get away," Davis said abruptly. "I'm going to see Grandfather." His mother clung to him, extracting a promise that he would be back that evening—even his father seemed anxious to have him there.

Davis didn't go directly to the captain's house. Instead, he went to the downtown newspaper office and bought copies of the last two weeks. Sitting in an outer office, he pored over the accounts of the trial. As he read, he realized his mother's analysis had been true: the trial was a showcase for the prosecution. The evidence was clear-cut—but the prosecuting attorney had kept Belle on the stand day after day, driving at her with every bit of power to expose her to the nation as a vile representative of the Southern woman—the Rebel who had no common decency.

Colonel Henry Wilder had stated under oath that Belle was little more than a prostitute, becoming his mistress for the sole purpose of gaining military secrets. Davis had some doubt about the colonel's testimony, for his own defense was that he was *used* by Belle Wickham. Davis could not understand why Belle's lawyer did not explore Wilder's role in the matter.

Belle's testimony was given word for word. When asked by the prosecuting attorney, "Did you prostitute yourself to Colonel Wilder to gain access to his papers?" she had replied, "Yes." When he demanded details, she said only, "I have told you I am guilty; I will say no more."

She admitted everything and made no defense for herself, Davis saw. The one thing she would not do was disclose the other Confederate agents who were working with her.

Davis felt dissatisfied, and left the newspaper office to attend the trial. The room was packed, but he bribed a guard and slipped in at the back, next to a thick-set Union major, who nodded at him. "Guess we'll get the thing over today, don't you reckon?"

"I suppose so," Davis replied, wishing the man would leave him alone.

The major continued to discuss the case, but fortunately the judge soon entered and the trial began.

There was an hour of legal maneuvering; then Belle was put

on the stand. Davis stared at her unwaveringly. She was wearing black, had lost weight, but was no less beautiful—only more so. Her face was thinner, which made her large eyes seem even larger, giving her an aesthetic appearance. *She looks like I've always thought a woman poet should,* Davis thought.

But her beauty did not mitigate his fierce hatred. He had been shocked at the intensity of the rage that had risen in him when he heard of her part in Lowell's death, for he had never hated before. Now he realized that it was not going to leave—this white-hot anger that made him rigid as he continued to stare at her.

He listened as the prosecuting attorney addressed the jury in his closing remarks, asking Belle to verify her vile deeds over and over. She answered each question quietly, admitting her guilt with no sign of emotion in her wan face. Only once did she break, and that was when she was asked, "And did you feel no guilt when you used an old man who loved you—who had, in fact, offered you the hospitality of his home—when his grandson, Captain Lowell Winslow, died as a result of your perfidious betrayal?"

Davis leaned forward as Belle dropped her head. The court grew very quiet, and finally she raised her eyes and suddenly met those of Davis! She had not seen him before, and her hand quickly went to her heart and her lips parted. In that moment, it seemed to Davis that the court faded from his sight, and all he could see were Belle's eyes. He tried to read her expression, but his anger welled up—and she saw it. Through numb lips she said, "Whether I feel guilt for what I have done is not a matter for this court."

The answer angered the crowd, and the prosecutor kept hammering on that issue for twenty minutes. Finally he stopped and wiped his brow, saying, "The prosecution rests, Your Honor."

"The defense may make its closing statement."

The defense lawyer was a seedy-looking man named Hankins. He spoke in a mumbling voice, addressing none of the points brought up by the prosecution. Davis could scarcely hear the man as he murmured something about the sanctity of womanhood, and how, after all, she was only a weak human being, and it would be good to show mercy. He finished by saying simply, "The defense rests, Your Honor."

The judge said, "The jury will retire to consider the evidence and bring back a verdict." Then he instructed them, which he did so quickly that it would be impossible for them to bring back anything but a verdict of guilty.

As Davis turned to leave, the major warned, "Better not lose your place. They won't take long on this one!"

Davis walked slowly to the captain's house, trying to shake off the anger generating from somewhere deep in his chest. He didn't know how to handle anger, but he knew that such rage was dangerous, apt to make a man do foolish things.

By the time he arrived at the house, he was under control, though only superficially. Deep down he seethed like a boiling volcano in the center of the earth, waiting only for some signal to burst forth, spilling the blistering lava that would scorch everything in its path.

When his grandfather came to the door, Davis saw that the captain had been sorely hurt. "My boy, come in!" the old man said. Davis was aware that the wise old eyes of his grandfather were studying him. Finally, the captain commented, "You're different. Changed inside."

Davis nodded. "I don't know what's wrong with me," he admitted. "I was crushed when I heard about Lowell's death—but I came to accept that. It's—it's that I can't—"

"You can't forgive Belle?"

"Can *you*?" Davis shot back. "She misused *you* most of all! Can you still forgive her?"

"Yes, I can," he replied. He leaned forward and his eyes pleaded with Davis to understand. "Son, I'm not far from the day when I'll stand before God. When I do, how can I face Him knowing that I had not forgiven someone?"

"But—she's evil!"

"Are we not *all* sinners, my boy?"

"Not like her!"

"Oh, not in the same way, yet we all have sinned. And the Scripture tells me that if I will not forgive those who sin against me, God will not forgive me."

"I can't, Grandfather!" Davis declared stubbornly. "It's asking too much."

"You must forgive *her* for her part in Lowell's death, just as she must forgive *us* for our part in her husband's death." Winslow saw the blind rage in his grandson's eyes, and he said with a voice that throbbed with pain, "My boy, I have lost one grandson. He died honorably, fighting for his country. But I will lose another if you continue this way, for it will make you bitter, and a bitter spirit dries up the bones. It makes the soul sterile and a man unable to give love or to receive it. You have always had a gentle nature, and I've loved you for it. Don't throw that away for the sake of cherishing a blind hatred that will destroy you!"

The old man continued pleading for a long time. At length he realized it was useless. "I will pray for you, Davis. You may have to reach the bottom of all that you are and all that you love, but I'm asking God to do whatever He has to do to your body—so that your spirit may be preserved!"

★ ★ ★ ★

Simultaneous with Captain Winslow's words, the jury read the verdict: "We find the defendant, Belle Wickham, guilty of treason against the United States of America."

The judge nodded. "Thank you for your verdict. The prisoner will please rise." He studied Belle's impassive face for a few moments, then said, "This court gives you the sentence prescribed by law. You will be taken from this place to Old Capitol Prison. From there, one week from this day, you will be removed and hanged by the neck until you are dead."

A sigh swept the room, but Belle's countenance remained impassive. She stood silently as the judge ordered, "Take the prisoner away."

As Belle was ushered out of the courtroom by a side door, the reporters fought through the crowd and rushed back to their papers. The defense attorney left quickly by another door, while the prosecuting attorney received congratulations from the crowd with a pleased expression.

"Get her out and into the wagon quick!" the sergeant-at-arms commanded, "before the crowd mobs us."

Belle was hustled down a dark hallway and almost pushed into a small courtyard, where a covered police wagon waited with two guards on the back steps and two on the driver's seat.

One of her guards opened the door, helped her up, then slammed the door and bolted it. "Get her to Old Capitol fast!" he commanded the driver.

"Yes, sir!" the driver, a tall man, answered. He spoke to the horses, and drove the wagon out through the opened gates—none too soon, for a crowd was already gathering. The driver slapped the reins hard across the horses and they broke into a run, scattering the mob as the wagon plowed ahead. A few tried to chase the patrol wagon, but it was useless, and they turned away.

Inside the wagon, Belle was thrown from side to side as the vehicle picked up speed. She braced herself by jamming her feet against the seat in front of her. Belle couldn't possibly keep track of all the turns they made. She just wanted to get it over with.

*I'm glad the trial's over!* she thought. *I only want a cell where I can be alone.* The drawn-out weeks under the cruel eyes of the spectators had been extremely painful. Her mind flashed back to the courtroom. *Davis was there—how he hates me!* That hurt, but the thought of Captain Winslow was like a keen knife piercing her heart.

Belle did not fear death—though she realized she probably would be afraid when the time came. *I hope the week goes quickly,* she thought.

Finally the patrol wagon slowed, and came to stop. She pulled herself together and waited. She could hear voices outside. Then the door opened and the sun struck her in the face as she stepped out, the tall guard holding her arm.

She looked around in confusion, expecting to see the prison, but saw they were in an alley. Just ahead was a buggy with a pair of bay horses stamping their feet.

"Belle!"

She whirled and looked up at the tall guard who had spoken her name. Ramsey Huger!

Her mind reeled, and her legs grew weak.

"Hurry, Belle. Get into the buggy!" Huger urged.

He rushed her to the buggy and lifted her in with one quick motion and jumped aboard. "Get out of here!" he called to the men who had watched them get into the buggy. They were all wearing street clothes. Ramsey himself had exchanged his guard's uniform for a suit.

"Where are we going, Ramsey?" she cried as the buggy tore down the alley and turned east.

He flashed his familiar smile, and reached over and hugged her.

"We're going home, Belle—home to Richmond!"

She shook her head. "Not there! They all hate me!"

"Not anymore, Belle," he smiled. "Your trial has been in every paper in the South—and you're the greatest heroine we've had since Belle Boyd!"

"I—I can't believe it!"

"You will when we get there." He gave the horses a cut of his whip and they broke into a dead run. "We've got to get you into some different clothes, and do some dodging. But when we get to Richmond, you'll see! The Yankees tried to destroy you, Belle, but they let the cat out of the bag when they told how you got the secret plans to our generals. Our men were able to use those plans to whip the bluebellies real good!"

"Ramsey, I wish I hadn't done it."

He looked at her, startled. "Don't say that, Belle! The South needs a lift—and you're the one who did it. The Dixie Widow—who outsmarted Washington and saved her nation's armies!"

She didn't believe it then—nor during the days they spent dodging the federal officers combing the country for the fugitive.

But a week later in Richmond, with her happy family at her side, a special ceremony was given in her honor. Only when Jefferson Davis pinned a medal of honor on her and she heard the wild cheers from the thousands who had gathered did the truth begin to sink in.

As she stepped into a carriage with President Davis and his wife and rode down the street, the cries of "Hooray for the Dixie Widow!" followed them. It seemed as if the whole city had turned out. But though Belle smiled and waved at the adoring crowd, there was no joy.

Her heart was heavy. Her mind in turmoil. For two visions were constantly before her: the face of Captain Winslow—and a Union soldier lying dead in Georgia.

PART TWO

# THE PRISONER

★ ★ ★ ★

## (May '63 – January '64)

# CHAPTER NINE

# "HE'S ALL WE HAVE LEFT!"

★ ★ ★ ★

"I'd hoped that Davis would be a comfort to you and Jewel after we lost Lowell," Captain Winslow said to his son Robert, "but it hasn't worked out that way, has it?"

Robert ran a hand through his hair with an air of desperation. "What's the *matter* with him, Father?" A frustrated note edged his voice. "He won't talk, he disappears for two or three days at a time—Jewel and I are about out of our minds!"

The two men sat beneath a peach tree in Captain Winslow's garden, where Robert had dropped by early one morning. It was May, when the peach blossoms were in full bloom, decorating the dusty blue sky overhead. During the past weeks, they had discussed Davis's aberrant behavior several times. Robert seemed to have aged years, the captain noted. His face was lined and his hands jerked with ceaseless motions.

"We'll just have to give him time, Robert," he said.

"Time! Why, he's getting *worse* as time passes, not *better*! Neither Jewel nor I realized how much Lowell meant to him."

"It isn't just that—though he was more devoted to his brother than any of us realized."

"Then what in the world *is* wrong with him?"

"He's angry, Robert—angry down to the bone!—and that's something Davis has never experienced before." Whitfield stood to his feet and looked down the street. "Here he comes now," he said as he saw a figure in the distance.

"At last!" Robert exhaled. "He's never had much starch, but at least he had common courtesy! Now, he doesn't seem to care what he does to his mother and me. She can't quit crying, and I've looked everywhere for him since he disappeared yesterday morning. Said he'd be back for lunch—but not a word from him!" He shook his shoulders in anger, then seemed to remember his father's words. "You say he's angry? About what?"

"About the world, I'd say. Davis has always stayed apart, never letting himself get involved. That's why he wants to be a writer—or thinks he does. A writer can stand on the sidelines and observe. He doesn't have to take sides, you see? If people go wrong or if things don't work out, why, he's not been a part of it, so he can't be blamed. I think Davis has done that all his life."

Robert nodded, watching his son come slowly down the street. "I believe you're right. And it would explain why he's refused to take any position in this war. It's as though he's kept himself above it."

"But now he can't do that, can he? His Olympian posture won't work anymore—because the war reached out and struck him down."

"You mean when Lowell died?"

"Yes. There's no way to be objective when you lose your flesh and blood."

Robert lowered his voice, a shrewd look in his eyes, as Davis approached the walk leading to the house. "And he's angry about that—and about the way that Wickham woman used us all?"

"Yes. He hates her. And it's that hate that makes me ache for him. He can't sort it all out. His brother is gone, and he has to blame someone, so he's focused on the South. But Belle is the symbol for the whole Confederacy. And that bitterness will destroy him if he doesn't get free." The captain added hurriedly, "Don't say anything about this, Robert, and don't nag him."

Robert nodded, and got up. "Well, there you are, Davis. I just dropped by to see if Father would come over for dinner tonight."

Davis halted, studied his father's face, then said, "I'm sorry I didn't get back yesterday."

Robert waited for an explanation, but seeing none was coming, said, "Oh, we figured you got tied up. I told your mother you'd probably been trapped by one of those young women she keeps shoving in your direction."

"No. I just needed to get away and think for a while."

"Of course!" Robert nodded, and got his hat from the chair. "Will you bring your grandfather over tonight?"

"Yes, of course. What time?"

"Early as you please," Robert replied. "I've been wanting to ask you about your writing, and this would be a good time to do it."

As he got into his buggy and moved away, Davis grimaced. "He's never been interested in my writing before."

"Give him a chance, boy," the captain responded gently. "Your parents are having a pretty rough time."

Davis was shamed by his remark, and said, "I know—we all are, I guess." He sat down in the chair vacated by his father and stared up at the peach blossoms. His suit was rumpled as if it had been slept in, and his eyes dulled with fatigue. The captain studied him, but didn't comment, knowing there was no way he could force the young man to open his mind.

After a few moments Davis spoke up. "I hope Mother wasn't too upset with me. I just lost track of time. I was having lunch and ran into a friend of mine—Professor Joshua Chamberlain, one of my instructors at Bowdoin."

"What does he teach?"

"He used to teach rhetoric. But he left to become a colonel in the Army of the Potomac—Corps V. Sure did surprise me," he added with a smile. "The last time I saw him he was fussing around trying to get us to organize our stiff little speeches—now he's trying to get me to join the Union Army!"

"Is that a fact? Are colonels doing their own recruiting?" the older man asked wryly.

"That's about the way it is, I guess," Davis nodded. "Colonel Chamberlain cussed Edwin Stanton—said he made a big blunder. Last spring he got the freakish impulse that the war was about over, so he closed down all army recruiting stations and stopped enlistments. He sure was wrong! With all the losses in the Shenandoah Valley, getting whipped at Richmond, and our heavy casualty lists, we're running out of men. And even when he opened the recruit centers again, there wasn't much business."

"The romance is gone," the captain nodded. "Always goes that way in a war. When the thing starts, it's all lemonade for the boys, every pretty girl coming out to kiss them goodbye, with the flags flying and the bands playing. But—when the dying starts, that all changes."

"That's what Chamberlain said." Davis thought about the conversation he had just had with his former professor, listening as the officer talked about the war. Davis would not have been so interested if Chamberlain had been a career officer; it was to be expected that the Regulars would be caught up in the struggle. But he knew Chamberlain had been opposed to the war. Now the tall, picturesque professor with his grave, boyish dignity and the clean-eyed, naive look of a happy professor had changed.

"I hate this war, Davis," he'd said as he sat at the table sipping coffee the day before. "I stayed out as long as I could, hoping somehow we'd find a compromise on the slavery issue—but when I saw that we never would, I joined up." He looked down humorously at his blue uniform and three-foot sword. "Never will look like a soldier, will I? But the Regulars can't win this war! It'll take men like me—and you, Davis. The South won't quit. We'll have to wear them down to the last Confederate before it's over."

Captain Winslow searched his grandson's face with intensity. But struck by an unexpected thought, said only, "I'd like to meet Colonel Chamberlain. Never knew a professor of rhetoric in the uniform of a colonel. I'll bet he can play a mean game of chess."

"How did you know that? He's a master at it!"

"Game takes logic—and usually those professors have that quality. Bring him around if you can."

"Not likely, sir. The regiment is pulling out any day. But we're supposed to have dinner tomorrow night, so maybe it'll work out. He'd like you—and you'd like him a lot." Davis stood up, saying, "We stayed up most of the night talking. He has a room at a hotel with two beds. That's where I spent the night. But it was a short night; I need a nap."

He went into the house, took off his outer garments and

stretched out on the bed, his eyes gritty, and sighed heavily. He could not sleep, but lay there trying to shut out the images that kept flickering across his mind. Mostly he thought of Lowell, of the good times they'd had together—and of his death in Georgia. When he first heard the news, his imagination was plagued by the unknown. But after talking with Colonel Taylor, he now could see the full picture. Lowell had been struck in the chest by a ball, the crimson blood pulsating over his uniform, running down to the ground—then his face had grown still. Davis reviewed the scene over and over. With a groan he pressed the heels of his hands against his eyeballs and tried to blot out the image.

Finally he drifted off into a fitful sleep, only to dream again—this time of Belle, a dream he'd had several times. She seemed to be before him, as beautiful as ever, but always tempting, her face twisting with a demonic cruelty. She would hold out her smooth white arms, whispering for him to come to her. Then as he moved toward her, she would point to something on the ground beside her, laughing. And when he looked, it would be Lowell—gasping and dying.

He woke up crying out "No! No!" in a choking voice. Shaking his head to clear his mind, he rolled out of bed and drank thirstily from the pitcher on the night stand. He paced the floor restlessly, stopping by the window to stare out. There he remained for over an hour, his mind flooded with angry thoughts. Abruptly, as if to shake off the tormenting voices, he turned and threw himself across the bed face down, and soon fell asleep.

He slept until noon, tried to write for most of the afternoon, but eventually gave it up. He found his grandfather reading in the parlor, and said, "Let's go uptown and see if we can find Colonel Chamberlain. Maybe we can persuade him to have dinner with us."

"Fine! Like to meet the man."

They found Colonel Chamberlain at the recruiting office. When he was introduced to Captain Winslow, he said, "I've always wanted to meet you, sir. Davis talked about you often when he was my student."

"We've come to recruit you for a meal, Colonel," the captain responded. "We're having dinner with my son Robert and his wife, and we'd like to have you join us."

"I'd like that!" Chamberlain agreed, then laughed, "I'm like a Baptist preacher these days, sir—always ready for an invitation to a meal." He rose to his feet, adding, "No business here today, so we may as well go. Take over, Lieutenant," he nodded to the young officer nearby.

The evening was a success, for the colonel's presence brought Davis out of his shell, much to the joy of his parents. Chamberlain was aware of the loss of the younger son, and after offering his sympathy, he focused on Davis. He spoke with humor about a few clashes they'd had in the classroom, told of some of the minor problems that Davis had never mentioned—including an incident involving a yearling calf that had been hauled up to the second-story bedroom of the president. His eyes twinkled as he'd looked at Davis. "The culprit was never convicted, but the entire faculty agreed that Davis Winslow was the prime mover in the incident!"

Robert looked at his son with fresh interest. "You never told me about that."

"Well, sir, it wasn't my finest hour—besides, it was never proved."

They were relaxing around the table after a meal that Chamberlain had attacked with the energy of a soldier. "Haven't had a meal this fine since just before Chancellorsville."

"Were you in action there, sir?" Robert asked.

"Yes, sir, I was." His brow puckered in a row of furrows. "It was a fiasco—again."

"We outnumbered the Rebels almost two to one, I understand," Captain Winslow remarked.

"Oh yes. We had about a hundred thirty-four thousand men at the beginning of the campaign—and we weren't green recruits, either. The army had been at the Seven Days, at Antietam, and at Fredericksburg. Lee had no more than sixty thousand at any time. Hooker took us across the Rappahannock and the Rapidan about twenty miles northwest of Fredericksburg."

Chamberlain was silent for a moment, then shook his head. "We had it all—the numbers, the terrain, the guns, everything! But we lost."

"What happened, Colonel?" Davis asked. "I can't understand

it. Time and again we have everything in our favor—and we lose! It's almost as if God is against us."

"I don't know about God, but Robert E. Lee and Stonewall Jackson were," Chamberlain replied dryly. "Hooker made lots of big talk. Called us 'the finest army on the planet.' And just before the battle, I heard him tell General Couch, 'It's all right. I've got Lee just where I want him. Lee's army is now the legitimate property of the Army of the Potomac.' " A strange expression lit Chamberlain's blue eyes. "It happened as soon as the battle started. Hooker caved in—just as Pope did at Second Bull Run, and Burnside at Fredericksburg. It's almost like black magic! As soon as our army meets Lee and Jackson, the generals become paralyzed."

"Well, Jackson was killed," Robert replied with satisfaction. "There's no one to replace *him*!"

"Yes," Chamberlain agreed. "He was unique, but don't forget, we lost seventeen thousand men and were humiliated in the eyes of the country—and of the world."

Jewel spoke up. "That many, sir—seventeen thousand of our men? How awful!"

"We've got to stop them!" Davis cried.

Chamberlain's head jerked up in surprise. Davis's face was pale, his eyes bright with anger. In the ex-professor's eyes, his former pupil's one fault was that he was too bland. Now Chamberlain saw the rage burning in the young man. He nodded. "Yes, Davis, we do. That's why I'm wearing this uniform."

"I'd like to line up every Rebel and blow them all to smithereens with cannon fire, Colonel!" Davis said between gritted teeth. "They brought this thing on because of that cursed slavery of theirs!"

Shocked by the ferocity in his voice, the others sat stunned. Chamberlain broke in gently, "It's easy to hate them, Davis, but I've found that I make a better soldier if I keep a steady head. I've had lots of hotheads in my command, and they usually don't last."

"So I discovered when I was a fighting man, Colonel," the captain said. "Oh, in the heat of battle when you're in a death struggle, most men go into some kind of madness, but a person can't keep living like that."

Davis set his jaw stubbornly, revealing the firm line of the Winslow look. He was still overweight, but he had lost some in the past few weeks. "I don't see how you can be halfway about fighting a war," he argued dogmatically.

"Please," Jewel begged quietly, "could we talk about something besides the war?"

"Why, of course!" Chamberlain said. "I must apologize, Mrs. Winslow. We soldiers get so caught up in the war, we forget there's another world."

"Why don't you and Father have a game of chess?" Robert suggested. "Davis and I will cheer you on."

The rest of the evening was pleasant, for Chamberlain was a cultivated man who could speak informatively on many subjects. He beat the captain in a hard-fought battle, offering to give him a chance at revenge any time. It was nearly ten before he left, and the captain decided to stay the night. "I'll see you tomorrow, Colonel," Davis said. He had been very quiet during the latter part of the evening, sitting beside his mother and listening as the other men talked.

"Well, it's too late to look at your writing tonight," Robert said. "But the colonel is an interesting man. Maybe tomorrow night, eh?"

"Perhaps," Davis replied vaguely, and said good night, retiring to his room.

After he left, Jewel commented, "Davis was in a better mood tonight, wasn't he?"

"Yes. I guess he needs bookish people like Chamberlain to draw him out," Robert nodded. "We'll have to work on that, Jewel—I mean, have people in whom he can talk with, like Colonel Chamberlain."

"I don't think Chamberlain will be here long," the captain said thoughtfully. "He seems to think the army will be moving out pretty soon."

"We'll have to make the most of him then," Jewel decided. "I've been thinking of having a special dinner, with some writers and professors. Davis would like that."

The captain didn't respond, for he had sensed a restlessness in Davis that he knew could not be assuaged by parties. He retired to his room and lay reading the Bible for about an hour.

Finally he laid it down, put his spectacles away, and blew out the light, feeling a heavy sense of oppression over his grandson. His prayer was mostly for the young man.

For the next five days, Colonel Chamberlain was a frequent visitor, both with the Winslows and at the captain's house. He actually had little to do, and enjoyed their company. Jewel and Robert were happy, and the dinner party she planned went off well. Davis seemed rather quiet, which wasn't unusual. He spent a great deal of the day with Colonel Chamberlain, and often spoke of him to his parents and his grandfather with an admiration they had rarely seen.

On Friday evening, the captain was again at his son's house for dinner. He had come alone, informing them that Davis would be there by six. Six came—but not Davis. Not until five before seven did he make his appearance.

When Jewel opened the door she saw both Davis and Colonel Chamberlain. As soon as the two men stepped into the parlor, Robert and Whitfield knew something was wrong. Colonel Chamberlain's face was intensely sober, while Davis's jaw was set in the stubborn expression he wore when he was determined to do something he knew would displease others.

Chamberlain said abruptly, "I apologize for this intrusion, but Davis and I have had some disagreement, and I wanted to—"

"Father, Mother," Davis broke in. "I'm enlisting in the army."

"No, Davis!" Jewel cried.

Chamberlain hastened to say, "I wanted to come with Davis, because you'll think that I talked him into enlisting." He shook his head. "Such is *not* the case, I assure you! As a matter of fact, I've used every trick of rhetoric I know to persuade him to postpone this decision."

Robert and Jewel began imploring their son to change his mind, to reconsider, to realize the possible consequences. The captain listened to their pleading patiently, but knew they were wasting their time. There was a mulish stubbornness on Davis's face, and his mouth was set like a trap. The longer they pleaded, the more obvious it became that he would not alter his decision.

His mother dissolved into tears, and his father became angry.

"You *always* nagged me to do this," Davis reminded them. "Now that I am, I don't see why you're so upset." Actually, he knew they were afraid of losing him, their last son, but he refused to let it influence him. "I've got to do it, so please be a little more reasonable."

Chamberlain spoke up. "As I said, it's not my doing, and if you ask, I will refuse to enlist him."

"Then I'll join another regiment," Davis said.

Chamberlain glared at him, then shrugged. "Well, there it is! If you would like, Mr. Winslow, I can make him my aide-de-camp. For whatever it means, I'll do my best to see he doesn't lead any foolhardy charges."

"That would be best—if he has to do it," Robert said sadly. He straightened up, forced himself to smile, and went to put a hand on Davis's arm. "Your mother and I—we didn't mean to be unfair. It's just—well, we'll worry about you."

"I know, sir," Davis replied quietly. "But I need to take this step. I couldn't live with myself if I didn't."

They made it through the rest of the evening, though it was uncomfortable. As Chamberlain left, Robert asked, "What's next, Colonel?"

"I think Lee will try a rather daring move to keep us away from Richmond. Most of the generals I know believe he'll probably hit us somewhere as far away from there as possible."

"Try to keep him safe, Colonel. I know that's nearly impossible in battle—but *he's all we have left*!"

"I'll do what I can, Mr. Winslow—but nobody who goes up against Robert E. Lee is safe!"

CHAPTER TEN

# Little Round Top

★ ★ ★ ★

Two months had passed since Stonewall Jackson's death in the woods at Chancellorsville, where he'd been accidentally shot by his own men. Vicksburg was slowly being strangled by Grant's iron fist. Overseas, the English observed carefully, watching for a sign to give support to the South. They almost decided to recognize the Confederacy after the Rebels won at Chancellorsville, but waited for a Southern victory on Northern ground.

Lee knew this and decided to strike. He had beaten the enemy back many times: McClellan, Burnside, Hooker at Chancellorsville; Pope at the Second Manassas; Banks in the Valley. But he couldn't mend the Army of Northern Virginia forever; the South had stripped itself of men, arms, and food. Lee had no alternative but to face the legions of Union armies that would come at him fully fed and equipped.

There was only one thing to do: strike at the heart of the North with all the strength he could muster, hoping to burst it asunder with one mighty blow. It was imperative that he carry the war up North, to the untouched fields where his tattered men could feed on the rich grainland and obtain shoes and clothing—take Washington if possible.

Lee was the most audacious soldier who ever wore a uniform, and now like a Mississippi riverboat gambler, he looked at his options. He knew his men. They had never been wholly beaten. He had driven four Union armies back within a year and broken the three top generals from their command. He studied his opponent's face—then put all the cards on the table. Win or lose—winner take all.

The decision made, Lee and the Army of Northern Virginia moved North, risking everything. In the words of a ragged sergeant in Jackson's old corps: "We'll give 'em the best we got at the ranch!"

They moved quickly, shouldering aside the shotgun militia, taking minor towns, paying out Confederate bills for supplies from Dutch storekeepers, who groaned at their personal loss.

In the North, Lincoln heard rumors of the army of tattered veterans on the move, and replaced Joe Hooker with General George G. Meade as commander of the Army of the Potomac. Meade, a Pennsylvanian, was tall, sad-faced, and austere. He had no flamboyance; his troops never cheered him as they did McClellan—but he was tougher than any of the previous Union generals who had confronted Lee. Like Grant, Meade could watch men die—then send in more who would die when the others fell.

As Lee moved north, he encountered Ellen McClellan, a Union woman with great courage. She had gained an audience with Lee to inform him that the people of her town were starving because the Army of Northern Virginia had taken all the food. He surprised her by immediately ordering supplies to be sent to the beleaguered town. On leaving, she asked for his autograph.

"Do you want the autograph of a Rebel?" he smiled.

"General Lee," Mrs. McClellan replied, "I am a true Union woman and yet I ask for bread and your autograph."

General Lee answered, "It is to your interest to be for the Union, and I hope you may be as firm in your principles as I am in mine," then gave her both bread and his autograph.

Another Confederate general, George Pickett, was leading his weary troops through Pennsylvania when a little girl burst out of a clapboard house, waving a tiny Union flag in explosive patriotic enthusiasm. Instantly, the general wheeled from the line, and taking off his cap, bowed to the child with all the grace for which he was noted, and saluted the flag of his foes. Then turning, he lifted his hand, and every man in the division doffed his cap and made that same salute.

The little girl stared at the ragged line of men, never expecting such courtesy, and then she cried out, "I wish I had a Confederate flag; I would wave *that* too!"

Later, Pickett was asked how he could salute the enemy's flag. He replied, "I saluted the womanhood in the heart of that brave little girl."

★ ★ ★ ★

It was now the end of June. As Lee advanced, Meade groped for his adversary. Through fogs of rumor and false report, the two armies fumbled for each other.

Their first encounter occurred at Gettysburg. The battle began casually—with a raid for shoes. A North Carolina brigade under an officer named Pettigrew moved toward the small town with no more noble ambition than to find shoes for the barefoot troops. They were spotted by a Union officer, John Burford, who had been tracking Lee's army like a hunter stalking a big cat. He sent a courier scurrying back to General Reynolds, commander of Union Corps I, who gathered his troops and attacked the Confederates the next day, July 1.

It was considered a minor skirmish, but more men were lost at Gettysburg than at Bull Run. General Reynolds was killed, and his Corps I lost half its number, either killed or wounded, as the Confederate General Heth overran the Yankees, who retreated to a fishhook ridge as the sun went down.

★ ★ ★ ★

Davis Winslow arrived at Gettysburg the next morning. He was considered the greenest Third Lieutenant in either army. Since the Twentieth Maine was down to only 300 men, Davis became the target for ridicule. Knowing nothing about the army, it was torturous training for the new recruit. Chamberlain had given Davis his first instructions, driving him day and night to learn his duties. He had been humiliated more than once. A bearded corporal taught him to shoot, but never missed an opportunity to degrade him. When given a horse with which to carry messages, he had fallen off—in full view of the regiment.

Another time he had gotten so lost that a courier had to be sent to find the missing messenger.

But he had endured—and learned. Having completed his training, Davis and the little column set out toward Gettysburg, through the soft green country, filled with orchards and big barns. They had been greeted with a band playing "Yankee Doodle" when they had crossed the Pennsylvania border, and people had handed out free food. A beautiful girl with long blond hair had rushed up to Davis, pressing a warm cake into his hand, and when the soldiers had greeted her with cheers, she had blushed and fled.

At noon they moved into Hanover. As they left they could see a haze against the horizon. "That's Gettysburg, Lieutenant," Chamberlain said, nodding his head. "The fighting's started, I think. That's gun smoke."

A thickness rose in Davis's throat. "Do you think we'll be in battle today?"

"No." Chamberlain shaded his eyes and looked at the sky. "Too late—but I reckon we'll be in the thick of it in the morning." He glanced at Davis and smiled. "I know what you're thinking. You're wondering if you'll run when the shooting starts."

Davis was startled. "How'd you know that?"

"It's what everyone worries about the first time he gets into a battle. It's what *I* thought." He stared down the road, waiting, as a rider thundered to a stop and handed Chamberlain a message. The colonel read it, and the rider sped off without another word.

" *'Proceed with all speed. Rebels will attack at dawn,'* " Chamberlain quoted. "We'll just about make it."

"Colonel, I feel so useless!" Davis exclaimed. "The greenest man in our whole regiment knows more than I do."

"Well, you're about to get a quick education," Chamberlain grinned. "When the fighting starts, you discover quickly that knowledge doesn't mean much. If it gets as thick as I expect, there won't be any fancy tactics. We'll line up and they'll line up on the other side, and the one who kills the most and the quickest will win the Battle of Gettysburg."

"What if I get separated?"

"You listen for our call. We've got our own special alert. Dan

Butterfield was a brigade commander under Hooker. He got tired of so many different bugle calls, so he wrote one just for our brigade. When you hear that, you come running. It's called the 'Dan Butterfield' and goes like this: 'Dan, Dan, Dan, Butterfield, Butterfield.' "

Chamberlain kept up a steady conversation with his officers as they moved on, more concerned about his raw third lieutenant than the others. At midnight the Twentieth Maine left the road and slept in the woods.

The next morning Davis awoke to see a group of men coming down the road, unarmed. "Reb prisoners," said Rankin, the first lieutenant. Davis wanted to talk to some of them as they paused for a rest, but he heard the call 'Dan, Dan, Dan, Butterfield, Butterfield,' and ran with the rest to form the line of march.

Chamberlain led them at a killing pace through a flat farm and a peach orchard, then through a high cornfield. They came to a brook, already filthy from so many men moving upstream, but they kept going. Finally they stopped to rest; off in the distance Davis could hear the sound of an occasional cannon. It was very hot, and sweat poured off him. Though he had lost weight in the weeks following his enlistment, he still carried twenty pounds of fat, and, unlike others, had not been hardened by long marches.

A courier arrived and spoke to Colonel Chamberlain. After reading the message, the colonel called his officers forward: "We've got to move quick! Double time all you can, and don't let anybody drop out!"

They raced forward, and after thirty minutes at the terrific pace, Davis was dizzy from the heat, and his legs trembled so badly he was afraid he would fall out. They made their way between rocks, on a narrow road, then to the top of a hill, where they were met by another officer. Davis was so close he could hear the conversation.

"Chamberlain, they're attacking the left flank! Sickles was supposed to be there, but he's not there! So you've got to do the job."

"Yes, Colonel Vincent."

"Come along and I'll help set your lines." Vincent led them down a ravine, and then onto a crest that afforded a view of the whole battlefield. "I'm putting you here, Colonel. This hill is shaped like a fishhook, and you're the part right at the tip of the barb. The whole brigade will form on your right." He paused, and said quietly, so quietly that Davis could barely hear him, "You are the extreme left of the whole Union line. You know what that means?"

"Yes, sir."

"You cannot withdraw—under *any* conditions. If you do, the line is flanked and they'll go straight up the hilltop and take us in the rear. You *must* defend this place at all cost."

"Yes, sir," Chamberlain said steadily, his eyes mild in the hot sunlight.

Vincent grinned. "Well, now we'll see how professors fight! Good luck, Chamberlain."

He rode off, and Chamberlain shouted, "Dig in!" The position was more than a hundred yards long. On his right the Eighty-third Pennsylvania was forming; on his left—nothing. The men dug in, piling up rocks for a defense, and soon the line was fortified. Having finished, they waited.

Davis was amazed at the calm of the veterans. They acted as if nothing traumatic was about to hit them. He wished he could be as calm, but his stomach churned every time he heard a cannon go off, or the rattle of musket fire. As the afternoon wore on, he thought of Colonel Vincent's order: *You cannot withdraw. Under any conditions.* What did that mean? He didn't have to ponder long. *To the last man—if necessary.*

Death and life beyond the grave had always been a philosophical speculation for him. But as he looked at the gray figures swarming like terriers below, preparing for a charge, the matter became intensely personal. His trembling hands perspired, his throat constricted, and his stomach churned. He thought of his father's assurance that such predicaments were for ministers. Now those words were empty. *If only—*

"Here they come!" The cry exploded in the air and sent a chill up his spine. Bullets rained around them. Rocks cracked. The Yankees dug in deeper—and waited. Davis and the other two lieutenants walked up and down the line. The men grinned at Davis, noting his pale face and jerky movements. He wanted to lie down behind the stones and hug the earth—anything to get away from the bullets zipping around them, but forced himself to walk confidently. *I may not know much—but I can stand up and ignore the fire,* he thought.

By now the Rebels, a myriad of gray-green-yellow uniforms, were rolling up en masse. Then for the first time, Davis heard the Rebel cry. It was a piercing scream that nearly made him drop his pistol, and the whole line dissolved in smoke and thunder.

His troops loaded and fired rapidly, like machines, and when a man in front of Davis dropped dead, Davis picked up the soldier's rifle and shot into the line of Confederates rushing upward in wavy ranks. The Yankees' fire was steady, hitting many of the gray targets below, but when one Rebel went down, it seemed as if three more emerged to take his place.

The attack continued with a ferocity Davis could not have imagined. Again and again the Rebels clamored up the hill, crawling over their own dead, and time and again the Maine regiment beat them back.

Suddenly the firing ceased and a voice called, "Winslow! Lieutenant Winslow!"

He whirled to find Colonel Chamberlain and the other two lieutenants staring at him in unbelief. "I guess you fought them off, Lieutenant," the colonel grinned. "Better save your ammunition."

"Why—!" Davis looked down the line at his troops. All eyes were fixed on him. Only at that moment did he realize the Rebels had pulled back. He dropped his rifle and got to his feet, feeling lightheaded. The silence was heavy and oppressive after the thunderous roaring of the canons and the rattle of rifle fire.

"I guess . . . I got carried away," he said lamely.

"I guess you did," Chamberlain smiled. He winked at another

lieutenant and said, "Perhaps if we had a few hundred more like Davis, we could attack Bobby Lee, eh?"

Laughter erupted, but Chamberlain sobered. "We're out of ammunition, I suppose."

"You're right, sir," Lieutenant Rankin replied, worry creasing his face.

"Send men out to collect all the ammunition they can from the enemy, but be careful. When you get back, add it to our supply and divide it up." He looked down the line sadly. It seemed that every other man had been killed or wounded.

"Sir, I don't know if we can hold them if they come back that strong," Rankin said.

From the statement, Davis realized the other officers weren't aware of the order given Chamberlain: You cannot withdraw—under *any* conditions.

Chamberlain didn't answer but gave orders to move the wounded back, and no sooner had they completed the task when the special call was heard: *Dan, Dan, Dan, Butterfield, Butterfield.* They rushed back and took up their positions just in time to meet the fierce charge as the Rebels neared the top of the hill.

The second attack was no less fanatical, and Davis soon ran out of ammunition. Running down the line, he frantically searched until he found a few balls and some powder, then sped back in time to help repel the last line. The Rebels withdrew, but this time they did not go far—only to wait until a new line of support caught up with them from below.

During the interlude, as the Rebels were reforming before their eyes, Lieutenant Rankin reported the shortage of ammunition. "Some of the men have nothing, sir," he said, his face gray. "Should we pull out?"

"We can't, Lieutenant," Chamberlain replied, checking the line. Davis followed his glance. If *they* went, the hill went, then the army—and the battle would be lost, as so many had already.

"They're beginning to move, Colonel!" Second Lieutenant Marsh yelled.

They all waited for Colonel Chamberlain's command to retreat, but he scanned the hillside at the lines of Rebels climbing up, and said casually, "We'll give them the bayonet."

Unable to comprehend his logic, they stared incredulously.

"They'll be tired, and we'll be going downhill," the colonel explained. "Rankin, you take the wing. We'll get them after they fire, before they can reload."

Davis quietly picked up a rifle, snapped a bayonet in place, and said, "Let's do it, men." That proved to be the spark Chamberlain needed.

The sight of the greenest man in the regiment moving forward either shamed the Twentieth Maine or fired them with courage, for up and down the line there was the clicking sound of bayonets being attached. Then Davis yelled and leaped over the rock barricade.

He never expected to get out alive, for he could clearly see the Rebels leveling their rifles, sending a barrage of bullets around them. He knew he was screaming at the top of his lungs, and so was every man who made the charge. They poured down the hill shouting, and in spite of those who fell, nobody stopped. Over the dead and wounded they flew, their bayonets gleaming in the sun.

As the Yankees plunged ahead, fearlessly brandishing their weapons, the enemy fell one by one.

The daring and unexpected assault drove fear into the Rebels' hearts, and they threw their rifles and fled down the slope in great bounds. The retreat began so abruptly that it seemed to have no beginning. The sight of that naked steel coming at them shook men who had endured the worst of the war, and they ran for cover.

It was over as suddenly as it had begun.

"Winslow," Chamberlain commanded, "check your men and return to your post!"

Davis took a quick count and found they had lost only six soldiers, though three more had been wounded. They reached the top, and cared for the wounded. Not more than twenty minutes later, an officer rode out from the timber behind them, his face wreathed in admiration.

"Sir," he said to Chamberlain, "that was magnificent! We saw it all from that hill back there. Colonel Gilmore wants to see you."

As they left, Chamberlain called, "Lieutenant Winslow, come with me. Lieutenant Rankin, see that the ammunition is handed out."

Davis followed him back to where the officer had tied some horses. He found mounting the animal awkward but bearable. When the three men headed for the ridge, Chamberlain remarked, "That was a stiff fight. If we were in the classroom, Winslow, I would give you an excellent mark for your work today." He added, "If you hadn't made that first move, I doubt if a single man would have gone down that hill."

"I didn't think we had any choice, Colonel."

"I'll mention your name in the reports—but I want you to know I'm glad you're in my command, Davis!"

They reached the crest and found Colonel Gilmore bubbling over with excitement. "By heaven, Chamberlain, how in the world did you ever get the idea to make a bayonet charge?"

"We didn't have any ammunition," Chamberlain said simply. "Sir, this is Lieutenant Winslow. He led the charge, as you perhaps saw. I might mention that he's new with our command. As a matter of fact, this is his first action."

"My word!" Gilmore exclaimed, extending his hand. "You deserve congratulations, Lieutenant!" He stood back and shook his head in wonder, then spoke to Chamberlain. "Colonel, I need one more thing from you—can you hold your position until support comes? That won't be long, I think, for I've already sent for Fisher. Should be here in a couple of hours."

"Yes, sir." Chamberlain looked around and asked, "Does this hill have a name?"

"Yes—Little Round Top," Gilmore replied. "Don't suppose you'll ever forget *that* name! By the way, could I borrow the lieutenant for a short time? I must get a message to the Sixteenth Michigan."

"Certainly," Chamberlain said, and turned to go, saying over his shoulder, "Winslow, report back when you've finished the mission."

He rode away, and Gilmore took a leather pouch from his saddlebag. "Just see that Colonel Harry McFarland gets this." He waved toward his left and added, "You need not report back to me, Lieutenant. When you've delivered the message, just go back to your brigade."

"Yes, sir," Davis said, taking the pouch and guiding the horse around and toward a line of trees covering the base of a rise. As he rode along, he had flashbacks of the battle, and found himself gripping the reins so tightly that his hands cramped. He was stopped several times by sentries, but had no trouble finding the Sixteenth Michigan. The colonel was a tall man with pale skin sunburned to a bright red. He took the pouch, read the message, and said, "This won't do!" He read it again, then shrugged. "Lieutenant, you'll have to take this to Major Shultz. He's down that slope in the forward position—right at the base of those trees. You see them?"

"Yes, sir."

"Deliver this to him, and then you can go back to your unit."

He turned away, and Davis moved across the line of men on the brink of the hill, noting that they had taken heavy losses. The slope was not steep at first, but when he was no more than 200 hundred yards from the crest, he came to a steep bank that ran straight across his path. He hesitated, not certain of his way, then moved his mount to the left. He followed the ravine for a quarter of a mile, but found no place to cross. Finally the ravine ran into a clump of scrub timber, and he thought he saw it flatten out. He ducked as he pushed through the timber and out to a small clearing. He sighed with relief when he saw he could cross.

Just as he reached the ravine, a voice came from his left: "Hold it right there, Yank!"

A shot of fear coursed through him, and he drove his spurs into the horse in a furious retreat. Four Confederates stood behind him, their rifles trained on him.

One of the Rebels stepped forward, a smile on his face. "Well, boys, guess what? Looks like we done caught us a courier! Now just step down off that hoss, sir, and let us relieve you of all that hardware."

There was no option—and Davis complied. After taking his gun, the leader said, "Well, lookee here!" He snatched the leather pouch out of Davis's pocket. "We got us a prize! Harry, you and me will take this feller back where the officers can question him. Tim, you and Simms stay here."

Thirty minutes later, Davis was in front of a tent, being questioned by a large bearded Rebel general. Only when one of the officers said "General Longstreet, look at this order" did Davis realize he was in the presence of the second ranking general of the Confederacy. He knew Longstreet had replaced Jackson, and was the man Robert E. Lee depended on most.

Longstreet read the message, looked up at Davis, and asked, "What's your outfit, Lieutenant?"

Davis knew vaguely that there was nothing wrong in giving that information. "The Twentieth Maine, General," he replied.

Longstreet eyed him for a moment. "When did you come into the line?"

Again Davis saw nothing wrong in answering, so he said, "Last night."

The general grimaced. "You see, Armistead," he said to an officer nearby, "I knew we'd moved too slow!" He looked back in Davis's direction. "I don't suppose you'd like to give us the other units perched on top of that hill, would you, Lieutenant?"

"No, sir. I wouldn't."

With a curt nod, Longstreet commanded, "Put him with the other prisoners, Major Lennox."

Davis was hustled away by a short, fat major and handed over to a sergeant, who took him through the Rebel lines to a group of prisoners, perhaps twenty in all. They were kept inside a rope corral with ten soldiers keeping guard.

"Hey, Lieutenant!" he was greeted almost at once. "What outfit?"

"Twentieth Maine," Davis replied. He found that most of them were from Sickle's Corps. One of them, a rawboned, red-headed lieutenant, came to stand by him. "Name's Ezra Lee. You hungry?"

"No."

The brief monosyllable drew a look of sympathy from the other. "Know how you feel. Felt that way myself at first—thinking of going to a Rebel jail for who knows how long. But we'll make it. How about a drink? We got a bucket over here."

"Sure. I'm Davis Winslow." Davis went with him to where one of the guards gave him a drink of tepid water. He had not realized how thirsty he was, and when he had downed all he could, he said to the guard, "Thanks, soldier."

"You're right welcome, Lieutenant." The guard was a small man with a bristling black beard. "We'll put you two with the other officers—soon as we catch us a few," he commented. "You can sit here if you've a mind to."

Davis sat down, and saw Lee hesitating, unsure if he should force himself on the newcomer. "Sit down, Lee. Tell me what's been going on."

Lee hadn't talked very long before Davis realized the man was a strange mixture of pessimism and optimism—comically so. One of the first things he said was, "Well, if we do die in a Reb prison camp, we won't have to be sceered of gettin' shot in a battle, will we, Winslow?"

"Guess that's sure enough," Davis grinned slightly, and this encouraged Lee to keep up a patter of conversation until they were moved about two hours later to the rear and put with another group of prisoners. One of them was Captain Perry Hale from Ohio. On the heels of this move, a Confederate lieutenant announced, "You men are moving out. If you try to escape, you'll be shot, so don't try it. Sergeant Willis will be in charge of your guards. Sergeant, get them out of the area at once."

Willis was a strong-looking man with a Springfield carbine in his large hands. He called out, "You heard the lieutenant—get movin'."

They left the area accompanied by eight guards and a wagon of supplies. Soon they were on the road leading out of Gettysburg. They were marched hard until late afternoon, when they halted and cut firewood to make a quick meal of bacon and coffee. After the meal, Willis announced, "We'll have to chain you up for the night." The news shocked Davis, but he realized the squad had no choice. All the men, except the officers, were fitted with a pair of handcuffs. One long chain was run through the chain loop of each man's handcuffs, then anchored at each end to a sturdy tree and left loose enough to allow some freedom of movement.

Then Willis called, "You officers, come over here. If you three will give me your promise not to escape, I won't have to chain you up."

"No, sir," they all said.

Willis wasn't surprised. "Well, you'll have to be chained then," he said and put the manacles on them, with a shorter chain that allowed freedom to lie down.

"Where will you be taking us?" Hale asked. He was a sturdy

man with pale blue eyes and a large mustache.

"You three will go to Libby, I reckon. The rest will go to Belle Isle."

In the North, both Libby and Belle Isle had been reputed as having inhumane conditions. Some even said it was better to get shot than captured by Johnny Reb.

Davis slept that night, and the next day they started their long, monotonous journey to Richmond. They marched all day, stopping at noon for a brief meal, then at night to eat and sleep. It was broken by one fragment of good news. A Confederate courier caught up with them on his way to Richmond. As he drank coffee, the Yankee officers heard him say, "We got whipped. The Yankees held on to that hill, and we had to retreat."

Hale whispered, "Well, we won anyway!"

When they entered the outskirts of Richmond many days later, the enlisted men were taken by the squad, while Sergeant Willis and one other guard took Davis, Hale and Lee to Libby Prison, a huge warehouse converted into a prison.

As the steel door clanged shut behind him, Davis was overwhelmed with a shroud of black despair. It seeped into the depths of his spirit with a crushing weight he'd never known before.

The prison was packed to capacity, but the three Yankee men stuck together, finding a bond with one another that was forged during their long journey. Each was given a thin blanket, and assigned to a large room, already packed with hungry-looking men. They ate thin soup and a single piece of cornbread, then lay down for their first night in Libby.

As Davis lay there in the foul-smelling air, listening to the grunting snores of the inmates and the cries uttered in their sleep, he found himself wishing he had been one of those who had died at Little Round Top. The future stretched out before him—a bleak line of spectral days, grim and cheerless, without end. Never again would he bask in the warm sunlight, never again breathe the exhilarating fresh air.

# CHAPTER ELEVEN

# CHIMBORAZO

★ ★ ★ ★

A veil of snow floated out of a leaden December sky as Belle approached Chimborazo. She had driven through the streets of Richmond early on her way to the hospital, and the thick blanket of snow that had fallen during the night muffled the sounds of travel so much that she seemed to have gone deaf. Instead of the clatter of iron wheels over the rough cobblestones and the clip-clop of horses, there was only a faint sibilance as she guided the buggy along.

Richmond itself on that Sunday morning had a strange mystic quality, due to the robe of pure white that clothed its grimy buildings and dirty streets. The sight of shops, factories, hotels, and the many buildings hiding their dark war-stained exteriors under a mantle of pure white, like a bride's mantle, caused Belle to think, *How often a beautiful outside covers ugliness and wrong!* She had been reading Shakespeare the night before, and the line flashed into her mind: "O what a goodly outside falsehood hath!"

She shook off the thought, stopped the buggy and got out, picking up the large bucket of soup she had made at home. She entered the hospital by a side door, and was immediately pulled out of a world that seemed pure and spotless into the world of sickness and pain.

Chimborazo was the largest military hospital complex in the world, with over 76,000 patients passing through it during the course of the war. Each of the five buildings had its dozens of wards. Belle was matron of Hospital Number 3, and her patients were from Virginia, Maryland, Arkansas, and South Carolina. They all had been mixed together when she first took charge, but she separated them into wards according to states because of the intense jealousy between them. If an Arkansan saw a Virginian receiving more attention, he would complain.

As she entered ward 17, the Arkansan ward, she was greeted cheerily. "Whatcha brung us, Miss Belle?" an emaciated boy no more than seventeen asked. He had yellow hair and gray-blue eyes that smiled when she looked at him.

"Home-made chicken soup, Lonnie," she replied. "And *you* get the first bowl." A protest went up from a long-haired man across the room, but she gave him a stern look. "When you let me cut that hair of yours, Coy, you'll get some attention."

Coy Willing was a tall lanky man from the Ozarks with a bandaged stump for a right arm. He shook his head stubbornly. "I promised my sweetheart I wasn't going to cut my hair till we won the war. You wouldn't want me to break my vow, would you, Miz Belle?"

She ignored him, went to the cupboard, took out a pile of dishes, and examined them to see if the orderly had washed them as she had ordered. For once he seemed to have done his job, and she ladled out some of the rich soup into one of them, and took it to Lonnie. He was lying flat on his back, and when she lifted him to a sitting position, she was shocked at how light he was. He had been brought in with critical abdominal wounds, his viscera bulging, and such patients usually didn't live long. Lonnie had become a challenge to her, and she worked long hours over the boy, keeping him from slipping away.

"Here, you've got to eat every bit of this, or I'll cut a switch to you."

"I'll try, Miss Belle," he said and began to swallow the soup as she fed him. Though his wounds had been terrible when he was brought from Gettysburg, he never complained. Now he was nothing but skin and bones, she saw.

The ward was quiet. Many of the men were still asleep.

Lamps burned softly on ledges over their beds. As she fed Lonnie, Belle glanced at the clean floor. She thought back to that first week and the filthy conditions of the wards. She had soon learned that the assistant surgeons would drink the men's whiskey supply, then lock themselves in their offices all day while the wounded died on their cots and the chamber pots overflowed.

She smiled, remembering the showdown she'd had with the ringleader. It had been in the middle of the afternoon, and a young Marylander had died in his own filth. She had stormed into the office of the assistant director of the hospital and in a voice that every patient, orderly, and assistant surgeon could hear clearly, she had scalded him verbally. He had blustered and threatened to have her removed, but she'd smiled coldly at him, saying, "We'll see who's removed, you sorry excuse for a human being! When I tell the President what sort of trash is in charge, you'll be out of this hospital—and I'll do all I can to see that you get drafted and sent to the front!"

He had sneered at her, but when President Jefferson Davis and his wife Varina marched into the Chimborazo the next day for a surprise inspection, the careless doctor turned pale. He turned even paler when after the inspection he was sent for by Dr. Keller Stevens and dismissed for incompetence. Later, word came back to the hospital that he had been assigned to Hood's division as a private. An older man named Elmer Gibbs had taken his place, and under Belle's direction the wards had been transformed.

Suddenly as she inserted the spoon into Lonnie's mouth, a spasm of pain seized him and he bit down hard, his body arching upward. She threw her arm around him and held him as he writhed in agony, his eyes closed, his lips a pale line. Finally he relaxed, and she took the spoon out of his mouth, saying, "That was a bad one, Lonnie."

"Not too bad, ma'am," he whispered. "I can't complain."

"You never do, Lonnie," she said, laying him down gently and smoothing his brow. "I'll bring you something for the pain if it becomes unbearable."

She went around the room dispensing the soup, giving a word of encouragement, and filing information about patients' conditions in her mind. The doctors were amazed at her ability to remember not only every patient but the fine details of their condition. Most of them didn't realize that in addition to the long hours she spent in the wards, she kept a written record of each man. She also wrote letters for many of them. In this way she felt as if she had come to know their families and their problems.

After all the men were fed, she walked over to Coy Willing with a basin of water and fresh bandages. He stared up at her with a stubborn frown. "I ain't gonna let nobody cut my hair," he stormed.

"If you want to look like a ridiculous fool," she shrugged, "that's fine with me." She sat down and removed the bandages, dropping them into a sack at her feet. As she dressed the stump, she remembered how she had reacted the first time she had seen a bad wound. She had become nauseated and run to the bathroom to recover. She had fought against the overwhelming desire to flee from the hospital. Instead, she had washed her face and gone back to the man, who had looked at her in surprise and muttered, "Ma'am, you don't have to do nothing for me."

"Yes, I do," she had said, and had proceeded to dress his wound. "If you can take a wound for our Cause, I can dress it."

The stump of Willing's arm had been infected when he first arrived, and she had feared gangrene, but it had healed nicely. She studied the knob of muscle, nodded and said, "The doctor did a good job on you. He left a nice pad of flesh over the bone."

"I reckon so," he growled in a lifeless voice.

"What's the matter?" she asked.

He picked at the cover with his remaining hand for a long moment before raising his eyes. "Miz Belle," he asked. "Do you reckon. . . ?"

She saw him struggle, and asked quietly, "What is it, Coy?"

"Oh, I jest git to thinking—about my sweetheart. You know? And the thing is—well, they's lots of fellers with two arms."

Belle stared at him. He had been in the ward for over a month, and had given her more trouble than any other patient. Now his arrogance was gone, and she saw the fear and doubt that had lain beneath his blustery behavior.

"A man is more than an arm, Coy," she said evenly, impulsively pushing the stringy hair back from his brow. "You're the same man you were before you lost that arm—no, better! Because you gave it for your country. If your girl loved you before, she'll love you more now." She saw the doubt flicker in his eyes, and said pertly, "If you'd get a haircut and clean up, we could get your picture made in your uniform and send it to her."

His eyes flared with hope. "Really?"

"Of course!" A humorous thought struck her. "In fact, we'll go down together, and you can have one made with me, if you like. That way you can make her a little jealous."

He stared at her, and his voice was husky as he whispered, "Really, Miz Belle? Would you really do that?"

Gone was the hard-talking exterior. She saw for the first time that for weeks he had been lying there covering up his fear with tough talk. Her eyes stung with tears as she took his hand. "Yes, I will—" A twinkle lit her eyes. "I will if I can cut that hair!"

He nodded, unable to speak, and she rose. "I'll be back with a pair of scissors a little later. And I'll find out about the pictures, too."

She moved from ward to ward, stopping at almost every bed, and finally went to the small office squeezed in between two wards. For two hours she worked on the paperwork accumulated during her absence. Several times she was interrupted by orderlies. She answered their questions and went back to the papers, working until she had gone through all of them. She had just sat back to enjoy a cup of tea when the door opened and her sister Pet burst into the room, pulling a Confederate officer with her.

"Belle!" Pet exclaimed. "Beau is back!"

Belle rose and walked around the desk to greet them. "It's good to see you, Beau," she smiled and put out her hand.

Beau Beauchamp held it in his own. "You're looking very well, Belle," he commented. "Your brothers send their love."

"They didn't come?"

"Not this time. But they'll be in Richmond in a few days, I guess. Nothing much happening now."

Pet jumped in. "Thad came with Beau, Belle. We're all invited to a party at the Chesnuts' tonight, and you've got to come." She lifted a sack, saying, "I've got to give these tracts out to the men.

Beau—you make her come, you hear!"

Belle smiled as she dashed out, saying, "I wish I had her energy, Beau. But she's young."

He laughed lightly, "What are you, an old woman?"

"I feel like one," she replied evenly. "But what brings you to Richmond?"

"Oh, nothing much is going on, Belle." He stretched and said thoughtfully, "It's almost like the Yankees and us wore ourselves out at Gettysburg. We've been moving back and forth from the Rapidan almost to the Potomac, just sparring all the time, but nothing big in Virginia. I came back for supplies, and to try to pick up a few recruits."

Belle poured him a cup of tea, and sat down, saying thoughtfully, "We've taken some hard losses this year, haven't we, Beau?"

He nodded. "Gettysburg was bad. We lost twenty thousand, killed and wounded. And the same day we retreated, July fourth, Vicksburg fell, then Port Allen down in Louisiana. That means that the Yankees control the Mississippi River now, and the Confederacy is cut right in two." His thoughts caused his brow to wrinkle, and he said, "Bragg lost a lot of men in Tennessee in September, so we're in bad shape in the West."

"It's going to take a miracle, Beau, for us to win."

"I guess that's so—but we can't quit." He put his cup down. "I hear about you, Belle. Everywhere we go they talk about the Dixie Widow."

"I wish they wouldn't call me that!" she exclaimed. "It sounds so—so much like something in a bad novel or a play."

He shrugged his heavy shoulders. "Too late. You became a heroine when you outfoxed those Yankees." He gave her a look that was half admiration and half reproach. "Belle, you sure fooled us all—and it wasn't really fair. You put on such a good act that I thought you'd really turned against the South. Wish you'd trusted me."

"Oh, Beau, I couldn't tell anybody. We've gone over that. Anyway, it's over."

"Not really," he argued. "The papers won't let it die down—and I hear there's going to be a play about it."

"Oh no!" she cried in vexation. "They *can't*!"

Agitated, she got up and paced the floor. She was more mature than she had been when he had courted her, Beau saw, for time had given her an air of calm assurance. He half listened as she railed against the newspapers, thinking, *Why, she's more beautiful than she was the first time I saw her at Belle Maison!*

She must have seen something of his thought in his expression, for she abruptly turned and said, "Beau, I've got work that must be done."

"I understand," he replied, getting to his feet. "But let me take you to the Chesnuts' dinner tonight."

She hesitated for a moment. "All right, Beau. I'll be ready."

His face flushed with pleasure. "It'll be like old times," he smiled, and left to find Pet.

She stared after him, wishing that she had said no, but he was a hard man to discourage. She was afraid he still fancied himself in love with her. She shook her head, thinking, *I've got to avoid that.*

★ ★ ★ ★

Richmond society, the rarefied segment of it, centered around the home of Colonel John Chesnut and his wife Mary. They had been among the wealthiest South Carolina planters at the beginning of the war and had moved to Richmond when Chesnut was elected to the legislature. The colonel was dominated by his impeccable Old World manners. His wife once told Rebekah Winslow: "My husband could see me—and everything that he loved—hung, drawn and quartered without moving a muscle. And he'd have the same gentle operation performed on himself and be just as stoic."

Mary Chesnut often exploded with disgust and impatience at the incompetence, stupidity, and inertia she witnessed in high places, but had such a beautiful and witty spirit that she was loved and admired by President Davis's wife, Varina. She had become a fast friend of Rebekah's, since their husbands were both close advisors of Jefferson Davis.

When Belle and Beau entered the large dining room at the Chesnut home, Beau exclaimed, "Would you look at that, Belle! There's General Lee—and General Hood!"

Belle smiled and drew him into the room. "They're at the

Chesnuts' often," she told him. "Hood is in love with a relative of Mrs. Chesnut's—over there with General Hood. Her name's Sally Campbell, but her close friends call her 'Buck.' "

"She's a beautiful young lady," Beau remarked. "But Hood—why, he's lost an arm and a leg! Surely she won't have him?"

"I think she might," Belle shrugged. "Mother says Sally's in love with him."

"If a man maimed like Sam Hood can win a young girl's fancy," Beau commented, his eyes boldly searching her face, "why, I guess there's hope for the rest of us."

"Beau," she countered, "I can't think of things like that anymore. I'll never marry again."

He shook his head. He carried the same bold, confident strength and assurance as always, so she didn't argue. "Look, there's Thad and Pet."

Thad stood to his feet, and Belle recalled how he had looked when he first come to Belle Maison—almost dead, and skinny as a rail. Now he was six feet tall, strong and healthy. His dark face broke into a smile as she approached. "Hello, Miss Belle," he said warmly. "We've been hearing all kinds of good things about you, the nursing and all."

When they were seated, Thad whispered in awe to Pet, casting a glance at General Lee, in deep conversation with Colonel Chesnut, "I can't believe I'm in the same room with General Lee. Just wait till I get back to the boys. Won't they be jealous."

"Not any more than when Lee pinned a medal on you—and made you an officer." She patted his arm and smiled. "Let's eat. I'm hungry."

The meal was delicious, and as they were finishing, Mrs. Chesnut and Rebekah Winslow walked over. Mary Chesnut was a small woman with hazel eyes and straight black hair. "Belle, I got the supplies for the hospital you asked for, but they were dear!" She sat down beside them, and motioned Rebekah to a chair. "I got a barrel of flour, a bushel of potatoes, a peck of rice, and five pounds of salt—and I had to pay sixty dollars for them!"

"In the streets," Rebekah said, "a barrel of flour sells for one hundred and fifteen dollars." She smiled at Thad and Pet. "By the time you two get married, it'll take all your pay just to buy a loaf of bread."

"Guess we won't mind the hard times," Thad smiled.

The conversation turned to other news. Deep in discussion, they were interrupted by a pleasant voice.

"Mrs. Wickham?"

Belle looked up to see General Lee standing beside her. She flushed. "Yes, General?"

He spoke very softly, his eyes kind as he watched her. He gave no sign that he was the most idolized man in the country. "I've just been getting good reports of your work from Colonel Chesnut. We are all in your debt, and I offer my grateful thanks for the sacrifices you are making for my men."

Belle nodded. "It's my privilege, sir, to be of service to them. I only wish I could do more."

"If you had been on the scene when our dear Jackson was shot, he might have lived." The thought of Jackson brought sorrow to his eyes, and he added, "He was a strange man. Next to a battle, he preferred a long Presbyterian sermon, Calvinistic to the core."

Then spotting Thad, he brightened. "Well, young man, you're still with us, I see."

"Yes, sir," Thad replied breathlessly.

"He's doing very well, General." Sky Winslow had come up in time to overhear Lee. He put his hand on the young man's shoulder. "He's a good soldier, and a good farmer. The food some of your troops have been eating is his doing."

"Is that so?" General Lee seemed surprised. "How does that happen?"

"He convinced me to plant corn and vegetables instead of cotton," Sky nodded. "When this war is over, this young fellow will show the South how to break out of the bondage of cotton."

"That's exactly what we must do!" Lee agreed. "Most of our planters are the real slaves, not the Negroes. They are held in serfdom by the banks in the East." He smiled at Thad. "I think I made a very wise appointment, sir." Pleased with the news about Thad, he nodded and moved away, leaving the room with Chesnut and Winslow.

Rebekah said, "That must make you very proud, Thad." She looked at Belle, adding, "And you too, Belle. Your father and I are so proud of you!"

"We all are," Pet said, going over to hug her. "You've done so much!"

Belle rose in agitation, her face pale. "Oh, I wish. . . !" Without another word she turned and left the room, with Beau following quickly.

"What's wrong with Belle?" Mary Chesnut asked, puzzled.

Rebekah sought to find an explanation. "I don't know, Mary. I think sometimes she's too caught up in the Cause. Ever since she came back from Washington, she's been different."

"I suppose being sentenced to hang would make one a little different," Mary conceded. "All the stories in the papers about the Dixie Widow! It's a wonder it didn't turn her head. Most girls couldn't take that much adulation."

"She hates it—all those stories," Rebekah said.

Mrs. Chesnut looked toward the door thoughtfully. "That captain is so handsome. He's an old beau of Belle's, you say? Perhaps he can help. They do make quite a handsome couple."

"She says she'll never marry," Pet put in. "That's why they call her the Dixie Widow. Married to the South and all that."

Outside, Beau assisted Belle into the buggy, then jumped in and took the lines. As they drove along the snow-packed streets, he thought about their past, but didn't speak until they pulled up in front of her small house. "Do you remember the New Year's Eve party—the one where Vance and I almost fought over you?"

She looked at him, took a deep breath, and pleaded, "Beau, you *must* understand—I'm not that girl anymore."

He leaned forward to peer into her eyes, and was surprised at the profound sadness. "Belle, we're both older, but for me nothing has changed. I loved you before you married Vance. That hit me hard—but I still care for you."

He put his arms around her and pressed his lips to hers, and for one brief moment she was passive.

"No!" she cried, wrenching herself away. The bitter cry erupted and she leaped from the buggy. "You don't want me, Beau! You don't know me—not anymore!" She ran to the house and slammed the door behind her.

Beau was stunned. Finally he shook his head and drove down the street. "She couldn't have changed *that* much," he argued quietly, and set his jaw with determination.

## CHAPTER TWELVE

# LIBBY PRISON

★ ★ ★ ★

"Davis! Look what I got for you!"

Holding a round object in his hand, Ezra Lee bent over the still figure under the blanket. There was no response, so he threw the cover back and began to pull the unconscious man to a sitting position.

"Look, it's an apple, Davis! A real honest-to-God apple!"

In the feeble light falling through the high, dusty windows, the cadaverous face bore little resemblance to the red-cheeked countenance of the man who had lain down for the first time on that same straw ticking in July. The eyes that blinked open were now sunken in the sockets and dull with fever. A thick reddish beard covered the emaciated cheeks that had once been round and rosy with health. Davis's full lips were shrunken to thin lines covered with sores. He slowly lifted a skeleton-thin hand to the fruit.

"Wha' you say?" Davis's head swam as he tried to grasp the apple. He blinked against the yellowish light, and would have fallen back had not Ezra held him firmly. Davis had been dreaming of riding in a carriage through a park in New York. Now to be recalled to the dank cell of a thousand rank stenches angered him. He tried to strike at Lee, but was too weak to make any impact.

Lowering Davis to lie on the hard pad, Lee stood up and said to a man nearby who had been watching, "Perry, he's in a bad way. I thought maybe the apple would make him feel better."

Hale looked at the twitching face of the sick man. He himself had lost thirty pounds since the three of them had arrived at Libby, but was still strong looking, though his face was as pale as theirs. He shook his head, adding, "I guess we better have another shot at gettin' him into the infirmary."

Ezra Lee had been lanky and rawboned in July when he had been captured, but the scanty diet at Libby had pared away every excess pound. Even though his face was shrunken, he was still relatively healthy. Hale's remark disgusted him. "What good will that do? LeCompt'll just laugh at us."

They stood over Davis Winslow, frustrated and angry—as they had been for the last six months of their imprisonment. Many times they had been told, "Thank God you're not in Andersonville—or on Belle Isle."

At first they were thankful, all three of them. They heard from former prisoners about the Confederate prison in Andersonville, in central Georgia—the huge open pen known as a living hell for Union captives inside its stockades. The prisoners were fed raw unsifted cornmeal filled with husks. Disease brought on by inadequate food, polluted water, and appalling sanitary conditions took a frightful toll. Scurvy, acute diarrhea, dysentery and gangrene killed men like flies. Day by day, prisoners carried their dead outside the stockade. The other prison, Belle Isle, a tent city on the James River, was no better. Every enlisted man kept on that isle described the place as horrible beyond human comprehension.

So in comparison, Libby was not as bad as those or their counterparts in the North, but the officers crowded into the old warehouse suffered many of the same conditions as the men at Andersonville—overcrowding, poor diet, lack of medical care, sicknesses that swept through the prison like wildfire.

Perry Hale had lived through them all, filling him with a seething bitterness. As he looked down at Davis, a dull hatred burned in his eyes. He had formed a special bond with Lee and Winslow, forged in the agony of Libby's dark, lethal cells. He was somewhat older than the other two, and of superior rank, so it had been natural that he would be the leader. Over the months, it was Hale who had been able to gain a few special privileges that had kept them from losing hope altogether. He had managed to sneak letters to their people, informing them of the men's whereabouts. And he had, by a means he never revealed, come into possession of enough gold to buy the three of them a few small comforts. In civilian life, Hale had been a wealthy manufacturer, and in prison had somehow gotten the gold through bribing the guards.

But now the money was gone, and Hale was frustrated to the core, trying to think of some way to help Davis. "We'll have to try it, Ezra," he decided finally. "Let's get him to LeCompt."

Lee shrugged, "All right," and bent over the unconscious man.

"You take him under his shoulders and I'll take his legs," Hale said. "We'll have to be real careful. There's not much left of him." The fever had raged through Davis for weeks, draining him of all vitality. His legs and arms flopped lifelessly as Lee and Hale carried him out of the cell into the large, packed room. They had to call out warnings, and in some cases shove their way through. The prisoners cursed and would have added blows, but Perry Hale's bulk and the captain's insignia kept the opposition down to mere curses.

Some of the men sat on the floor playing cards, some stood around talking, and others just slouched against the wall, staring dully at the floor. There was a hum of voices from the large gathering of skeleton-like men in blue suits. How long each man had been incarcerated in Libby could easily be discerned by the way his uniform fit. Though every prisoner had on all the clothing he possessed, he still resembled a scarecrow.

Lee and Hale had to go to the third floor to get to the infirmary, and by the time the two had navigated the crowds and struggled up the stairs, they were both winded. They staggered along the corridor until they came to a set of double doors marked with a sign INFIRMARY. "Get the door, Ezra," Hale said, taking Davis's inert form.

Lee opened the door and the two men entered a large room with over thirty men waiting on the benches that lined the walls. A sharp-featured man with narrowly spaced eyes looked up as they approached. Glancing carelessly at Davis, he asked, "Winslow again?"

"Yes." Hale answered, and straightened his back. "He's got to have some help, Coulter."

"You know the rules, Hale," the guard returned. "First come, first served. You'll have to wait your turn." He picked up a pen. "What's his first name—and his number?"

"Davis Winslow. Number 3320," Lee replied. No more information was necessary, so the two men turned and bargained for a spot to lay the emaciated form down. They sat down with a sigh of relief, and Lee wiped his face with a ragged piece of cloth. "This won't be no good," he observed, "but at least it's warmer in here."

"Not warm enough," Hale said. "Remember how we griped about how hot it was when we first got here? Judas! I'd like to have a little of that heat now!"

Lee grinned. "Perry, you'd complain if they hanged you with a new rope!" He glanced down at Winslow and his face sobered. "Shore has gone downhill, ain't he? Remember what a fine, big feller he was when we got here?"

"He wasn't as tough as most of us, Ezra. You and me, we'd had to tough it out, but Davis is a rich man's son, and studying at Oxford—that kind of life doesn't get you ready for Libby."

Two hours passed. Finally Coulter called, "Hale, you can take Winslow in now."

They rose stiffly and picked up Davis, carrying him awkwardly through the single door.

Harry LeCompt looked up at them, then said briefly, "Put him on the table." LeCompt was thirty-two, a slender man with black eyes and straight black hair that hugged his skull. He was not a doctor, but a former medical student. No one had ever determined how far he had gone in his medical studies; some said a few weeks, but others swore he'd done almost the entire course.

He had one leg that was conspicuously shorter than the other, so he limped as he came across the room to examine Davis. The limp had kept him out of the army, of course, but it had embittered him as well. Hale had talked to LeCompt on several occasions, and had discovered that his one goal in life was to leave Richmond and finish his medical studies. He had hinted that he would like to study in the North when he got the money.

"His leg looks worse," Lee observed.

"Let's see." Davis had taken a deep, tearing cut from a rusty nail two months earlier, and it had become infected. Nobody healed well at Libby—some very minor cuts went septic, some caused amputations—even death.

The leg was swollen like a balloon. LeCompt jerked the bandages away, and Davis moaned and cried out as the dried bandages pulled the flesh loose.

"Careful there, man!" Perry exclaimed. He saw that Davis's eyes were open and said, "Take it easy, boy. We're going to have that leg dressed."

LeCompt stared at the leg and shook his head. "I'll clean it out." He poured some antiseptic solution out of a large brown bottle into a basin, and cleansed the leg quickly and efficiently. He looked at the raw wound and the dark streaks running up the leg, and shook his head again. "Not good! Not good at all!"

As LeCompt rebandaged the leg, Lee asked, "Ain't there something else you can do for him? He needs to be in a hospital."

"Of course he does!" LeCompt snapped. He finished the dressing and stepped back, his black eyes moving over Davis's flushed face. "He's got a burning fever, and he's not far away from blood poisoning or gangrene."

"Put him in the hospital," Hale urged.

"There are twenty beds in the hospital," LeCompt said flatly. "And every one of them is filled with a man who's in even worse shape than your friend. There's nothing I can do."

Hale glared at him. "Look, I don't have any money now, but I'll get some. I swear it. Get him in and I'll pay you for it."

"I can't do it!"

"You've done it before," Hale argued under his breath. "And you'd do it now if I had the gold."

Not bothering to deny the charge, LeCompt simply said, "I have other men to see, Hale. Take him out."

The two prisoners' eyes blazed with anger, but there was nothing they could do. They lifted the unconscious man and passed through the outer office, into the hallway. When they finally got Davis back into the dark cell, he came to and asked, "Where—where we going?"

"Why, we done been, Davis," Lee replied. "See that new bandage? We got you all fixed up—and look here, I got you an apple! See there?"

Davis stared at the apple. "Where did you get that?"

"Oh, a leetle ol' major from the Sixth Ohio thought he could play poker, and I disillusioned him. Here, you eat this thing."

"Cut it three ways," Davis said weakly.

"No, you eat it all," Lee insisted, but no amount of persuasion would work, so Lee divided it roughly, and the three sat sucking the sweet juice, forcing themselves to eat a fragment at a time.

"I got one of the seeds," Davis smiled with satisfaction. "It'll last an hour." He looked at the other two and grinned. "Never thought I'd enjoy an apple seed so much." His face was almost hidden behind the busy growth of reddish beard, but they saw the old Davis coming back.

"We ought to be hearing from your father soon," Hale commented. "He's a congressman, so he'll know how to handle things."

"He's in the wrong Congress, Perry," Davis said. "I doubt if he gets the letters, anyway."

Hale felt the same way, but would not admit it. "It's just a matter of time. Pretty soon you'll get a call-out, and that's the last Ezra and I will see of you. You'll be back in New York eating at Delmonico's."

"Just a matter of time," Davis agreed with a faint smile, and then did what most of the fever-stricken men did—he fell asleep without warning.

"One of these days, Perry," Ezra said slowly, "he's going to go out like that—and just not wake up."

"No! He'll make it!" Hale tucked the blanket around Davis's body and declared fiercely, "God won't let him die here in this hellhole."

"He's let a heap of men die here," Lee said. There was no anger in his voice—only an air of resignation that came with time in Libby.

"His father will do something." Hale struck his hands together angrily. "It's just a matter of time!"

Gazing at him curiously, Lee nodded. "Well, if blood poisoning don't set in, and if he don't get gangrene—and if that fever don't get no worse—and if he don't get the cholera that's started—why, I reckon ol' Davis will make it."

"It's just a matter of time!" Perry Hale insisted stubbornly.

## CHAPTER THIRTEEN

# A PROPHECY FOR THAD

★ ★ ★ ★

For Thad Novak, New Year's Day arrived, not by celebrating but by getting shot.

The regiment had been sent to Tennessee to help hold the line after Bragg had been beaten. Lee had been apprehensive that the Yankees might mount a full scale assault toward Richmond, but nothing came of it. The Richmond Blades were part of the line strung loosely from east to west across the northern border of Tennessee, but there was no fighting to speak of.

Thad had been assigned a section covering some two miles, a gap in the Berland Mountains that Colonel Barton thought the Yankees might use, and he sent the company in a sweeping movement to spy out the Yankees' position. Thad had ridden ahead of his men to explore a grove of trees, using one of the few horses fit to ride. Surprised by a stiff blow on the right side of his chest, Thad thought he had run into a low-hanging limb; then he heard the sound of a shot and realized he'd been hit.

He grabbed the saddlehorn to keep from falling, and at the same time saw a small group of Yankees scurrying out from behind a clump of boulders about a hundred yards away, firing at him. As he wheeled the horse, a bullet knocked his hat off. Digging the spurs into his horse, he hunched down and dashed for safety, hearing the popping of gunfire behind him.

Tom Winslow, now first sergeant, had already moved the men forward. "Lieutenant," he cried, his face alive with excitement, "let's go get 'em!"

Thad slid off his horse and waved his arms. "Tom, take the left; Dooley, you take the right. I'll keep the center."

"Hey, you been shot!" Dooley exclaimed, seeing the blood on Thad's chest.

"Just a scratch—forward!"

There had been lively action, but they captured a nest of Yankees, including one lieutenant and a dozen privates. The officer, a fresh-faced young man on his first assignment, was chagrined. Tears ran down his cheeks as Thad talked to him on the way back to camp. "Aw, now, it's no disgrace to be captured," Thad said gently. "I did some time in Old Capitol Prison in Washington myself."

Captain Beauchamp was pleased with the capture, but he was concerned about Thad's wound. The surgeon examined it and found that it was not serious. The bullet had struck the ribs and skidded off, sloughing some flesh with it. "Going to hurt like fury," he said as he finished taping Thad's chest. "Don't use that arm too much for a few weeks."

"Get your gear, Thad," Beauchamp said. "I'm sending you back to Richmond."

"Why, I'm not hurt that bad, Captain!"

"Maybe not, but somebody's got to take these prisoners back. I'll want to send a few letters, so be ready to pull out early in the morning. Oh yes, Major Benning of Tennessee Company was telling me they had a brush with the Yankees last week and one of his officers was wounded. He's in bad shape, but you can take a wagon. Think four men will be enough guard?"

"Yes, sir." He hesitated, then asked, "I'd like to take Corporal Young."

Beauchamp grinned. "I thought you might! All right. I'll give you the letters in the morning. Send Young over to pick up the officer from Major Benning today."

When Thad told Dooley their assignment, he yelped, "By granny, we'll be gone like Moody's goose, Thad!" and left immediately to get the officer. Thad chose three other men—which was not easy, for every man volunteered for the job!

By the time Dooley returned, Thad was busy packing his gear. Approaching Thad, Dooley said, "I got the lieutenant, but he's real poorly. Took a slug in the belly and one in the arm. The arm ain't bad, but the other trouble is bad. Don't look to me like he'll make it through two clean shirts."

"I better take a look." Thad followed Dooley to the wagon, and found a very sick man. "I'm Lieutenant Novak," he said. "Looks like you've been having a hard time."

"I'm Owen Morgan." Thad had to lean forward to hear the man's faint voice. There was a hollow look in the deep-set eyes and traces of red on his cheeks that Thad didn't like. His arm was in a sling, and he was almost unconscious.

"We'll get you to a doctor quick as we can, Lieutenant." Thad turned and said, "Corporal Young, fix the lieutenant a good place to sleep in my tent. And get some hot food down him."

Morgan tried to get out of the wagon, and would have fallen had not Thad and Dooley caught him. "Blasted nuisance!" he whispered as the two men bedded him down.

"He ain't in no shape to make no trip," Dooley commented. "He's weak as a cat whose ninth life is draining out of it."

"We'll *have* to take him," Thad said. "You draw enough supplies to get us to Richmond, and we'll try to make good time."

That was his plan, but it didn't work out that way. The first day over the rough roads almost killed Morgan. He couldn't stifle the cries of pain the jolting caused, though he tried.

The next morning, Thad said, "Dooley, get what food you need from the supplies and take the prisoners on to Richmond."

"What'll you do, then?"

"I can't stand to hurt this poor fellow. I'll take it slow—stop if I have to. Probably have to find some house where they can take us in—him anyway. I'll write this down as an order for headquarters."

Dooley left the next morning, saying, "I'll tell that pretty little ol' gal of yours you're on your way, Lieutenant!" He led the little company away, and Thad went over to where Morgan sat with his back to a tree, watching them.

"Better have some more of this bacon, Morgan," Thad suggested, squatting beside the fire.

Morgan took a swallow of the black coffee, but said nothing

for a while. Finally the officer spoke up. "Sorry to slow you down."

"Aw, we Rebels got to stick together." He took a bite of bacon and added, "I'm in no big hurry."

Morgan sipped the coffee, then shook his head. "No, I don't believe that. Not many would care much about a dying man."

"You're not dying."

Morgan didn't answer, but there was a fatalistic set to his face. He ate little, but drank cup after cup of coffee. After the fourth cup of the brew, Thad said, "We'll just mosey along and if it gets too bad, say so and we'll take a break."

They spent three days heading north, stopping often when Thad saw the man grimace in deep pain. Every night Thad would change the dressings on Morgan's arm and stomach. But as the days went by, he realized the man was getting no better, so when he finished dressing the wounds one night, he said, "We'll stop at the next farm until you get better."

"You'd leave me?"

"I couldn't do that," Thad replied slowly. "I'll see you're all right, Owen." They had somehow gotten to a first-name basis during their talks around the fire at night. "All this jolting in this blasted wagon is tearing you to pieces."

All day Morgan had been practically in a coma, lying in the back of the wagon. He looked across the campfire now and said slowly, "It won't matter, Thad. I've known for a time that I wouldn't make it."

"That's just a feeling, Owen."

"I'm Welsh, Thad—what you'd call Irish." Morgan closed his eyes, seemed to go to sleep, then opened them again. "My people have had second sight—a lot of them. My mother saw my father the day he died—and he was six hundred miles away. She was sitting in the kitchen, and he came in and said, 'I'll be waiting for you, Kathleen,' and then he left."

"A dream, Owen," Thad suggested. Such things made him nervous, so he added, "Don't speak of dying."

Owen Morgan gave him an odd look and asked, "Are you afraid to speak of it, then? But we all come to it. For me it'll be soon, maybe for you many years—but we all come to it." He looked up at the cold January skies and said, "My sister told me it would happen. When I left Wales, the last thing she said at the boat was, 'Goodbye, Owen. We will meet in heaven.' "

Thad looked up abruptly. "Are you a man of God, Owen?"

"Why, of course!" he replied proudly. "My people are chapel, nonconformist. I was saved in a revival when I was sixteen."

"I was saved last year," Thad said quietly.

"Ah, I knew it!" Owen nodded. "There's something of Christ in you—no matter that you're a soldier."

"How'd you get mixed up in our war, Owen?"

Owen didn't hesitate but began relating his story, halting often when a spasm of coughing tore through him. The coal mines had gone out on strike, and he'd come to America looking for work. "I wound up as a gambler on a Mississippi riverboat. Made a lot of money," he said. "Then I enlisted in a burst of misguided patriotism. But it's God's will," he hurried on as he gazed into the fire. After a while he sighed. "I'd like to sleep now, Thad."

Thad helped him roll into his blankets, and then sat for a long time peering into the fire, wondering why some things happened the way they did. He was disturbed about Owen, for in the few days of their journey, Thad had found himself drawn to the Welshman.

The next morning he could not awaken Morgan. The ashen appearance on the man's face frightened Thad, but unable to do anything else, he made a fire—and waited. Just before noon, he heard Owen call weakly, "Thad." He rushed to the sick man and knelt beside him. Owen's breath was shallow and his eyes rolled upward.

"Owen!" he cried, and the eyes began focusing on Thad. They were strange eyes, filled with a mystery he could not read. "Owen!" he cried again, "what is it?"

Morgan stirred and lifted a hand. "My friend . . ." he whispered. "You've . . . been good . . . to me."

Grasping Owen's hand, Thad began to tremble. He'd seen men die before, some in terrible ways, but this was different. He felt as if he'd been punched in the stomach. "Owen, don't give up!" he begged.

"It's my time," Owen murmured, pausing for breath. "Thad, I give you what I leave on this earth—God has told me you will have a use for it. Send the other half to my mother—Kathleen Morgan—County Cork—the widow of Michael Morgan. And tell her . . . I'll be waiting for her—with Father."

Thad watched as the man took a deep breath and looked up at the arching sky.

"I'm coming—Lord!" he whispered quietly, joy filling his eyes. Slowly he relaxed and his eyes fluttered—then he was still.

Numb, Thad sat for a long time, tears running down his face. Greatly moved by the event, he carefully laid Morgan down and got to his feet. He had been in the presence of God—of that he had no doubt. He bowed his head and thanked God for this brother at his feet.

He wrapped the soldier in a blanket and buried him beneath a large oak in the middle of a clearing. With the mound at his feet, Thad prayed, then turned and loaded the wagon. He drove the team hard that day, and made camp by a brook, breaking the ice to get water to make coffee. He ate a little and read a chapter from his dog-eared Testament. A thought struck him, and he went to the wagon and got the knapsack Morgan had brought with him.

It was an ordinary army knapsack, and contained Owen's personal effects, including several pictures, one of them a full-faced portrait of a strong-looking woman with warm eyes and a determined chin. It was signed Kathleen Morgan, but even without the name, Thad would have known her as Owen's mother.

He read several letters from her, and two from a girl who signed her name Angharad Gruffydd. He wondered at the strange name, and read only a part of one of the letters, for it was a love letter and he felt like an intruder.

There was a pouch with forty-two Confederate dollars, nothing else. And he remembered Owen's insistence that his mother receive half the money. But since it was so little, Thad decided, "I'll send it all—everything in here."

He started to put the knapsack down when a lump in the bottom attracted his attention. He felt inside—nothing. He turned it upside down and peered within, noticing that the seams along the bottom had been taken out and replaced with different thread. Carefully he pulled the thread loose and discovered papers stuffed between the inner and outer linings.

He reached in with two fingers, grasped a paper, and pulled it out. Holding the paper up to the fire, he blinked and gasped, for what he held was a crisp U.S. greenback worth $100. Quickly he pulled the other notes out with trembling fingers and counted them.

"Six thousand two hundred dollars!" he gasped, and realized this was Owen's winnings from gambling. Thad knew little about money, but one thing he was sure of: *this paper was as good as gold.* As a matter of fact, it could be exchanged for gold under certain circumstances. Mr. Winslow had done so more than once. The Confederate currency was practically worthless, but Thad held a fortune in his hands.

*What did Owen say as he was dying?* Thad questioned, staring at the money. Slowly the words seeped into his mind, like a prophecy:

*I give you what I have on this earth—God has told me you'll have a use for it.*

Slowly Thad gathered up the bills and stared at them once more before tucking the bunch into his inside pocket. Two days later he caught up with Dooley and the others, and two days after that they reached Richmond. Thad arranged for the prisoners to be taken to Belle Isle; then he reported to headquarters.

"Letter for you here somewhere, Novak," a fat lieutenant greeted him. "Been here for about a week."

Thad took the letter gingerly, stared at the writing, and went outside. He didn't recognize the script, but read the short note quickly.

December 5, 1863
Lt. Thaddeus Novak
Third Virginia Infantry

I am hoping this letter will reach you soon, for there is an urgent matter I desperately need help with.

My grandson, Lieutenant Davis Winslow, has been a prisoner of war in Libby Prison for six months. He is critically ill, and I fear he will die if he does not get proper medical care.

Will you go to him? It may be impossible for some reason that I cannot know. But if you could go, it would mean a great deal to me and to his parents.

I have thought of you so often, and pray for your safety. God keep you safe until this terrible conflict is over!

Sincerely,
Captain Whitfield Winslow

Thad read the letter twice, then wheeled and walked back into the headquarters building. Two hours later, after a determined effort and a stubbornness that would not be ignored, he left with a pass permitting him to visit Lieutenant Davis Winslow, prisoner of war at Libby Prison.

## CHAPTER FOURTEEN

# A SLIGHT CASE OF BRIBERY

★ ★ ★ ★

Ezra Lee looked up from where he was slumped against the wall, shot to an upright position, and jabbed Hale with a pointed elbow.

"Keep your elbows to yourself!" Hale grunted.

"Perry. Lookee what's here!"

Hale roused himself. Across the crowded room in the direction of Ezra's wave, he saw a Confederate officer moving slowly toward them, searching the faces of the men as he came.

"Seems to be looking for somebody," Hale remarked. "Maybe the Rebels are coming here to do some recruiting. I hear they're down to old men and boys now."

Lee rubbed his whiskers. "Well, another month in this hole, and I might consider it."

The officer was no more than ten feet away now. Hale scrutinized the man's dark face as he looked around and called out, "Anybody here know where I can find Lieutenant Davis Winslow?"

Surprised, Hale and Lee jumped to their feet. "We can take you to him, Lieutenant," Hale said.

"I'd be obliged," the officer told them. "I'm Thad Novak."

"I'm Captain Perry Hale and this is Lieutenant Ezra Lee," Hale nodded, and was surprised when Novak stuck out his hand. Hale and Lee grasped the young officer's hard grip, and Perry motioned, "He's back in one of the smaller cells."

Thad followed the two men across the crowded room, out into a corridor, and down a wide hall to the end.

"He's in here, Lieutenant," Lee indicated.

Thad entered the twenty-foot-square room. Sack mattresses were laid so close together that only narrow aisles served for movement. Several men were at one end of the room—some talking, others playing cards on their cots. Thad gave them all a searching glance. None resembled Davis.

"He's over here," Hale informed him, stepping over to a far corner of the room where a man lay wrapped in a blanket. He leaned over, giving the still form a gentle shake. "Davis—a visitor to see you."

Thad came closer. The man did not move. "Is he unconscious?" he asked, leaning closer to get a better look.

"Off and on. He's been real bad for a long time, Lieutenant," Ezra said. "Sometimes he don't wake up for a couple of days at a stretch."

Hale tapped softly on the man's cheek. "Wake up, Davis."

Thad's eyes widened at the sight of the man. "Why, this isn't Winslow!" Thad had pictured Davis as he last saw him—a robust healthy man, overweight, with red cheeks and glowing eyes.

*This man is a wreck!* he groaned inwardly. His frame looked like parchment stretched over bones. His face was a skull, the muscles shrunken, making the bones stand out like ledges. The deep-set eyes, dull and lifeless, were round balls staring out of cavernous sockets. The lips, covered with sores, were pulled back, exposing yellowed teeth. Stench reeked from the man.

"Guess he don't look much like you remember him," Lee remarked grimly. "But it's him all right."

Appalled, Thad squatted down, the other two men joining him. "I—I can't believe it!" he gasped. He started to speak, then glanced at Davis, not wanting to say anything that would hurt him.

"He can't hear you, Lieutenant," Hale said. "Even when he does wake up, he doesn't even know Ezra and me half the time. Too much fever."

"What's wrong with his leg?"

"Got punched with a rusty nail some time back. Never has healed. He'll likely lose that leg—if he lives long enough."

Thad's mind raced as he was forced to revise his plans. He had expected to find a man who was able to move swiftly, but now he knew he would have to find another way.

He studied Davis for a long moment, then looked up at the pair. "You two are friends of his?"

"We came to Libby with him," Hale replied. "Man needs friends in a rotten place like this or he won't make it." He gave Thad a direct look. "What's your interest in him, Lieutenant?"

Thad balanced the question in his mind, wondering what to say. They were the enemy, but he had to have help—and these two men were obviously Winslow's friends.

Finally he said, "His brother did me a good turn once."

Ezra nodded. "Well, you sure got a good chance to pay him back, Lieutenant. This boy ain't goin' to make it unless he gets help. He'll be dead in a week—if he lasts *that* long."

"I reckon you're right," Thad responded. "I got a letter from his grandfather, asking me to try to help him."

Instantly Hale asked, "Would that be Captain Whitfield Winslow of Washington?"

Startled, Thad nodded eagerly. "You know him?"

"No, but I've been writing him a lot, trying to get some help for Davis."

Thad decided he'd have to trust the two, and said in a hushed tone, "Let's keep our voices down. I came to see if I could get him some better care, better food—but that won't be enough."

Hale and Lee expressed doubt. "You got another idea, Novak?" Hale asked.

Thad nodded, speaking softly. "We've got to get him out of here or he'll die."

"You could maybe get him transferred to another prison," Hale suggested. "But I doubt he would be any better off there."

"No. We have to get him out," Thad told them. "Out of prison and into a hospital where there's a doctor and medicine."

"Escape?" Hale couldn't believe what he was hearing. "He can't even sit up! And they guard this place like we was worth solid gold. Nobody's *ever* made an escape from Libby."

"There's only six doors in the whole place," Lee added. "And always at least two guards at each door. Most of us are in poor shape to do any running—but even if we were, where'd we go? Libby's right in the middle of Richmond, which is swarmin' with your troops. A man wouldn't get two blocks before he was picked up."

Thad shook his head stubbornly. "There's always a way to do a thing," he said. "All you got to do is find it."

"Well, you better find it quick," Hale told him. "I've gotten right fond of Davis. Anything we can do, just say it."

Thad sat down on the floor to ease his side, which was beginning to ache. He noted their quizzical expression, and grinned. "One of your friends raked my ribs with a ball last week. I'm still a mite sore. Now, tell me about this place."

"Tell you what?" Lee asked.

"When you eat, when visitors come, who the guards are—everything. Don't leave anything out."

Hale grinned and sat down, "Well, we don't have any pressing engagements, do we, Ezra?"

"Nary a one."

For over two hours Thad listened. Sometimes he would ask a question and carefully consider the answer. Once Davis woke up and stared at him, but didn't recognize him or the others. Lee raised him up for a drink of water and he lay right back and closed his eyes.

Finally, Hale said, "Well, that's all I can think of, Novak." He looked at Thad. "You got any ideas?"

"Just a little one." He reached into his pocket, took out a single gold coin, and handed it to Hale. "Maybe that will buy some food or something to help. Use it for all of you, Hale."

"By the good Lord—that's a ten-dollar gold piece!" Lee gasped. "I ain't seen no gold in so long I done forgot what it looks like! We can get some decent grub for that, Lieutenant!"

"And some medicine from LeCompt, too," Hale added.

"That's the doctor you mentioned?"

"He's no doctor," Perry shrugged. "He sure does want to be, though."

"How's that?" Thad listened while Hale told him about LeCompt's burning desire to get away from the prison and into medical school. When he was through, Thad said, "I'll be back tomorrow."

Lee watched him go. "You reckon he meant that, Perry?"

"I think he did. He's got kind of a set look in his eyes." Hale looked at the gold coin he held. "If it wasn't for this piece of gold, I'd think I dreamed the whole thing." He rolled the coin around in his hand and smiled. "Let's see what it'll buy, Ezra."

★ ★ ★ ★

Thad had gotten the gold piece by exchanging Morgan's money. The bank teller had snapped the greenback and stared at him. "We don't see many of these."

"It's good, isn't it?" Thad asked.

"Of course, it is." He counted out ten gold pieces and said gloomily, "Wish our Confederate money was as good."

"I've got to send some money to a friend in another country. Would it be just as good to send greenbacks as gold?"

"Oh, a letter of credit would be better for that." He explained the mechanics of the exchange, ending by saying, "Best not to send cash through the mail." Thad decided to get Mr. Winslow to help with the matter of sending Morgan's money to his mother.

"If a fellow were going to the North, then," he had asked casually, "Greenbacks would be as good as gold?"

"Gold is always best—but this greenback will spend anywhere in the North."

★ ★ ★ ★

Thad had left the bank with some satisfaction. Now after his visit with Davis and his friends at the prison, he walked around the rest of the day, trying to formulate some plan to get Davis out. He had been given no assignment at headquarters, so there was no need for him to report for duty. The nine gold coins jingling in his pocket gave him a good feeling. He had never had even one gold piece, and since he had no other money, he decided to use one of the coins for a meal and a hotel room. He went to the Ballard House and reserved a room for a few days, then to the dining room for a meal. As he lingered over coffee, he considered asking Sky Winslow for help, but could find no way to justify it. Anyone caught aiding in the escape of a Union officer would be in serious trouble. "Can't even let Pet know what's going on," he murmured as he left the dining room.

The streets were crowded with poorly dressed people. The years of being cut off from the outside world showed in frayed cuffs and skirts. The blockade had drawn so tight that only an occasional ship made it through—and most of those were loaded with arms and ammunition. The scanty diet showed in the faces of many, Thad noticed. Walking back to the hotel, he could feel the gloomy atmosphere. No longer did Richmond hold the gay celebrations she had when the war first started.

When Thad retired for the night, he found it impossible to sleep. His mind went round and round, but nothing seemed feasible. Around midnight he dozed off but awakened several times, still seeking desperately for some plan to free Davis. He woke up in the morning with a start, and as he swung his feet to the floor, he *knew* what to do. When the idea came he didn't know—perhaps he dreamed it—but the whole plan was there.

He spent some time reading his Testament and praying—longer than usual, ending his prayer with the words, "Lord, Owen said the money was for a purpose. I ask you to use it to get this man out of prison and save his life."

He got up, dressed rapidly, and left the room, carrying half the greenbacks in his pocket. The rest was still stowed away in the knapsack in the room, where he felt sure it would be safe until he could return.

The pass he had from headquarters got him into the prison without any problems, and he asked the guard, "Where'll I find the infirmary?"

"Third floor."

He climbed the stairs and asked another guard, who directed him to the double doors marked INFIRMARY.

The sharp-featured man at the desk looked up, startled.

"Like to see Mr. LeCompt," Thad requested.

"About what?"

"Guess I'll tell him that," Thad answered, giving the man a steady look.

Reluctantly the orderly got up and disappeared behind the

inner door. "There's an officer to see you, LeCompt," he said. "He won't say what he wants."

LeCompt raised his eyes from where he was changing a patient's dressing. "That's good," he said and waited until the man hobbled out on a pair of crutches. "Is he some kind of inspector?"

"He won't tell me nothing."

"Well—send him in. Hold the other patients until he comes out."

When the orderly left, LeCompt sat down at the small desk, wondering what would bring an officer to *his* little kingdom. He was not worried, for he was so underpaid that he could not be easily replaced. He was surprised, however, when the door opened and a lieutenant entered. He was very young, which meant he was not high on the medical staff.

"I'm Lieutenant Thad Novak, Third Virginia Infantry."

LeCompt leaned back and eyed him, saying curtly, "What can I do for you, Lieutenant?"

Thad had gone over this scene many times, uncertain as to the right approach. He had finally concluded that it would be best to be straightforward.

"One of the prisoners here is a friend of mine," he said. "I want to help him."

"How did you get to be friends with a Yankee officer?" he asked, curious.

"I've known his family a long time. We both come from the same state—New York."

LeCompt's eyes widened in surprise. "You're from New York? That's unusual." He shrugged and added, "There's not much I can do. Of course, better food and care is available, but it'll cost a little money."

"I'm not interested in a little help, Dr. LeCompt," Thad replied, fully aware the man was no doctor. "My friend is in bad shape."

"What's his name?"

"Davis Winslow."

"*Winslow*?" The name jarred him. "Well, you're right about him. He's in terrible condition—though I've done the best I can," he added defensively. "This is an impossible job here, Lieutenant. The food is terrible, and they keep shoving new prisoners into an already overcrowded condition."

Thad nodded and pulled out the leather case. When he removed ten of the bills and saw LeCompt's eyes devour the money, he plunged in. "I've got a thousand dollars in greenbacks here, LeCompt," he said evenly. "I'd spend every dime of it to help Winslow make it."

The man's eyes fastened on the bills like a leech. He seemed hypnotized, unable to speak. Finally raising his face to Thad, he said in a husky voice, "Why, I think I can do something, Lieutenant. We have a small hospital here, and I—"

"That's no good," Thad interrupted. "He'll die if he doesn't get to a *real* hospital."

"I can do only so much, Lieutenant," LeCompt argued. "With that much money I can buy some drugs and make sure he gets proper care."

Thad paused, then pulled out another sheaf of bills. He had divided them into three packets for just this occasion. "Here's another thousand dollars—in U.S. greenbacks." He added them to the other bills, fanning the money out so it covered the top of LeCompt's desk. "Now," he said, "I'll pay two thousand to get him out."

"*Escape*?" LeCompt whispered, and looked at the door. "You're crazy!"

Thad stared at him, saying, "I may be, Doctor, but I'm the richest crazy man you've seen lately. How many chances do you have to make all that money for one day's work?"

LeCompt jumped to his feet and started for the door. "I'll have to ask you to wait here, Novak. The warden would like to talk with you, I'm sure."

He reached the door, expecting Thad to stop him, but when he heard no protest, LeCompt turned back to see the officer grinning.

"Go get him, LeCompt," Thad challenged.

The man hesitated, then said angrily, "What kind of a fool do you take me for? You're obviously here to trap me!"

"You really believe they're thinking a lot about that?" Thad asked. "How many bribes have been taken here at Libby? Just petty stuff, I'd guess. You're not important enough to tempt."

"In that, you're right," he replied bitterly.

Thad took advantage of the man's admission and said quickly, "I'll lay it all out for you, LeCompt. I've been talking to a couple of Winslow's friends—Hale and Lee—and they tell me you want to get out of this place to become a *real* doctor."

"I never said that!"

Thad ignored his statement, and indicated the money. "There's your chance. You can shake off the stench of this place, go north and become a doctor."

"Impossible!"

"Don't you know about Winslow's family? He's the last son, and his father's a rich man—a congressman. His grandfather's well off—a retired naval hero. They can get you into any medical school in the country with a single word!"

"That may be—but there's no way it can be done. Nobody can steal a prisoner from here."

Thad noticed that the argument had shifted, that LeCompt was not arguing about the *way* but the *means*. He leaned forward. "If I show you a way to do it—will you do it?"

"I tell you, it's impossible!"

"Guess you don't want to get out of here and be a doctor as bad as Hale thought." Thad reached down and scooped up the money.

"Wait!" LeCompt put his hand out, and licked his lips. "I'd do anything to get out of here—but there's just no way to get a prisoner out."

Thad lowered his voice to a whisper. "No way to get a *living* prisoner out, maybe—but dead ones go out all the time, don't they?"

LeCompt's eyes bulged in surprise. "Yes, they do," he admitted.

"That's the way Winslow goes out—in a coffin."

Again LeCompt looked at the money and shook his head. "I see what you're getting at—but I can't risk it."

Thad played his last card. He pulled the remaining sheaf of bills from the leather case. "My last offer, LeCompt—five hundred more. All I've got. Take it or leave it."

He added the money to the cash on the table and watched LeCompt's face. *He's too much of a coward to do it,* he thought.

LeCompt sat there weighing the odds—the dangers versus

the opportunity of leaving Libby, studying in clean classrooms, being called "Doctor."

Time seemed to crawl. Finally LeCompt spoke. "It'll have to be soon. He might die any time." He was a brilliant man in his own way and had already formulated a plan. "This is what you must tell Hale and Lee to do . . ."

Thad left the office twenty minutes later. Half the bribe money was in LeCompt's pocket, the rest to be handed over at the last minute of escape. Thad stalked down the hall, going immediately to the cell where the three were kept.

Scanning the cell as he entered, he saw the other prisoners were in the outer room.

"He's better today, Novak," Hale told Thad as he approached. Then he turned and said, "Davis, the lieutenant is here."

Novak squatted down so he could see the sick man's face. The eyes were clear. "Good to see you feeling better," Thad said.

Davis focused his eyes on him a moment, then asked in a thin voice, "My grandfather sent you?"

"That's right. I'm the one your brother saved from a firing squad."

"I—remember." Davis licked his lips. "If you see my grandfather, tell him I appreciate what he did."

Thad smiled faintly, lowering his voice. "You can tell him yourself, Winslow."

Davis shook his head. "I won't make it. Too far gone."

"You're leaving tomorrow." When Winslow stared at him without comprehension, Thad said, "It's all set up."

"You got him transferred?" Hale frowned. "I told you another prison wouldn't be any good."

Thad turned to face the pair, studied them carefully, then murmured softly, "You two are leaving with him. That's the only way we can pull it off."

"That's crazy!" Lee said, trying to keep his voice down.

"Just what LeCompt said," Thad grinned. "Now, listen to me, because we get only one shot."

For over an hour, they rehearsed their part of the escape plan, and by the time the Confederate lieutenant rose to go there was hope in their eyes. Leaning close to Davis's ear Thad whispered,

"Next time I see you, you'll be a free man!" He rose and quickly left the cell.

Stunned silence enveloped the three. Finally Davis murmured, "It doesn't matter so much about me—but I thank God that you fellows are getting out."

Hale shook his head. He was Presbyterian, and there was a stubborn look on his face as he gazed at the other two. "This is no accident," he announced firmly. "God is in it."

"Amen!" Ezra added fervently.

CHAPTER FIFTEEN

# A NEW PATIENT

★ ★ ★ ★

A single candle flickered in the cell, emitting a pale light that did little to break the darkness. Some of the prisoners had gone to the larger outer hall to play cards, where a few lamps burned—lamps that were always turned off by the guards at ten.

Hale forced himself to wait until he heard the guards come down the hall, enter and peer about with the aid of a lantern, then leave. That meant it was about midnight; the next cell check would not come for two hours. He steeled himself to lie still for another thirty minutes, listening to the groans of the men and going over the plan in his mind.

"Perry—you reckon it's about time?" Lee whispered, sitting up.

Hale's shadow was outlined against the wall where he hunched. "I think so. See if Davis is awake."

"I'm awake," Davis acknowledged.

Perry rose up cautiously, and Lee did likewise. "All right, let's do it," Hale said. "Davis, keep your eyes shut, and try to hold your breath when the guards challenge us."

"All right."

"Here we go." The two men moved toward Davis, picked him up, and moved away from their beds. There was so little room that it was impossible to keep from brushing against the limbs of other prisoners, and more than once one of them grunted. Lee bumped one man's arm so hard, the man sat up, growling, "What's going on?"

"Davis—he's real bad," Lee whispered. "We're takin' him to the infirmary."

The man sighed, lay down, and they made it to the door. In the hall outside, a guard was sitting beside a table. He was reading a book by the light of a lantern, and as they moved down the hall, he jerked his head toward them. Snatching up his rifle, he demanded, "Who's there?"

"Hale and Lee," Perry answered. "We've got Winslow with us. He's dying, I reckon."

"Come closer," the guard commanded.

When they were even with the light, the man bent forward, staring at Winslow's face. Davis was completely limp, his head bobbing as they moved, his mouth open. "Well—take him on then."

They continued down the hall as the guard went back to his book. The men reached the stairs and began to climb. They rested on the second floor, then moved to the third. Another guard challenged them as they moved toward the infirmary. "Who is it?"

"Hale and Lee. We got a man bad off."

"LeCompt won't be on duty till eight. You know that."

"He looked at this one yesterday," Hale told him. "Said to bring him in if he looked like he was going." Then he paused and added, "I think he's scared it's cholera."

The guard took a step backward, for the very threat of the dread disease brought a surge of fear. "All right. Stay here. I'll see if he'll look at him."

He walked down the hall and entered the room used for a hospital. LeCompt had a small room wedged in between that and the infirmary. The guard knocked on the door, paused, then knocked again. Finally LeCompt opened it a crack, his hair wild and his eyes half shut.

"What do you want? I just got to sleep."

"Couple of prisoners, LeCompt. They've got the man who may have cholera."

LeCompt seemed to come awake. "Have them bring him into the infirmary."

The guard returned to where Hale and Lee stood waiting with Davis in their arms. "Take him into the infirmary," he said, keeping well back as they passed. He didn't even offer to open the door as they entered. "It better not be cholera!" he muttered angrily, taking up his station at the door.

LeCompt came into the infirmary immediately and said hastily, "Bring him over here—on the table." He unlocked a cabinet, pulled out a bottle and poured a glass half full of fluid. He brought it over and handed it to Davis, saying, "Drink this—all of it."

"What is it?" Hale asked.

"Laudanum!" LeCompt snapped. "Just do what I tell you." When Davis hesitated, he urged, "Drink it! It'll put you out. You're supposed to be dead, so I don't want you making any noise inside that coffin."

Davis gulped it down. Almost at once the powerful drug began to work. He grew dizzy and felt a roaring in his ears. "Perry," he whispered.

"What is it?"

"If this doesn't work, I want you to know—how much—I appreciate you—and you, too—Ezra. It's—it's . . ."

He slumped back, and LeCompt said, "He'll be out for hours." He stared at the door. "I hope this works."

"Just get us out of this place, and you're free," Hale told him. "What's next?"

"There's a stretcher in the supply room—through that door," he said. "Go get it." Lee moved to get it, and LeCompt opened a cabinet and pulled out a paper sack. He put his coat on, saying, "Put this sack under him somewhere."

When they had arranged Davis's limp body on the canvas stretcher, LeCompt said crisply, "I've got to get a burial permit from the warden. You wait here."

He left quickly—and didn't return for what seemed like an eternity. His face was pale as he held up a paper. "I've got it!—let's go."

They moved out of the infirmary, and the guard inquired, "Is it cholera, LeCompt?"

"Yes, I'm afraid so."

The guard avoided them as they passed, and as they walked

down the hall, they heard him say loudly, "Well, I ain't stayin' here—not me!"

LeCompt took a deep breath at the stairs. "That was rough. I thought he was going to make us wait until morning, but I told him it'd cause a panic among the guards."

"He'll do that—all by himself," Hale projected. "What's next."

"The workshop."

"Why there?"

"Because that's where the coffins are made. I hope to heaven there's one left!"

He led them past several guards. The permit worked like a charm. The last guard carried a lantern and preceded them into a large room. "There's a couple of coffins, all right," he said, waving his lantern toward the pine boxes.

"You men get one of them," LeCompt ordered.

Lee and Hale put Winslow's limp body down and moved to the two coffins. The top was nailed on, and Hale said, "Got to have a hammer to get this off."

"Tools are over there," the guard said, indicating a bench. While Hale went to get it, he said, "What's the hurry, LeCompt? Couldn't this wait till morning?"

"Why . . . I just think it'd be better if . . . if he didn't stay in the prison any longer than necessary."

He was being purposely mysterious, and was relieved at the guard's immediate reaction.

"What'd he die of?" he demanded, stepping back.

"I can't say. Warden's orders."

The guard glowered at him, then walked over to peer down at Winslow. The other men stood with bated breath. Then the guard cursed and fled the room, rasping, "Get him outta here! The wagon's over there!"

"Quick—get him inside!" LeCompt snapped, removing the hidden sack containing hospital uniforms. After they had put the "corpse" inside, he said, "Nail the lid on."

Lee took a hasty look at Davis's pale, still face before nailing the coffin shut.

"All right, get it on the wagon—wait, put these uniforms on it first."

The men snatched the white uniforms from LeCompt and

tossed them on the low four-wheeled wagon used for this purpose.

"Now—put the coffin on top."

The coffin was heavy, but the men worked swiftly, and LeCompt cried, "Let's go!"

Hale and Lee grabbed the long tongue of the wagon and pulled it past the guard, who gave them plenty of room. They rolled down the hall; then as they rounded the corner, LeCompt said, "Quick! Get into those clothes."

Hale lifted one end of the coffin while Lee pulled the uniforms out. They pulled off their rags and put on the uniforms, shoving their rags under the coffin.

"So far, so good," LeCompt said. "But we've got one final post." His hands trembled as he pointed. "Don't say a word—either of you."

He took a deep breath, limped down the hall ahead of them, and opened a set of double doors. When the other two passed through, they saw they were in an outer office. Two guards sitting on a bench jumped up.

"I have a special order from Warden Holmes," LeCompt stated before they could challenge him.

One of them, a burly man with calico eyes, fixed his eyes on LeCompt, then unfolded the paper and read it.

"What's it say, Nick?" the other asked. He was a small man with heavy burnside whiskers.

"Says to get this feller buried."

"What's the big hurry?" the other demanded.

"Guess *you* better answer that, LeCompt."

LeCompt shrugged. "You better go wake Holmes up and discuss it with him, Simmons."

"Wake up *that* man?" Simmons snorted. "Not much! Open the door, Shorty."

The other slid the bolt, and LeCompt ordered, "This way, and be quick about it!"

In the thick darkness only a few stars shone in the sky. Both Hale and Lee felt weird, for they had not been outside for over six months. "Sure feels good, don't it, Perry?" Ezra whispered.

"Sure does!"

"We go this way—he's supposed to meet us," LeCompt informed them.

The iron-bound wheels of the wagon sounded like thunder to them as it rumbled over the cobblestones. Expecting to be stopped at any minute, their eyes swept the area.

"There's a buggy of some kind over there," LeCompt whispered.

They moved closer and a low voice called out, "LeCompt?"

"Here! Be quick!"

"You made it!" Thad was ecstatic as he leaped to the ground from the wagon seat.

"Hurry. Put the coffin on the wagon," LeCompt ordered.

"No, take Davis out, and put him on the bed," Thad said. "He can't stay in that coffin." He reached into his pocket, pulled out the pouch, then handed the bills to LeCompt. "Here's the rest of the money."

As LeCompt took the bills, Hale asked, "How're you going to account for two missing prisoners, LeCompt?"

LeCompt's face broke into a smile. "I'll be far from here by the time the news gets out. I'm leaving *now.*" With that he turned and limped down the dark street.

"We'd better get moving ourselves," Thad urged.

Hale had thought to bring the hammer, and he quickly removed the lid. They all looked at Davis, and Thad exclaimed, "He looks dead!"

"Just drugged," Hale said. "He'll come out of it."

They lifted Davis into the back of the wagon, wrapped him in wool blankets; then all three hopped into the front.

"Be light pretty soon," Thad said as the wagon moved down the street. "You fellows'll have to hide out. I got a couple of rooms in a run-down boardinghouse. We'll go there first and get you fixed up."

By the time he pulled up in front of a dilapidated two-story house, he'd gotten the full story of the escape. "God was with us," Hale said as he ended the tale.

"I reckon you got that right," Ezra added.

"I'll go ahead and make sure nobody is up," Thad said. He leaped out of the wagon and was back in a few minutes. "Let's go." They carried Davis inside to a small room lit by a single lantern, and shut the door.

Thad bent his head close to Davis's face and listened for a

moment. With a smile he raised his eyes. "He's breathing." Then he walked over to some packages that lay on the floor and said, "You two are leaving town in a couple hours. I've got you some clothes—had to guess at the sizes." Thad had bought two dark suits, complete with white shirts and ties.

"Hate to put on clean clothes without washing that prison filth off," Hale complained.

"You'll have to do with hands and face for now," Thad grinned. "And you'll have to shave that brush off your faces."

While they cleaned up, Thad took Owen Morgan's uniform and managed to squeeze into it. It was not a good fit, for Morgan had been a smaller man, but it would have to do.

Soon both men had shaved and stood clothed in their new outfits. "I swear, Captain Hale," Lee exclaimed in delight, "you look like a preacher!"

"And you look like a Philadelphia lawyer," Hale grinned.

"There're a couple of suitcases with some other stuff in them," Thad said. "And a couple of heavy overcoats and hats." He took out a sheaf of bills, divided them, and handed half to each man. "This ought to get you out of our territory."

Hale stared at the money, then looked at Thad with a strange expression. "You're doing a lot for a couple of your enemies, Novak."

Thad shifted uncomfortably. "I don't think of it like that, Hale. Way I see it, the enemy is death—and we're working together to keep Davis Winslow out of his way."

"What about Davis?" Ezra asked.

"By the time you're on the train, he'll be cleaned up and in the hands of the best doctors in Richmond."

They waited until six before leaving the hotel. Dawn was just breaking as they put Davis into the wagon and drove off. As they moved toward the river, Thad said, "This train takes mostly supplies toward the south. I put some Confederate money in with the other so you won't make anybody suspicious. Don't know where you'll wind up, but anywhere is better than Richmond."

They got to the station and waited until the train's whistle blew a warning blast. "So long," Thad said, shaking hands with them. "Be careful—I've got too much invested in you two to lose you now!"

"It's going to be hard for me to fight from now on, Thad," Hale said, uncomfortable at the thought. "I wouldn't like to think I was shooting at *you*."

"The same here," Ezra added. "I didn't know there were any Rebels like you around." The whistle blew another warning, and Lee said, "About Davis. I'd like to know if he makes it. Send me a letter, will you? Address it to Sickle's Corps. I'll get it."

The men had to run to make it, but with one short sprint they hit the steps and clung to the door, waving at Thad until the train moved out of sight.

Thad flicked the reins, and the horse moved down the street. It was not far to Chimborazo, and by the time Novak pulled up in front of the hospital, the sun was up.

He tied the horse, walked up the front steps, and asked the first orderly he met, "Where can I find Mrs. Wickham?"

He took the instructions, wound his way around the maze of buildings, and came to one marked Number 3. As he stepped inside, the first person he met was Belle Wickham. She was carrying a pitcher in one hand and had towels draped over her other arm.

"Why—Thad!" she exclaimed; then her face sobered. "Is something wrong? Someone sick at home?"

"No, Miss Belle. Far as I know they're all right. Can I talk to you?"

"Of course. Come this way." She led him to her office, put the things down, and asked, "What's the matter?"

"Well, I just came in from duty. Got a scratch on my side—" He saw her look of alarm and said hastily, "Oh, it's nothing, really. But I brought back an officer, and he's in terrible shape. Going to die if something don't happen."

"You want us to take care of him?" Belle asked.

"Well, yes, but I know about all this red tape," Thad went on. "By the time we get all the papers and stuff, he'll be dead. And besides, they might stick him in someplace with some sorry help. If I could ask a favor, Miss Belle, I'd like for you to see to him personal."

Belle gave him a direct look. "It would be against regulations, Thad."

"Yes, ma'am, I know." Thad had no arguments, and stood

there with his hat twisted in his big hands. Finally he said, "This fellow is special to me."

Belle dropped her head, unable to face the plea in Thad's dark eyes. She knew he was right about all the red tape, and suddenly the maverick streak in her broke through. "One of my boys died last night. I've got a bed available. Where is your friend?"

"Outside in my wagon."

"Bring him in while I get the bed ready."

She left, wondering how she would justify this action to the officials, but didn't worry much. They would never fire her, she knew. By the time she got the bed changed, Thad was coming in with the limp body of the officer in his arms.

She motioned toward the bed, and Thad laid him down. As Belle moved forward, Thad stepped back to watch her reaction. He knew she had met Davis Winslow. He remembered the time Captain Winslow had brought him to Richmond, and Belle had entertained him at a dance.

He had known all this, had weighed it in the balances, and finally decided that it was a gamble he had to take. But now as she bent over Davis, he wondered if he'd been a fool. *Even if he is a lot skinnier—and has a beard, Belle's not a fool! She'll recognize him for sure.*

But when she turned back after looking at the sick man, her eyes held only concern. "He's in bad shape, Thad. I'm not sure you got here in time."

"I been worried, Miss Belle," Thad told her, and a great surge of relief welled up in him. "His leg is real bad."

"Help me undress him," she urged, and the two soon had the unconscious man in a clean hospital gown. Thad felt strange about pulling a man's clothing off in front of a woman, but Belle was long past such modesty. She looked down at the soldier and shook her head. "I want Dr. Stevens to look at that leg right away. You stay with him, Thad."

Fortunately she wasn't there when Davis began tossing on the bed. Thad saw the man's eyes open, so he leaned over him. "Are you all right, Davis?"

"I—guess so." His voice rasped and he looked around. "Where am I?"

"In a Confederate soldiers' hospital, Davis."

"Am I—under arrest?"

"No! No!" Thad replied, bending over and whispering, "Davis, this is Chimborazo Hospital. I had to bring you here—but the only way I could get you in was to tell them that you're a Confederate officer."

Davis tried to comprehend as the young man related their successful escape. Focusing his eyes on Thad, he shook his head. "It'll never work. They'll find out."

"Maybe so, but it's a chance we have to take, Davis—the only one you've got. Now you listen to me. I can't stay with you. I've got to go back on duty, but if you keep your mouth shut, they won't find out. I got papers for you. Just remember you are Lieutenant Owen Morgan. Got that? Owen Morgan."

"Owen Morgan," Davis whispered. He closed his eyes, then opened them again. "Thad—did Perry and Ezra get away?"

"Sure did! On their way right now!"

A smile split Davis's shrunken lips, and he lifted a hand, which Thad squeezed. "Thad—thanks for—everything. Grandfather will be glad."

Thad lifted his head and saw Belle coming though the door, and he cautioned, "Don't forget—keep your mouth shut, Davis. Here comes the matron. Can you do it?"

"Yes."

Thad didn't know all the details of Belle's experience as a spy in Washington, but he knew a little. His biggest fear was that Belle would recognize Davis; another, that Davis would be so filled with hate toward her for deceiving his family that he would give himself away. Thad stood ready to silence him if he should make a mistake.

"Miss Belle, he woke up," Thad said. "I'd like you to meet Lieutenant Owen Morgan. This is Mrs. Belle Wickham, Owen."

Belle looked down into Davis's ravaged face. "I'm glad to meet you, Lieutenant."

Davis felt as if he were in a dream. He had spent months hating Belle Wickham; now she was bending over him. He had an impulse to shout, to scream, calling her all the names that had run through his mind. He glanced at Thad. The agonized look on Thad's face stemmed the vitriolic flood. He took a deep breath and nodded slightly.

"I'm glad to meet you, Miss Wickham," he said weakly.

PART THREE

# THE MASQUERADE

★ ★ ★ ★

(January '64 – April '65)

## CHAPTER SIXTEEN

# BACK TO THE WORLD

★ ★ ★ ★

Day arrived with piercing light and the noise of movements about Davis. Hands touched him, and sometimes when his leg was handled, great fiery shards of pain seemed to devour him. The light hurt his eyes, and he would try to slip back into the warm darkness—but the hands would not leave him alone. He grew angry, thrashing his head from side to side as they put food into his mouth, but they kept on relentlessly until he swallowed it. The hands were soothing, sometimes applying cool cloths to sponge his fever-hot body. This was the best part of his day.

The nights were long tunnels of blackness, a warm hiding place to slip into and be oblivious to everything until the light returned to disturb him. He dreamed often, but could not distinguish between the visions that fluttered through his mind and the times he knew he was lying on a real bed in a body that cried out with every movement.

One face appeared in both his dreams and his infrequent moments of consciousness. More than once a vision of a woman with dark hair and eyes like ebony pools would flicker through his mind—then he would open his eyes to find himself looking into that face. And he was always disturbed when he saw her, either in a dream or when conscious, her face so close he could see the tiny flecks of light in her dark eyes. During those times, he would stare at her, wondering why her face confused him. He wanted her to tell him something, but didn't know what it was. Sometimes she spoke, urging him to eat; other times she would sit silently beside him, and he would lie there studying her face until finally sleep would overtake him and he'd drift off into a dream of some time in the dim past—and she would be there, too.

One day he awoke—suddenly. One moment he was in the dark tunnel; the next, lying on a bed staring at a man and a woman who were standing beside him.

The man was tall and thin, and had a shock of snow-white hair and a pair of steady hazel eyes. "Well, now," he said in a rumbling bass voice, "he's decided to come back to the real world, Miss Belle."

Davis glanced at the woman, and memory flooded back. He remembered some of the escape from Libby, and Thad warning him to be quiet, that he was here under the guise of a Confederate officer. What was the name? He couldn't remember, but Belle furnished it.

"Well, Lieutenant Morgan, how do you feel?"

Davis licked his lips, considered the question, and replied, "Hungry."

The doctor chuckled deep in his chest. "Well, he's going to make it, I reckon." He picked up a black bag from the bed. "Get some real food down him, keep the dressings changed."

"Yes, Dr. Stevens."

He started walking to the next patient, then swung back. "Lieutenant, you behave yourself! I've invested too much time and effort in you to lose you at this stage—and Miss Belle's done more, so you mind her, you hear?"

The doctor turned to the patient on the next bed, and Belle said to Davis, "I'll get you some solid food for lunch."

He nodded. Davis lay studying his surroundings as the doctor and nurse moved from patient to patient. It was a long, narrow room with windows along one short wall. He could see the black, bare branches of large trees, dripping with the slow rain that fell slantwise. The other three walls were bare except for shelves over the beds, some of them holding lamps with blackened chimneys. Two rows of beds stretched the length of the room—all occupied by patients in gray gowns. Some of them, he saw, were sitting up, but most were lying down.

"You finally woke up, didn't you, sir?"

Davis turned his head to find a young soldier with yellow hair and blue eyes looking at him shyly. He had a thin face with a childlike countenance, and Davis said, "Guess so." He remembered the name Thad had spoken. "I'm Owen Morgan."

"Yes, sir. My name's Lonnie Tate."

"How long have I been here, Lonnie?"

"Why, it's been nigh onto a week since you got here, Lieutenant." He lifted a hand so thin Davis could see the blue veins like a lacy network on the back, and counted the days off on bony fingers. "That's right, sir, this is Tuesday and it was last Tuesday they brought you in."

Davis blinked his eyes. "Don't remember much." He looked down at his leg, which was not very swollen anymore. Moving it cautiously, he grimaced at the pain, though it was no longer as fierce. Carefully he rolled over on his side facing the boy, and asked, "You get hit bad, Lonnie?"

"Well, my arm's all right now, just about—but my belly's still not right." He lifted the blanket and exposed a mass of bandages crusted with blood. He studied his abdomen, then shook his head. "Most fellers would have been dead already with a hit like I got—but Miz Belle, she jest wouldn't give up on me."

A shiver ran through Davis at the sight of the wound, and he was glad when the boy lowered the blanket. He knew Lonnie had spoken the truth—that intestinal wounds from the tearing action of minié balls were usually fatal. The balls were conical lead slugs weighing over an ounce, and caused fearful damage—smashing long bones into fragments and ripping through the body with deadly effect.

"Where's your home, Lonnie?" he asked.

"Jasper, Arkansas. Guess maybe you ain't never heard of it?"

"No, I don't think so."

"Well, it's in the mountains. We got us a farm there, some of it's sort of hilly, but we got 'bout forty-five acres of good bottom land. And Pa's got his eye on a farm that jines ourn. Reckon he'll buy it—and when I get home, I'm goin' to get to farm it myself."

"That sounds good." Davis smiled at the boy's excitement,

and lay there as Lonnie outlined exactly how he would plant his crops and raise what he called his "critters" for meat. The monotone made Davis sleepy, and he was paying little heed to the boy until he cried out. Lonnie was clawing at his stomach, his face contorted in pain.

"Doctor!" Davis called, looking wildly toward the door. He continued to yell for help until Belle came running into the room. She saw the boy's distress and rushed over to pull his hands away from his abdomen.

"Let me be!" he screamed. "It itches!"

But she restrained his hands with all her strength. "Don't fight, Lonnie!" She looked up and saw an orderly entering the ward. "Elmer," she called, "come hold his hands." When the man had a firm grasp on Lonnie, Belle reached up to the shelf over the boy's bed, poured some cloudy liquid into a glass from a brown bottle, and forced it between his jaws. "Don't let him go," she whispered in prayer, her hands trembling as she worked.

Finally the orderly said, "It's taking hold now, Miz Wickham. You want me to stay with him?"

"No, Elmer. You go on with your work. I'll change his bandages while he's asleep."

"Yes, ma'am." Elmer Gibbs was in his sixties, a small, kind-looking man. He studied the boy's twisted face, saying quietly, "Poor boy!" Then he left the room, and Belle pulled a chair to the bedside and sat down.

She was very pale, Davis saw, and her upper lip beaded with perspiration. When Tate lay still, she rose and went to a cabinet beside the door, returning with bandages and a basin of water. She removed the soiled dressing and washed the wound. As she worked, Davis noted that the flesh was pulled away from the raw lips of the wound, exposing the intestines. Finally she applied some medication and put on fresh bandages.

Putting the blanket back over the boy's slight form, she leaned back and closed her eyes. As she sat there, Davis studied her, and memories of Lowell swept over him. He had been admiring her skill—and her willingness to face a raw wound—but now he thought of how she had brought about the death of his brother, and the hatred that had been dormant during his sickness revived.

He rolled over on his back, closed his eyes, and didn't look up as he heard her walk away. For a long time he lay there, thinking of Lowell, and the anger and bitterness grew. He tried to think of something else, but he could not quell the rage that rose when he thought of Belle Wickham.

Finally he napped, and was wakened by Gibbs, who fed him some boiled chicken and a bowl of peas, which he ate hungrily, then fell into a deep sleep. He was awakened later by another orderly, and saw that it was dark outside. "Got some supper for you, Lieutenant," the man said, and Davis roused himself to eat more chicken and drink some buttermilk. "What time is it?" he asked.

"Six-thirty." The bushy-browed orderly with a droopy mustache answered. "You want some more? Miz Wickham says to give you all you want."

"No, thanks. That's plenty."

The orderly left and Davis looked up to see a man with one arm missing regarding him curiously from the bed directly across the room. "Howdy, Lieutenant," he said. "I'm Coy Willing—Third Mississippi."

Davis nodded and gave his name, and the lanky Willing said, "You sure gave everybody a time around here, Lieutenant Morgan. We all thought you must be a general at least, the way Miz Wickham had everybody hopping. You must be real important."

"No, not very," Davis replied. He moved his leg, and pain shot through him, catching him off guard. He groaned, and lay back until it passed.

"Leg still bothering you, ain't it, sir?" Willing nodded. "Dr. Stevens wanted to take it off. You know that?"

"No, I didn't."

"Wal, he did. Him and Miz Belle got into an orful fuss 'bout it. Never seen Doc Stevens get so mad! They stood right there over you and fought like two yard dogs!"

"I didn't hear it."

"Naw, you was out, but you gotta thank Miz Belle, 'cause she just stood there and let Stevens holler, and just kept saying no until he give up." He shook his head in admiration. "She sure is a stubborn woman."

Davis looked down at his leg with a strange feeling. He had

never feared death, but he *had* feared being left a cripple. The thought of it had haunted him, and he remembered saying to Perry Hale when the leg had become swollen and infectious, "Don't let them cut it off, Perry. I'd rather die than drag myself around for the rest of my life."

Willing asked, "What's your outfit, Lieutenant?"

Davis suddenly realized he had no idea. A wrong word could be fatal, so he closed his eyes, murmuring, "Sure am weak . . ." and pretended to doze off. He heard Willing say, "He's weak, ain't he, Frank?" but lay there quietly until somebody came and turned out the lamps. He did sleep then, but it was no longer like a long black tunnel with no end.

* * * *

The next morning Davis awoke to falling snowflakes lacing the black branches with intricate patterns and thickening the limbs like blankets of down. At ten o'clock he looked up to see Novak coming toward him.

"You look good," Thad said, noting the improvement. Then he added for the benefit of the other patients, "How do you feel, Owen?"

"Going to live, Lieutenant," he replied. "Sit down." When the young man had pulled a chair close, Davis said carefully, "I've been pretty sick. Can't seem to remember much."

"Well, you were in bad shape, but things'll start coming back." He reached into his pocket, pulled out a paper, and said with a slight wink, "Letter came for you." Davis looked puzzled, then opened the envelope and read the words: "Second Lieutenant Robert Owen Morgan, Company H, the Maury Grays, First Tennessee Regiment. Colonel Hume R. Field, commanding officer." Running his eyes over the paper, Davis realized that it was the information he needed about the real Morgan's background. He glanced at the bottom of the page and saw the personal data, such as the fact that Morgan came from Wales and had been a gambler on a riverboat.

He looked up with gratitude. "Thanks, Thad. I needed this."

"Reckon so, Owen," Thad said with a droll look in his eyes. Then he smiled. "I got a note from Hale and Lee. They made it home all right. Said for you to take care of yourself."

Davis's eyes widened, and he said softly, "Thank God for that! I've had some anxious thoughts about it."

"'Course, you know how Hale is—always thinking that God's in control of everything." Thad added, "The more I think about it, the more I'd like to agree with him."

Davis glanced cautiously at Lonnie, who was sleeping soundly, and at Willing's bed, empty at the moment. Not wishing to take any chances of being overheard, Davis lowered his voice. "My family will get a report saying I'm dead, Thad. I've got to get word to them."

"Better wait till you're on your feet and we can figure a way to get you out of here, Davis. If the record keeping is as bad at Libby as it is everywhere else, you could be back home before your folks get a letter. I'll think on it, but right now it'll be better to lay low."

"Guess that's right," he replied, casting his eyes at his leg, trying to estimate how long it would keep him down. Frustrated, he groaned. "Got to get out of here as soon as I can."

Novak studied him shrewdly. "You've got a pretty big hate for Belle, don't you?"

"Why shouldn't I?" Davis asked defiantly. "She used me and my family—and she killed my brother."

Thad refused to argue, though he wanted to say that Lowell could have been killed on any account. Instead, he said, "Looks to me like she balanced the account by saving your life."

Davis stubbornly clamped his lips together. He was in the grip of emotion, and logic had no power to move him. The long months he had spent in Libby had blocked off all normal activities, leaving him with nothing to do but dwell on the past. His sickness and the dreary routine of the place had quickly dulled his sharpness of mind, and his hatred for the South and for Belle, as a symbol of it, had fed upon itself. Now he desired only one thing—to get back to the war where he could express his anger by fighting the Confederacy.

*No use talking to him,* Thad thought. *He's so eaten up with hate he can't even think straight.* After a few more minutes, he decided it was time to leave. "Not much going on right now, Owen," he said in a normal tone. "Looks like I'll be around Richmond for a spell. I'll drop in from time to time."

Davis felt a quick pang, knowing he owed the young man his life, but he could find no way to express it. He nodded. "All right, Thad."

As he went to find Belle, Thad had an uneasy feeling about Davis. Physically he was much improved, but inside, the man was filled with a burning anger. If they were to get by with this masquerade, it would take a cool head—the one thing Davis lacked now. He found Belle in her office. "Hello, Nurse Wickham. Looks like you've pulled it off with Owen."

Belle looked up from her desk. "He's going to make it—but it didn't look like it for a while. Is he awake?"

"Sure. I had a talk with him." He slouched back against the wall and asked casually, "How long you figure he'll keep that bed tied up?"

"He's not over this thing yet, Thad," she warned. "He's nothing but skin and bones—and though that leg is better, it's still touch and go. I'd say a month would be the best he could hope for—if everything goes well."

Thad masked the dismay her words brought, saying only, "Well, he's on his way—thanks to you, Belle." He stood up to leave. "I'll be around for a spell, so I'll come in and check with him as often as I can."

"Pet will be glad," Belle smiled, and walked him to the door. Snowflakes were still falling, and as he got on his horse and rode off, Belle lingered, watching the snow swarm across the yard. On an impulse she walked off the porch, turned, and made her way down the walk running parallel with the building. The flakes bit at her face and melted on her lips like wax.

She had always loved the snow, though there was little in her world. She remembered as a young child, waking up to find the dark earth transformed into a fairyland of glistening crystal. Some of that same feeling swept over her now as she walked. The world was quiet, sounds muffled by the soft, downy blanket that covered everything.

Finally, the cold numbed her face and she turned back. As she passed one of the windows, a patient in Davis's ward saw her from the window. "There goes Miz Belle! Lookee there!" he exclaimed. "She looks like a ghost—wearing that black in all the snow!"

Davis caught just a glimpse of the dark figure outlined against the white before she disappeared.

Lonnie, who had just awakened, asked, "Did you see her, Lieutenant Morgan?"

"Yes, I did, Lonnie."

"She's something, ain't she now?"

Davis didn't answer—he couldn't.

CHAPTER SEVENTEEN

# HOSPITAL VISIT

★ ★ ★ ★

Most of Richmond's population had gathered on the Capitol grounds to greet a large number of returned prisoners. It was a cold, blustery February day. Sky and Rebekah were standing close to the platform where the speeches were customarily made. "It doesn't seem very humane to make the poor men come out and stand in this cold when they've already suffered so much, Sky," Rebekah commented. "Why couldn't they have the reception inside?"

"Couldn't get as many people inside for the politicians to speak to." Sky looked disgustedly at the members of Congress who were gathering on the platform. He shook his head and muttered, "Seems to me they could have visited the wounded in the hospital if they're so concerned about our men. Bunch of vultures looking for votes!"

"I know, dear," Rebekah said, squeezing his arm. "But the President will be here. *He's* not one to put on a show." She was aware of her husband's growing disillusionment with the government the past months—as she herself had been. The first two months of 1864 had brought no good news from the military, for the Yankee armies were drawing the net tighter on all fronts. It was time, Sky said repeatedly, for the South to pull itself together in a determined effort—but just the opposite seemed to be happening. The states were refusing to send arms and supplies for Lee's army, holding them back for their own units, and Sky had nearly gotten into a duel with one governor who had kept the warehouses full in his own state, while the Army of Northern Virginia and the Army of Tennessee went barefooted and hungry.

Sky scanned the senators on the platform, then shrugged in a gesture of disgust. "Well, Rebekah, we have to honor the boys who've come back—but I don't see how a long-winded speech is going to help—"

"Oh, look, Sky—there's Belle!" exclaimed Rebekah, breaking into Sky's diatribe.

"Where? Oh yes, I see her." At the same time Belle spotted them, and Sky motioned for her to come over to where they were, but she shook her head firmly. "Well, she won't come up here," he said.

"She hates attention," Rebekah commented. "Let's go stand with her. I'd like her to spend the weekend with us at Belle Maison. She needs a rest."

"You *know* she won't do it," he said as they pushed their way through the crowd. "She's working too hard. Spends fifteen hours a day at that hospital."

They finally made their way to her, and greeted her. She was wearing black, as always, and put her hand on the arm of a worn, middle-age woman beside her. "Father, Mother, this is Mrs. Donaldson—Emily, I'd like you to meet my parents—Mr. and Mrs. Winslow."

The woman nodded nervously "How do you do?" and took the hand Rebekah extended. "Emily's son, William, is one of my patients," Belle informed them. "She's hoping her husband will be one of the returned prisoners."

"He was took at Gettysburg, I heard," Mrs. Donaldson said. She lifted a basket, adding, "I brung him somethin' to eat. My Tom was always a careful feeder."

Rebekah caught Belle's glance and saw they were both thinking the same thing: *He probably wasn't so careful in a Yankee prison.* But Belle shook her head slightly; just at that moment a smattering of applause broke out.

"There they come," Sky said.

A column of men, preceded by honor guards with flags flying, appeared. They walked up the steps to a reserved section on one side of the platform; and the honor guards, all carrying muskets with bayonets in place, stepped down to form a line below. As the President and Vice-President mounted the platform, the people gave another round of applause. Jefferson Davis began to speak almost at once, his high tenor voice easily carrying over the crowd.

"He's looking poorly," Rebekah whispered to Sky. "How pale he is!"

"A little good news from the front would bring some color," Sky murmured. "As well as less criticism from the papers here at home."

Davis gave a short speech, specifying a tribute to the sacrifices of the gallant soldiers of the Confederacy. A cheer from the crowd—and the prisoners who were able—followed. Then the President stepped back, and the people moved forward to greet the prisoners.

As Emily Donaldson hurried off in search of her husband, Belle said, "I hope she finds him. It's all she lives for."

Rebekah took in the scene, her heart sad. "How worn they all look!"

Indeed, the men were a tragic sight—forlorn, gaunt, shrunken. Most of them were so emaciated their clothing hung like sackcloth, fluttering in the sharp winter breeze. Many stood as if rooted to the ground, unable to comprehend their surroundings or the world they had been dead to for so long. Others had a restless, wild look, their eyes mirroring a longing to run away from the noise and the press of the crowd.

"Look!" Sky cried. "There's Gil Hardee!"

Sky rushed up to a small man standing off to one side. "Gil! By heaven, it's good to see you back!" He put his hand out, smiling broadly, but Hardee stared back blankly. Sky dropped his hand, and his smile faded.

Gil had grown old and sick. The young man who had been so eager to join the Richmond Blades was no longer the same. He and his twin brother Robert had been two of the young aristocrats who could hardly wait for the war to start. Young, wealthy, and full of life, they had gone as officers in the Third

Virginia at the same time Sky's own two sons had joined. The fire that had flamed in Gil Hardee was gone. The cheeks, once rosy and full, were sunken. He had lost most of his teeth in prison, and his eyes were dull and fearful.

Carefully, Sky put a hand on the thin shoulder, feeling the sharp bones through Gil's new uniform, and said gently, "Well, my boy, I'm glad you're home. It's been hard, I know, but we'll get you back in shape in no time."

Hardee slowly nodded, but didn't speak. Sky went back to Belle and Rebekah, depressed and sad. "He's like a dead man," he reported—"like most of these men. They've been ground to pieces and will never fight—"

"Look!" Belle broke in. "I think she's found him!" She pointed to where Mrs. Donaldson was coming toward them, a tall, thin private in tow.

"He's here, Miz Belle!" the woman cried, tears streaming down her face. "My Tom—he's back!"

The man was thin but, unlike Hardee, his eyes were bright and he grinned from ear to ear. When he was introduced to Belle and her parents, he said in a strident voice, "Why, I knowed all the time I was comin' back!"

"By the looks of the prisoners, prison must have been hell," Sky commented.

"Oh, it wasn't no Sunday school picnic," Donaldson voiced; "but I'm ready to go back and even it up on them bluebellies!"

"Come on, Tom," his wife urged. "William is going to jump out of that bed when he sees you."

As the couple left, Belle watched them with wonder in her eyes. "I never thought he'd be here," she said quietly. "It's good to have a happy ending once in a while, at least."

"Is her boy very ill?"

"No, he'll be out soon."

"Belle, you need a rest," Sky interjected. "We're going to the country for a few days. Why don't you come with us. We haven't had any time together lately."

She smiled and shook her head. "I can't right now, Father. Maybe in a few weeks when I get some more help."

They tried to persuade her, but she was adamant. Finally Sky said, "Why don't we get something to eat before we go to the hospital with you."

They went to the best restaurant in town and had a delicious meal. When they left, they stopped to buy some items for the prisoners—a large supply of newspapers and a few books, some bakery goods, and cotton for bandages (going to three stores to find enough). As they came out of the last store, Sky said in disbelief. "You'd think the one thing in this world we'd have plenty of is cotton—but it's getting hard to find, like everything else."

"Plenty of it on the docks," Belle replied. "I read in the paper last week that the President is urging farmers to plant food instead of cotton—just what Thad said a long time ago."

"He was right, too." As they got into Sky's buggy, he told them how well things had gone at Belle Maison in the fall. "Thad's idea to plant corn and raise cattle and pigs saved our hides," he said. "We paid off quite a bit of the debt on the place—and the food helped our men in the army. If we have another good year or two, we can really get rid of some paperwork."

"If we last that long," Belle commented, then put her hand on her father's arm. "I'm sorry. I—I just get a little discouraged sometimes."

"No wonder," he sighed. "Attending those poor fellows day and night, with so many of them dying. I don't see how you do it, Belle!" He studied her and said cautiously, "You're not the same girl anymore. If I remember, the most serious problem you used to have was whether to wear a blue or a pink dress to a ball—and you pulled a real tantrum if you didn't get your way. But now you deal with death every day. Everyone in Richmond—and the South, for that matter—admires you."

His words stirred her for a moment, and she hung her head. "It's the men who pay the price. I just do what I can."

Rebekah longed to say more to Belle, but dared not. That morning at breakfast she and Sky had discussed how withdrawn their famous daughter had become. "She's hurting inside," Rebekah had remarked as they lingered over their coffee. "It's not just the loss of Vance, Sky, though that hurt badly. She hasn't been the same since her traumatic time in Washington. That whole episode took the life out of her."

"She can't bear any mention of it," Sky noted. "People praise her for her work as a Confederate agent, but she freezes up."

"Yes, she does, and have you noticed she hasn't been to church since she came back, Sky?"

"She never was too much for church. It was kind of a duty for her."

"Well, whenever you mention the Lord or church, her eyes get a strange look—and her face pales. I think she feels some kind of terrible guilt. But she'll never talk to us about it."

★ ★ ★ ★

The visit at the hospital was rewarding. Both Sky and Rebekah noticed how everyone's face lit up as Belle passed by, addressing each man by name. The three went from ward to ward, passing out the bakery goods and newspapers. As they came out of one ward and prepared to go into another, Belle remarked, "It's good of you to do this. They love cake and are dying for something to read—but just having visitors is what gives them a lift."

"Is the young officer Thad brought in still here?"

"Oh yes. He's in this very ward. Come along and I'll introduce you."

She led them into the room, saying, "Men, this is Mr. and Mrs. Winslow—my parents. I don't suppose any of you could down a piece of cake, could you?"

A noisy cheer erupted, and arguments broke out about who deserved the largest piece. As the Winslows walked toward the end of the room, a tall lanky soldier sitting on his bed called out, "Hey, Mr. and Mrs. Winslow, lookee what I got!"

The man showed them a framed picture on the table beside his bed.

"Why, that's very nice, my boy," Sky said, admiring the portrait, which was of the young man and Belle. He was seated and she was standing beside him, her hand on his shoulder.

"He was supposed to send it to his sweetheart," Belle smiled. "But he fell in love with himself and couldn't bear to part with it."

"Didn't know what a handsome feller I was till Miz Belle had this took," he admitted. "Anyway, I had another one made and sent it to my girl." His face broke out into a rueful grin, and he shook his head sadly. "Made her plum green with envy, it did! But we're gettin' married soon as I get back—and that's right off."

They congratulated him, then Belle moved to a bed just opposite. "This is Thad's friend, Lieutenant Owen Morgan. My parents, Lieutenant."

"Happy to know you, sir," Sky said, shaking the thin hand.

Rebekah added, "Thad told me to make sure Belle takes extra good care of you."

"She's doing that, Mrs. Winslow."

The man was tall, but very thin. His face was covered by a thick, bushy reddish-brown beard, with crisp hair the same tint. He considered them out of a pair of brown eyes, deep set and intent. He spoke so softly that Rebekah had to lean forward to hear as he added, "I owe a lot to Lieutenant Novak—and to Mrs. Wickham, of course."

"Father," Belle suggested, "why don't you let Mother visit with the lieutenant? One of your old friends, Ray Stallings, is in the next ward."

"Why, of course." Sky plucked a newspaper out of the bundle under his arm and gave it to Davis. "You may want to read this later."

After Sky and Belle had moved on, Rebekah said, "Can you sit up, Lieutenant?"

"Yes. I'm doing much better."

"Now, let me see, I've got some chocolate—and this caramel is very good, the men say; or maybe some of this angel food would suit you."

"Chocolate would be fine, Mrs. Winslow."

She sorted a thick wedge of the chocolate cake from the others, then looked around. "There's no plate, I'm afraid—but I'll bet you'll manage."

He took the cake and ate it quickly, trying not to spill. As he consumed the delicacy, she reported on Thad's activities, concluding with, "He's managed to stay on here in Richmond, though I don't know how! He and Pet—that's Belle's sister, you know—they spend a lot of time together. They're such a fine young couple!"

"Is Miss Pet like your older daughter?"

"Oh no. Not at all!" Rebekah replied. "They're as different as night from day. Pet's always been a tomboy. Never cared anything about parties or dresses. Of course, she does now a bit more. But she and Thad are so compatible—and will do well when they get married. Both love farming."

"Your other daughter is very efficient," Davis said carefully. "She's quite well known, isn't she?"

Rebekah seemed disturbed at the question, her eyes troubled. "Belle was a very flighty girl while growing up. Cared for nothing but parties—and was very sought after." She paused hesitantly. "She hates all the talk about being a spy—but tell me about yourself, Lieutenant Morgan," she said, changing the subject. "Thad says you're from Ireland."

"Well, yes, I am."

"You don't sound very Irish."

"I-I've been away for a long time, Mrs. Winslow."

"You have a family?"

She drew him out, thinking what a shy person he was. Both Thad and Belle had spoken of the man's critical condition when he was first admitted to Chimborazo—mentally as well as physically. Thad had warned her, "He's kind of mixed up. Keeps forgetting things—and it bothers him, so if you go see him, don't press him too hard."

She didn't question him further, but for the next twenty minutes talked about current happenings until Sky returned. She took Davis's hand as she said goodbye. "I'm so glad you're making such good progress, Lieutenant Morgan. You must pay us a visit while you're in Richmond—as soon as you're up and about."

He nodded and promised to do so. After they left, he picked up the papers with rather unsteady hands. When Belle's mother had first looked at him, he thought she had a gleam of recognition in her eyes, and fully expected Rebekah to cry out, "Why, Davis Winslow—what are you doing here?"

It was still a miracle that he could face these people and not be recognized. But when he looked into a mirror later that morning, he realized why. Belle had brought a mirror and a pair of scissors, saying firmly, "You can keep that beard you're so attached to, Lieutenant, but it's got to be trimmed. You look like a wild hermit! Now get out of that bed and sit in this chair."

He had protested, but she had pulled the blanket back, and soon he was sitting there as she trimmed his beard. "Leave it long, please," he pleaded.

"You're as vain as a peacock!" she laughed, but agreed.

As she worked on his beard, moving his face from one position to another with quick and firm hands, her face was uncomfortably near. He studied her intent expression carefully.

*How can a woman so evil be so beautiful?* he wondered—not for the first time, however. She was biting her full lower lip with perfect teeth in deep concentration, and he could not help admiring the smooth planes of her lovely face. Her eyes were fixed on his beard, but as she shifted them, Belle caught his gaze and smiled. "Now see what sort of barber I am," she challenged.

He took the small mirror, looked at his image, and was surprised. There was little to remind him of the plump-cheeked smiling man he'd been before his imprisonment. The cheeks were still thin, the eyes sunken, and the hard-set mouth almost totally foreign. He handed her the mirror. "It feels better," he admitted. "Thank you, Mrs. Wickham."

She noted he never called her "Miss Belle," as most of the patients did. He was a mystery, with his distant air and reserved manner. He never smiled, and made few friends in the ward. She thought it was because he was an officer among enlisted men, but the reticent manner went deeper than that. The Irishmen she had known had been outgoing. But Morgan, while not sullen, kept himself firmly behind a mask, polite but unapproachable.

She put the shears down and said with a slight smile, "Now, let's see if that leg will work."

Startled, he asked, "You mean—walk?"

"Well, you can't lie in that bed the rest of your life, can you? Come on, get up and let's try a few steps."

He slowly rose to his feet, and she stepped beside him. "Put your arm around my shoulder," she commanded. "Come on, Lieutenant, I won't let you fall."

"The room's spinning," he said faintly. But he wanted to walk, so he did as she said, putting his right arm around her shoulder.

He took one step, swayed, and she put her left arm around him, holding him firmly.

"That's good, Owen," she coached, using his given name for the first time. "Very good! Now another . . . that's it!" She led him out to the aisle, turned him carefully, and they moved slowly along as the men in the beds called out encouragement: "Go to it, Lieutenant!" . . . "Run him this way, Miss Belle!"

Finally she turned, and they walked back to the bed. Davis was concentrating on staying upright, but at the same time, he was acutely conscious of her firm body pressing against his, of the warmth of her arm around him. And the pressure of his own arm around her shoulder was disturbing. He made the final turn, and she helped him sit down on the bed and he shifted his legs up.

"You've made a good beginning," she said. "We'll do a little more tomorrow."

"I—I think I can manage by myself," he replied.

"You will *not* get out of that bed alone, Owen Morgan! Do you hear me?"

"Yes, but. . . !"

She put her hands on his shoulders and pushed him down; and as he went back, she brushed her hands across his lips.

"You've got chocolate cake all over your mouth—just like a little boy," she quipped. Then she picked up the shears and moved away. "We'll walk some more tomorrow."

Davis tried to read the newspaper, but had difficulty concentrating. For a long time he thought of Sky and Rebekah, of Thad and Pet, of his parents and his grandfather—and of the dark eyes of Belle Winslow. For once, the anger he usually felt did not come.

## CHAPTER EIGHTEEN

# DEATH IN THE NIGHT

★ ★ ★ ★

Every day Davis grew stronger, and by the time March blustered in, driving the snow away, he was able to walk with the aid of a cane. He had suffered Belle's assistance only a week, then had rebelliously insisted on making his own way.

"Let's see you do it, then," she had said with a smile. "We need your bed. No room for a healthy man in this place."

He mused about Belle's comment as he hobbled along the walk one Sunday afternoon, savoring the tang of air that drove the dead leaves along in front of him, like ghosts fleeing from an enchanter. He stopped, balanced on his good leg and, swept by an unexpected sense of well-being, took a sudden swing at the leaves. "By George, it's good to be on my feet!" he exclaimed. He glanced around quickly to make certain nobody had overheard, then continued his walk.

*No room for a healthy man in this place,* Belle had said. The thought returned, and he moved slowly along under the huge oaks that lifted bare arms to a leaden sky. *I've got to think of something—and soon,* he mused. His recovery, Dr. Stevens had proclaimed, was "nothing short of miraculous," his leg healing faster than any of them had expected, and the flesh filling out his frame so that he no longer looked like a skeleton.

*I've got to get away from here.* It was not a new conviction, but before, it had been impossible. He could not have crawled on board a train, to say nothing of riding a horse. But now that he could walk better, though stiffly, he tried to think of some way to get out of Richmond.

As if in answer to his dilemma, he saw Thad riding up the road, and waved his stick to catch his attention. The young man rode up, dismounted and tied his horse to the picket fence. "Well, Davis, this looks promising!" Thad said with a smile. "How long have you been able to go outdoors?"

"My maiden voyage, Thad," Davis replied. "I'm beginning to feel more like a human being. Come on, walk with me, but take it easy." The two moved slowly along the walk, and Davis added, "This is the first time I've been able to say a word out loud since January without being afraid I'd be denounced as a spy."

"You've done a good job. I sort of fished around with the Winslows to see if they thought you looked familiar—but they don't have any suspicions at all." He peered at Davis carefully. "You sure don't look anything like you did when you were here with your grandfather. I always think of Davis Winslow as a fat man, with baby-faced red cheeks, always smiling. Now you have the appearance of a mature fellow, maybe ten years older."

Davis nodded. "It's been a freaky thing, Thad. Makes me feel creepy—but it saved my life, so I'm not complaining."

"I got a letter from Perry Hale last week. I brought it along—think maybe you ought to read it." He handed it over to Davis.

February 21, 1864

Dear Thad,

I write to tell you that I am back on duty—and so is Ezra. We are stationed outside Washington, waiting to be reassigned. And I thought you would like to know. I went to see our friend Captain W. yesterday. He is in good health, but is quite sad over his loss. The letter came last week telling him of the death of his grandson in the prison, and the entire family is taking it hard, as you might expect. His daughter-in-law is prostrate, he said. I wanted to comfort him, but was uncertain as to how to do it. If you can think of anything I could say to him to assuage his grief, write at the address below. I will be here for at least three more weeks and will be happy to give any message you think good to the family.

Give my best to our young friend, who is mending well by this time, I hope. Lee and I will never forget him—nor you, Thad. Mr. Lee pokes fun at my strict Calvinistic theology, but as the poet says, "God's in his heaven, all's right with the world!"

Sincerely,<br>
Captain Perry Hale<br>
Maddox Hotel<br>
Washington

"I'm glad about Perry and Ezra," Davis said; "but I wonder if it hurts your conscience any—letting two of your enemies escape."

"Not a bit!" Thad assured, taking the letter. "This letter is sort of in code. He's asking if he can tell your people you're alive."

"Yes, I know." Davis moved his stick back and forth, paused, and said, "It would be dangerous. Bad as I hate to see them suffer, I think they'll just have to stand it until I can get away."

"Up to you now, Davis," Thad shrugged. "How long you figure that'll be?"

"Belle dropped a hint that I'd have to let someone who's worse off have my bed. I'd better leave the hospital as soon as possible. Maybe I can make it like Perry and Ezra. Just shove me on a train, and I'll try to get to one of the border states. From there I can make it back to our lines."

"Not till you can navigate better than you're doing now," Thad insisted firmly. "If you get caught impersonating a Confederate officer, they won't waste much time on a trial. You'd be shot out of hand."

"Well, I've got to do *something,*" Davis countered.

"I'll try to find a place for you to stay for a few days," Thad said. "God's brought you this far, Davis—He's not going to lose you now!"

Davis kept his head down, and when he finally lifted his eyes to meet Thad's gaze, there was an intensely sober expression on his face. "I've wondered about that, Thad. Guess you have too, as many men as you've seen die. Why did *they* die—and not us?"

"I don't know the answer to that, Davis," Thad replied thoughtfully. "Don't really think anyone does. But since God did bring me through alive, I figure He's got something in mind for me."

"That's what the preachers say," Davis sighed, and changed the subject, saying, "I promised one of the patients I'd be at the service this afternoon, Thad. You remember the young fellow in the bed next to mine?"

"He looked pretty sick when I saw him," Thad remarked.

"He suffers all the time. At night I can hear him gritting his teeth to keep from crying out and disturbing the rest of us." A bitter taste rose to his mouth. "I can't do a *thing* for him, Thad—not a thing!"

"Reckon I know what that's like, Davis. Sure eats on a man, don't it?"

"Maybe you'd like to come for the service?"

"Sure would." Thad turned and walked into the building with Davis, and when they entered the ward, the Methodist pastor, Reverend Tyler Eubanks, was just getting ready to start. He saw Thad and came to him eagerly. "Lieutenant! You're an answer to prayer. Help me with the service, will you? You do the singing and I'll do the preaching!" He nodded at Davis, saying, "This young man is the best gospel singer in the Confederate Army, Lieutenant Morgan. And one of the most faithful members of my church. How about it, Thad?"

"Do what I can, Reverend Eubanks," Thad replied.

After the preacher opened the service with a brief prayer, Thad's clear tenor voice filled the room with the old gospel songs. Most of the men, Davis saw, tried to join in, but it was a thin, pitiful effort. He himself made no attempt to sing, but sat holding the paperback hymnal up for Lonnie.

Tate's face was overcast by a gray pallor, and he could only whisper the words, "There is a balm in Gilead." And when they sang "Amazing grace, how sweet the sound, that saved a wretch like me," tears filled his eyes and trickled down his cheeks.

As Thad sang, Belle came in and stood with her back to the wall. She didn't sing, but watched the men with an unfathomable expression in her violet eyes. Once her gaze met that of Davis, and as they looked across the room for that one moment, he felt intuitively that she was the loneliest person present. Not that anything showed in her face, for the texture of her skin and the stillness of her countenance made her seem like a porcelain statue. Finally Thad moved to one side and Reverend Eubanks opened his Bible and began to speak.

Belle looked at the minister so strangely that Davis did not listen to the words at first. As always, it was a tremendous struggle for him when she was around, for inevitably he thought of Lowell. Each time that happened, a refrain would go on inside his head, a voice that said over and over again: *She's the one who killed him—she's the one who killed him.*

Ignoring the sermon, Davis stared at Belle, the same refrain "she's the one" hammering at his skull. Time had done nothing to kill the pain when he thought of his brother, nor had it made his hatred of Belle grow less. There had been moments when he was moved by her selfless attention to the broken and dying men in the ward. He had seen her fight for a boy's life for hours, as if her own soul depended on it. Hour after hour, in his own ward, she had labored over an older man named Hooker who lingered for two days before dying. During that time she rarely left his side. When the man had died, Davis watched as Belle stood by his bedside, her face not fixed in a set expression as it usually was, but soft and vulnerable as if feeling all the pain in the world at her defeat.

Now he thought of those times, the weeks of ceaseless care given him, remembering that today he was not a cripple because she had waged a war with the doctor to save Davis's leg. He knew all that, yet the bitterness was strong; even as he stared at her, thoughts of her infidelity and cruelty washed away all tenderness, causing him to turn his head away and listen to the preacher.

". . . and so, our most important task on this earth," Reverend Eubanks was saying, "is not to make money or get an education, nor any of those things that are of some importance in this life. No, those pursuits must give way to that which is, according to the Word of God, *most* important—finding forgiveness for our sins." He opened his Bible and read: "A certain ruler asked him, saying, Good Master, what shall I do that I may have eternal life?" then looked up and said, "That is the question every man must ask of God: 'How can I be forgiven and know God as my Savior?' "

Davis let most of the words flow by. His eyes were on Lonnie, who was drinking in the preacher's words as if they were life to him. *Wonder what's going on in the poor boy's mind,* Davis mused. He himself had not paid much attention to such things, having been content with a nominal assent to the basic truth of religion. From time to time he had felt a vague alarm, when thoughts would arise about death and judgment, but not since he was a very young boy had he really felt anything like the fear of God.

His head jerked up at the preacher's next words. "Some of you may spend eternity in hell, cut off from God, because of *one* idol. I don't mean that you would bow down to a statue made of clay; none of you here would be so foolish. But consider, for example, the words of Jesus in Mark, chapter eleven. It says: 'And when you stand praying, forgive, if you have ought against any: that your Father also which is in heaven may forgive your trespasses.' "

Eubanks lifted his head and swept the faces of the men who were turned to him. "That's what you want, for the Father to forgive you, isn't it? But listen to verse twenty-six—which, in my own mind, contains the hardest word in the Bible: 'But if ye do not forgive, neither will your Father which is in heaven forgive your trespasses.' "

He closed his Bible and stood there—tall, solemn, compassionate. "Those are terrible words—*If ye do not forgive, neither will your Father forgive.* Think of that! There are millions in hell this morning, I fear, who could have known the mercy of God—but they would not forgive. There are, God help us, millions in both the North and the South who have grown bitter in their hearts and are now rotting with hate against a human adversary. They fall under these words: 'neither will your Father which is in heaven forgive. . . .' "

Davis gave an involuntary glance at Belle, and a strange emotion shot through him as he thought of his adamant hatred for her. He tried to wash the minister's words from his mind, but could not.

"You say that your son has been killed by the Yankees, or your brother or father? 'Must I forgive even *that*?' The scripture rings out, 'If you have ought against any . . .' You will not be forgiven by God if you do not forgive! 'But that's more than a human being can do!' you say. No, it is not, for Jesus Christ proved that it can be done. Do you remember His cry as they crucified Him? I know that you do! 'Father, *forgive them!*' And do not say that He could do it because He was God, for that is what the Incarnation meant—God became *man*, and it was as a *man* that Jesus forgave His enemies!"

Davis's hands began to tremble, and he clasped them together like a vise so no one would notice. The words of the Bible rang in his mind: *If you have ought against any.* Never had he been so shaken—not in battle or in any crisis. Fear flushed through him, and he gritted his teeth and looked down at the floor, trying to thrust the fear from his mind.

Thad was watching Davis, and knew instantly that God was moving on the man. He bowed his head and began to pray, asking God to bring a sense of need so great that Winslow would cry for salvation.

Belle, too, was watching, and a strange sensation went through her as she saw the tormented face of the man she knew as Owen Morgan. It was the first time she had seen him show any emotion, other than that strange oblique light which sometimes came into his eyes when he looked at her. Now she pondered the brokenness she could not understand.

Finally, the minister ended his sermon with a plea for every person to turn his heart to God. "No matter what is keeping you from God, it's not worth what you're paying for it. Jesus Christ is your only hope for time and eternity. I beg you to forgive those who have offended you, and let God forgive you the way He longs to!"

Davis sat as though transfixed, lost in his silent struggle, and responded only when Lonnie reached out to touch him.

"Lieutenant? Are you all right?"

"Why—yes, Lonnie," Davis replied quickly. He saw Thad coming toward them, and pulled his shoulders together in an attempt to cover the weakness that had assaulted him. "This is Lonnie Tate, Lieutenant Novak."

Thad took the chair offered him and began to talk with Lonnie, and Davis got up, found his cane and moved out of the ward. The hall was crowded with visitors, and he edged his way through until he reached the porch, where he was taken aback to find Belle, standing with her back to one of the pillars, staring out across the lawn.

She heard the tap of his stick and turned to face him. "Hello, Owen," she said quietly, then turned back.

Davis stood there, in a quandary. He wanted to leave, but that seemed graceless. Yet she showed no desire to talk to him, so he hobbled off the porch and moved along the walk again. Nearing the corner, he looked over his shoulder and saw her in the same position, motionless as a statue. He circled the hospital, and when he came back, she was gone. He sighed with relief. He didn't want to talk with her or anyone else, so he avoided everybody by finding a bench under one of the trees where he could sit locked in his own thoughts.

★ ★ ★ ★

That night he awoke with a start, confused as to where he was or what had aroused him from a sound sleep. Then his eyes adjusted to the dim lamplight at the end of the ward, and he turned his head, peering to his right. "Lonnie—are you all right?"

Hearing only a faint sound, Davis carefully swung his feet out of bed and leaned over to see better. Lonnie was staring up at the ceiling, his body racked by great tremors. Davis made a lunge at his cane, and hobbled out of the ward and down the hall. Usually one of the orderlies was nearby. No one in sight! He moved quickly along, calling, "Orderly!"

A door burst open, and Belle cried, "What's the matter? Are you sick?"

"It's Lonnie! He's very bad."

She ran lightly down the hall, and by the time he got to where she bent over Lonnie, Davis's leg was throbbing with pain. He ignored it and went to his bed, standing there as Belle bent over the boy. She had moved a lamp on the shelf over his head; and by the flickering light, Davis saw that Lonnie's eyes were set, fixed on the ceiling. "Is he dead?" he whispered.

"No—but he's going, I'm afraid."

She held her hand on Lonnie's forehead, staring into his face.

Davis's legs suddenly gave way, and he dropped on the bed, fear knotting his stomach. "Isn't there *something* to do?" he asked.

Her eyes were filled with an enormous sadness as she looked at the dying lad. "No. There's nothing anyone can do."

The words hit Davis like a blow. He clamped his lips shut, wishing there were some way he could run away from it. But there was no escape, and as the two waited, they could hear the raspy breathing growing fainter.

From time to time tremors would shake Lonnie, but they became less and less frequent, and each less potent. Davis feared that each one would be the last, and shut his eyes every time the fragile body arched upward in a spasm.

A long time passed, and then Lonnie opened his eyes. "Hello—Miss Belle," he whispered.

"Lonnie. . . !" she said, choking with emotion. She bit her lips to stop the tremble, all the while stroking his forehead.

He turned his head, and his eyes were calm as he said, "Lieutenant, is that you?"

"Yes, it's me, Lonnie."

The boy's lips curved in a smile, and he closed his eyes as he moved his head back. He seemed to be resting. In a moment he opened them and studied Belle's face. He reached out a thin hand and carefully touched her cheek, then whispered, "It's time, ain't it, Miss Belle?"

She blinked. "Time for what, Lonnie?"

"Why—time for me to go," he replied, and seemed surprised that she would ask.

"Oh, Lonnie! Lonnie!" she cried, and he felt the hot tears falling on his face.

He touched his cheeks, and shook his head. "Why, Miss Belle—it ain't no call for you to cry—not for *me*!" His voice got stronger, and he nodded at her. "I been wishin' to go for a long time now. I hurt so bad. . . !" Then he raised his hand to her cheek again. "But you been so good to me, Miss Belle—so very good!"

She caught his hand and pressed her lips against it, but could not utter a word. Davis watched as the tears flowed from her tightly closed eyes over the boy's hand, and felt his own hot tears rise to his eyes.

"You know what, Miss Belle?" Lonnie said in a voice filled with wonder. "It don't hurt no more!" He turned his head to smile at Davis. "Ain't that wonderful, sir?"

Davis managed to nod, but could not speak. He reached out his hand and Lonnie placed his in it. "You're such a good man, Lieutenant!" Lonnie whispered, resting his hand in Davis's. It felt like a bird's claw to Winslow. "All this time you've been so good to me! I reckon—the good Lord—will have to reward you—now that I'm—leaving."

He arched, gave a great cough and cried out. Both Davis and Belle thought he was gone, but the tremor passed and he said, "You two—you been my best friends—outside of family. I sure do—thank you . . ." He paused, his head pushing back into the pillow. His eyes opened wide and he whispered faintly, "Tell my ma—I'll see her—in heaven!" Then his eyes began to close, and a smile crested his lips, as if he had thought of something very wonderful.

". . . and I'll—see you, Miss Belle—and Lieutenant . . ."—he whispered so faintly they could barely make it out— ". . . I'll see—you too . . ."

The smile remained on his lips, and he gave one great sigh—and lay still.

Belle put the lifeless hand on the boy's chest, and Davis got his cane and pulled himself to his feet. They stood there looking down at Lonnie's ravaged features, and suddenly Belle gave a great choking sob and turned blindly toward Davis. Without thought, he put out his free arm and she fell against him. As he held her, he felt the quick loosening of her body and the onset of her crying. She would have fallen, he knew, if he had not supported her, for her strength had drained from her. It was as though the iron control he had noted in her had slipped away with the spirit of the dying boy.

He continued holding her, letting her weep. Finally she straightened up and her expression changed from softness to a self-willed pride.

"I'll have someone come for him," she said, and left the room without a backward look.

Davis returned to his bed and lay looking at the face of the dead boy. He had grown very fond of Lonnie and felt the vacuum left by someone whose life had made a difference—in Davis's life and others.

"Goodbye, Lonnie," he whispered softly into the darkness.

CHAPTER NINETEEN

# LOVE NEVER CHANGES

★ ★ ★ ★

Lonnie Tate's death saddened the entire ward, for the gentle young man had become a favorite.

But it was Belle Wickham whom Lonnie's passing had influenced most. She had seen death in all forms since coming to Chimborazo, and had considered herself capable of meeting any situation. However, the constant pressure of the hospital had been building up in her unconsciously. She carried a facade that successfully disguised any damage the hurt, the pain, and the deaths did to her spirit. But by nature she was a gentle, loving person, who eventually broke under the barrage of grim blows accosting her.

Immediately after Lonnie died, Belle went to her office and attempted, as she often did, to shake off the grief that always engulfed her. Never had she allowed anyone to see her as she wept over the patients, but many nights were spent struggling to keep from giving way. More than once she had come within a hairsbreadth of quitting her job, but the next morning, apparently calm and steady, she showed no sign of the struggle.

When a tree falls in the forest, it immediately begins to decay—from the inside. Time passes with no apparent effect, but the destructive elements are at work. The winds and the rains batter the outside; the tiny borers attack the core. After some time a hunter sees it, and to his eye it is solid and healthy, but when he steps on the tree, it gives way, revealing the destructive damage to the life within. It took many months to break down the strength of that tree; it was not the pressure of the man's boot—that only exposed the damage done by time and the enemy.

In somewhat the same way, Lonnie's death had been the final pressure that broke Belle. It was not his death alone, but all those that preceded his that caused the total breakdown of her defenses; and though she struggled all night to steady herself, by dawn she was still sitting in her chair, trembling with weakness and unable to face another day.

Elmer Gibbs arrived early to get supplies, and when he entered Belle's office, she was sitting motionless, her eyes underlined by dark circles, her face haggard and pale. He hesitated, then said, "Miss Belle, we're out of lint. You want me to go downtown and see if I can get some?" He waited for her answer, but she stared at him vacantly. "Ma'am?" he asked, "is something wrong?"

Still she sat there, saying nothing. Finally she got up and walked to the window. Gibbs was disturbed, for it was not like her. He waited for a few moments, and when he received no answer, he turned and walked down the hall to the kitchen where he found Dr. Stevens drinking a cup of coffee.

"Doctor," he said anxiously, "Miss Belle—something's wrong with her."

"Is she sick, Gibbs?" Stevens asked, lowering his cup.

"I don't know. She won't talk—and she looks bad."

"I'll go see her." He put his cup down and walked rapidly to Belle's office, where he found her still staring out the window. When she didn't respond to his presence, he said, "Belle. . . ?"

After a long moment's pause she turned. Her face was set in an abnormal grimace, her eyes wide, the whites prominent circles surrounding the irises. *Emotionally paralyzed.*

"What's wrong, Belle?" Dr. Stevens asked.

"Lonnie died last night," she said slowly, dragging the words out.

"Yes. I heard about it when I arrived. Too bad! Such a good-hearted young man."

She didn't speak, but her mouth twisted uncontrollably, and she covered it with her hand and wheeled.

He caught her arm as she attempted to run out of the room, held her, and said firmly, "I'm sending you home for a few days' rest, Belle."

"No! I can't do that."

Dr. Stevens shook his head. His eyes were concerned, but there was a rough firmness in his deep voice as he said, "You don't have any choice, I'm afraid. You've been working too many hours—which I've warned you about." She began to shake her head, and he raised his voice, saying, "You've done good work here, and I don't want to lose you. And that's what'll happen if you try to go on like you've done the past few months. You're a casualty, Belle. You need rest or you'll fall apart."

"What will happen to the men if I go?" she asked in a tight voice.

"What will happen to them if you crack up for good?" Stevens demanded. "We'll get along for a week or two. Go home and don't even *think* about this place for a while. Then when you've had a good rest, you can return and resume your duties."

He had to argue for a time, but slowly she gave in, and he drove away with her in his buggy. He was a friend of the Winslows as well as their family doctor since he came to Richmond.

"My house is over that way, Doctor," she protested as he turned toward the west side of town.

"You're not going there," he said firmly. "I don't want you all alone. You'll do nothing but brood. I'm taking you to your parents. They've been complaining for a long time how they never get to see you. Well, now they're going to—and don't argue with me!"

The fact that she accepted his decision without flaring up was evidence to Stevens that she was not herself. He had fought many a battle with Belle over matters at the hospital, and was well aware of the vein of steel that ran through her. She would never have given in so easily to his decisions if she had not been weakened in some way he didn't understand.

Rebekah met them at the door, and saw the serious look on Dr. Steven's face as he said, "Rebekah, this young woman is going to stay away from the hospital for two weeks. She's been doing the work of two people, and it's time she had a rest. You think you can hold her down and teach her how to be quiet for a time?"

"Oh, this is ridiculous, Doctor!" Belle objected. "There's nothing wrong with me!" But she could not control the trembling of her hands.

Rebekah ignored Belle's words and said, "I'm so glad you've come. We've wanted you to visit us, you know. Pet's gone to Belle Maison for a while—and this place is so lonely."

"Good. You take care she gets out some, Rebekah," Stevens nodded. "I'll talk with you later in the week."

"Oh, Dr. Stevens," Rebekah said as he turned to leave, "Thad was at church last night, and he mentioned that his friend Lieutenant Morgan will be leaving the hospital."

"That's right. He's made a good recovery and doesn't really need to be in the hospital anymore. Did Novak say where Owen would be going?"

"He knew our boys were gone, so he asked if we might put the lieutenant up for a time. Sky said it would be fine, so if you approve, we'll just let him stay here."

"He's a lucky young fellow," Stevens replied and grinned at Belle. "You see, Belle? You'll still have at least one patient to practice on!" He turned to leave, adding, "I'll have someone bring him out this afternoon."

Neither Rebekah nor Stevens saw the expression that swept Belle's face at the mention of Lieutenant Morgan, and by the time Rebekah took her arm, saying, "Now, let's go over to your house and get your things," she had recovered.

Part of Belle's agony over Lonnie's death was her mortification at her collapse, weeping helplessly in the arms of the tall lieutenant. Something about him had always made her uncomfortable. He had a way of looking at her out of his steady brown eyes that was disturbing, though she could never figure out why. She had prided herself on her control, and to have shown weakness before anyone was repugnant to her—but to dissolve completely before *him* in a fit of helpless dependency had shamed her deeply.

The two women stopped by Belle's little house, picked up the things necessary for the visit, then spent an hour shopping for a few items. As they moved in and out of the stores along the streets of Richmond, many people stared at Belle, whispering, "There she is—that's her, the Dixie Widow." Belle ignored them, but was relieved to get back to the house, where she helped her mother with a few simple household chores.

"It's nice out today, Belle," Rebekah said later. "Why don't you take a walk around the neighborhood?"

"I think I will, Mother."

"I won't be here when you get back," Rebekah added. "I have a meeting at two. Perhaps you'd like to read that new novel by Dickens—*David Copperfield*."

Belle agreed, and left. Although dark clouds were beginning to roll over the mild April skies, she strolled for two hours along the side streets of Richmond. When distant thunder announced the coming of rain, she made her way back to her parents' house. By the time she was within a few blocks of home, the heavens seemed to tilt, sending a solid stream on the town. The streets soon filled, washing away in a gurgling stream the trash and the winter's leaves.

Belle stopped, closed her eyes and lifted her face, letting the rain wash over her face. Her clothes were instantly soaked, but she did not notice. The drops coursed down her cheeks like a river, mingling with the torrent of tears dammed up over the long winter. Like a frozen mountain stream melting under the spring sun, so her rigid coldness turned to warmth.

Finally, she took a deep breath, wiped her eyes, and walked rapidly to the house. She grabbed several large towels on her way to her room, where she stripped and dried herself until her skin tingled. She was putting up her hair when she heard a knock at the door downstairs. Hurriedly twisting her dark mane into a thick roll, she pinned it up as she ran down the stairs, calling, "Just a minute!"

Opening the door, she blinked in surprise. "Why, Lieutenant, come in." She looked past him to where Elmer Gibbs sat in the buggy. "Thank you, Elmer!" she called and stepped back. "You're almost as wet as I was, Lieutenant Morgan."

Davis stood uncertainly, as if trying to decide whether to walk away or stay. With a gesture of surrender, he limped across the threshold. After he'd shrugged out of his coat, Belle took it, saying, "Come on into the kitchen. Mother's got a fire in the stove."

She pushed a chair out for him, and brought a piece of apple pie and a steaming cup of coffee. Nervously he reached for the beverage, and she saw he was very uncomfortable.

"This place will be a lot better than Chimborazo, Owen," she said, taking a sip of her coffee. "Besides, Mother's cooking is fantastic."

He moved slightly in his chair, his thin face reflecting the rebellion he had felt since Dr. Stevens told him it would be better to leave the hospital. "This—wasn't my idea," he blurted out. "I feel like a tramp."

Belle shook her head. "You won't when you get to know my parents. Any man who's shed his blood for the Cause is a welcome guest in their home."

The words stung like sharp barbs. Now more than ever he wanted to leave. But he knew he had no choice. "I'll try to stay out of the way as much as possible," he promised in a tight voice.

Her mind flashed back to the previous night. "I—I was very upset last night, Owen."

He dropped his eyes. "We both were."

Conscious that he was referring to her outburst that night, she decided to speak frankly about the incident. "I don't often give way—as I did. I'm sorry you had to be the brunt of my hysteria."

He looked up in surprise, shaking his head. "I don't think of it that way." His lips moved in a half-embarrassed smile, and he admitted, "You weren't the only one who cried for Lonnie."

Belle couldn't believe what she was hearing. The men of her family were not given to public displays of emotion. That was considered unmanly, and Davis's simple admission intrigued her. Her firmest concept of Owen Morgan was that he was not emotional, for he had always kept his distance from everyone. Not once in the weeks she had known him had he ever dropped the habitual austere manner, and now to hear him admit weeping over someone seemed out of character.

"He was very brave," Davis murmured. "The day before he died, he told me how much he longed to go back to Arkansas and make a crop."

He continued to speak of Lonnie, telling her how the boy had asked him to write the family. Belle listened quietly, sharing some of the things that had endeared Lonnie to her heart. Time flew, and before she knew it her parents were back.

"Why, Lieutenant," Rebekah said as she entered, "how nice that you arrived so soon!" She turned to Belle, "Would you take Dan's room upstairs so that Lieutenant Morgan won't have to climb steps?"

"I'll show you the guest room, Lieutenant," she said, leading the way.

Returning to the kitchen, Rebekah commented, "Belle, I'm glad Thad thought of this. It'll be nice to have someone to cook for."

The evening meal went well. Sky and Rebekah were so happy to have Belle home that they talked more than usual, unaware that Belle and their guest said very little. After supper Sky escorted Davis to the parlor while the women tidied up the kitchen.

Davis maneuvered Winslow into telling some of the tales of his youth on the western frontier, and when the women joined them, Belle asked her parents to relate the story of their courtship. Davis sat entranced as he heard how Sky had guided a wagon train load of "Mail Order Brides" from the East to Oregon. Rebekah had been one of them, and at the end of the journey, they had fallen in love and married.

"It sounds like a very bad novel," she smiled at her parents. "I'm convinced you made it all up—and you were probably only a dull shoe salesman from St. Louis."

Sky laughed and reached for Rebekah's hand. "I can't help it if it sounds crazy," he said, giving Rebekah a gentle smile. "I've enjoyed every second of it!"

Rebekah stood to her feet, laughing. "I could remind you of a couple of times—!"

"I refuse to remember!" he said, leaping up. He grinned at Davis, saying, "Make her wait on you, Owen. She's like a mother hen with all her chicks gone."

The Winslows retired to their rooms, and Davis commented thoughtfully, "You are blessed, Belle."

"They are wonderful, aren't they?" Then feeling uncomfortable alone with him, she rose and said, "I'll see you in the morning, Lieutenant."

He slept poorly that night, guilt slicing at him. He tried to assuage it by thinking he was not there to spy out any secrets, but that did not seem to ease his mind. Finally he fell asleep, vowing to leave as soon as possible.

But his leg was worse the next day, and Belle diagnosed it as overuse. "You're pushing too hard to get well—and in the long run it will take longer," she had told him firmly.

He forced himself to spend long hours in bed reading, and when he tired of reclining, Belle prepared a place in the parlor where he could sit comfortably with his leg raised. The change was gratifying and he continued reading until he had devoured every book in the Winslow library. Noticing Davis's eager pursuit, Rebekah said, "I think Mary Chesnut has all the books ever published. I'll bring you some. What are you interested in?"

"Oh, anything."

Without delay, she returned with a large stack of books, including novels, poetry, travel books, sermons, and biographies. He immediately submerged himself in the reading material, and the long rainy days passed unnoticed as he lost himself in book after book. To Rebekah's surprise, he finished the stack in less than a week, and she made another trip, bringing back twice as many.

Belle found herself tense for a few days, worrying about the nursing needs at the hospital, but slowly she began to relax. She went for long walks, refused invitations to parties, and finally began to read—not one of her most enjoyable pastimes. She had never been an avid reader, so had no particular interest. Davis had recommended a novel, *Pride and Prejudice,* which, to her surprise, she liked. He gave her another, *Jane Eyre,* and after she finished it, she told him, "I don't like this one."

He smiled at her. "That's because you identify yourself with the heroine."

She stared at him puzzled. "Jane Eyre! I'm like *her*?"

"Not plain like Jane—nor poor." Davis studied her for a moment. "You're like her in character. Both of you are very determined women. When Jane made up her mind, she wouldn't allow anything on God's earth to change her."

"She was very religious—and I'm not."

"All of us are firm in what we believe in," Davis said. "For

Jane Eyre it was religion. For you it's the Confederacy."

They discussed the book for about an hour, and finally Belle remarked, "I never knew books were about people—I mean *real* people."

"The good ones are," he said.

That had been the beginning, and Sky and Rebekah were pleased to find the pair involved in long conversations about books. "It's good for Belle," Sky voiced. "She's much more relaxed, isn't she, Rebekah?"

The second week passed, and on Friday Sky arrived home with a guest for supper. "Here's Beau!" he announced as he entered the kitchen where Belle and Rebekah were preparing supper. Rebekah greeted him warmly, giving him a hug, but Belle's hands were covered with flour, and she said quietly, "I'm glad to see you, Beau."

"I've got only a week," he said, staring at her, thinking that she looked more beautiful in an apron with her hair tied up loosely than most women fully gowned for a ball.

Sky drew him away into the parlor to discuss military matters and to introduce him to the Winslows' house guest, who was sitting with his leg up, reading by a large lamp. "Lieutenant Owen Morgan—Captain Beau Beauchamp."

"Keep your seat, Lieutenant," Beau said, bending down to shake hands. "Glad to see you've recovered so well. Major Benning told me he was sure you'd die on the way."

"Major Benning?" Davis repeated, then recovered quickly. "Why, I guess I did look like a poor bet when I left the company. But as you can see, I'm doing all right."

Davis listened carefully, but said little. He had memorized Thad's brief and incomplete background information about Morgan. *It's a good thing Morgan was in the Army of the Tennessee,* he thought. *I'd be in real trouble if he'd been in Beauchamp's brigade!*

He tried to excuse himself, but Sky wouldn't hear of it. "You'll want to hear what's happening with the army, Owen."

Beauchamp shrugged, and his face was not happy as he gave his opinion. "Grant's the man now for the Union. He's the best Lee's ever had to face, and it looks as if he's building up to hit us with everything he's got."

"I think that's right, Beau," Sky nodded. "Most of the staff officers think he'll send the one army to get Joe Johnston in Tennessee, and that'll he'll bring the Army of the Potomac here to fight Lee."

"He'll never whip General Lee!" Beau responded with pride in his eyes. "Grant's done all right in the West, but he's never come up against Robert E. Lee. He'll go down like Pope and Burnside."

Sky looked at the young man doubtfully, but said nothing. He knew how thin the lines of Lee's army were stretched, and how desperately short supplies were—on the front and at home. Still he said nothing, but sat there letting Beau speak.

Rebekah and Belle came to join them, and Beau, of course, had to give a complete report on Mark, Tom, and Dan. Rebekah listened to every word, her hands twisting in her lap; but the fear she fought to control showed in the lines in her face.

Changing the subject, Beau asked Belle, "What have you been doing with yourself since you took a vacation from the hospital?"

"Oh, nothing much," she shrugged.

"She's become quite a reader, Beau," Rebekah smiled. "When she was in school I had to threaten her with a switch to get her to read anything. Now she's got her nose in a book every spare minute."

"Oh, Mother," Belle protested, "it's not that bad!" She gave Davis a nod. "There's the *real* bookworm."

Beau turned his gaze on Davis, studying him as if he were a strange specimen. "I didn't know you fellows from the Army of the Tennessee were such scholars, Morgan. Were you a schoolteacher or something before you joined up?"

Davis shifted uncomfortably, not knowing for certain what to say. But they were all waiting for him to speak, and he answered, "Oh no. Just picked up the habit along the way. Kills the time, you know."

Belle said, "I never really thought that books meant much. To me they were just stories to entertain people—but Owen's got me to noticing how they can help you to look at life."

Beau raised his eyes at her use of Morgan's given name, but merely asked, "How's that, Belle?"

"Oh, I don't know—yes, I do, too." She began to tell how Morgan had suggested she read some of James Fenimore Cooper's novels about the frontier. "At first it was just exciting Indian stories, but after a while I began to see that it was more than *that*." Her eyes grew bright as she spoke of how, for the first time, she understood Cooper's books were about America—how it grew, and the tragedy of the Indians who lost their way of life in the process. She mentioned the way she had wept when the noble Mohegan recited the elegy of his race.

"Why, the Indians had to go, Belle!" Beau broke in sharply. "We could never have grown to be a great nation if we'd let a few thousand savages keep all the land."

Belle stared at him, then said, "That's what *I* always thought, Beau, but as I read the book I was able to see the Indians' side of it. And I guess that's what I'm learning through books."

Beau admitted grudgingly, "Well, I guess maybe novels can do that, but I think poetry's a farce. I've tried to read some of the stuff, and can't make head nor tail out of it! Why can't they just *say* what they mean instead of beating around the bush?"

Belle laughed. "That's exactly what I told Owen!" She turned with a smile to Davis and said, "Tell Beau what you told me about poetry."

"I don't think the captain needs a lecture from me, Miss Belle," Davis protested.

"Well, then, if you won't, I will," she said saucily, and proceeded to enlighten Beau on interpreting poetry. "Poets don't say what they mean, because some things can't be put into words," she told him. "For example, when Father wants to tell Mother how much he loves her, how can he do it?"

"He can say 'I love you,' " Beau grinned. "You wouldn't expect him to spout poetry, would you, Rebekah?"

"Yes, I would!" Rebekah responded unexpectedly.

"Well, I'll have to start saying 'thee' and 'thou' and learning how to make rhymes," Sky joked. "Or better still, I'll hire a poet to write me a poem for you."

"That's not what you did on your last anniversary," Belle countered. "At that party you said it right out loud for everyone to hear. Remember? You lifted your glass and said, 'Rebekah, most people drink the best wine first—but you and I, we've saved the best till last!' "

"Why, that's not poetry!" Sky protested, his face beat red.

"Yes—it is," Rebekah insisted quietly. She took his hand and added, "I've thought of it almost every day since you said it. It told me more about how you felt toward me than anything you've ever said."

Sky looked at her, then nodded, "Well, bless me! It's true!"

"See, Beau?" Belle said triumphantly. "What Father said would *seem* to be about drinking wine—but it's not. It's about love."

Beau plunged in, and for half an hour he and Belle argued about poetry. Rebekah caught Sky's glance, and knew they were both thinking that Belle was more alive than she'd been since her time in Washington.

Finally Beau said, "Well, I guess I'm just a thick-headed soldier. I guess the best a woman will ever get out of me is a plain 'I love you.' " He glanced sharply at Davis, a half-angry challenge in his eyes. "I suppose *you'd* dash off a poem about it, eh, Morgan?"

"No, I'm no poet," Davis answered with a shake of his head. "The best I could do would be to copy one from a real poet."

"Secondhand love?" Beau jibed. "Sounds like pretty weak stuff to me."

Belle asked, "Which poem, Owen? What's your favorite poem about love?"

"Oh, I don't know. Shakespeare's Sonnet Number 116, I suppose."

"Do we have a copy?" Belle asked.

"I haven't seen one," Davis replied.

"Do you know any of it?" she insisted. "You do! I bet you can say the whole thing!"

"Let's hear it, Owen," Rebekah urged.

"I never memorized it, but I've read the poem so often, I think I remember most of it. Let's see, it goes something like this:

Let me not to the marriage of true minds
Admit impediments. Love is not love
Which alters when it alteration finds,
Or bends with the remover to remove.
Oh, no! It is an ever-fixed mark
That looks on tempests and is never shaken;

It is the star to every wandering bark,
Whose worth's unknown, although his height be taken.
Love's not time's fool, though rosy lips and cheeks
Within his bending sickle's compass come;
Love alters not with his brief hours and weeks,
But bears it out even to the edge of doom.
If this be error and upon me proved,
Then I never writ, nor no man ever loved.

Davis's voice fell away, and he looked around the room with embarrassment.

"I don't understand much of it," Belle said quietly. "But I like the part where it says *love is not love which changes when it finds alterations.* She looked at Davis, her lips parted, and then asked, "Is that what it means, Owen, the part about rosy lips and cheeks being cut down?"

"I think so." Davis shrugged and added, "I guess that's why I like it. I've seen so few people who loved without reservation. Men who say they love, but when the woman grows older, he leaves her for somebody younger." He knew he was talking too much, but added impulsively, "That sort of thing's not love at all!"

Sky stared at him in wonder. Finally he said, "Owen, that's what I've always *wanted* to say, but never could find the words for it!"

Davis got to his feet, picked up his cane, and said, "Mr. Winslow, you've just given the best definition of poetry I ever heard! Well, I've bored you enough. Good night, sir. Good night, Mrs. Winslow." He turned to Beau and shrugged his shoulders. "Don't tell anyone about this stuff, please, Captain Beauchamp. It's a weakness I have, but it could be worse. I could hold up trains or do something I could be jailed for."

Beau laughed mirthlessly. "I won't let it get out, Morgan."

"Good night, Owen," Belle said, and after he had left, her parents talked for a brief time, then bid the pair good night and retired.

Beau and Belle talked for a time about her brothers, about Pet and Thad. Finally they went to the kitchen for a glass of lemonade. "Let's go out where it's cooler," he suggested, leading the way to the porch.

"This is nice, Belle," Beau commented. "Gets pretty noisy at camp. Tonight you can almost cut the silence with a knife."

"It is quiet."

They spoke softly, watching the clouds race across the sky. A full moon had come out to smile down on the rain-soaked earth, and the smell of honeysuckle and moist earth filled the air.

"Belle, I've worried about you."

"Worried about me, Beau?" she asked in surprise. "Why, I'm all right, Beau."

"You are *now,* but the last time I was home you were pale as a ghost and half sick." He moved closer, his eyes resting on her lovely face. "You were all tensed up, too, as if you were scared or something."

"It's a difficult job. All that death—and men hurting all the time."

"I know. I wish you wouldn't go back to it."

"Not go back?" Belle stared at him, incredulous. "Why, I've *got* to go back, Beau. It's my job, just like being a soldier is your job. Anyway, what would I do with myself if I didn't go back?"

He took a deep breath and wrapped his arms around her. "You could marry me, Belle."

Totally off guard, she lifted her face to him and he bent his head and kissed her. She felt like a fragile flower in his powerful embrace, and was so moved by his kiss that she surrendered and leaned against him, letting him have his way. He felt her response, and pulled her closer, his lips demanding.

Suddenly she jerked away, whispering, "Beau! Let me go!"

As though not hearing her, he said, "Belle, I love you! Marry me!"

She shook her head, and pushed him back with a violent surge. She walked to the end of the porch and stood with her hands pressed to her lips, her back rigid.

Beau came to her, put his hands gently on her shoulders. "Belle, I've loved you all this time. Is it Vance? Is that why you draw back?"

She shook her head, and when she turned, the lively expression that had been on her face all evening was gone. Her mouth was drawn into a thin line, her eyes dull. He was alarmed and mystified by the transformation. "What in the world is wrong with you, Belle? Tell me!"

"It's—nothing you can do anything about, Beau," she whispered. The weariness in her voice that he remembered from the last time he'd been home was back.

His voice was ragged as he demanded, "Is it another man?"

"No. It isn't that." She moved around him, but he caught her.

"Why won't you marry me, Belle? Maybe you don't love me enough—but that'll come. I'll *make* you love me!"

She gazed at him, her eyes vacant, and said in the loneliest and most forsaken voice he'd ever heard, "I'm not fit to marry you, Beau—not fit to marry any man!"

# CHAPTER TWENTY

# Two Meetings

★ ★ ★ ★

"I've got to make a break for it, Thad," Davis stated. "Sooner or later somebody from that Morgan's outfit is going to come looking for me."

The two men were standing outside the Winslow house speaking quietly. Thad had come for the evening meal, and while the women were washing the dishes, Davis had pulled him outside.

"That leg's not healed yet, Davis," Thad protested.

"It's good enough. I can even get by without a cane now." Davis flexed his leg carefully, and looked at Thad. "People are beginning to wonder, to talk about why I'm staying around here. No, I've got to leave."

Thad nodded slowly, for he had been thinking along the same lines. "All right. We'll look for a break. But they're watching the lines real careful now. Checking everybody's papers closer than ever—especially on the trains."

Davis moved restlessly, shifting his shoulders. "I'd have gone before, but if I got caught, you'd be in trouble. They'd want to know why you brought a Union officer to Richmond dressed in a Confederate uniform."

Thad raised his wide mouth in a grin. "Lightning don't strike twice, I always heard. I've been tried for treason once, so I don't reckon it'll happen again." He sobered and said, "I'll think on it. We'll come up with something."

Pet and Belle burst through the door, laughing. Pet ran over to the two men and took Thad's arm, saying, "We're going to Mary Lou Taylor's house. She and Howard are announcing their engagement this week. And she asked especially that you two come along."

"Oh, Pet—"

Pet ignored Belle's reluctance. "It'll be good for you—and you, too, Owen. Do you good to get your noses out of books. Besides"—Pet's smile disappeared, and she shook her head sadly—"there won't be many there, Belle. So many men are at the front, or . . ."

Belle knew Pet had intended to say "killed," so she blurted out, "I suppose I could go for a quick visit. Are you able to walk that far, Owen? It's only four blocks."

Davis had no intention of going, but she took his arm, and he found himself walking with her behind Thad and Pet. They spoke little on the short walk, and the party itself was not a strain. But once when Davis and Belle sat watching the young people playing a game, Belle said, "They make me feel as if I'm a millon years old." She looked around, and added, "I'd like to go home now if you're ready."

They said their goodbyes and made their way down the street in silence. A faint light in the west still lingered, and the air was filled with the sound of crickets. When they got to the house and mounted the steps, Belle said impulsively, "It's so hot in the house. Let's sit in the swing for a while," indicating a place beside her. "Does your leg hurt?"

He hesitated, then sat down, replying, "Not much."

He had wanted to say something to her, but had never found the right moment. Now he sought for a way to broach the subject. Finally, he began. "Belle, I always disliked having people thank me for anything—and I've noticed you do, too."

She was surprised he knew her that well, and gave him a quizzical look. "It embarrasses me."

"Then one of us is going to have to give in, because I've got to say something about the way you've helped me." He avoided her eyes, adding, "For the sake of helping my own feelings, I guess I'll have to ask you to be generous and ignore your own."

"Why, it wasn't all that much, Owen," she protested.

He turned quickly and without thinking took her hand. She was surprised, for he had never touched her, but she listened silently.

"Yes, it was. It was a great deal—at least to me. If you hadn't fought for me, I'd be a cripple right now. You kept Dr. Stevens from amputating my leg." He held her hand, and she felt the strength of it as he unconsciously gripped it tighter. "I don't think I could have lived like that, Belle."

"I'm glad it didn't happen, Owen."

"I was a dead man when I came to you, Belle," he said slowly. "I don't know what will happen from now on—but you're the one who gave me life, and I—I thank you."

She sat motionless, his hand tightening around hers. "I'm glad you're alive."

He suddenly became aware that he was gripping her hand, and released it instantly. He had always been nervous around beautiful women, and the sight of her face in the dusky light made him mute. In the silence, a truth hit him with lightning force: *I don't hate this woman anymore!*

He had lived with a fierce bitterness so long that the revelation left him breathless. *When did I stop hating?* His mind raced, and another thought came to him, and he asked, "Do you remember the sermon the minister preached in the ward about not hating?"

"Why, yes, I do." She looked at him carefully, wondering what had brought that to his mind. "It was on the same day Lonnie died." He was struggling with something, and she asked quietly, "Did it mean something to you, Owen?"

"I think it did," he nodded. "I've been hearing over and over again one thing the preacher read from the Bible that day. Something about if we have 'ought against any,' God won't forgive us."

"That's very hard, isn't it? Most of us have some hard feelings we can't get rid of."

"I was carrying a deep-seated hate, Belle," he went on. "It was eating me alive—and I didn't even know it."

"And—it's gone now?"

He considered her question, and there was a shocked expression on his face as he turned to face her. Slowly he nodded, saying, "I don't know why, or even when it happened—but it's gone."

She assumed he had been filled with hatred for the Union, and said quietly, "I hated the North when my husband was killed." She looked down at her hands, then back up to him. "I was so filled with bitterness that I think I lost my mind for a time. Hatred can do that to you."

He stared at her curiously. "How did you get rid of it, Belle?"

The question troubled her, and she rose to her feet and walked to the railing. He, too, got up and moved to stand beside her. "Did I say something wrong?"

"No!" She bowed her head, and when she answered, her voice was so faint he was forced to lean forward to hear her words. "I let my hate make me do something so evil—!"

Her voice broke into a sob, and she moved blindly away from him and entered the house. Bewildered, he wondered what could have broken her. "She's hurting bad," he murmured. For a long time he remained on the porch, trying to figure out how the bitterness and hatred had been purged from his own heart—and what brought such a terrible remorse into the once proud Belle Wickham's life.

He didn't understand his own deliverance, but he knew it had something to do with God, for he had never forgotten how shaken he had been when the preacher read the scripture. *Something happened inside me that day,* he thought, and he shook his head, determined to find the answer.

★ ★ ★ ★

The company came back from the Tennessee front, and Pet immediately began a campaign to have a grand party at Belle Maison. "It can be my engagement party, Papa," she wheedled. Unable to resist, Sky had given in.

He defended his actions that night to Rebekah. "We owe it to Pet and Thad. After all, a man doesn't marry off a daughter every day in the week!"

Rebekah had needed little urging. "It may be the last chance we'll have for a long time, Sky." She smiled and said, "Let's do it up right. Pet's never given a bean for parties and dresses. We'll make it a party people will talk about for years!"

Belle Maison came alive in its pride once more, swarming with grinning slaves who cleaned and decorated and cooked from early until late. Belle, yielding to Pet's pleas, put off going back to Chimborazo, and the three joined to make preparations for the ball.

It was to be a two-day party, with some of the young people staying overnight, so the house was a whirlwind as bedding was aired and floors scrubbed. Hams were boiled in cider, and the last of the wine removed from the wine cellar. A blockade runner had made it through the line of Union warships to purchase silk for Pet's dress. When Sky heard the price Rebekah paid, his jaw had dropped.

When Davis arrived with Thad at Belle Maison, he wondered at the excited smiles on the black faces. After the two were settled in a room, Thad took Davis on a tour. At the slave quarters, he was interested in meeting Toby, the giant black man whose freedom he knew had been purchased by Thad.

"Mistuh Thad!" Toby exclaimed as the two men entered the compound. At once Thad was submerged in a sea of smiling black faces. Davis stood to one side studying the scene, and as the hands reached out to pat the tall Confederate, Winslow could see no sign of the misery so often portrayed in the novels and papers of the North. The blacks were healthy and seemed to be far happier than many of the mill workers he'd seen in his own homeland. Their voices were rich with laughter, the kind that erupts from deep within, and there was no mistaking the genuine affection the slaves had for Thad Novak. Davis thought perhaps that was because the young man had been kind to Toby. But he saw that same respect and affection shown toward the owners of Belle Maison.

Toby guided them around the farm, proudly pointing out the new improvements. They met Sut Franklin, the surly overseer, who shook Davis's hand with a limp clasp and left abruptly. Davis had seen the flash of resentment in the overseer's muddy eyes as he looked at Thad. Later, when Thad left briefly, Davis asked, "Toby, what's wrong with your overseer? He's not very friendly."

"He don't lak Mr. Thad, suh," Toby answered quietly. "He didn't lak it when Mistuh Thad got Mr. Winslow to plant corn 'stead of cotton. Reckon he's skeered fo' his job."

Davis studied the dark face."What about you? I understand you're a free man. Will you stay here after the war—or go to the North?"

Toby shook his head firmly. "If de South win, I stay here and work fo' Mistuh Winslow till I can buy my wife and boy free."

"And if the North wins?"

Toby looked up at him quickly, and Davis realized that no white man had ever suggested such a thing—that the South might lose. He knew that an uprising of the slaves was the recurrent nightmare of the people of the South, and it was common knowledge that thousands of slaves had already been lost through the Underground Railroad.

"You is Mistuh Thad's friend, he say," Toby replied, "and I tell you, suh, de South ain't nevuh gonna be de same, not lak it wuz befo' dis wah."

"How's that, Toby?"

They were walking along in the fields where a group of field hands were working together, singing as usual in rhythm. Toby paused. "Listen to dat singin'," he said, and Davis turned to hear what the slaves were singing.

Don' you see 'em comin', comin', comin'—
    Millyns from de oder sho'?
Glory! Glory! Hallelujah!
    Bress de Lawd fo' ebermo'!

Don' you see 'em goin', goin', goin'—
    Pas' ol' massa's mansion do'?
Glory! Glory! Hallelujah!
    Bress de Lawd fo' ebermo'!

"It's just a spiritual, isn't it, Toby? One of their religious songs?"

Toby stared at Davis—seeming to weigh him somehow, then nodded as if he had made up his mind. "Dat's whut it use to be, but most of de slaves sing another verse. It goes:

Jordan's stream is runnin', runnin', runnin'—

Milyuns sogers passin' o';
Linkum comin' wid his chariot.
Bress de Lawd fo' ebermo'!

Toby's deep bass voice ceased, and he added softly, "Freedom—it's a funny thing, now. If a man don' nevuh have it, why he don' miss it. But evah slave in de South done heard 'bout it now, suh." He paused and added with a far-off look in his eyes, "Reckon dey ain't nobody gonna evuh be satisfied without it no mo'."

Thad came back and Toby said no more, but later on when the two soldiers walked back to the big house, Davis told Thad about the conversation, and asked, "Thad, do you think the South has a chance?"

"To win the war? Why, I don't reckon so, Davis—though I've never said it to anybody else. We're pinched in from all directions now. Grant's army is getting bigger every day, and ours is getting smaller."

That was Davis's opinion, too. "Why don't you give up? It would save so many lives!"

Thad replied quietly, "If it was up to me, I'd lay my gun down and never pick it up—but I don't guess the South will quit, Davis. Too much pride in men like Jefferson Davis and Robert E. Lee."

Novak's words depressed Davis. He said nothing, but as they came back across the yard, which was already crowded with horses and buggies as the guests poured in, he pulled Thad to a stop. "I've been thinking about a way to get out of here," he said.

"What's your idea?"

"I'll tell everyone I've had orders to report to my brigade. I'll get on the train in this uniform, but someplace along the line, I'll get off the train."

"What then?" Thad asked. "If our people catch you trying to get across the lines in that uniform, they'll think you're deserting. And if the Yankees get sight of you, they might shoot you and ask questions later."

Davis shook his head stubbornly. "Any way I try, it's going to be a risk, Thad. Can you get me some civilian clothes—and enough money to buy a horse?"

"I reckon so, but what—?"

"I'll get off the train and change clothes. Then I'll walk until I can find someone who'll sell me a horse. After that, I'll make my way cross country until I get back to the North."

Thad bit his lip, thought about it, and said slowly, "It's your say-so, Davis. But it could get you in a bad fix." He studied Davis for a moment. "I've got the cash in our room. I'll give it to you tonight. You can pick up some clothes at a store in town—but the party won't be over until late tomorrow night."

"Be a good time for me to leave," Davis nodded. "Everybody will be busy here. I'll leave a note for you, telling them I got a quick call to rejoin my unit."

They slipped into a side door to avoid the crowd, and as Davis wrote a note, Thad pulled a pouch of gold coins out of his coat pocket. "The last of Owen Morgan's money," he said, handing it to Davis. "Guess this will cover it."

Davis felt awkward but took the money. He looked at the youthful face of the man who had risked so much for him. He struggled for words, then gave a rueful laugh. "I owe you too much, Thad. No way I can ever pay you back." He put out his hand and gripped Thad's, saying, "God bless you, Thad!"

Novak studied Winslow's face. "Something's different about you, Davis. You're not all filled with hate—like when I first met you."

Davis smiled. "That's right. I don't know how to explain it, but the hate's gone. That's something else I owe you, Thad. If I hadn't come here, I think I'd have carried it with me all my life. I may not see you again—but I'll get word to you somehow when I get back."

"Maybe you'll run into Hale and Ezra," Thad smiled. "Now, guess we'd better get down. I'm the victim of this party, you know!"

They went down the stairs and found the house spilling over with guests. Davis had to be introduced to the Winslow boys, and he shook their hands soberly as if they had not met before.

Afterward, he stayed in the background, which was not difficult, for the rooms were crowded. Long tables loaded with food and drinks flanked one side of the room, and the house servants dashed through the crowd, constantly carrying china dishes and cut crystal glasses. He saw the Chesnuts, and as usual Hood was there keeping his eye on the young woman he was courting.

A small group of musicians took their station at the far end of the room, and soon the room was filled with sprightly music. Couples spun around the room, the gray uniforms of the soldiers serving as a foil for the brilliant colors of the women's gowns.

Davis stood beside the fireplace, watching the smooth dancing of the couples over the polished floors. The women looked like proud dolls scissored from colored paper, with hoopskirts as wide as the front door. They pointed their toes and flirted with their bright eyes, spinning around the room like flying feathers. To Davis it seemed they all had the same voice—lazy Southern voices, thick as honey.

The men were the remnant of Southern gentry. He knew, though it did not cut his heart as it did others, that they were but a faint echo of what had been when Sumpter fell. Many like them—proud, handsome, daring—lay under the soil at Bull Run and Antietam, at Gettysburg, and half a hundred other spots of bloody ground.

He watched as Belle went to stand beside her mother at the punch bowl. As always, she was wearing black. Even from where he stood, Davis could see that no other woman in the room was half so beautiful. Time and again an officer would approach her, ask for a dance, and receive only a smile and a shake of her head. Davis saw Beau Beauchamp approach her and say something. She hesitated, but shook her head again. He remained beside her, his face flushed, but eager.

Finally Davis heard Sky's voice calling for quiet, and looked up to see him standing with Thad and Pet. The music stopped, and the murmur of voices trailed off. "Welcome to Belle Maison, all of you!" Sky said. He bowed his head at the enthusiastic applause that followed his words, then held up his hand for quiet. "My wife and I have the pleasure of announcing the engagement of our daughter Patience to Lieutenant Thaddeus Novak of the Richmond Blades!"

A deafening cheer erupted, and for some time the young couple was so overwhelmed with hearty congratulations that further speeches were impossible. Finally Sky got the floor long enough to say, "If every father were as proud of his daughter as

I am, it would be a better world. I can't think of a man in the world I would trust her to than the one who holds her hand. That's my speech. Now let's hear from you two!"

Thad swallowed and looked around the room. "I'm getting the most beautiful and sweetest girl in the world!"

Pet blushed at his words. She was wearing a pale blue gown of pure silk, with dark blue trimming at the bodice and around the skirt. A pair of sparking red rubies adorned her ear lobes, and a matched pendant hung around her neck. She was more beautiful than anyone had ever seen her. "I'm so happy!" she said. "I—I wish all you girls here could find a husband!"

Laughter sprinkled through the room, and several men grinned at the young ladies, who pretended not to notice. The music began again and Davis went to congratulate the couple. For the next hour he watched the dancers until he felt as if he had done his duty. Passing out one of the doors leading to the large court on the east side of the house, he crossed the flagstones, headed for the back of the house, intending to enter that way.

He was startled when a voice said, "You're leaving early, Owen."

Turning quickly, he saw Belle standing in the shadows. Her black dress made her difficult to see, but her pale face glowed with the reflection of the full yellow moon rising over the trees.

"We seem to spend a lot of time in the evenings on porches," he said, coming close to her. "No swing on this one, though."

She leaned back against the house as though she were exhausted. "It's so sad, isn't it, Owen?"

"Sad? The party?"

"Yes."

"Why, I think Pet and Thad are having a wonderful time. She looks so beautiful."

"Yes—and so vulnerable!" Belle moved away from the wall, turned and gazed at the moon. "Next week he may be dead."

Davis fixed his eyes on her pale face, wondering at the sadness in her voice. "That's true—but it's always been true, Belle. It always will be. Every man and woman have to risk that. What did Bacon say? Oh yes: 'He that hath wife and children hath given hostages to fortune.' "

She came closer to see his face better. "What does that mean, Owen?"

"Why, if a man doesn't have a wife, she can't hurt him. He can't lose her. But I've never liked the alternative."

"Not having anyone to love?"

"That's right. A man—or a woman—can get pretty badly cut up by someone they love. But the only other way is to be a hermit. Build a wall around yourself and say to everybody, 'Keep out!' "

She mulled that over—her expression changing from sadness to bitterness. "Some of us need walls!" she defended.

"No, I don't believe that." He shook his head. "What most of us need to do is knock the walls *down*—not build them up." The look of poignancy on her face touched his heart, and he asked, "Belle, what's wrong? You hinted at it the other night, and now all this about walls."

She started to leave, but he caught her arm. She bit her lip, uncertain as to what to do—run or stay. She relaxed and moved to the railing. "Owen," she began, "when you first came to the hospital, your spirit was almost as hurt as your body."

He blinked in surprise. "That's right, Belle!"

"You hated me, didn't you?"

"I—ah. . . !" He paused, realizing he couldn't tell her the truth.

"I think I know," she went on quietly. "You heard about the time I was in Washington. It's been in all the papers. Did you read about the trial?"

"Yes, I did, but—"

"Then you know what I did—that I prostituted myself." She dropped her head and began to tremble. "Well, it was true—what the papers said I did. And I don't blame anyone for hating me." She lifted her eyes, soft with pain as she murmured, "You couldn't despise me any more than I do myself, Owen."

"Belle—it's not like you think!" he said, but he saw the self-loathing, and without a thought put his arms around her and drew her close. She was struggling to keep from weeping, her head pressed against his chest. "Belle, that's not why I hated you. I was a fool! What you did was for your country. No man could ever fault you for that!"

She drew back hastily. "No. You're just being kind. No man would want me after what I've done. He could never forget!"

Davis shook his head, but just as he was about to speak, footsteps sounded to their left. Both of them stepped back quickly. Davis began talking at once about the food. Belle was just able to wipe the tears from her face when Beau Beauchamp rounded the corner of the building. He saw them instantly and stopped dead.

"Perhaps," Davis went on, "it was those oysters, Miss Belle. I didn't eat . . ." He paused, looked at Beauchamp, and said, "Oh, Captain—Miss Belle is not feeling well. She got so faint I thought the fresh air might revive her—but it's probably something she ate."

Beauchamp looked perplexed, and would have spoken, but Belle broke in, "Beau, I feel—terrible. Would you please tell my mother I'm going to bed?"

"Oh, I'll do that," Davis offered. "Perhaps you'd help her to her room?"

Davis spun around and left, and Belle touched her handkerchief to her face again.

"Are you very ill, Belle?" Beauchamp inquired. "I can get Dr. Malone to have a look at you."

"No—I just want to lie down, Beau."

He escorted her to her room, and came back to speak with Rebekah.

"Lieutenant Morgan told me," she informed Beau. "I'll go see her."

"She didn't seem ill earlier," Beauchamp commented.

"I guess it *was* the food," Davis replied. He moved away, but felt the eyes of the big officer follow him.

CHAPTER TWENTY-ONE

# THE END OF THE MASQUERADE

★ ★ ★ ★

Davis pretended to be asleep when Thad entered the room that night. After the young man's breathing grew slow, Davis reviewed the scene with Belle. He would be gone from Belle Maison within a matter of hours, and the fact that he would not see her again disturbed him. *How could the deep bitterness he had held for the girl vanish so quickly and so completely?* he wondered. He wrestled with this until he fell into a fitful sleep, leaving him more tired than when he'd gone to bed.

He washed his face, dressed, and went downstairs to find a small crowd eating breakfast from the long tables in the ball room. Belle was not there, but Sky Winslow motioned him over. "Have something to eat, Morgan."

"Guess I could have something," Davis said. He consumed a portion of bacon and eggs and two biscuits. As they ate, Winslow spoke of the future of Belle Maison. It was evident that the man's heart was at the plantation, not in politics.

When they had finished, Davis asked, "Do you know where Thad is this morning?"

"He left to go to the stable, I think. Mare is about to drop her foal."

Sky moved across the room to speak to Colonel Barton, and Davis went outside. He headed toward the stables, where he found both Thad and Pet, along with Dooley Young.

"You shore do look better than you did last time I saw you, Lieutenant!" Dooley exclaimed. "I never thought you'd make it to Richmond alive."

"Almost didn't," Davis replied.

Dooley squinted at him, and bobbed his head in surprise. "Had it in my mind you was a smaller man—but I guess you was all shrunk up with the mullygrups."

Thad broke in quickly, "This mare is sired by Dooley's best stallion. We figure to make a million dollars racing her colt—if he ever gets here."

"Mind if I hang around?" Davis asked.

"Glad to have you," Thad said, adding, "This mare is going to be slow, I reckon."

His words were prophetic, for by noon the mare still hadn't delivered. When two o'clock came, Davis said with a significant glance at Thad, "Like to take a little ride, Thad. Think I might borrow a horse?"

Thad nodded toward the bay gelding tied under a large oak. "Take mine, Lieutenant. He's already saddled."

Davis hesitated, then nodded. "Thanks—for everything, Thad."

He swung into the saddle and rode toward the house. Tying the gelding to the hitching post, he started into the house, but stopped when Rebekah appeared at the side of the house and called his name.

"What is it, Mrs. Winslow?"

"I've got to talk with you. Come this way."

He followed her, mystified—and was even more confused when she walked to his room and entered. He followed, and she said, "Close the door."

"What's wrong?" he asked.

Rebekah looked at him and said quietly, "You're not Owen Morgan."

Davis blinked, caught off guard. He was totally unprepared for such a possibility, and couldn't think of a reply. His heart began to race. Finally he asked, "What makes you think that?"

"Because I know who you really are."

"Who am I, then?" he asked steadily.

"You're Davis Winslow." She spoke with an iron certainty, and he decided the masquerade was over.

"How long have you known?" he asked, looking at her curiously, yet strangely without fear.

"I've been uneasy about you for a long time, but I didn't know who you were until today."

"How'd you find out?"

"Last night you mentioned something about my sister Louise."

He nodded slowly as he recalled the incident. "You told me about her when I was here with my grandfather."

"Yes. When I finally figured out where I'd seen you, I went to your room to face you. I checked through your things—and I found this."

She removed something from her pocket and held it toward him. He took it and nodded. "I thought it would be safe to keep it. Looks as if I was wrong." It was the small Testament his grandfather had given him. The inside page was inscribed to Davis Winslow and signed by his grandfather.

He carefully put the Testament in his pocket and asked, "What are you going to do?"

"Why did Thad bring you here?"

He told her the story, concluding with, "I didn't know what he was doing. When I woke up in Chimborazo, I couldn't stand the thought of being in a Confederate hospital. But Thad saved my life. Thad and Belle."

"It'll ruin Thad if you're discovered."

"Yes, I know. That's why I'm leaving right away." He looked her full in the face. "Rebekah, you must believe me. I'd never do anything to hurt any of your family. I've got Thad's horse outside. When you stopped me, I was on my way here to get my things." He told her about the plan to make his way back to the North, and added, "I suppose someone will write asking about Owen Morgan—but all anyone here will know is that he boarded the train and left."

Rebekah's eyes filled with tears. "Davis! I've been terrified!" She attempted a smile, partially succeeded, then stood examining him. "I—I thought all sorts of things."

"That I was a spy? I don't wonder. But Thad will tell you all about it." He hesitated. "I came here filled with hate, Rebekah, but it's gone now. I don't understand it myself, but it's all gone."

"I'm glad, Davis," she murmured, putting her arms around him. "Thank God! Thank God!"

He held her, knowing she had been tormented by fear of the disaster he might bring to her family. Finally he said, "I've got to hurry, Rebekah. The train pulls out at five o'clock—and I've got to be on it."

"All right." She stepped back and studied him silently. "Davis . . . I think you ought to tell Belle the truth before you go."

He stared at her. "Why?"

"I can't put it into words, but part of it has to do with your brother's death. She still blames herself for that. She never talks about it, of course, but I think she's so filled with guilt that it's killing her. If you could tell her you forgive her for your brother's death, I think it would help her get over it."

He shifted nervously. "It may backfire, you know. She could take me for a traitor and denounce me."

"That's possible." Rebekah's eyes had a poignant plea. "It might mean your death if that happened, Davis." She paused. "Perhaps you could write her?"

"No," he decided. "I want to tell her face-to-face." He began to stuff his things hurriedly into his small bag. "I need to see her alone."

"All right, Davis. She's sharing a room with Pet and another girl, but I'll send her out to the spring house."

"I'll be there."

He moved to pass her, but she caught him and looked up into his face, saying, "God go with you, Davis!"

"And with you," he said quietly, and left the room, slipping down the back way and around the house to the gelding. He strapped the small bag behind the saddle and led the horse to the spring house, which was behind the big house, off to the left under an elm tree.

He tied the horse and paced back and forth, wondering desperately if he were doing the wise thing. Belle was a strange woman—at times impulsive and quite capable of turning him over to the military if she thought it was the thing to do. He knew that her love for the Confederacy was strong, had been strong enough to cause her to give up her life to preserve it.

A movement caught his eye, and he turned to see her coming from the house. She hurried toward him, a question in her eyes. "Mother said I should see you, Owen. She says you have something to tell me."

He made up his mind, and knew there was no easy way to say it. Yet he paused, trying to find the right words.

"What is it, Owen?" she urged, fear clutching her. "Are you in some kind of trouble?"

He looked at her searchingly. "Belle, you've done more for me than any human being on this earth—except perhaps Thad Novak. You two saved my life—and now I think you may regret it."

Belle's eyes opened in disbelief. "Owen! What are you talking about? You look so strange." She put her hand on his arm. "Please, tell me what it is."

"All right. I'm not the man you think I am." He watched carefully, looking for any indication she had been suspicious of him. He saw only confusion. Squaring his shoulders he dived in. "I was a prisoner in Libby, Belle."

"Libby!" she whispered, her lips tightening. "But—that's impossible!"

"Thad got me out of there, Belle. I was so near death I didn't know much about it, but that's what happened. He bribed a medical attendant, and they took me out in a coffin. So far as Libby prison is concerned, I'm dead and buried."

Belle touched her temple with an unsteady hand, and her voice rose as she asked, "But why would Thad do such a thing—for a Yankee?"

Davis paused, then said tonelessly, "He did it because my brother saved his life, Belle."

His words seemed momentarily unintelligible to her, for she looked at him blankly. But as he watched, he saw the truth dawn—first in her eyes, then across her face as the enormity of it hit her. She cried out in unbelief, "No! No! It's not so!"

She was shaking all over, and he urged, "Belle, let me tell you all of it. Sit down."

Belle obeyed blindly. She sat motionless as he traced the story. He told her frankly how he had joined the Union Army out of blind hatred, and how even when he came to Chimborazo he had been little better. He told her how Lonnie's death had affected him, and again how the hatred had left him.

"I don't know when I stopped hating, Belle," he finished, watching her face. "It had something to do with that sermon, as I told you before. But whatever happened, I don't have any hate anymore—not for anyone or anything."

The sound of laughter came to them faintly from the house, and he turned to look in that direction. When he faced her again, she was regarding him in a different manner. Not anger—but not gentle either. She said slowly and in an ultra-controlled voice, "Why did you tell me all this? Why didn't you just go away?"

"Because—I wanted to be honest with you."

"Honest!" she cried. "That's a fine word for you to use!"

"You've got no reason to trust me. But God knows I wouldn't hurt you or your family!"

She jumped to her feet, her face strained. She looked at him for a long moment, then breathed deeply. "I don't know what you'd do," she finally said. "I thought I knew you—and now I find out that everything's been a masquerade."

"Not all of it, Belle," he countered.

"How can I ever believe anything?" she whispered. "I had just started to feel—something for you. And now I discover that it was all nothing!" Tears gathered in her eyes. "Oh, why didn't you just leave!"

He longed to touch her, to hold her, but he realized he couldn't. He sighed. "I wanted to tell you something."

"Tell me what?"

"I wanted to tell you not to spend your life grieving over the past. Don't tear yourself apart over what's done." *That isn't what I wanted to say!* shot into his mind. Suddenly he knew what had happened to him. It took him off guard, like the force of a hammer blow.

She eyed him carefully and shook her head. "Just throw off the past—as if it were a worn-out coat? Don't you think I haven't *tried*? It doesn't *work* that way—not with me, anyway. I told you what I've done. Do you think all that will just fade away?"

Davis was listening quietly, but at the same time he was conscious of the truth that had just come to him. It was not a new thing, he realized, but something that had been building up for a long time.

Yet he knew it was hopeless. She was regarding him quizzically, waiting for him to speak. His lips seemed frozen. Never had he said anything that would cost him more—but he must speak.

"Belle, I've learned to care for you."

Her lips parted in astonishment at the unexpected revelation. She stood transfixed as he continued.

"Yes, I hated you when I came—but every day I watched you. I never saw a woman who gave herself to others as I saw you do. Day after day, I watched you, Belle, hoping to see you fail! I remember when you cleaned up Tommy Hopper, and I thought, *Lord, how can she do it!*"

Belle dropped her eyes. "It was my job," she murmured.

"No, the orderlies did *jobs,*" he said firmly. "It was more than that, Belle. It was a calling. I think that's what they call it." He slowly reached out and lifted her face. "Belle! Belle!" he whispered, "I know you can't believe it. I didn't realize myself until this minute that I love you."

"You *can't* love me!" she argued, almost angrily. "You're my enemy—and even if you weren't a Yankee, I still wouldn't believe you!"

She turned to leave, but he caught her, forcing her to face him. "I've got to go. But you listen to this. You may think I'm the world's worse liar. I've given you no reason to think any differently. But I'm telling you that I love you. I know my brother is dead, and you blame yourself. I can't sort out all the crazy things about this war. I guess God will have to do that; but think what you will, believe it or not—I love you, Belle!"

Her eyes mirrored her unbelief. "You love *me*? With the kind of love in that poem?"

He nodded. " 'Love is not love which alters when it alteration finds.' " He studied her face. "We Winslows are one-woman-sort of men, my grandfather says. I've never told a woman I loved her—and I don't expect to tell another one."

She drew away from him, and cried in a voice charged with pain, "Oh, Davis, go away! I don't believe anything anymore! Please go!"

He nodded slowly. "I'm going, Belle. But this isn't the end—just the beginning."

"Can't you see how hopeless it is?" she whispered.

He shook his head. "That's not what *I* believe." With one sweep he caught her to him and kissed her. Her soft lips were still under his when he stepped back.

"Goodbye, darling," he said as he swung into the saddle. He lifted his chin, said "Goodbye!" again, then pulled the horse around and rode off.

Belle stood motionless for only a moment before running out to catch the last glimpse of him. Not until he was a distant dot on the horizon did she turn back to the spring house. She paused to look at the spot where they had talked, her face damp with tears, her mind reeling.

She returned to the house without a backward look and went straight to her room. When she opened the door, Rebekah was waiting for her. "Mother. . . ?" she said and fell weeping into Rebekah's arms.

Rebekah held her, rocking slowly as she had done when Belle was a child. And as she held her, she prayed fervently, *Oh, God! Don't let her be lost! Bring her to yourself!*

## CHAPTER TWENTY-TWO

# The Homecoming

★ ★ ★ ★

Captain Whitfield Winslow stood up slowly and dusted the dirt from his knees. Straightening his back carefully to ease the protesting muscles, he grunted with satisfaction as he surveyed the line of roses he had been mulching. The flowers were two years old now, and had made it through the harsh winter. The captain smiled. Delving into the rich, black soil was one of his joys.

*Not so many years left to do things like this, though,* he mused. *At eighty-one—the end's not as far away as it was.* But the thought did not trouble him. When he had been on active duty, he had gone to battle with the knowledge that he might not be alive at the end of the day; now he faced a more certain fate with equal equanimity. He remembered a line Davis had read to him about death: "By my troth, we owe God a death, and he that pays this year is quit for the next."

He liked that thought, and repeated the words as he moved down the row of roses set in strict military fashion along the front walk, stopping now and then to touch one of the crimson blossoms. He limped markedly, for the broken ankle had never completely healed. Entering the kitchen, he washed his hands and gulped down two glasses of cool water.

His back still ached, but he refused to lie down. Instead, he fixed a strong cup of coffee, picked up the latest newspaper, and returned outdoors to sit in the small courtyard on the east side of the house. It was merely a cubicle of space, large enough for a table and four chairs, but it was shielded from the street by a lath screen and protected from the hot sun by a spreading elm that touched the eaves of the house.

Easing himself into the chair, he opened the paper and began to read, sipping his coffee as he scanned the war news. Not much had changed in the long months since Gettysburg. Finally he laid it on the table and closed his eyes. The bees he kept in two hives were busily flying about, singing in a high-pitched key as they passed. In the hedge to his right, the mocking birds chirped, and the colony of martins nesting in the two-story house he had built argued and bickered in their amiable way.

The captain was more tired than he cared to admit, and the warm sun, combined with the soft sounds of June, soon caused him to drop his chin on his chest. He dozed lightly until a faint sound of knocking aroused him.

He jerked his head up with a start and looked toward the front door. From where he sat, he couldn't see who it was, but he had ordered some fresh beef from the butcher and assumed it was Billy McMannis, the delivery boy.

"Come round to the side, Billy," he called. He picked up the cup, took a sip of the cold coffee, and turned toward the sound of footsteps on the walk, saying, "Put the meat in—Chamberlain!" he exclaimed as the tall blue-uniformed officer emerged through the narrow slit in the screen. "What are you doing in Washington?"

The sun was behind the man's back, and Whitfield thought it was his old friend. But when the captain rose to his feet and took a step forward, he saw he was mistaken. It was not a general, but a lieutenant. The captain couldn't see the face clearly because the sun was peeping through the trees from behind the man's head, catching Winslow directly.

Shading his eyes with his hand, he peered at the officer and demanded, "Yes? What is it?"

No answer.

"Well, speak up, man!" he grumped. "What is it?"

The officer stepped forward. "It's—it's me, Grandfather!"

The world plunged into an eerie stillness. He stood as if transfixed, staring into the face he had grieved over every day for the last months. The silence rang in his ears and a dizziness swept over him, causing his knees to buckle.

Catching himself he whispered, "Davis. . . !" Reaching out in stark unbelief, he was enveloped by a pair of strong arms.

"I'm back, Grandfather!" Davis said thickly. He helped the old man sit down, realizing the shock had been almost too much. "I'm back," he repeated. The pale cast of the strong old face of his grandfather alarmed him.

"Let me get you some water," he offered, and started for the kitchen.

"No." Winslow's voice was unsteady, but he lifted his shoulders and pulled himself up straight in the chair. "I'm all right."

Davis sat opposite him. "I wanted to send a wire to break the news, but I was afraid you'd be alone when it arrived." He put out his hand and the captain grasped it, holding on as if he were afraid Davis would vanish. "Just sit there for a minute. Then I'll tell you all about it."

"Have you seen Robert and Jewel?"

"I just came from there. It was—hard," he said, stumbling over the word. "I saw Father first, and then he went in and broke it to Mother. I don't think either of them can believe it, though." A smile touched his lips, and he added, "They almost refused to let me come over here."

Whitfield Winslow had led an eventful life, but nothing had shocked him so much as the sight of his grandson's appearance. He stared at him, his throat constricting. He put his other hand over Davis's in a steel grip. "I know how they feel," he said quietly. "I'm afraid if you leave, I'll wake up and find it's all been an old man's dream."

"I won't leave," Davis promised, squeezing the gnarled hands.

"Tell me about it—all of it!"

For the next hour Davis gave a detailed account of his escape from Libby. "I should have found some way to let you know I was alive—but I was afraid it would get Thad in trouble," he said.

"You did the right thing, boy," Whitfield nodded emphatically. "That young man, he's the Winslow stock—the real thing!"

"You're correct about that," Davis nodded. He went over his first days at Chimborazo, emphasizing Belle's role. "I'd be either dead or a one-legged cripple by now if it hadn't been for her."

"You've forgiven her, I see." The captain's eyes lit up with approval. "That was what frightened me, Davis—your terrible hatred for her. It was killing you inside. But now it's all gone?"

Davis hesitated, then said what he had not told his parents—what he had not intended to tell anyone—"It's . . . more than that, Grandfather." There was a note in his voice that made Whitfield look at him with surprise. "All the time I was in the hospital, I watched her. Later when the Winslows took me in, and she was there, we spent a lot of time together. We talked much about books, and—well, I got to know her."

He found it difficult to say what he wanted, so his grandfather did it for him. "Are you trying to tell me you love the girl?"

Davis nodded. "Yes—but she doesn't care for me."

Whitfield studied Davis carefully. It had been less than a year since he had gone away, but little remained of the rosy-cheeked boyish look. Instead, his face was lean and marked with suffering—suffering that had made him into a man. His deep-set eyes were steady and filled with wisdom, the clean lines of his face, once hidden, now apparent.

"She's suffered a lot, boy," he finally stated quietly. "I've always felt she was a fine woman. But it may take some time."

"It'll take that," Davis agreed. "It'll take a miracle, too."

"Well, there *are* precedents." Whitfield's face creased in a smile, and he gave Davis's shoulders a hard slap. "There's one sitting in my garden! Now, tell me how you escaped from the South."

"That was sort of a miracle in itself, I think," Davis answered. "It was almost too easy! I boarded the train in a Confederate uniform, rode as close as I could to the lines, then got off. I put on civilian clothes, got rid of my uniform, and started walking. The first farm I came to, I bought a horse. From there I just eased around until I found an opening. Soon as I got through to our side, I asked for the Twentieth Maine. It was a two-day ride, but I made it."

"I'll bet Chamberlain got a shock at the sight of you."

Davis smiled at the memory of how he had walked into camp to find Chamberlain in a staff meeting, wearing the insignia of a general, which he'd received in June. He had taken one look at Davis and shouted, "Good God! He's come out of the grave!" Davis repeated this to the captain, and said, "For once that man lost his scholarly reserve!"

"How'd you account for being reported dead?"

"Oh, I just said I'd bribed a guard to let me go out in a coffin. I didn't mention Thad, of course, so they think I'm somewhat of a hero." He laughed. "He found a uniform and sent me away right off. My leg's not all that steady, so you'll have me on your hands for quite a while, I think."

"My boy, I thank God for your safe return."

Davis stared at the floor. "Well, Perry Hale would say God's been in it all the way."

"Hale's a good man, and I agree," the captain nodded.

"I've changed my views about God," Davis stated abruptly. He told how the sermon he'd heard had affected him so powerfully, and asked, "Do you think it was God who took all the bitterness out of me? I didn't call on Him, or make any kind of public profession."

"Davis, only God can do a thing like that. It's not in the power of man to change his own heart."

"But—am I a Christian, then?" Perplexity creased his brow and he added, "Most of the Christians I know have some kind of experience. They call it 'getting saved.' You've told me about how you came to know God—and nothing like that's happened to me."

"God's not in a box, Davis, though lots of people would love to put Him there. He's an infinite God, and I think He deals with people in many ways. It's a mistake to think that every man has to have the same experience in all the details. You've read the Bible. You know He didn't deal with Abraham as He did with David. Paul had a spectacular experience with Jesus on the road to Damascus, while other people have a more simple conversion."

Davis shook his head. "Something in me is different—but I still don't feel—I don't feel God, somehow."

The captain smiled and nodded his approval. "Why, boy,

most of us have to go through some sort of struggle to find God. I was miserable for two years, fighting God all the way. I know now He was after me, and I was doing everything I could to keep from being caught!" He studied Davis carefully. "I think God came knocking at your door in that hospital, Davis. And He gave you just a little taste of what He's like by removing the hate. But that's not the end of it."

Davis mulled the words over. After a while he nodded, his face sober. "I've been thinking about that. It seems like I'm—well, sort of half finished. What do I do now?"

"You give your life to Jesus."

"But—*how*?" Davis was disturbed, and his confusion was evident.

"I guess that's what you and I will have to talk about, Davis," the captain replied. "One thing I know for sure—when a man is ready for Christ to do something in him, it's not a long affair. It doesn't take God long to save a man—but sometimes it takes quite a spell for the man to get his heart *right* for God to do something. I think what you'll be doing for the next few days or maybe months is getting ready."

Davis looked doubtful. "Well, I've got the time—and I've got a good teacher," he smiled. "Now, let's get *you* ready."

"Me? Ready for what?"

"Why, the prodigal's come home!" Davis got to his feet. "Mother's killing the fatted calf for me—and we've both got to be there for the feast." Then he amended his words. "On the other hand, I guess I'm sort of a cross between the prodigal and Lazarus, wouldn't you think?"

"A little of both, my boy—a little of both!"

* * * *

The rest of the summer sped by, and Davis stayed in Washington. He had no inclination to leave and was glad when he was assigned to a desk job—a job that in his opinion had no meaning or value, except that it allowed time with his grandfather and the family.

His stay with his parents was rewarding, for the breach between them was totally healed. They were so filled with joy over his miraculous appearance that nothing was too much for them to do for him. Sometimes it seemed a little smothering, the way his mother clung to him. Davis, however, never showed any displeasure. He grew close to his father also, and they spent many evenings together, often dining out or going to the theater.

But it was the visits with his grandfather the young man prized most. The two studied the Bible constantly, and Davis was astonished to discover how much he understood.

Attending church had always been a duty, but by the end of summer Davis was a fixture, along with his grandfather, in the Presbyterian church where the captain had taken Belle. He often saw President Lincoln, and once had shaken hands with him after the service.

But it wasn't until late summer that he found the answer he'd been seeking—and it didn't come as expected. For months he'd been examining his life, trying to find his way to God. At times he grew desperate, for nothing seemed to happen. Still, he had kept on, and one Sunday morning as the minister preached on the cross of Jesus, Davis was greatly moved. He said nothing to his grandfather, but walked the cold streets for an hour after returning home.

The captain had been surprised when Davis appeared at three o'clock. His face was somewhat paler than usual, and as soon as he entered the house, he said in a tight voice, "I've found Christ, Grandfather!" He paced the floor as the old man waited, a broad smile on his weathered face. "I was thinking of the sermon, about the cross, and I'd just about given up on ever having any kind of real experience with God—like you had. As I was crossing Oak Street, all of a sudden, I just felt like God was there!"

"Even more than in church, eh?" the captain nodded.

"Yes, much more. And I just said, 'God, I'm not sure about much, but I know that Jesus is the Son of God—and that He died for me—so please forgive me and make me what *you* want me to be.' "

Davis was alive with excitement as he went on. "And He did it! He did it, Grandfather! Oh, it wasn't like Paul's experience—not like yours either—but I *know* Jesus came to me there on Oak Street!"

Whitfield's eyes were moist, his lips trembling, but he said firmly, "Davis—the devil is going to tell you in the days to come that you *imagined* it all. He always does! So what you better do is go back to that crossing and put an *X* on the spot where you called on God—and then when the devil comes, you can take him to the exact spot and tell him, 'Right *there* is where it happened!' " He embraced his grandson, saying exuberantly, "My boy! I'm so happy for you! So happy!"

After that, the two spent even more time together, and when Davis was baptized in the church, his parents stood beside the captain. And for all his professed agnosticism, Robert wiped his eyes as he saw the happy smile on his son's face.

The week after he was baptized, Davis received his orders to rejoin his company, which was being thrown into the final struggle around Richmond. Everyone knew, now that Grant had fought Lee and the Army of Northern Virginia to a standstill at the Wilderness, Spotsylvania, and Cold Harbor, that the war could have only one end. The South was fighting valiantly, but the massive armies of the North now encircled the heart of the Confederacy. Hood's Army of the Tennessee had been destroyed at Franklin and again at Nashville, so all that kept the frail fabric of the Southern Confederacy intact was the thin gray line Grant presently faced at Petersburg. When that fell, Richmond was doomed, and when Richmond fell—the war would be over.

"I've been called to join my unit at Petersburg, Grandfather," Davis said. He stared at the summons and shook his head. "I wish I didn't have to go."

"God will be with you, Davis," the captain encouraged. "He's brought you this far, and He won't let you down now."

"I'm not afraid of dying—you know that," Davis told him. "But I am afraid of killing other men. I just want to be a help to the people there. How can I fight against men like Thad?"

Davis left the next day, and the last thing he said was to his grandfather as the train pulled out of the station, "I'll be back—but pray that God will use me!"

CHAPTER TWENTY-THREE

# THE END OF IT ALL

★ ★ ★ ★

Belle had ceased to notice the rumbling of cannons that had become part of Richmond's existence. For almost ten months, Grant had hammered at the thin line of Confederates with little success. Belle had heard her father say, "If Grant knew how thin our lines are, he'd drive through them tomorrow!"

But Lee shifted men from place to place, often managing to strengthen a weak point minutes before the Federals attacked. Grant had grown desperate at one point during this time, and in July of the previous year had resorted to a wild scheme of Colonel Henry Pleasants', a mining engineer in civil life. Pleasants was a member of the Forty-eighth Pennsylvania Infantry, composed largely of coal miners. They dug a tunnel over 586 feet long and laid a powerful mine directly under the Confederate position. The mine exploded, but when a poorly led colored division tried to invade the gap, hundreds died in what came to be called "The Crater."

On March 25, General Lee made a valiant attack on Fort Stedman, but was driven back by strong Union reinforcements. Six days later, Grant's hard-driving general, Sheridan, won against the Confederates at Five Forks, and Grant immediately ordered a general assault at dawn of April 2. The night the attack broke through, the Army of Northern Virginia left Petersburg and

Richmond and set out on the road to Appomattox.

* * * *

Every bed at Chimborazo had been occupied for months, for the toll of the siege resulted in heavy casualties. When there were no more beds, men lay on the floor with blankets as cots. Even then there was not enough room. The pressure of Belle's tasks had kept her from brooding on who was winning as she heard the rumble of the guns a few miles away, but on the morning of April 2, her routine was broken.

That morning one of her patients, a small Texan named Sam Dempsey, asked if he could go to church. He had lost a leg at the battle of The Crater, and had healed slowly. "I promised my ma I'd go real faithful, and I ain't had no chance to go in a long time, Miss Belle."

Realizing Dempsey's condition would not be helped by the journey to church, she was uncertain. She had been on duty for over forty-eight hours, broken only by short naps in her office, and the strain had built up in her. A quick decision came to her, and she said, "I'll have to go with you, Sam. I promised my mother I'd go too."

The prospect of getting the wounded man to St. Paul's Church was difficult, but Belle managed by using a wheelchair and having Elmer Gibbs take them by wagon.

When they arrived, Gibbs asked, "Could I go with you, Miss Belle? Reckon a little preaching might do me some good."

"Of course, Elmer." She walked beside the chair as Gibbs wheeled the soldier. The church was crowded, and she hesitated when she heard a familiar voice. "Sit with us, Belle," her father said. "There's room in the aisle for this young fellow." Belle felt conspicuous as they moved down the aisle to the front row where her mother and Pet were already seated—next to the President! Her lips parted in surprise. President Davis immediately rose and stepped from the pew to acknowledge Dempsey, who was speechless. He turned to Belle, saying, "God bless you for your faithful service, Mrs. Wickham," then resumed his seat beside his wife.

The service began, and although Belle was so exhausted she could not concentrate on it, she was gratified to see that Dempsey did. He sang the hymns lustily, though off-key.

Belle had to strain to stay awake during the long sermon. More than once, she nodded and awoke with a jerk, embarrassed, but no one seemed to notice.

She had just closed her eyes again when she was aware of movement to her left. A young lieutenant was handing a note to the President. As President Davis read the message, Belle could see his lips pale and draw to a thin line. He suffered, she knew, from neuralgia, and the pain was evident in his eyes. He turned and said something quietly to her father, then rose, spoke to his wife, and the two followed the young officer out.

Belle heard the words faintly as Sky leaned over to Rebekah. "It's the end. Lee's army is in retreat."

The minister saw the impossibility of continuing his sermon, and dismissed them abruptly. Gibbs hurriedly wheeled the wounded boy out, and the Winslows followed. As Elmer assisted Dempsey into the wagon, Sky spoke. He was not flustered as most of the others seemed to be. It was as if something unpleasant, though long expected, had come—and he said as much.

"We'll have to be ready for hard times. The Union troops should arrive soon."

"What is the President going to do?" Rebekah questioned.

"He's leaving immediately—for Greensboro." A grim look swept across Sky's face. "He hopes to reorganize and carry on the war, and asked me to accompany him."

Dismayed, Rebekah groped for words. "Will—will you go, Sky?"

"No! It's over, Rebekah. Thank God, it's over!" he uttered, and turned at once to the crisis at hand. "Things'll get out of hand in Richmond. A great number of hoodlums have been gathering here, and there's sure to be rioting. I'm taking all of you to Belle Maison."

"I can't leave the hospital, Father!" Belle objected. "The war may be over, but there are still thousands of helpless men. Take Mother and Pet."

"I think I'd better stay," Rebekah said. "Some of the orderlies will run when the Union troops arrive, won't they, Belle? Sky, you take Pet—"

"I'm staying, too!"

Sky stared at them helplessly. "Guess we'll all stay! I'll have to go by the Capitol and tell the President what I'm going to do; then I'll come."

Sky left and the rest went to the hospital. Rebekah's words had been prophetic, for two of the orderlies in ward 3 had already fled, according to the patients. A grizzled veteran named Sid Hawkins, with both arms bandaged, said, "They skedaddled out like ol' slewfoot was after 'em, Miss Belle." He lowered his voice. "Some of the fellers are a little on edge—what with the bluebellies comin', so they say." He looked at his arms, adding, "If I jest had *one* of my arms, I'd be able to help."

"You can help, Sid," Belle told him. "The men trust you. Tell them I'll be right here—and so will my parents and my sister."

"Is that a fact, ma'am?" Hawkins' homely face brightened. That'll shore calm the fellers down, you bet!" He moved around the ward, speaking to the men, and Belle did the same. The serenity of the three women relieved the panic, and Belle decided, "Let's bring their meal now. It'll keep their minds off the Yankees—at least today. It might be a little harder tomorrow."

They worked all afternoon, and at dusk Sky stopped by. "Well, the President didn't like it—but I told him I had to do what I thought was my duty, just as he did."

"How are things downtown?" Belle asked.

"Terrible!" he snapped. "It's out of control. Mobs are rioting in the streets, plundering stores, and setting buildings on fire. Nobody to stop them." He glanced at the wounded men and said quietly, "I hope they don't get any idea of coming here, but I convinced a few of the militia to come with me, telling them I had enough repeating Spencer rifles for all. Guess we could put up a good fight if we had to."

The night passed slowly. Each minute they expected the rioters would pour in, and about midnight a tremendous explosion rent the air. "That's got to be the arsenal," Sky said grimly. "Nothing else could make that much noise." The roar drowned out all the other sounds and awakened every patient.

They moved through the wards, speaking calmly to the men. "What if the Yankees come, Miss Belle?" a young soldier asked. "What if they set fire to the hospital? Some of the fellers couldn't get out."

"We'll not let that happen, Donnie," Belle assured, but the thought had occurred to her—and to all of them—more than once. She walked outside, scanned the troops, and moved over to where her father was standing, a pistol thrust into his waistband and another in a holster at his side. He was staring at the red sky, all lit up with flames billowing into the inky heavens. They both were pretty sure the ships and ironclads in the harbor were in flames as well, and it looked as if every building in Richmond were ablaze.

"Do you think they'll come?" Belle wondered.

"I think they will," Sky replied. "It would be better if the Federals came. Their officers would have some control over them."

"But Sherman didn't stop on his march to the sea. And they burned Columbia to the ground even when they were ordered not to by the officers."

"This is Grant's army, not Sherman's. Grant's men are used to obeying orders. But I don't think they'll come soon enough. They'll be chasing Lee." He gazed at the burning city. "The mob will soon be here, Belle. Keep your mother and Pet out of the way. A group like that doesn't have any morals. The scoundrels would kill a woman as fast as they would a man."

Belle didn't answer for a moment. Her thoughts were with the helpless men inside. Finally she said, "I never thought I'd see the day I'd pray for Yankees to come."

"They won't, they'll be chasing Lee."

★ ★ ★ ★

Sky Winslow was correct. Ulysses S. Grant was chasing Robert E. Lee and his Army of Northern Virginia. The wily gray fox had never been pinned down by a Union force, but Grant was determined to surround Lee and destroy his army, and had instructed all his staff officers to let nothing prevent that.

The Twentieth Maine, under the command of General Chamberlain, was part of the force Grant ordered to pursue the tattered remnants of Lee's army as they moved away from Richmond. Chamberlain came back from meeting with Grant, and his staff gathered around as he relayed the order. "Lee is headed for Amelia Court House, it seems. We're to harass the troops in every way. General Grant says Lee must not be allowed to escape."

"Not much chance of that, sir," Colonel Grimes shrugged. He can't have more than twenty thousand men, and most of them are out of ammunition. He's in a trap this time."

"Yes, I believe that's right, Colonel," Chamberlain nodded. "But we will carry out our orders. Prepare to move out at once."

The officers broke away instantly, calling out loudly for the men to fall in. Chamberlain stood there, thinking of Lee's moves, when he was interrupted by his aide.

"Sir?"

"Yes?" He turned and saw Davis Winslow. "Well, we're almost home, Lieutenant," Chamberlain smiled. "Good to think that in a few more hours the war'll be over."

"Sir, I want permission to accompany Colonel Sizemore."

The request brought a frown to the general's face, and he asked with some irritation, "Sizemore? He's going in to secure Richmond, isn't he?"

"Yes, sir. I'd like to go with him."

"What's this about, Davis?" Chamberlain had been close to Winslow for some time, but since he had rejoined the Twentieth Maine after his escape, there was more substance to the man. They had seen little action, but Winslow had been faithful in every respect. Now Chamberlain stood there wondering why the request.

"It's going to be bad for people in Richmond—the civilians, I mean." Davis spoke rapidly, a sober intensity in his brown eyes. "You don't need me, sir, but I think there are some people in town who do."

Chamberlain knew a little of the story of the Southern branch of the Winslows, gleaned from the captain, and he thought carefully. "It would be very irregular. I don't see how you could have any good effect if you were attached to Sizemore's brigade."

"I could try, sir!"

Chamberlain eyed Winslow intently, remembering Little Round Top. He had felt so ineffectual when he gave the order for the bayonet charge—and visualized Davis Winslow leading that charge. *If Davis hadn't gone,* he thought, *I think all of us would have been killed—and I sure wouldn't have been promoted to general later if it hadn't happened!*

"Winslow, I tried to teach you logic in a classroom . . ." He hesitated, then grinned. "Now I'm going to do something completely illogical. Don't know what General Grant will say, but I'm going to detach thirty cavalrymen under your command. I order you to take that force, enter Richmond and secure any element that needs securing." He slapped Winslow on the shoulder, demanding, "Is that order flexible enough for you?"

"Yes, sir!" Davis responded. "Thank you, sir!—and would you give me that order in writing?"

"Yes—and you be sure you burn it—after you get your business done!"

* * * *

"The mob of hooligans is coming this way, Mr. Winslow! Must be two, three hundred of 'em!"

Sky had come out of the hospital immediately when Belle had told him, "One of the militia men wants to see you."

The sixty-year-old man was out of breath, and had to pause before he could add, "They're setting fire to every building as they come!"

"Thanks, Jennings. Will you and the rest of the men get your rifles loaded?"

"Why, Mr. Winslow, you don't aim to *fight* them, do you?" Jennings gasped.

"I hope not. Some of them will have more manhood than to burn a hospital." Then Winslow said evenly, "But I'll kill the first man who sets a torch to this place if I die for it the next second."

Jennings smiled unexpectedly. "Well, one advantage of bein' old is you ain't got a heck of a lot to lose if you get killed. I'll get the men ready."

"Good man!" Sky smiled. His face sobered as he turned to Belle, looking much like his Sioux grandfather must have—stern and deadly, Belle thought. "Well, the war has come to us, hasn't it?"

"Father, don't—"

He saw her fear for him, and it touched him. "Why, Belle, how could I look your brothers in the face if I didn't stand up for their wounded comrades?" He looked down the street, and his eyes narrowed. "That's them, I think. Take care of your mother."

He moved off the porch to join the small group waiting for him. They were all old men, except for one young fellow who had only one arm. He had no rifle, but he did have two cap-and-ball dragoon pistols stuck in his belt. "You're loaded for bear, young man," Sky smiled.

"Name's Jack Post, sir. I lost this here arm at Shiloh, but I got twelve little arguments fer them fellers if they don't behave."

The others laughed nervously, and Sky said, "I hope they'll listen to reason. If they don't, I intend to kill as many as try to attack this hospital. Now listen carefully, because we don't have much time. Every mob like that one has a few men who keep the fire going. Wipe those out, and it's like shooting a man in the brain."

"How'll we know which is them?" Post demanded.

"They'll be in front urging the others on. Now spread out—don't set the fireworks off. Don't fire until I do—no matter what happens! That's important. Now, get behind some kind of cover."

The men scattered, poking their Spencer rifles out from behind trees.

Sky planted his feet like a sentry as the first wave of men appeared—five or six, he saw. They seemed to be studying him; then one of them waved the others back, and waited, staring at the hospital buildings, always dropping his gaze back to where the single man stood in front of the largest structure.

Soon he was joined by more men, many of them carrying torches. He motioned to the buildings on both sides of the street, and with a wild yell, a few men rushed to the buildings, broke the windows and tossed the torches inside. The mob grew steadily. Finally the leader called out, "Let's go!" and the whole mass moved down the broad street straight for the hospital.

The leader was a huge full-bearded man wearing a pistol in a holster and carrying a shotgun in one hand. He bared his teeth in a rash smile as he continued to advance, the rowdy men at his heels. Most of them were carrying rifles or pistols; others carried torches, which flickered in the early light.

The burning city behind them seemed to fuel the violence in

the faces of the men, and they yelled and cursed as they advanced, filling the street and spilling over on the sidewalks. When they came within thirty feet of Sky, they halted, moving restlessly. The shouting died as they cocked their heads toward the big man, trying to hear what he was saying.

"Well, lookee what we got here, men!" he jeered. He cast his eyes around; then seeing no other force than the single man and the few defenders, he spat out, "Mister, you got five minutes to git!"

Sky Winslow didn't move. He made a solid shape against the white buildings. His voice was steady as he spoke. "This is a military hospital. There's nothing of value for you."

"You hear me?" the leader roared. "Git out of the way or git killed!"

The mob cheered, but Sky waited until the voices dwindled to a mutter before he answered the challenge. "I wonder what kind of men you are? You'd set fire to a hospital filled with wounded men who fought for you? I thought we had *men* in the South—not a bunch of yellow dogs who'd attack helpless men!"

His slashing words cut and stung, and he saw a few men begin to waver. Somebody called out, "Let it go, Cutter! There ain't nothin' in a hospital we can use."

The big man whirled. "Shut your mouth or I'll shut it for you, Hayes!" He lifted his voice. "He's lying, men! Right in there is grub and whiskey, and them soljers got money and gold watches. Let's go take it!"

The crowd began surging forward, and Cutter took two quick steps ahead—then jerked to a stop as he found himself looking down the steely muzzle of the Colt that had leaped into Sky Winslow's hand. His mouth opened to yell, but nothing came out. The crowd stopped abruptly.

"He's only one man, Cutter!" a tall ruffian in a black suit cried.

At once Sky called out, "Post, if that man who just spoke opens his mouth one more time—put a bullet in his brain!"

"Yes, sir!" Post answered. "I got a bead right between his eyes! He'll be in hell if he opens his big trap—even to sneeze!"

The tall hoodlum froze, and swiveled his head to see that he was covered by a grinning young man who looked anxious to pull the trigger.

A mutter went over the crowd, and a squat burly man inched a couple of steps toward Cutter. "We can rush 'em—!"

"Kill that man if he moves, Jennings!" Sky yelled.

"Yes, *sir*!"

Sky knew it couldn't last, so he thrust the pistol back in his waistband and taunted, "Cutter, do you have the guts to fight me? Or do you just shoot women and wounded men?" The man blinked, his eyes loaded with the wrath to kill. Sky raised his hands above his head, calling out, "You've got a shotgun in your hands—all you have to do is turn it and pull the trigger. Go on, Cutter. Show these men you're not a gutless coward!"

Cutter's sweat shone in the sunlight, but he didn't move. He had seen the revolver leap into the hand of the man in front of him as if by magic, and he began to back away. That might have been the end of it, but one of the men in the second rank lifted his gun and fired at Sky.

Winslow felt the slug rake his side, half turning him; but it was not a fatal blow, and he yelled, "Let them have it!"

Even as he yelled he drove a slug at Cutter, who had leveled his shotgun and was in the very act of pulling the trigger. Sky's bullet caught him in the mouth, and the shotgun flew up, exploding its charge high as he fell back, dead before he hit the ground.

Sky's men were on a hair trigger, loosing a hail of bullets at the first ranks, dropping at least half a dozen in the street. A yell of rage and fear rang out, and the mob began to return the fire. Those in front, however, lunged back, trying to get away from the gunfire that searched the street with a deadly effect. Man after man fell, and the cries of the wounded spread panic.

Sky felt a bullet pluck at his coat, and heard others whizzing around him. "Get off the street!" Post shouted, and Sky dived for one of the elms. The mob saw it, and somebody raged, "Get 'em!" The whole mob surged against the blistering fire, shooting steadily. Sky saw one of the militia go down with a bloody face. Then Jennings arched backward, gave a high-pitched cry and fell.

"We can't hold 'em, sir!' Post yelled. He took a snap shot and a man dropped instantly, but they were coming fast—too fast.

Suddenly a shrill sound rose above the yells of rage and the firing, and Sky turned. Down the west side of the street, a body of mounted Union men were charging, with sabers flashing. They hit the mob with locomotive force, and man after man went down from the slashing blades.

Sky yelled. "We'll hit from this side!" He snatched his second revolver from his belt and headed for the street, firing all the way. The rest of the militia joined him, and the mob was caught in the pincers. But the sight of the naked steel was too much for the hoodlums, so they dropped their guns and scrambled back to the city.

The mounted men dispersed the rest of the frantic mob as a wolf might scatter a flock of helpless chickens, and then the officers rode off.

Rebekah came running out of the hospital and threw her arms around Sky. She was joined almost at once by Pet and Belle, and he heard his little band of defenders giving a cheer. He grinned at Post. "Your arguments were quite convincing, soldier!"

"Sky! You've been shot!" Rebekah cried out, noticing his bloody vest. "Quick! We've got to get you inside."

"Not yet," he said and walked over to look down at Jennings. "You did well," he murmured. He checked the other casualties, commenting, "They were soldiers, weren't they?"

"Here come the Yankees!" Post cried, adding with a strange look on his face, "Ain't never seen any bluebellies who wasn't tryin' to kill me."

The officer called out "Halt!" and swung out of the saddle.

Sky moved to meet him, holding out his hand. "Sir," he said, "we are in your debt. You must—"

"Mr. Winslow—are you all right?"

Sky stared at him dumbfounded.

"It's Davis Winslow, Sky!" Rebekah exclaimed.

Sky tried to speak—with some confusion, for he had not recognized the tall, lean, bronzed officer as the overweight son of his relative.

Belle felt as though she were going to faint, and turned to flee into the hospital, but Pet grabbed her arm and pulled her with her. *It can't be possible!* Belle thought, gazing in unbelief.

"You have General Chamberlain to thank, sir," Davis continued. "He allowed me to bring the detail in to protect the citizens."

Then he saw the blood on Sky's clothing and exclaimed, "You've been hit, sir!" At the same time his eyes fell on Belle, and he said, "Mrs. Wickham, I think your father should see the surgeon at once."

Belle nodded, and took her father's arm. "Yes—thank you, Lieutenant."

She found Dr. Stevens waiting just inside the door. "Come along, Sky," he urged. "I'll have a look."

While the doctor attended her father, Belle headed for the wards to tell the men what had happened, but stopped at her office to regain control of her emotions. Finally she took a deep breath and left the little cubicle, stopping to talk to Rebekah and Pet, who were waiting with Davis near the doctor's office. "How's Father?" she asked.

"I'm all right—just a scratch," Sky said, emerging from Dr. Steven's surgery.

He stared at Davis and shook his head. "I never thought angels wore the uniforms of lieutenants in the Union Army, Lieutenant Winslow."

"You were right to think that, Mr. Winslow," Davis remarked. "But tell me, what can we do to help? Looks as if the whole city's on fire."

"I don't think that mob will be back," Sky told him. "When do you think your troops will get here?"

"In a day or two. Colonel Sizemore will be the officer in charge. He's a fine man. You can be sure he'll keep the peace." Davis shifted awkwardly, saying, "I'll go post the men around the hospital."

The Winslows stared after the retreating officer. "What is it about him that seems so strange?" Sky asked. "He doesn't look like himself."

Rebekah broke in. "He's older, that's all, and he's been through a lot. Come along now, Sky. You're going to get some rest, exactly as Dr. Stevens ordered. I imagine the house is burned, so Belle will find you a cot here."

Glad to have something to do, Belle busied herself finding places for everyone to sleep. She worked throughout the seemingly endless day, and didn't see Davis again. Pet informed her he'd gone with some of his men to check conditions in Richmond.

Later when Belle and her mother were alone, Rebekah asked, "Are you going to talk to him, dear?"

"I don't know, Mother," she replied, exhausted. Closing her eyes, she added, "I don't see what good it will do."

The next afternoon she was walking across the yard to another building when she saw Davis ride up and dismount. He headed straight toward her ward, and she knew intuitively he'd come to see her.

"Davis!" she called.

Winslow turned and came to stand before her. His eyes were tired, she noted as he pulled off his hat. "I'm leaving Richmond, Belle."

An unexpected twinge cut at his words. "Why—why are you leaving?"

"I have to rejoin my unit. Colonel Sizemore arrived with his troops, so you won't have to worry about any looters."

Their last meeting flashed into her mind, and she blushed. She had never expected to see him again—and certainly not under these circumstances. Struggling to find words, she said hesitantly, "You . . . saved them all, Davis. All those wounded men!"

"I doubt the mob would have burned the hospital."

"Yes, they would have. They were *insane.*" The silence was so strained she wanted to flee, but he stood there looking at her in that peculiar way of his. Finally she murmured, "Thank you . . . for the men, and for my family."

When he didn't respond, she flared, "*I* can't say any more! Why don't you *say* something?"

"I said everything to you the last time we talked, Belle." He smiled and asked slowly, "Do you remember?"

"Yes," she whispered, avoiding his eyes.

"What did I say, Belle?"

She raised her eyes and he saw the pain, fear—and something he couldn't put his finger on. Drawing a deep breath, she replied softly, "You said . . . that you cared for me."

"I did. And I haven't changed my mind."

"I . . . it won't ever—"

"Goodbye, Belle," he broke in, brushing her cheek with his hand. "You're the most wonderful thing in my life—and *nothing* is going to alter that—just like the poem says."

He turned to go, and she cried out impulsively, "Davis—will I see you again?"

He looked deep into her eyes and said in a firm voice, "You're going to see me for the rest of your life, Belle."

PART FOUR

# The Preacher

★ ★ ★ ★

## (October '65 – April '67)

CHAPTER TWENTY-FOUR

# The New Banker

★ ★ ★ ★

Belle shivered and snuggled her coat around her throat as she drove the rickety wagon down Cherry Street. Winter lurked over the horizon like a hungry wolf, and the sharp breath of a chill October wind numbed her hands and lips as she drew up in front of the Planter's Bank. Her father was waiting, sitting on the seat of a wagon in front of the bank. He leaped off to hitch her team as she got down.

"Cold this morning," he remarked. "I brought your heavy coat." He was wearing a brown suit, the cuffs of his trousers and sleeves slightly ragged. "Toby sent a wagon load of greens for the hospital, and we butchered that old red bull. I brought about half of it, but I can't answer for it. Probably tough as shoe leather."

Belle smiled and gave him a hug. "Bless you! The men are so tired of chicken! And they love greens."

The hospital had thinned out dramatically after Lee had surrendered at Appomattox, and now after six months, only those who were unable to travel remained. With the collapse of the Confederacy, there had been no support for the hospital, and it was only through the gifts of local farmers that the men were able to subsist. Most of the plantations had been stripped by the invading soldiers, despite efforts by Union officers to control them. Even the majority of the cattle and hogs had been "liberated" by the Yankee soldiers. The Winslows, however, had not complained, for none of their buildings had been destroyed, as was the case with some.

Sky took Belle's arm. "Come along with me and meet the new banker. I'll leave the greens and meat at the hospital after I finish here."

"Is Planter's Bank really out of business?" Belle shook her head sadly. "Richmond's almost a ghost town." The blackened outlines of buildings bore little resemblance to the former prosperous, busy city. Many lots were piles of rubble with only black chimneys left, pointing skeletal fingers at the sky. Of the remaining buildings few were occupied. Merchants with little to sell and weary of refusing to accept worthless Confederate money had closed their doors.

"It'll come back, Belle," Sky encouraged. "The bank's been taken over by a New York group. Now, let's meet the new president." He opened the door, adding, "His name is Moody. He's a strong Methodist, so we'll be seeing him quite a bit at church."

"Hello, Max," he greeted the middle-aged man sitting behind the front desk. "Like to see the president if he's not busy."

"I'll see, Mr. Winslow." The clerk disappeared through a door at the rear, and was back almost at once. "Be just a few minutes, Mr. Winslow. Sit down and have a cup of coffee." He motioned to the two, then spoke to Belle. "How are you, Mrs. Wickham?"

"Just fine, Mr. Wayne. Tell your wife the men were delighted with the cakes she sent."

"Wish we could do more—but it's a little slim right now." He sat down and took a sip of coffee, considering them over the rim of his cup. "Guess things are pretty tight at Belle Maison."

"Going to be a hard time, Max, but we'll make it with the help of the good Lord."

Wayne's face darkened. "Going to have to be God, I reckon. Lots of folks losing their farms. Been a steady stream of them coming in ever since Mr. Moody got here."

"Anybody we know?" Sky asked.

"Noel Roberts and Ben Lattimer. Good men, but they just had nothing to start with—and Milton Speers."

"Speers!" Sky was stunned. "Why, he's got one of the biggest plantations in Virginia!"

"All mortgaged—and most of his money was in slaves, you got to remember. He may get out of it with a little, but not much."

Just then someone came out of the president's office, and Wayne nodded, "You can go in now."

Sky and Belle were greeted by a huge man. "I'm Asa Moody," he said, coming around the desk. The man was at least six feet two or three, and massively built, more like a wrestler than a banker. His heavy square face held a pair of guarded eyes, and his hand, Sky noticed as he shook it, was soft and well cared for.

"Glad to meet you, Mr. Moody. This is my daughter, Mrs. Belle Wickham."

Interest flared in Moody's eyes, but he said only, "Happy to meet you, Mrs. Wickham. Here, sit down, and we can talk." He returned to his chair and leaned on his desk. "I understand you folks are Methodists?"

"Yes," Sky nodded. "We attended St. Paul's for the last few months, to be with the President. But we'll be back at St. Andrew's now."

"Fine! Fine! I'm a newcomer, of course, but Mrs. Moody and I were distressed to see the small crowd last Sunday. I trust you and I can work together to build the church."

"I'd like that," Sky responded. "Our place is about twelve miles out of town, but we're anxious to see the church prosper. Of course, we haven't had a minister for the last year, which hasn't been the best."

"I talked to the bishop about that," Moody commented. "He promised me he'd send a pastor within a month." His gaze shifted to Belle. "You've done an efficient job at the hospital, Mrs. Wickham, from all accounts. Now that it's being phased out, perhaps some of your talent could be used for the church."

Belle immediately knew Moody was aware of her past, and she gave him a steady look, saying, "I'll do what I can, sir."

"I'm sure you will. My wife is having a little get-together for the ladies of the church next Wednesday. She's very good at getting things organized. Six o'clock, she said. Please come, and tell your wife about it, will you, Mr. Winslow?"

"Yes, I will."

Moody nodded, and a change swept his countenance. Sky could see that the man had an aptness for cataloging things, putting every element into its proper place. The church business was taken care of—now on to the next item.

"I've been going over your notes." He opened a brown cardboard file, pulled a sheaf of papers out, and scanned them. "Some go back quite a ways, don't they?"

"Yes, they do."

As Sky answered the questions, Belle noticed that the banker's friendliness had been replaced by abruptness. The former president had been a warm, personal friend of Sky Winslow's, and most of their business was conducted in a casual manner—but that was not the way it was going to be with Asa Moody.

After checking the figures, jotting down several numbers on the sheet of paper in front of him, Moody looked up. "It's a serious problem, Winslow. Very serious." He rocked back in his chair, considered the sheet again, and frowned. "There's no way we can continue in this fashion."

"What do you propose, sir?" Sky asked quietly.

Moody spread his hands in a helpless gesture. "I came here to save this bank. In order to do that, I must be firm. Many will call me a hard man—but if the bank goes under, ninety percent of the planters in this county will lose their land. Slavery is the culprit, of course."

"I've always said that."

Moody gave him a hard look. "Strange that a man high in the Confederate government would have those sentiments. But, be that as it may, I am forced to stick to a certain line. It may seem harsh to you, but my board and I see no other way to save the bank—and the economy of the state."

"What do you propose?" Sky asked again.

"Basically, two things. First, all notes must be paid off in six months. Second, loans will be advanced only on money crops—which means primarily cotton."

Anger washed over Sky. "You couldn't have found a better way to ruin the planters if you'd spent your life thinking about it!"

Moody was not offended, and sat with his eyes fixed on Sky. "It's hard—but there's no other way. The strong will survive, and the weak will go down."

Belle spoke up. "I thought the Christian way was to help the weak, Mr. Moody."

Her quiet question broke through the banker's cold facade, and he lifted his head, a touch of color rising in his heavy cheeks. "That's theologically true, Mrs. Wickham, and I wish we could always do so—but in business we have to act in the best interest of the institution."

"Cotton got us in debt in the first place, Moody," Sky said. "It takes a lot of workers, and with the slaves gone, that means hiring white labor and freed slaves. We would have to borrow large sums—and then the crops might fail. It's little better than a slow way to bankruptcy. As for paying the notes off in six months, why, there's not five men in this county who can do that!"

Moody sat there shaking his head stoically. "As I say, it seems harsh, and I know I'll be vilified. But the board has spoken, and I must carry out their instructions."

Both Sky and Belle were sure the board would do exactly what Asa Moody told them, and not vice versa, but Sky realized it was useless to argue. He rose to his feet, took Belle's arm and said, "Thank you for you time, sir."

"I'm sure a man of your character will be able to weather this, Winslow," Moody told him, then slipped out of the role of banker. "We'll see you in the services this Sunday? Fine! I'm looking forward to our fellowship. When the new pastor comes, it seems likely we'll have to help support him."

As Sky and Belle left the office, Max Wayne gave them a sharp look, but said nothing.

"What did you think of him?" Belle asked when they got outside.

Sky shrugged, his face filled with doubt. "He's not going to bend one inch, Belle—not *that* man!"

"How can he be so amiable one minute, and so hard the next?"

"Guess he's learned how to throw up a shell. Maybe bankers have to be that way." He made an effort to smile. "But God is able. We'll be all right, Belle."

She gave him a quick hug. It hurt her to see the heaviness on his face. She smiled roguishly. "Mother and I will go to the ladies' meeting. We'll charm Mrs. Moody so completely she'll make that old husband of hers do exactly what we want him to do!"

Sky laughed. "Come out for supper this week. Spend a couple days if you can. Pet'll like having you help plan her wedding. It's still set for December, but she's tried every trick in the book to get Rebekah and me to move it up."

"I'm happy for them," Belle said. "They won't have much, but they love each other so much it won't matter, will it?"

Sky hesitated, for Belle rarely talked about marriage. Her own had been so brief that she had not had time to build a home. She seldom referred to her husband, and Rebekah had once confessed to Sky that Belle's marriage had been too hasty—which had been his own thought. Now he said carefully, "Beau still coming around trying to get you to marry him?" He knew very well he was, but wanted to get his daughter's reaction.

"Oh, I see him pretty often," she said, and bit her lip nervously. "He ought to marry one of those Huger girls. Both of them are madly in love with him."

"He doesn't seem interested," Sky replied. He peered quizzically at her. "What about you, Belle? Do you care for him at all? He's waited for you a long time."

The question disturbed her, and she shook her head. "It's all I can do to take care of my patients—and you!" she added. She turned and walked away, calling back, "Tell Pet I'll be out tomorrow."

Late the next afternoon, Belle went as promised and was surprised—and a little suspicious—to find Beau there. But he greeted her casually as she came into the house. "I didn't know you were coming, Belle!"

"Hello, Beau," she smiled. "I have to come home once in a while to get a good meal. How have you been?"

He shrugged. "Why, pretty well, I suppose. I get sick of my own company and inflict myself on my friends. An old bachelor can wear his welcome out in no time."

"Nonsense!" Sky exclaimed. "Always glad to have you. But I've got some bookwork to do before supper. Belle, Pet's out feeding those black chickens. I doubt if you'll be able to get her into a dress for her wedding, but you've got to try!"

Belle laughed, "Let's go see the chickens, Beau—and the blushing bride."

He joined her, and as they walked toward the barn, his eyes shifted across the field. "Looks like Tom and Dan fixing the fence over there. Where's Mark?"

"He's with Thad somewhere out looking for pigs and calves to buy."

Beau grinned ruefully. "Funny, isn't it, Belle? Six months ago we were all giving orders. Now we're building fences and hunting for pigs." He looked down at his own hands and sighed. "Guess I'm not cut out to be a planter."

She looked at him sharply. "Are you in trouble, Beau—with your plantation?"

"Isn't everyone?" he shrugged. "Your father told me about the visit to the bank. I got about the same story." Beauchamp was a volatile man, his emotions rising and falling like a yo-yo, and the mention of the bank sobered him. They walked along silently for a time as they made their way past the barn and turned toward the chicken yard where Pet was broadcasting feed to a flock of small black chickens.

"I've been thinking of selling out," he blurted out, adding, "This country is like a cemetery, Belle! Everything we used to love is dead."

"What would you do, Beau?"

"Oh, I don't know. Head for California, maybe. I hear San Francisco's a lively place." They were almost to the wire fence and Pet looked up and waved. "Belle," he said, his words rushed, "Haven't you ever thought of leaving here? Making a brand new start?"

"I've thought of it," she replied, and then seeing the hope leap to his eyes, added, "But I have my work—and this is my home."

"Not much left of it," he uttered dolefully.

"Look at my chickens!" Pet exclaimed as the couple reached them. "Aren't they beautiful?"

"Kind of smallish, aren't they?" Beau remarked.

"Don't say anything until you've tasted a genuine Black Winslow," Pet challenged. "They go all the way back to one of our ancestors—Miles Winslow. I'm going to get rich from them!"

she announced proudly. "You just wait till supper, Beau Beauchamp. You've never eaten fried chicken until you've eaten Black Winslow!"

Turning to Belle, she said, "I hate to leave the little flock, but I want to show you the pattern for my dress—and some samples of material we just got. Sure is a lot of fuss. Wish we could just run off and get married."

"Pet! Be sensible!" Belle admonished.

"Oh, I am! I just hate to wait."

They spent the next hour talking—Belle mostly listening—studying patterns, looking at material, and planning the wedding reception. In spite of Pet's desire for less "fuss," she was filled to the brim with details and jumped from one subject to the next almost without pausing to catch her breath. When Rebekah stuck her head in the door, calling out "Time for supper," they couldn't believe the time had flown by so fast.

"Gosh, Belle! You must be deaf, listening to me rattle on!"

Belle hugged her. "I'm happy for you, Pet. It'll be the most beautiful wedding ever held in these parts. Now, let's go downstairs."

They ate in the small dining room, and for once the entire family was present. Sky prayed a short simple grace, as was his habit, then said, "Pitch in. Beau, see what you think of this Black Winslow breed of chicken."

Beau tasted it, smiled and said, "Why, it's delicious, Pet! You may get rich after all." He grinned at Thad. "How'd you like to be married to a rich woman, Thad?"

"Wouldn't bother me a bit!" Thad announced readily. "I was reading in the Bible last week that in the Old Testament days when a man got married, he didn't do any work for a whole year."

"What *did* he do?" Beau questioned.

"Bible says all he did was please his wife." He grinned at Pet and asked slyly, "How'd you like that?"

Pet made a face at him and laughed. "I'm pretty hard to please, I'll have you know."

Rebekah looked around the table. "I doubt if there's another family in the country who's been as blessed as we have," she said. "Three sons—no, four, counting you, Thad! And all of you came out of the war alive and whole."

"That's right," Sky nodded. "I know so many who had only one son—and lost him." The thought sobered him and he looked at his family. "God be thanked, for it's His doing."

Tom asked quickly, "What did the new banker say, Pa?"

Sky told them the conditions Moody had laid down, and Tom exclaimed, "Why, that's crazy!"

"We can't make that much money in *five* years, much less in six months!" Mark added heatedly. "Nobody can meet terms like that."

"You know what he's doing, don't you?" Beau spoke up. "He'll foreclose on us, and then his friends from the North will buy our land cheap through the bank."

"I don't think he's planning that," Sky countered mildly. "He's a hard man, but I don't believe he's dishonest."

"Doesn't have to be," Beau argued. "It's not *illegal* for him to call our notes—but it's not right! You mark my words. The next few years the buzzards from the North will swarm all over Virginia, all over the South! They've already started. I'm not saying Moody's that kind. But there'll be plenty of crooks who'll take everything they can get."

"If Lincoln had lived, it would have been different," Sky said regretfully. "John Wilkes Booth did his best to ruin the South when he shot the President."

"Maybe," Beau nodded, his face sullen. "Andrew Johnson is a different sort. Never went to school a day in his life—and he's made it clear he hates Southern aristocrats. He'll wipe us all out if he can." He looked around and added in a different tone of voice, "We've got to take care of ourselves. Nobody else gives a pin about us!"

Mark leaned forward and asked curiously, "You're talking about the White Knights, Beau?"

Beau nodded emphatically, and struck the table with his fist. "Yes! It's the only way we're going to stay alive in the South. And I think you all ought to join us as soon as possible."

The White Knights was a secret organization that had sprung up throughout the state almost as soon as the war had ended. It was composed of young white men, almost exclusively ex-Confederate soldiers. Their meetings were secret, as was the identity of their members, but everyone had heard of their activities. They met at night and donned white hoods and capes, then rode throughout the area to leave warnings for those who broke what they considered the code of the South. For the most part, this seemed to mean Negroes who were "uppity" and demanded their new rights, but it also included whites who showed any favoritism for the former slaves or for the federal government.

Sky considered Beau, conscious that his family was waiting for him to respond. Many of his friends had already asked him to join the knights, and he knew that sooner or later he would have to make a decision. "I guess we've all heard about that organization, Beau," he said slowly. "Some of the thinking sounds good—but I won't join the White Knights."

"Why not?" Beau demanded.

"For one thing, I couldn't be a part of any movement that has to hide its face. If a cause is good, it's not necessary to hide one's identity. I was proud of the Southern Confederacy, and I never kept it a secret."

"I was proud, too, sir," Beau argued. "But this is different. The North is in control. Any man who acts against the laws will be arrested at once. That's why we wear masks. We've *got* to fight—and we can't do it if we're rotting in a Northern jail!"

Mark spoke up quietly. "Beau, we lost the war. Now we've got to make a place for ourselves back in the Union."

"Not me!" Dan snapped. He gave a defiant look around. "I think Beau's right. We've got to fight for ourselves."

"Dan sees it," Beau insisted. "And sooner or later you all will. Just wait until they start this *reconstruction* they're talking about! Why, there'll be laws you won't believe, Sky! I *know*!"

Sky stared at him, a hard clear light in his dark eyes. "I won't *ever* be a party to night-riding with a hood over my face, Beau. That's final."

Beau's face flushed. "Not speaking for myself, of course, but you may make some enemies. People look to you, and they'll expect you to support them."

"And if I don't, they may come calling on me some night?"

"I didn't say that, sir!"

"But it's the way it works, Beau," Sky countered. "When a group looks for power, they draw a little line around themselves and say, 'Come in with us—or you're the enemy.' Everybody is either a sheep or a goat—no middle ground. Beau, I'd advise you to stay out of it."

Beauchamp set his jaw stubbornly, but he said no more.

Rebekah broke in. "Pet, have you and Thad got all your wedding plans made?"

"Not much to do!" Thad said before Pet could speak. "She's going to have the dress and I'll have the ring, and the cake and refreshments will be there, but . . ." He grinned at Pet and jibed, "We'll have everything except a preacher to marry us!"

"Better elope and find one," Tom grinned. "The way I hear it, the preacher's the one indispensable element in a wedding."

"Well, you can set your minds at rest about a preacher," Sky offered, relieved at the change of topic. "Moody told us that the bishop promised him we'd have a new pastor within a month."

"And who will it be?" Rebekah asked.

"Moody didn't know. But if I've got the banker's number, he'd order a preacher the way he'd get a suit from a tailor! Right, Belle?"

"I wouldn't be surprised," Belle agreed. "He's that sort of man, I think." She smiled and added, "I can see his order now: 'Send one Methodist preacher. Conservative in views, stuffy in private life, willing to live on pittance. Ship C.O.D. to St. Andrew's Methodist Church. Merchandise may be returned if not satisfactory!' "

They all laughed, but she warned, "Wait and see!"

CHAPTER TWENTY-FIVE

# NEW PREACHER

★ ★ ★ ★

With the wedding only a week away, and no preacher in sight to perform the ceremony, Thad took quite a bit of ribbing. "Maybe you could get the Baptist preacher—or even the Episcopalian priest to tie the knot," Tom suggested to him and Pet.

"No, Pet's a pretty strong Methodist." He grinned at her. "She's not real sure a wedding's legal without a Methodist spouting the words. But I aim to be married even if I have to kidnap the governor to do the job."

Asa Moody had been promising the church the new pastor would arrive before Christmas, and on Sunday, December 11, he stood up in church and waved a letter. "Bishop Taylor's letter came yesterday. He's got the field narrowed down to two men, and the one he selects will be in our pulpit next Sunday morning!"

The congregation spent all week discussing the new preacher. As Max Wayne put it, "If that poor preacher could hear what's expected of him, he'd turn tail and run to the cannibals in Africa!"

Sky agreed. "Sounds as if they expect him to preach like John Wesley, work like a mule, and live on air."

The next Sunday, the church was almost full. It was cold, and the two wood-burning stoves glowed with heat as the congregation filed in much earlier than usual. People who hadn't been to church in months were there to evaluate the new pastor, and Moody said with some satisfaction to Sky, "Well, now, this is the way I like it! A good crowd!"

"I guess for some it's the first time since last Christmas. The preacher come in yet?"

"Yes. Last night."

"How'd he strike you?"

"Haven't met him yet. He pulled in late and went to the hotel—but he sent word he'd be here for the morning service." Discontentment spread across his face. "This thing hasn't been handled right, Winslow. I told the bishop the minister ought to go before the leadership of the church *first;* then if they didn't approve, it wouldn't be so awkward getting another man."

"Let's hope this one will be satisfactory so we won't have to trade him off on a newer model."

Time for the service to begin came, and Moody nodded at the song leader. They sang two songs, and Moody became more and more restless. Finally the front door creaked, and Moody stood up and said loudly, "Come right to the platform, Reverend! Your church is anxious to meet you."

A few of the congregation, mostly the Winslows, resisted the temptation to swivel their heads as the new pastor walked down the aisle. Belle heard Mary Ann Peterson whisper, "My! He's too good-looking to be a preacher!"

Pet leaned over to Belle. "Heaven help him if he's not married! He'd probably make *one* maiden happy, and the *rest* hate him!"

Belle smiled and looked up as the minister passed her. He was wearing the customary black suit, and he was tall, but she couldn't see his face. He kept his back to the congregation as he met Moody, conversing briefly.

Then he turned and every Winslow gasped. Davis Winslow!

"Did you know this, Sky?" Rebekah whispered.

"No!"

Moody looked at the congregation and said smoothly, "Since I've not had the pleasure of meeting our new pastor before now, I think it might be well if he introduced himself. This is Reverend Davis Winslow, and he tells me he is no stranger to some of you. Reverend, we welcome you to St. Andrew's!"

Davis stepped to the platform and placed his large black Bible on the pulpit. Looking out over the congregation, he seemed to be evaluating them as carefully as they were weighing him.

Finally he said in a strong voice, "This is the most exciting moment of my life—and the most awkward! A friend of mine told me how he felt the first time he met his future wife's parents. He said he was as nervous as a long-tailed cat in a room full of rocking chairs!"

A titter swept the congregation as Davis continued. Belle looked around to see that most of the church members seemed pleased, but *she* wasn't. She couldn't reconcile this man with the memory of the one who had kissed her, saying, "I care for you." She desperately wanted to flee, but she was trapped.

"We'll soon get to know each other better," Davis said, "but since Mr. Moody asked that I introduce myself, I will do so. I am thirty years old, not married, and in good health." This information quickened the interest of most women who had marriageable daughters, but he went on without a pause, "My parents are Mr. and Mrs. Robert Winslow of Washington, where my father is a representative in the Congress of the United States. Some of you may remember when I visited Richmond with my grandfather some years ago."

More whispers.

"Some of you are also remembering that my brother Lowell came to this city to testify on behalf of Thad Novak—who I see is here this morning."

Davis's eyes rested on the Winslows. Belle felt the weight of his glance. For a moment he hesitated before adding, "It is sometimes dangerous for a minister to have members of his family in his church, but my connection with the Winslows is distant. Sky, of course, is part of the Southern branch of the Winslows —while my own family has made its home in the north for many years."

Several of the church members who had looked on the new pastor with some satisfaction, now scrutinized him more closely. Smiles faded, and Davis lifted his chin, saying in a firm voice, "Yes, I am from the North—and as some of you know, I served as an officer in the United States Army."

A disturbance in the back interrupted Davis. Belle saw Hiram Coggins moving out of his pew, herding his wife and two children ahead of him. His face was red with anger as he turned to face Davis. "I fought you from Bull Run to Five Forks, Yankee—and I'll never darken the door of this church again until the bishop gets enough sense to send us a man of our own kind!" He turned and raked the congregation with his eyes, adding, "And the rest of you ought to leave like me and my family! You, Henry—you lost two boys and a son-in-law to the bluebellies! You gonna sit there and listen to a man who maybe killed them?"

Henry Cooper was a small man who rarely spoke in public. The church waited with bated breath. Would he follow Coggins? Henry had no sons left to carry on his name, and his wife was past childbearing age. His eyes met those of Davis. The new pastor did not flinch. A silence fell across the room, and everyone realized that the fate of the young minister lay in Henry's hands. Almost every family had lost some relation to the war—a son, a brother, a father—and the bitterness of four years of struggle hung heavily in the room.

Finally Cooper shifted his eyes to Hiram Coggins and in a mild voice said, "Hiram, my sons are gone. Nothing can bring them back. But I've got three girls, and I aim to do my best for them—and for this church." He gave Davis another quick evaluation and nodded, "The bishop's not a fool, Hiram. He knew what this man would be facing when he sent him—and he's my pastor until he proves himself unfit."

Coggins glared with outrage, whirled, and screamed, "Be a fool if you want! I refuse!" He stalked out, and two other families followed, giving Davis a withering look as they left.

Davis bowed his head for one moment. When he raised it, he spoke quietly to Henry Cooper. "Thank you, sir. I have some idea of what that cost you." Then he stepped out from behind the pulpit and came to the edge of the platform. There was an assurance in his manner that in no way resembled the young man who had visited the Winslows years earlier; and as he spoke, Sky measured him with fresh interest.

"You have been wondering why the bishop waited so long to send you a pastor. When he comes, he will no doubt inform you. I can tell you what he told me—that it was the most difficult choice he's ever made. Why send a Yankee, a former officer in the United States Army to pastor a people who have just fought a bitter war against the government?" A smile creased Davis's face, and it made him look younger. "That was exactly what I asked him. He had narrowed the choices to me and a man from South Carolina—a former chaplain in the Army of Northern Virginia. When he said he was sending me to Richmond, I begged him to choose the other minister!"

Not a sound was heard. Every eye was fixed on Davis. "He told me God had directed him in the matter, and that was that. But we discussed it at length, and I think I know what was in his heart. There are hard times ahead for the South—and he believes that only as the wounds of war are healed will there be hope for her people."

He searched their faces, and his voice took on a different tone. "I didn't want to come to this church. I have had no experience. I am a novice and will have to continue my biblical studies as I pastor the church. Frankly, I am not wise enough to pastor a church of this size; it would have been my desire to go to a small church for an apprenticeship. But the bishop persuaded me, believing there was something I could do here, and I will do my best. Some of you are already convinced I will fail—but I want to make you one promise. While I am your pastor, I will preach the truth as I hold it, and I will serve you as faithfully as I can. But if at the end of six months, a majority of the membership feels I should step down, I will do so."

Jaws dropped in surprise, and he smiled. "That's not the Methodist way, but I made it clear to the bishop it would have to be, and he agreed." Then he said, "Now I am introduced to you. You will introduce yourselves to me very soon, and as we serve the Lord Jesus Christ together, it is my prayer that our judgments of one another will not be whether we wore a blue or a gray uniform—but whether we manifest the simple love of the Savior of the world! In the time that is left, turn in your Bibles to the Gospel of Mark, chapter eleven, verse twenty-two."

He opened his Bible and read, " 'Have faith in God.' " He continued with several more verses, and then Belle heard him say, " 'If you have ought against any . . .' " Startled, she looked up to find his eyes fixed on her—and she knew he was thinking of the afternoon Chaplain Eubanks had preached on the same text at Chimborazo. It was that night Lonnie had died, and the memory of how Davis had held her in his arms and comforted her leaped into her mind. Her face flushed, and she dropped her head, unable to hold his gaze.

His sermon was brief, using scripture after scripture, illustrating the need for forgiveness. To nourish unforgiveness and hatred, he told them, would lead not only to rejection at the judgment seat of God but destruction to the person himself here, in this life. The person harboring the bitterness would be more harmed than the one to whom it was directed.

He closed his Bible and said quietly, but with an earnestness that shone in his eyes, "I know what bitterness and unforgiveness can do to a person—for it came very close to destroying me. I hated someone with such violence that it ate away everything good in me—and if Jesus Christ had not come in to save me and take away that hatred, I would probably be in hell right this minute. But He can heal the brokenhearted. He can set the captives free. And it is to that power, which He alone has, that I must look—and everyone in this church if we are to face the difficult days ahead."

Davis concluded with a simple prayer, and dismissed the congregation. Many left without coming to meet Davis as he stood at the front of the church, while others, including the Winslows, stayed to welcome him.

Belle desperately wished she could avoid him but realized she would no doubt be seeing him often.

"Got work for you, Preacher," Thad said after greeting Davis. "Pet and I are getting married next Friday afternoon at Belle Maison. Sure am glad you got here! I was beginning to think we'd have to import a Baptist!"

Davis smiled. "Guess it'll be a first time for all three of us. I'll probably be more nervous than the bride."

"I'm glad you're our pastor, Reverend Winslow," Pet enthused. "I *know* we're going to have a revival in the church. You wait and see!"

Sky thrust out his hand as he and Rebekah reached Davis. "I'm glad to see you—but you really gave me a jolt. Feels kinda strange having a relative as a pastor."

"You know too much about us," Rebekah added, taking his hand.

"And you about me," Davis responded, remembering when she had confronted him with his true identity. Then he nodded to Belle, who was hanging back, and said, "My grandfather will be happy to hear you're in my church, Mrs. Wickham. He thinks highly of you."

As always any reference to her time in Washington brought a flash of guilt, but she said only, "How is he?"

"Very well. He'll be coming to Richmond—or so he says. I'll be petrified to preach with him here!"

"He's very proud of you, I'm sure," Belle commented. "I remember what great friends you are."

Pet took Belle's arm and said eagerly, "Brother Winslow, Belle is helping me with the wedding plans. You two will have to get together and work it all out."

Davis caught Belle's look of doubt, and replied, "I'm afraid that responsibility will have to be Mrs. Wickham's. Just getting through the ceremony will take all my energy."

Relieved, Belle said simply, "It'll be a beautiful wedding."

Asa Moody had been visiting with some of the people and now came to Davis. "You'll have dinner with us, Reverend, won't you? We've got a lot to go over."

★ ★ ★ ★

Davis was thankful for the approaching wedding, for it kept him busy—and gave him breathing space. He was well aware that not only the members of his own church but nearly all of Richmond were discussing the bishop's strange choice. Davis met pastors of other churches, most of whom could not conceal the doubt in their eyes. Two ministers refused to speak to him, and five families of St. Andrew's resigned.

"Don't worry about them, Preacher," Moody encouraged. "They're soreheads and would only cause trouble. We're better off without them." Davis saw that the banker viewed the church members in much the same way he did his customers. He had the same careful way of looking at a man and estimating how much could be squeezed from him. But the man was cheerful, and being a Yankee himself he was delighted that Winslow had come.

Davis met with Belle at the Winslow home for dinner, at Sky's insistence, the following Thursday night. But before their meeting, Rebekah approached him as he was standing at the window in the parlor, waiting for Belle and Pet to come downstairs.

She smiled faintly and asked, "How do I address you? As Mr. Winslow . . . or Reverend Winslow . . . or as Lieutenant Owen Morgan?"

A sadness flashed in his eyes at her query. "I can't believe that somebody hasn't actually seen through my masquerade, Rebekah. Are they all blind?"

"I think we see what we expect," she replied. "Nobody thought about the overweight, smooth-shaven Davis Winslow when they looked at Owen Morgan. They saw a man skinny as a rail with gaunt cheeks and a bushy beard. Now when we look at you, we see an older version of the young man who was here a couple of years ago. You've put on weight, the beard is gone, and your whole manner is different from what we saw when we looked at Owen Morgan."

"It was wrong," he said. "I still feel somehow that it wasn't right to deceive all of you."

"Remember Joseph in the Bible, Davis? How his brothers feared him after he revealed himself to them? They'd sold him for a slave—and their lives were in his hands. He said, 'You thought evil against me, but God meant it unto good, to bring to pass, as it is this day, to save much people alive.' If you'd died in Libby, what would have happened when that mob came? I think they'd have burned it down—with the loss of many lives."

"I'm glad you can look at it in that light." He hesitated, then said, "I feel very—strange is the word, I guess—when I'm around Belle."

"What else do you feel about her, Davis?" Rebekah asked, her eyes fixed on him.

"I—I think you know," he murmured. "I love her. But she feels nothing for me."

"Don't give up. She's been very hurt."

"I know. But it's going to take a miracle."

"We need a sackful of miracles, don't we, Pastor Winslow?" Rebekah ticked them off on her fingers. "We're going to lose this place if God doesn't do something about the mortgage. You're going to be ousted from St. Andrew's if about 200 people don't learn to accept a Yankee as their pastor, and Belle is going to dry up if she doesn't learn to accept herself."

Davis opened his mouth to speak, but at that moment Pet and Belle entered. "Oh, Davis!" Pet cried, rushing in, "I've decided I can't call you 'Reverend'—except when others are around. After all, we *are* cousins, aren't we?"

"I suppose we're sort of fifth cousins, or something like that. My grandfather will be happy to inform you when he comes. First names are better, I think. Do you agree, Mrs. Wickham?"

"Of course." Belle gave him an odd look that Rebekah didn't miss, then asked, "Shall we go over the details of the wedding?"

Though Davis had declined at first to assist in the planning stage, the three spent an hour and a half working on details. In the midst of their discussion, Rebekah stuck her head in the door and called out, "Pet, come help me set the table."

Pet was happy to escape, saying, "You two will have to do the rest. Besides, Belle knows what I want."

Belle looked fondly at her sister's retreating form. "She's so excited about getting married. It's funny, she never cared at all for parties or dresses—like the rest of us did." She turned back to Davis, and her expression changed. "I feel so utterly—confused! When I saw you in church last Sunday, I wanted to die."

"I knew it would be hard on you, Belle," Davis replied. They were sitting opposite each other on overstuffed chairs. As always, her delicate, flawless beauty had a powerful effect on him, but he said only, "Are you angry, Belle—because I came?"

"N-no." She hesitated, then added, "But for some reason, I'm afraid, Davis. It's like living around a bomb that might go off any second!"

"Yes, I know the feeling," he said ironically. "But I sense that it won't be more than six months."

Startled, her eyes opened wide. "Why, I didn't know you were that sure to fail!"

"Like your mother says, Belle, we need a whole bunch of miracles."

"One happened when you saved the hospital," she responded. Her eyes sparkled at the thought. "I'll never forget how you came charging down the street into that mob!"

Davis smiled at her expression. "I wish everything were as

simple. Not too hard to fight that kind of battle. Others aren't so easy."

She dropped her eyes, feeling uncomfortable. She knew he referred to the two of them. Finally she excused herself. "I'd better help Mother and Pet."

Suppertime was delightful, and Davis felt accepted by the Winslows. He saw no malice in anyone—except perhaps Beau Beauchamp, who was a guest that night. During the meal he maintained an uncharacteristic silence, but after dinner when the men met in the parlor, he began to question Davis about the intentions of the North.

"I hear that Congress is going to demand that ninety percent of the population of any state will have to sign loyalty oaths before the state will be readmitted," Beau said. "And it's common knowledge that many powerful men want to establish a military rule over us."

"I haven't heard anything like that, Mr. Beauchamp," Davis replied. "I think it will depend on how the South behaves."

"We've got to obey—or take the consequences?" Beau shot back. "They'll strip us bare if we sit around with our hands in our pockets."

Sky tried to head off the argument he saw coming. "Beau, we have to be patient. We have friends in the government. It won't be easy, but for the next few years, we need to work at rebuilding our state."

Beau would not be pacified, and rose hastily, saying, "Thank you for the evening. I'll be at the wedding, Thad."

"Doesn't look as if he'll calm down, does it?" Tom remarked as Beau walked out. "And he's got lots of company."

"Somebody has to fight for the South," Dan defended heatedly. His cheeks were flushed, and he stared around defiantly, adding, "I'm going to join the White Knights myself!"

Sky stared at him hopelessly. He had argued the matter with the boy until there was nothing left to say, so he turned to Davis and stated, "I believe your father will have great influence concerning the reconstruction of the South." That ended the argument.

Davis left the Winslow home thinking about the various members of the family. Dan's determination to join the White

Knights showed a crack in the family solidarity, and Mark had told Davis about leaving soon to take a job on the Union Pacific railroad. The foundations were crumbling—not only for them but for the whole South.

The wedding on December 23 was everything Pet had hoped for. The house was filled with friends, and though the family had spent nearly all they had, Sky and Rebekah regretted none of it as Thad and Pet said their vows.

Pet, in a shimmering white gown, and Thad, in his new gray suit, made a handsome couple. The only nervous person seemed to be the minister!

After Belle and Davis had waved goodbye to the newlyweds, who had driven off for a week's honeymoon, Belle said, "I wasn't sure you were going to make it through the ceremony."

"Never was so scared in my life," he grinned. "They really are a fine couple, aren't they?"

"Yes. So in love!" She shook her shoulders in a gesture of rebellion. "I always feel let down after a wedding. It's always so anticlimactic! And there's all that cleaning up to do!"

"I'll help, Belle," he volunteered. "I'm probably better at that than I am at performing wedding ceremonies," he laughed.

"You did wonderfully well," she said. "Your words about marriage—did all that come out of a book?"

"Some of it," he admitted. "Remember the part about love that is real love never changing?"

Her eyes mirrored the doubts bombarding her. "You really believe that, Davis? That love is that strong?"

"Yes, I do," he murmured. "But it's rare to find that kind of love in this world of ours."

## CHAPTER TWENTY-SIX

# ON THE WAY HOME

★ ★ ★ ★

The ministry of Reverend Davis Winslow provided a form of recreation for the citizens of Richmond during the cold days of January and February. His congregation gathered regularly to hear him preach, and for every die-hard Confederate that shook the dust of St. Andrew's from his feet, one or two curious visitors would slip into a back pew and listen with curiosity to the Yankee preacher.

Dooley Young was one of the first of the rural people to come, but he did not slink in and claim a backseat. He marched into St. Andrew's with his hair slicked back, his huge mustache brushed, and an innocent look in his bright blue eyes. He sat beside Thad and Pet and sang with unbridled enthusiasm, though off-key. After the service he grabbed Davis's hand and with a vigorous handshake said, "Parson, that sermon took the rag off the bush! I ain't heard such good preachin' since I was a feeler for the Baptists over at Donaldson."

"A feeler?" Davis asked, puzzled.

"Why, shore! At all the baptizin's, I got out in the creek to feel around for a shallow spot for the dippin'!" Dooley grinned and passed though the door, calling over his shoulder, "You turn your wolf loose next Sunday morning, Reverend. I'll bring you a hull bunch of sinners to work on!"

True to his word, the following Sunday the church was banked by two pews of Dooley's relatives and friends, and they continued to attend. "Ain't got no preacher out our way," Dooley's mother, a short, heavy woman with eyes like her son, said. "You think you might hold us a camp meetin' come spring, Reverend?" A sadness clouded her pleasant face, and she added, "Real bad times. Our young'uns ain't got no school and no church. What's to become of 'em, Reverend?"

Davis couldn't forget Mrs. Young's question, and for several days he struggled for a solution. He decided to visit the settlement where Dooley's people lived. It was cold by the time he reached Belle Maison. Thad spotted him from where he was repairing a fence, and called out, "You're turning blue, Preacher! Get off your horse and come inside. We'll get you something hot."

Rebekah and Belle joined them at the kitchen table. "Good to see you," Rebekah nodded.

"I am really on my way to see the Youngs—but this coffee sure is welcome." Davis sipped some more of the bitter brew and said, "Mrs. Young told me there's no school for any of the children."

"That's bothering Dooley a lot," Thad said. "He's got a whole passel of brothers and sisters. From what I hear, those folks are having a hard time just making it through the winter. The men haven't been home to make a crop for a long time."

Davis finished his coffee, and asked for directions to the Young place. Thad scratched his head and began giving some rather lengthy directions. "Ah, this is too complicated. Guess I'll have to go with you."

"I'll go, Thad," Belle spoke up, then covered her impulsiveness by saying, "Hitch up Maggie to the light buggy while I change clothes." She dressed warmly in woolens, put on a heavy overcoat, pulled on a stocking cap and knitted gloves and hurried downstairs. "I'll be back soon, Mother," she called to Rebekah.

"Take some of these cookies to Asa and the rest of the children," Rebekah suggested. "Have a good time." She watched out the window as Belle crossed the yard to where Thad and Davis were waiting, got into the buggy, and the two disappeared down the road.

The air was cold for March, but there had been little snow. "Never been down this road," Davis commented. He saw someone plowing far back off the road, and when the man waved, Davis waved back.

"That's Toby," Belle nodded. "He's going to make his own crop this year. He worked out some arrangement with Father." She hesitated. "If we have to move, I suppose he'll have to go as well."

"I hope that doesn't happen."

"I think it will." A note of finality edged her voice. "There's no way we'll have the money to pay the bank, Davis. I told Thad once that it was foolish putting all the work he does into a place he'll not be able to keep, but he just told me, 'I'm not giving up on God.' "

"Good way to think," Davis replied. "I'm doing about the same thing, I guess. Plugging along with the church work, all the time something's telling me, 'Take it easy! You won't be here more than a couple more months.' " He changed the subject abruptly: "What about the hospital, Belle?"

"They closed everything except one small wing. Most of the patients had left, and there wasn't enough work for all of us."

"Thousands of men will never forget you, Belle," he said quietly. "I'm one of them."

She brushed his comment aside and began speaking of happenings around the farm. They left the main road, and soon were on a makeshift, rutted lane leading into the thick scrub timber. That gave way to larger trees. By now Davis was quite lost. "If you leave me here, I'll never get home," he said ruefully.

"These are real backward people," Belle told him. "Poor as church mice and proud as Lucifer! They're very suspicious of outsiders."

"They might not take kindly to a poor Yankee invading their territory," Davis said. "But I haven't been able to forget Mrs. Young's question."

They continued winding their way through. "Look! I think I see light ahead," Davis said.

"There's the house," Belle pointed as they left the heavy woods and entered a cleared field. "Isn't that Dooley riding over there?"

"Looks like it."

The rider waved his hat, and rode full tilt to meet them. "Well, I wish to my never!" he exclaimed with a wide grin. "If it ain't the preacher and Miss Belle! Come on in. I reckon you're just in time for some dinner."

"We can't—" Davis broke off as Belle's elbow jabbed into his ribs. He caught the tiny shake of her head, and amended his speech. "Well, you can trust a preacher to drop in right at dinnertime, can't you now?" As Dooley turned to dismount and enter the house, Belle advised, "Don't ever refuse what people give you, Davis—especially those like the Youngs. They may not have much, but they'd be hurt if you didn't share it."

"Good thing you came along," Davis told her as he helped her out of the buggy. "Keep an eye on me, will you?"

Children of all ages sprinted from every direction. They scooted through the front door, and raced from around the house. One tow-headed boy of about ten jumped out the window over the porch and slid down the sloping shed roof, falling loosely on the ground, then got up and joined the others, staring bashfully at the visitors. Mrs. Dooley emerged from the house, smiling enthusiastically. "Come in the house, Reverend—you young'uns make a path, for mercy's sake! You act like you ain't never seen a preacher before."

Once inside, Davis and Belle were almost forced to sit down by the burst of hospitality Mrs. Young considered good manners. The room was large and scantily furnished with items made by a clever home craftsman. The floor consisted of wide pine boards, with cracks so wide Belle wondered how the tiny feet of the baby tottering along the floor kept from getting caught in them.

Dooley leaned against the wall, and the children scattered to corners where they could get a clear view of the visitors. All had an almost comic family resemblance—undersized, the same pale blue eyes, yellow hair, and large ears, including the girls. Davis commented later, "They all look like sugar bowls with two big handles!"

"Pa'll be in directly," Dooley said. "He jest came in from trotlining over on Ten Point. Got a big mess of bullhead catfish. Lem'me name all these here young'uns for ya." Everyone had two names—Asa Roy, Billy Joe, Mary Sue . . . When he had introduced them each one, he grinned. "You won't be able to recall which is which. I get mixed up my own self sometimes."

Mrs. Young and two of her daughters, both about fifteen, scurried around preparing the meal, while Dooley kept Davis and Belle entertained with tales of his hunting feats. Davis was entranced by the little man, and Belle smiled as Davis set one of the smaller Youngs on his lap while Dooley told about his dogs—all awesome, it seemed.

"What's your best dog, Dooley?" he asked.

"Guess I'd have to say it's ol' Blue," Dooley drawled. "He's gettin' on a bit, but all in all, he's about the best bird dog ever drew breath." He scratched his head, remembering an incident. He went on to tell a tale of ol' Blue's feats, how he'd chased a bunch of quail into a hole and then released the birds one by one so Dooley could shoot them with his shotgun. The longer he talked, the longer and wilder the story became.

By now Dooley had Davis's rapt attention. The extraordinary exploits of such a dog must have been something to behold!

Belle suddenly loosed a peal of laughter, a silvery sound, that surprised Davis. His face grew red as saw that everybody in the room was grinning at him. "Dooley Young!" his mother admonished as she came sailing out of the kitchen with a long wooden spoon waving in his direction, "Don't you be aggravating the pastor with them lyin' stories of yours!"

Davis joined in the fun at his expense. He didn't mind. It made the room seem less alien now. The door opened shortly, and a short man in worn overalls entered. Reuben Young greeted the visitors, and seeing the meal of catfish, greens and cornbread already on the table, invited them to be seated. The long table was made of rough pine planks. No two plates were alike, and the tableware ranged from a silver fork, black with age, to Dooley's Arkansan toothpick, a Bowie knife over a foot long that he had carried all through the war.

Davis enjoyed the dinner immensely and complimented Mrs. Young. After the meal they sat around drinking sassafras tea, a new experience for Davis, and he said, "Sure is good tea. Guess you wonder why I came out here. I've been thinking about something you said in church last Sunday, Mrs. Young."

"Me, Reverend?"

"Yes. You said the children are getting no schooling."

"That's a sad truth, Brother Winslow," Reuben nodded. "We had a little school here—'bout four years ago, wasn't it, Ada? But the schoolmaster went off with Jackson and got hisself killed at Chancellorsville."

"Sech a fine young man!" Ada remarked. "But they wouldn't be no way to pay anyone anyways."

Dooley speared a biscuit with his huge knife, spread some honey over the fragments and transferred a morsel to his mouth. "I sure have been grievin' over these young'uns, Preacher. We thought about movin' to town—but we're not town folks."

Davis shifted uncomfortably on the bench he shared with Belle and three of the children. He wanted to help, but didn't want to raise false hopes. *These people have been hurt too much already,* he thought, and had almost decided to say nothing of an idea that had been in his mind for the past week.

"You have an idea, Reverend Winslow?" Belle asked, and he gave her a quick glance, long enough to see that she was encouraging him to do anything he could to help the Youngs.

"Well, I'm not sure," he replied. "I've got a diploma somewhere back home that says I'm qualified to teach a little bit. I've never done it, but I'd be willing to give some time if you think it would help the children."

The room became so still Davis thought he'd violated one of the obscure mountain credos. Both parents stared at him as if he had dropped out of the moon. Dooley and the rest of the family as well seemed struck by Davis's words.

He dared not look at Belle, and mumbled, "Well, I just thought it would be—"

He broke off as Mrs. Young began to cry. Mr. Young patted her shoulders, explaining to Davis, "Preacher—if you could teach my kids to read and write—"

Dooley raised his head, his face sober. "Preacher," he said, "I ain't never been a religious man. But for months I been listenin' to my mama pray that God would send somebody to teach these young'uns. I never thought it would happen." He stopped, then said huskily, "But I don't reckon I'm ever gonna forget that the good Lord ain't forgot about us out here in the woods!"

Davis reddened. "I'm glad to hear you say that, Dooley—but really, you're all making too much out of my offer! I can't come full time. I thought we could work out some sort of schedule when I could take a few days off from the church—say, three mornings a week, maybe—and at least do something." He laughed. "It'll be the first time my education's done much good."

"Reverend, would it be all right if a few other childrens came along with ourn?" Reuben asked. "We got some kinfolk who're jest as anxious as we are to get some larnin' for their childrens."

"Why, not at all. As I told you, I'm not much of a teacher. I guess I can do pretty well with the reading and writing, but arithmetic is like a foreign language to me."

Belle looked at the eager faces around the table and said impulsively, "I'm a terrible speller—but I did very well with arithmetic." She smiled at Davis. "Could you use an assistant, Reverend Winslow?"

"Why—of course!" he nodded in delight.

When they left the house, it was decided that on three mornings a week Dooley would bring the children to Belle Maison for lessons. That would cut down on the long trip for Davis, and Belle volunteered to get a large vacant building in order. They both felt a little overwhelmed.

"I'm a little frightened, Belle!" Davis confided. "We've got them all excited—and I don't have any idea how we're going to do it."

Belle was feeling very warm and happy. "We can do it, Davis! I *know* we can!" She talked rapidly about the job that lay ahead—desks, benches, maps and supplies. Her face was alive with anticipation—just like the old days when he had first seen her. Her eyes were clear, without the veil of reserve he had grown accustomed to, and her cheeks glowing, both from the cold air and the excitement that bubbled over.

He stopped to rest the horse at a small creek when they were halfway to Belle Maison. She turned to face him, unconscious of the picture she made in the blinding sunlight. Her hands flew as she described the plan for the schoolroom, and once unconsciously gripped his arm. Her lips, reddened by the sharp air, were tender and enticing.

All of a sudden she gasped with shocked surprise and embarrassment. "Good heavens!" she laughed. "I haven't taken on like this for years!"

"I'm glad we're doing this project together, Belle," he said, smiling. "I would never have offered if you hadn't urged me on. It's going to be good, isn't it?"

She nodded, tiny lines furrowing her smooth brow as she thought about possible opposition. "But—will the church let you do it, Davis? Some of the members are very jealous of the pastor. They think since they're paying his salary, he ought to spend his time with them."

"I have no idea, Belle," he shrugged. "Never been a pastor before. But I don't think this project is an accident. I believe God is in it, and it's about the clearest sign He's given me that I'm on the right track."

She studied him a moment. "Is it that way with you? You seem so confident about things."

"Not about details, just the big things." He watched the horse drink, trying to think how to say what he was feeling. "I know that God came into my life and made me a whole man. I know that He wants me to serve Him. And I know He brought me to this place for this particular time. The rest . . ." He smiled at her. "Well, I'm just walking in what little light He gives me, Belle. I was beginning to get a little desperate—but this idea of a school! And you offering to help!" He reached out and put his hand over hers. "I'm thankful for you, Belle!"

She felt the warmth of his hand, and was swept by a haunting guilt—a black, horrible, dreary, hopeless feeling that never left her for long. She shivered and lifted her eyes to his. He saw the pools of pain and grief.

He had prayed for an opportunity to speak to her, had asked for wisdom to say words that would lead her to the truth. Now he was afraid—afraid that he would overstep the boundaries she had placed around her spirit. If he crossed those lines, would she build the walls higher and stronger than ever?

But her eyes were begging for help and assurance, so he plunged in. "Belle, I've got to talk very straight to you. You may hate me for what I'm going to say, but God has given me a love for you—not just as a man for a woman, though that's there, too—but that other kind of love that a man can have for another person."

His voice was low, and seemed to rake along Belle's nerves, and she shuddered. His hand was still on hers and she knew he could sense her weakness. Two forces pulled at her: the strong impulse to shake him off, to insist they hurry on home. It was the same power that had driven her to hide behind a facade that shut out everyone. Words throbbed in her mind: *Don't listen to him! He wants you to be something you can never be!*

The other force was something new—an intense desire to listen, to let him bring her out of the darkness that had blighted her life for years. She loathed herself. And something within her cried: *This is your last chance!*

Davis's voice broke into her thoughts. "Belle, I hated you after Lowell died. You and the South. I wanted to kill you all." The memory of his past brought pain into his eyes. "And then by some miracle I wound up in the hospital. God met me there. He was so gracious, Belle! I didn't find Christ the day the chaplain spoke of forgiveness, but it was a first step. I called on Him later, in the middle of Oak Street in Washington—and Jesus Christ came into my life."

Belle closed her eyes and whispered, "I've heard that so often—but what does it *mean,* Davis? How can a man who died two thousand years ago come into your life?"

With deep compassion he said, "That's part of the miracle, Belle. The greatest miracle of all is that God became a man, and His name in the flesh is Jesus. None of us can really understand that, no matter how learnedly we may speak of it. God in man! It's too big for us, Belle, and so is the other miracle. In somewhat the same way that God put himself into a human body, Christ will put himself into us if we will let Him."

"How can I—after what—I did!" Belle began to sob in great choking cries.

"You committed adultery?" he asked. "So did the woman at the well in John four, but Jesus forgave her. The woman in chapter eight of John was *taken* in the very act of adultery, yet Jesus said, 'Neither do I condemn thee.' You see, Belle, you think your sin is *worse* than anyone else's, that you're not as *good;* therefore God doesn't love you. But that's not true! If you could believe just *one* of the hundreds of God's promises to us, you would see how much He loves you. Romans five says: 'But God commendeth his love toward us, in that, while we were yet sinners, Christ died for us.' Can't you believe that, Belle? Christ died for *you*! He *commendeth* His love, He proved it by dying for you."

He spoke earnestly about the cross, and she wept until it seemed as if her body were torn in two. "Belle!" he encouraged, "stop doubting God. Just ask Him to save you. That's all I did—that's all any of us can do. I'm going to pray for you, and I want you to pray for yourself. Just call out to Jesus as if you were drowning and He were standing there watching you, waiting for you to call!"

Davis prayed, softly and loudly. Time went by and he was conscious only of his strong desire to see her surrender to God. Tears flowed as he poured out his heart for Belle.

Then slowly, quietly he became aware of the silence around them. Belle had stopped crying, and her eyes, no longer filled with pain and guilt, were alight with wonder and joy.

"Belle?"

She felt weak—as if she had just come through a long illness and the world seemed distant and fragile. But she had a peace in her heart unlike anything she had ever known. Her lips parted and she asked, "Is this what it's like? I feel so—so free, Davis!"

He threw his arms up in a shout of joy and wrapped them around her. "Yes! Yes, Belle, that's what it's like! Like coming out of a dark, foul prison into a room filled with clear light!"

She touched her cheek tentatively. "Will it last, Davis?"

"Yes! It will last, Belle. You've come into the house of God—and you'll never leave it!"

## CHAPTER TWENTY-SEVEN

# THE WHITE KNIGHTS

★ ★ ★ ★

"She's a different girl, Rebekah," Sky commented. The two were sitting outside the kitchen watching Belle playing a game of Red Rover with the children. "Never thought working in a school would make her so happy."

"It's not that," Rebekah said. "It goes much deeper. The school is just an outlet."

"Yeah, I know—but that schooling thing really helped Davis get the confidence of the church—and it's given new life to Belle." He frowned, "Of course, it's been hard too . . ."

She nodded. The school had been so successful that even Asa Moody and a few others couldn't protest the pastor's time spent on the project. For it had brought new people into St. Andrew's—not just the Youngs and their relatives, but townspeople who couldn't believe a graduate of Yale University would drive into the country to teach a bunch of ragged children.

Dooley Young's conversion played a major role in the church's attitude. He had been soundly converted, and was now one of the most visible—and audible—members of St. Andrew's. What he lacked in theological knowledge, he made up for with energy and enthusiasm. He took scripture quite literally, and was known "to go out and compel them to come in"!

On the first day of school, Davis and Belle were flabbergasted to see thirty-two children, ranging from age five to eighteen. The teachers attacked the project with enthusiasm. Soon several members of St. Andrew's caught the fire and volunteered to help in any way.

Asa Moody dragged his feet at first. But when he saw what effect the school had on the church and the publicity it brought St. Andrew's, he began underwriting expenses.

Things flowed smoothly until Toby broached a touchy subject. The former slave had helped a great deal with the physical needs of the school, and it was natural he would think of his own people. But the question caught Davis off guard on his way home one day.

"Mistuh Winslow," Toby said, hailing him from the roadside, "kin I talk to you?"

"Why, certainly. What is it, Toby?"

"I been thinkin' 'bout my boy, Wash." He bit his lip, struggling for words, then looked Winslow right in the eye and declared, "I wants my boy to learn how to read an' write."

It dawned on Davis that he himself had not given one thought to the black children. No one had. Of course there were fewer blacks because many had left for the North, but looking at Toby, Davis felt a flush of guilt for not having anticipated the need.

"Well, I don't see why we can't do something about that, Toby," he replied. "We've got plenty of room around here, empty buildings that could be turned into another school—and the church members have been willing to help."

Toby's eyes mirrored his unbelief. "Dey won't be so quick to he'p black young'uns," he prophesied.

That, Davis soon discovered, was an understatement. The first explosion came when Asa Moody roared at Winslow, "What! Why, you *can't* be serious, Pastor!" He had been sitting behind his desk at the bank where Davis had cornered him, and he shot up from his chair. "In the first place, that's the job of the federal government—and *they'll* take care of it! In the second place, if you do a fool thing like that, you'll lose most of the goodwill you've built up since you've been here." When Davis stubbornly insisted that he was going to do it, he saw another side of Asa Moody. The big man's eyes narrowed, and he said in a steely voice, "Winslow, remember your promise to the church? If they didn't vote to keep you on after six months, you'd leave?"

"I remember."

"Well, you start a school for black kids, and you can pack your bags. I'll vote against you myself!"

Most of the church members had not been so adamant, but the Sunday after the black school started, the attendance was down by at least one-third. Moody had immediately called a meeting, where Davis was confronted by six of the leading men of the church—all handpicked by Moody, to be sure. After a stormy two-hour session, Moody had left with an ultimatum—get out of the business of educating black children, or be prepared to find another church.

Toby came to him, his face stiff. "Reverend Winslow, I knows you done yo' best—but dey ain't no need fo' you to git yo'self run off. I 'spect we bettuh close de school."

"Like blazes!" Davis Winslow looked up at the giant black and said, "I'll see them all in—in China before I close that school!"

The Winslows, of course, stood behind him. However, at supper one night an unpleasant fact was mentioned. They had been talking about the future, and Mark remarked, "Well, if we get kicked off Belle Maison by Asa Moody next month, it's pretty plain that the black school will go as well."

"We're not whipped yet, Mark," Sky stated. "I've made applications for loans at several out-of-state banks."

"If we can't get a loan from our local bank, Pa, how can we get one from people who don't know us?"

His logic was hard, but Sky was not deterred. "I've asked the Lord to help us keep this place, and I believe He will—but if not, I'll put you in a wagon, Rebekah, and we'll hit the trail to Oregon."

"We did it once," Rebekah smiled fondly. "And you're as good a man now as you were then."

Belle said little, but the next day she broached the subject to Davis. They had sent the pupils home, and were now sitting outside the spring house, watching the swifts fly around the house. "Davis, what if we do get evicted? How would that please God?"

He looked at her sharply. She was not angry, only puzzled. "Well, you do something else, Belle. This is a big world, and we serve a big God. If He wants to put the Winslows someplace else, you can bet that place will be just the ticket. You know what the Bible says: 'All things work together for good to those who are the called according to his purpose.' "

"I guess I just don't know what His purpose is," she smiled faintly.

"Neither do I for the most part. But we'll find out soon enough. It looks pretty grim, but one thing is certain: When things get bad enough, they can't get any worse."

But things did get worse three days later. Sky woke up one morning to find a note pinned by a knife to a tree in the front yard. He pulled the knife free, opened the note, and read: *Get rid of the nigger-loving Yankee preacher and his school—or we'll come calling*. It was not signed, but at the bottom was a poor drawing of a helmet with a plume, and under it was written *The White Knights*.

His eyes blazed and he stalked around the house, rage filling him as it had not done in years. He slowed his steps, trying to calm himself as he approached the school and walked inside. "Reverend Winslow," he said, "will you step outside for a minute?"

Davis was conjugating the verb "to eat" for a small group. He handed the chalk to the oldest girl, saying, "Caroline, see how far you can go with this verb."

"What is it?" he asked when they were outside.

Sky handed him the note and watched carefully as he read it. Davis handed it back, saying, "I've got quite a collection of this sort of garbage."

"You've gotten them too?"

"Ever since the school started. That didn't surprise me, but I didn't think they'd threaten you." He studied Sky's angry expression. "It may be best if we move the school—leave you out of it."

"Not likely!" Sky snorted. "I almost wish they would come calling, Davis. I'd like to pull a few masks off and see what kind of men hide behind them—but I guess I already know."

"Are you going to tell your family?"

"Yes. They've got a right to know what's happening."

That evening after supper, Sky told them. He had sat at the meal, enjoying their banter, and the family's discovery of Belle's new joy. Finally, he leaned forward and said, "I hate to bring a sour note, but there's something I need to warn you about. This morning there was a note pinned to the big oak in front of the house."

Mark lifted his head and demanded, "What was it, Pa? The White Knights?"

"Yes. I wanted you to know, because they may come for a visit."

"I hope I'm home, Pa!" Tom exploded. "I'd like to furnish the reception."

Dan remained mute, rebellion evident in his face. He had been away from home often, several nights at a time, and Sky was fairly certain his son had been with Beau.

"What'll we do if they come, Sky?" Rebekah asked.

"Have to see how it goes, I guess," he replied, sadness edging his voice. "Not all knights are bad men. Just misled. But some are troublemakers filled with hate left over from the war. They're the ones who'll raise the ruckus."

"They made one of their 'visits' two nights ago to Little John's cabin," Thad said. Little John had been one of the Winslow slaves. He had taken his wife and four children to a cabin on the old Speers plantation.

"What happened, Thad?" Mark asked.

"They came after dark and pulled Little John out of the cabin. Said he was getting too uppity, so they tied him to a tree and whipped him. Told him the next time he'd get a bullet."

"Oh, how awful!" Pet cried. "They wouldn't really shoot him, would they, Papa?"

"May come to that," Sky replied. "But if they come here, I want you young firebrands to show some judgment. Don't open up on them and start another war."

They said little about the note from the knights for the next few days, but Dan became more withdrawn. Belle noticed it, and found him staring out of the parlor window one rainy day. She pinched his arm playfully. "Dan, you ought to find yourself a sweetheart. You need something to worry about. How about that

McClain girl, the one with the big eyes. I think she's going to give some man a lot of grief. Why don't you have a try?"

Dan turned swiftly, picked her up and carried her across the room and set her on the high mantel over the fireplace. Grinning, he admonished, "You talk too much."

"Dan! Let me down!" she pleaded.

"Nope. Stay there until you improve your manners," he commanded, walking away.

"Oh, Dan, *please* don't leave me up here! I might fall!" she begged. The mantel was narrow and she kept her balance only by pressing back against the bricks.

He laughed, reached up and plucked her down. "That's the way to treat a talky woman, I guess."

She looked up at him, taking in the fine blue eyes and the trim strong body. "You are a handsome old thing," she smiled. "You can do a lot better than Ellie McClain."

He sobered, and said quietly, "Guess my prospects aren't too good, Belle. Another month and I'll be leaving."

"Oh, Dan, it may not come to that. Father may get a loan that'll tide us over."

"I hope so, Belle—but I'm leaving anyway. Going to Texas."

"Texas! Why Texas?"

"Better than here." He grimaced bitterly. "Don't tell the folks. I haven't said anything to them."

"Does it have anything to do with this White Knight business, Dan?"

"No. But I think Beau and the knights are right and the folks are wrong."

"What about whipping Little John?"

"Oh, that may happen, but if enough good men take part, they will make sure everything is done right."

She put her hand on his arm, saying gently, "Dan, I hope you don't go. I hate to see the family breaking up. There's Mark going to work on the railroad, and now you're talking about leaving."

"Guess the war ruined everything for us, didn't it?" Then he looked directly at her and asked, "What about you, Belle? What'll you do?"

She knew he was curious about her sudden happiness, and

she said with a trace of embarrassment, "I'll be all right, Dan. After I lost Vance I just crawled into some kind of black hole and told the world to leave me alone."

"You've sure changed," he commented. "Is it that Yankee preacher?"

She flushed and hesitated. Slowly a smile softened her lips. "He's been a big help to me, Dan. He helped me find my way back."

"Are you in love with him?"

"Oh, Dan, I don't know!" Belle exclaimed. "I've just got my life pulled together. I was so far from God and so unhappy, and Davis showed me how to find Him. It's too soon to talk about things like that—and, anyway, we were talking about you, not me."

"I'll be leaving, Belle," he shrugged. "I feel out of place around here."

Three nights after this conversation, the White Knights struck.

Belle and Davis had spent all evening going over plans for the school. Since it had been so late, he decided to stay over. Belle went to bed and fell asleep as soon as her head hit the pillow.

She awakened instantly out of a deep sleep by the sound of several gunshots in the distance. Jumping out of bed, she ran to the window and saw a glow in the east. She heard others calling down the hall, and threw on her clothes and raced down the stairs just as her father and the other men left the house.

"What is it?" she asked her mother.

Rebekah was pulling on her coat, and paused only long enough to say, "Trouble at the quarters." She left, and Belle hurried after her. Davis was ahead with her father, and when she glanced back, she saw Pet and Thad running out the door.

The moon was full, casting a golden light over the pathway leading to the quarters. As they came closer they could hear the horses stamping and blowing and men calling out.

As she dashed past the hog lot, Belle saw the flicker of torches immediately behind the small rows of cabins lying in a shallow hollow. When she reached the crest, she paused, restrained by Rebekah and Pet.

Between the rows of cabins facing each other, men on horseback were drawn up in two rough lines—all bearing torches and wearing white hoods with holes cut for eyes. Six men had dismounted and two of them watched as the others dragged a black man across the yard.

"It's Toby!" Belle cried. Even as she did, she saw her father and the other men move down the hill toward the houses. She tried to get closer, but Rebekah held her back.

"Hold it right there!" Sky's voice rang out.

The men dropped Toby abruptly.

Sky moved into the space between the two lines of mounted men, holding his pistol. Davis was at his side, but unarmed. Sky's sons and Thad stopped at the end of the rows, fanning out. Mark had a pistol, the rest rifles.

Two hooded men on foot wheeled to face Sky and Davis, about ten feet away. One knight, dropping his hand to the pistol in his holster, yelled, "Winslow—get your people out of here!"

Sky stood like a pillar, the high planes of his face outlined by the flickering shadows cast by the torches. He held the Colt loosely at his side, the careless ease of his body giving a sinister warning.

"You're on my land," he said evenly; and although he didn't raise his voice, it carried across the yard. "Let that man go and get off."

The large man shook his head and cried out, "You've been warned, Winslow! We aim to show you that this is a white man's country!" He turned to the twin lines of riders, and the sight of them spurred him on, for he turned his head and said to the four men holding Toby, "Get on with your business!"

They obeyed instantly, one of them jerking a length of rope around the post; the other, throwing a lashing around the struggling Toby.

Sky said in almost a conversational tone, "If that man is not released at once, Henderson, I'll put a bullet in you." He had recognized the voice of Rance Henderson, a small-time local lawyer. He'd had dealings with him several times during the war, never pleasant. Henderson had not been in the army, though he had been an agitator to pull out of the Union.

Henderson laughed, not seeming to care that he'd been recognized. He waved a big hand at the two lines of armed men and jeered, "I guess you haven't counted how many men are here, Winslow. Now, you just move on back. This is just a warning visit." He motioned with his hand, "Tie the nigger up."

Belle had often heard of her father's youthful exploits, and knew his expertise with a pistol. But neither she nor anyone else in the crowd was prepared for what happened next. In a movement so smooth it was almost impossible to see, like the strike of a rattlesnake, he drew his gun and fired.

Henderson screamed and swung to one side, sending the torch he held in his left hand cartwheeling. The bullet had struck with deadly accuracy. He threw the other hand up to ward off the next bullet, but Sky calmly lowered his gun, holding it casually at his side. "I could have put that bullet in your brain instead of the torch, Henderson," he said. Then the anger he'd bottled up boiled over, and he lifted his voice as he looked over the mounted knights. "You men are wrong! I think some of you are my friends and neighbors—but I'm no friend of any man who covers his face and tortures helpless people. Now got off my land!"

The echo of his voice had not died before one of the men called out, "Let's give *him* a dose of the whip!" Several voices rumbled approval, and Mark warned from where he stood, "That one's my meat when the ball starts." The man who had spoken snapped his head around and spat out, "I ain't afraid to die, you nigger lover! Let it start, Henderson!"

Henderson half turned, facing Sky again. He was noted for his fits of rage, and had shot two men in duels. Every man there knew the Winslows had no chance whatsoever if Rance gave the signal—and most of them expected him to begin the action.

But Henderson could not forget the unearthly speed of Sky's draw, and shivered as he thought of the instant shot that had blasted the torch out of his hand. He hesitated, longing to kill the man who stood in front of him, but unable to shake off the knowledge that if he touched his gun, he was a dead man.

The rider who had spoken called out again, "Well—what's it going to be, Henderson?"

Sky smiled thinly. "Your boss is trying to decide whether this is a good day to die."

He slid the gun gently at Henderson and saw the big man falter. Doubt rounded his shoulders, and in the end, Henderson dropped his head and moved to his left.

"Bluffed out!" the rider who had spoken to Mark cried out, and then yelled, "Well, *I* ain't!"

Sky had kept his eyes fixed on Henderson, but Mark saw the angry rider lift his pistol. "Look out, Pa!" Mark shouted. But none of them were ready. The unexpectedness of it all caught them flat-footed.

Even as Mark cried the warning, he knew it was too late.

Davis had no gun, but he threw himself forward and caught Sky by the shoulders to push him out of the line of fire. But the shot came the exact moment he reached Sky and struck Davis high in the back. It drove the breath from his body, and sent a cold streak of pain through him as he fell to the ground. From seemingly far away, he heard another shot and the sound of a woman calling his name. He felt hands pulling at him—then he slipped into smooth, black silence.

## CHAPTER TWENTY-EIGHT

# DAVIS GETS A SHAVE

★ ★ ★ ★

"Richmond! Richmond! All out for Richmond!"

Robert Winslow had been gazing out the window of the coach, dismayed with the terrible devastation of the city. At the conductor's announcement, he pulled himself up and began gathering the luggage, saying, "We made pretty good time." He helped his wife to her feet. "It looks as if we might have a time finding a hotel room. From what I can tell, most everything's been burned."

"We'll find something, Robert," Jewel assured him. "It doesn't matter so long as Davis is all right."

Captain Whitfield Winslow cocked an eye approvingly at his daughter-in-law. He got to his feet and stretched his stiff leg. "You've handled this trouble very well, Jewel." He smiled and patted her shoulder. "Davis will be all right. The telegram said the wound wasn't mortal."

Jewel's face was tense, but since the telegram from Sky Winslow telling them about Davis's injury, Jewel Winslow, for the first time in many years, forgot her own ailments—real and imaginary. She had handled the crisis better than her husband. Robert had been so shocked that he was unable to make the instant decisions he was noted for. It had been Jewel who had announced adamantly as soon as the news came, "We're going to

Richmond!" Her determined response had galvanized Robert into action, and they were on the next train out of Washington.

Now as they descended the coach to the brick pavement of the station, they were greeted by Sky and Rebekah. "Glad you've all come!" Sky said warmly.

Rebekah put her arms around Jewel, which caught her off guard. She was not accustomed to gentle expressions of affection—particularly from strangers—and *most* particularly from ex-Confederate women.

But Rebekah's face was filled with such compassion as she said, "My dear! I'm so glad you've come!" that Jewel found herself relaxing. "Davis will be so glad to see you all!"

"He's awake then?" she asked, her hand at her throat. The telegram had been carefully worded to give no alarm, but Jewel had found herself unable to break free from the pangs of fear. She had been afraid to get off the train, thinking her son might have died before she saw him.

"Oh, yes!" Rebekah smiled. "He gave us quite a fright—but after the first night he awoke with a clear mind. Actually, I've been feeling very bad about sending you the telegram. I knew it would frighten you, Mrs. Winslow—but the wound did *look* bad—"

With relief Jewel broke in, "No, Mrs. Winslow. I—I'm so happy that he's doing well, but I'd have come anyway!"

Sky laughed. "Hey, everybody here has the same last name, so using it's going to be a confounded nuisance. I move that we dispense with the formalities. Sky and Rebekah—Robert and Jewel, all right!"

"What about Whitfield?" the captain demanded, but Sky shook his head firmly.

"No, sir, you're an *institution*—and I'm not about to call an institution by its first name." He urged them along. "The carriage is over here."

Sky led the way, and when they were all aboard, he took the reins and urged the horses on. As they made their way along Cherry Street, Robert said, "I was in Richmond ten years ago." He looked at the blackened shells of the burned-out buildings and exclaimed, "Terrible! Terrible!"

"It'll be rebuilt," Sky replied.

Robert was dubious. Changing the subject, he asked about Davis. "What actually happened? You said he was shot."

"There's a group called the White Knights." He told the story in full detail, leaving out none of the unpleasant ones, but stressed at the end that Davis had saved Sky's life.

"What happened to the man who shot him?" Jewel wondered.

Sky paused. "He won't be making any more midnight calls on folks," he remarked. "He was killed as soon as he fired—and that discouraged the rest."

They continued down the road in silence. Noticing the countryside, Robert said, "Why—we're on our way out of town, aren't we? I thought we'd find a hotel before seeing the boy."

"No need of that when we've got plenty of room at Belle Maison," Rebekah told them. She smiled at Jewel. "I knew you'd want to help take care of Davis, so your room will be just down the hall from his."

"Why—we can't put you out like that!" Robert protested. But neither his nor Jewel's protests swayed their relatives.

"I'll bring you back to Richmond tomorrow if you insist" was the only concession Sky would make.

Both Robert and Jewel had come prepared to keep a formal air with their Southern relatives, but the frank, warm hospitality of Sky and Rebekah made that impossible. Neither Robert nor Jewel had been in favor of Davis's decision to go into the ministry, but as they heard the enthusiastic praise from their hosts, they began to relax their views. It was, both had agreed, *much* better than being a writer!

As they passed through the fields lining the road and were informed that they were part of Belle Maison, Robert was puzzled. "Isn't it about time for spring plowing, Sky?"

"Yes, it is." Sky wondered how much to tell them. "Guess you'll learn about it soon enough, so you may as well hear it from me."

He spoke briefly about the problems that beset them, including his refusal to go along with planting cotton. He concluded, "I don't see any future in going back to a one-crop system. That's what created the need for slavery in the first place. What I'd like is to diversify—but the bank won't agree."

"Why, I think you've got the right!" Robert exclaimed. "Have you tried to find financing any other place?"

"Sure—but there's not a line of investors waiting to put their money into farming in Virginia right now," Sky answered.

Robert studied his relative with a new interest. He had been a hardliner on the war, but had not considered the South's future. The burned-out ruins of Richmond, the fields gone to weeds, and the crisis of the planters were a graphic picture of the hardships that lay ahead. He said no more, but saw that his father was looking at Sky Winslow with a steady approval.

"Here we are," Sky announced. Both Jewel and Robert were impressed with the grace of the two-story white house, despite the fact that the fields around it were untended. When they all got out of the buggy, Sky said, "Rebekah, take them in, will you? I'll be right along."

They entered through the large foyer, and down a hall to the left. "This will be your room, Captain," Rebekah said. "And this is yours," she added, opening a door across the hall for Robert and Jewel. Then she walked to the door at the end of the hall and peeked inside. Smiling, she nodded to Davis's parents. "He's awake. Go on in."

The two men allowed Jewel to precede them. Jewel's first glance was at Davis in a big bed, with the sunlight falling on him. He was sitting up, getting a shave from a lady in a black dress. The woman immediately stepped back to a walnut washstand. Without a glance at her, Jewel rushed to her son's side, unable to speak.

"Mother!" he murmured when she straightened up. He was paler than usual, but his eyes were bright. "And Father—!"

Robert took his hand. "Son—you're looking very well!"

As the couple bent over Davis, Captain Winslow glanced at the woman in black. He walked over to her, put his hand out and said with a warm smile, "Belle! How good to see you!"

Belle saw Davis's parents swivel in her direction, but she said evenly, "Thank you, Captain. You're looking well." Then she faced Robert and Jewel. "I thought I'd finish with Davis before you got here." She put the straight razor in her hand on the washstand, and moved to leave the room.

Both Jewel and Robert had been adamant in their refusal to

listen to Captain Winslow's defense of Belle Wickham. She was, in their minds, a perfidious woman who had abused their hospitality, and was to some extent responsible for the death of their youngest son. They had held this attitude despite the letters Davis had written, giving them full details of how she had helped with the school.

Davis felt the awkwardness and said, "Wait, Belle." She paused and he motioned to his half-lathered face. "You can't leave a man in this condition! I look like something in a freak show!"

Belle hesitated, then said, "I'll come back later." She gave his parents a steady look, but said nothing as she walked out, closing the door with a soft click.

Davis picked up the towel she had left on the bed and wiped the lather from his face. "Well, Grandfather, you came along to inspect the damage, I expect?" He dropped the towel and grasped the captain's gnarled hand in his.

"I didn't know being a Methodist preacher was such a dangerous occupation," the captain voiced. "Not a lot safer than being in the army, is it?"

"I guess I'm just accident prone," Davis grinned. "Sit down, everyone! Mother, come sit by me."

"I don't want to jar your wound," she protested, but did as asked. She dabbed at some excess lather and laughed, "I'd finish shaving you if I weren't afraid of cutting your throat."

"I'm sure I'll be able to handle it in a day or so," Davis said. "The bullet didn't hit the lung or break any bones—just sort of angled out. My right side is tender, though. Can't move that arm very well. But tell me, how long will you stay?"

"I don't know," Robert replied. "Your mother got us on the train so quickly that I don't think we brought enough clothes for more than a day or two."

"Oh, you're not getting away so easily," Davis protested. "I'll be in the pulpit a week from Sunday—and you're going to hear me preach *once* at least!"

They had talked for half an hour when Rebekah came in and said, "Time for the patient to rest—and you all may want to also."

Davis hated the idea, but Rebekah won, escorting Robert and

Jewel out. The captain lingered long enough to say, "Boy, I'm proud you shed that bullet—and I'm looking forward to hearing a Winslow preach the gospel."

"Grandfather, try to talk to the folks—about Belle, I mean."

"I'll try," he promised.

As Whitfield fell asleep, he thought, *After coming so close to losing Davis to a war prison and a bullet, it'd be a shame if Robert and Jewel refused to accept the woman he loves.*

When the captain awakened later, Robert and Sky had left to tour the plantation. Rebekah was in the kitchen with Pet and Lucy, the house servant, fixing supper. "Belle's gone down to the schoolhouse, Captain," Rebekah told him. "It's that big, whitewashed building over there beside the pasture fence. Why don't you go let her show you the school she and Davis have worked so hard on?"

"Like to see it," he agreed, and ambled across the yard toward the building. Spring was in the air, and he stopped once or twice to look at the tiny flowers breaking through the black dirt, wondering what they were. The schoolhouse door was open, and he stepped inside. "Came to see your school, Belle," he announced as she lifted her head from where she was washing the windows. He looked around and nodded, "Looks real good."

She came to stand beside him. "It's been hard—but it means so much to the people here. They have so little—and they're desperate for their children to have some education."

"How many do you have?" When she told him the number enrolled and their ages, he was surprised. "How do you teach them with such a big range in ages?"

She appreciated his interest, and showed him the materials and books. As she explained how they operated the school, he watched her face. *How she has changed,* he thought. *She is still beautiful, but there's a serenity she didn't have before.* During her time in Washington, Belle had shown a restlessness she failed to conceal from him.

"That's about it," she said.

"You and Davis should be very proud, Belle. It's a wonderful thing you're doing."

"It's Davis who did it," she hastily replied. "I just help a little."

The captain had been known as one of the most aggressive

seamen in the U.S. Navy, and he had not changed. "Belle, Davis is in love with you."

"It can never come to anything, Captain!"

He saw the flush in her cheeks at his statement, and undaunted, bore right in. "Why not? Don't you care for him?"

"Oh—!" Agitated she walked to the window, and he followed. "Too many things have happened." She smiled briefly as a memory came to her. "One thing you'll be glad to hear, I think. Ever since I went to church with you that time—when the President was there—I've been running away from God. But it's different now. I've found Jesus Christ."

"Wonderful!" the captain exclaimed. "I can see the change in you." He put his hand on her shoulder. "Don't give up, Belle. God hasn't brought you this far to let you fail. My son and his wife—they'll come around. You'll see!"

Belle had always been impressed with Whitfield's calm faith in God. It bolstered her own, and she felt much better as they walked back to the house—until she saw Robert and Jewel. At the sight of them, the guilt returned, but the captain's words sustained her. And she went immediately to check on Davis.

"Come in!" he said. "I'm about ready to get out of this bed—and I can't stand being partly shaved! I feel like half a man."

"You're staying in that bed until Dr. Stevens gives you permission," she admonished. "I'll finish shaving you, though. You *do* look silly!"

She got hot water, lathered his face, and picked up the razor. She began moving it down his cheeks with a steady hand. She had learned to shave men at Chimborazo, and thought little of it, but her presence was disturbing to Davis.

His pulse raced at Belle's nearness, and he watched her violet-hued eyes follow the strokes of the razor. Her smooth, creamy skin and lovely lips were enticing. He could smell the faint odor of lavender, and he was acutely conscious of her hands on his face.

She was startled when he reached up and took her wrist. "Be careful!" she exclaimed. "You'll make me cut you!" She looked into his eyes. Her lips parted with surprise and her eyes widened at his expression. "Davis . . . don't," she faltered, and tried to pull her hand away.

"Belle, I can't go on like this," he said, tightening his grip. "You're so beautiful—and I love you so much!"

Her heart leaped and her face flushed, but she shook her head. "You've got to forget me."

"No. I can't ever do that, Belle. Winslow men don't forget the women they love. When I'm an old man, I'll still think of you—just as you are now. But if you don't love me, then I must leave. You don't know what it's like—loving someone and not being able to have that love returned!" He paused and the silence seemed almost palpable. He broke it by saying, "Belle, if you can't love me—tell me so!"

Belle sat motionless, feeling weak and confused. There was a pleading in his warm brown eyes she couldn't deny. For weeks she had struggled with her feelings for him, and now she felt her defenses crumble.

"I—I do love you, Davis, but . . ."

He put his arm around her and drew her to him. She dropped the razor and with a sob threw her arms around him. He held her tenderly until she grew still. But when she pulled back, her eyes wide with wonder, he murmured, "You're going to marry me, Belle—no arguments. I know I'm about to be kicked out of a church, and my parents have wrong feelings—and twenty other reasons why we shouldn't—but there are *two* reasons why we should. First, God is in it. I'm still old-fashioned enough to believe that He's got His hand on us."

She picked up the towel and wiped his face, then hers, smiling through her tears. "And the second?"

*"This!"* he grinned. He pulled her close and kissed her softly—thoroughly. It sent a spasm of pain through his wounded side—and a quiver of joy through her heart.

CHAPTER TWENTY-NINE

# THE WEDDING SUPPER

★ ★ ★ ★

The engagement of Davis Winslow to Belle Wickham made a profound impact on Richmond. When Davis first announced it in his pulpit, the church members gasped in unbelief. But as they left the church, they burst into uncontrollable chatter.

The headlines of the Richmond papers screamed: DIXIE WIDOW TO MARRY YANKEE OFFICER! Other newspapers in the South picked it up—killing any desire Davis and Belle had for a quiet wedding.

Belle was reduced to tears, but the captain brought great comfort. "Let 'em carry on all they please, Belle," he said, finding her weeping one morning. He put his arms around her, and when her sobs subsided, gave her his large handkerchief and chuckled. "I know it's a pain, but it'll pass. After all you've gone through, what does a little gossip mean? You've got the Lord, you've got Davis, and you've even won Robert and Jewel over—and that's a miracle!"

Belle knew it was true. She had not known how Davis had shared with his parents the story of his time in Chimborazo. But they had listened, and taken time to get to know Belle. She had been shy at first, but both Jewel and Robert had made a special effort, and it wasn't long before Belle's courage and her sweet spirit won their hearts.

In fact, Robert and Jewel had become warm friends with Sky and Rebekah, and the entire family had accepted them without reservation. They had put off their return to Washington in order to attend the wedding, which Davis insisted on having as soon as possible.

The captain looked at Belle and added, "I'm going to give you a wedding present."

"I don't want you to spend a lot of money on us."

"It's not for Davis—it's for you, Belle." Then he assumed a stern expression and said sharply, "And I don't give a continental what you want! At my age I'm entitled to be spoiled, and I'll have my way in this—or know the reason why!"

His vehemence was intriguing. "What in the world is it?"

"You'll see when I give it to you!" No more was said until a week before the wedding. One day while she was peeling potatoes in the kitchen with Pet and Rebekah, Captain Winslow called in a stentorian voice from the parlor, "Belle! Come out here—and the rest of you women!"

"Why in the world is the captain yelling?" Pet asked, and the three rushed to the parlor. Whitfield was standing in the center of the room holding a large item covered with cotton.

"Belle, here's your wedding present," he grinned. "Remember what I told you—I'm apt to have a spasm if you give me any argument! Now, help me get this thing off."

He held one end high, and Belle untied a drawstring at the top, and the cotton fell to the floor. Belle gasped—as did Pet and Rebekah.

"It's—beautiful!" she whispered, reaching out to touch the shimmering pure silk of the most beautiful wedding dress any of them had ever seen.

It was an unusual color, a pale silvery blue, with fine white lace at the neck and wrists. The captain, obviously very proud of his choice, said with satisfaction, "That came all the way from Boston. I had Lucy snitch one of your dresses for size to send with the order, so it ought to fit."

Belle could not believe her eyes. She took it from the captain and held it up as she faced them. Her dark hair and coloring set the delicate blue off perfectly.

"Exquisite, Belle!" Rebekah marveled. Pet was ecstatic, and

took it from Belle for a closer examination.

"Thank you—for everything!" Belle whispered, putting her arms around the captain. She kissed his cheek and said with a roguish smile, "What made you think I wouldn't take it? I'm selfish!"

★ ★ ★ ★

The nuptial supper was held at Belle Maison the night before the wedding, which was to be at St. Andrew's.

Davis smiled broadly at the applause as he and Belle entered the dining room. After seating Belle, he took his place beside her and commented, "There are lots of Winslows here tonight." His gaze swept across both families. "And as Tiny Tim once said, 'God bless us every one!' "

The table was laden with food, and after Davis asked the blessing, they wasted no time. Sky was immensely happy to have his family all together. After the main meal was finished, and they sat drinking coffee over dessert, he said, "I ought to make a speech, but I was never much good at that. However, I want to say how happy I am to have you here, Robert and Jewel—and you, of course, Captain!" He looked around and a slight shadow crossed his face. "We may never be around this table again just like this. But I want to thank God for letting us have each other."

Robert replied quietly, "Thank you, sir, and unaccustomed as I am to public speaking—"

Laughter erupted around the table, cutting off his words. He waited until it died down, and continued. There was a strange look in his eye, for the days with the Winslows had changed him. He had never seen such a loving family, and their commitment to Christ had silenced him. He had, as a matter of fact, been forced to reevaluate his agnostic views. His father's solid Christian life had long been a testimony to him, making Robert feel that his own vapid moral values were nothing in comparison. Seeing Davis's firm determination and the steady Christian values exhibited in the lives of Sky and Rebekah, and their children, had been somewhat of a shock to him.

"I don't think any of you can know how much it's meant to me—and to Jewel—being here, being members of your family. I didn't know such warmth and love existed. All my life I've heard my father talk about 'The House of Winslow,' but I'm afraid it meant very little to me. Now—it is very meaningful!"

Whitfield Winslow rose to his feet, fierce pride shining in his aged eyes. He said slowly, "I've always been proud to be a Winslow—but never so much as tonight! Much of my life has been spent studying the men and women who bore our name—and we've had our share of rascals, I tell you! But there's always been a man or a woman named Winslow who'd stand in the gap. Many of our men have shed their blood for this country, and many of our women have had to send their sons and husbands off to die."

He paused a moment, then went on. "I guess it'll always be that way. This country will never be safe for us. Remember how Jefferson put it? 'The price of liberty is eternal vigilance!' So this country will have to fight for what we hold true—over and over again!" He raised his head in pride. "But as long as America has men and women like you, the Republic will stand!"

He sat down, a little embarrassed at his own eloquence, but his family nodded approval. Sky spoke again. "As I say, we may never meet around this table—"

"Just a minute, Sky," Robert interrupted. He stood up, looking apprehensive, and after getting an approving smile from Jewel, he pulled a paper out of his pocket. "I don't know how you all are going to take this, but it's something my wife and I have felt we should do. I—I hope you won't be offended, Sky and Rebekah."

All eyes were fixed on him, especially the captain's. He knew his son well, and had never seen him at a loss for words. He was hesitant and nervous as he peered at the paper.

"I can't think of anything that would offend us, Robert," Sky smiled.

Robert took a deep breath and held up the paper. "I've been going behind your back, I'm afraid, Sky. Never could stand a man who meddled in the affairs of others—and now I'm as guilty as sin!" He grinned unexpectedly. "I'll make a clean breast of it. I didn't like the way Asa Moody proposed to handle your mortgage. Went by to talk to him, but he's a pretty stubborn fellow. So—I sent off a couple of telegrams to a friend of mine in the banking business. He asked for details, and I wrote him a long letter." He paused. "Well, you take us in, and I shove myself into your business! But Warfield, my banker friend, didn't think much of Moody's ways either. So, he bought your note from the bank here."

"He did what, Robert?" Sky asked, perplexed.

"He bought your mortgage and issued another from his own bank." Robert handed the paper to Sky. "This is it."

Sky took the note. "What are the terms?"

"Same interest—but the payments are spaced out over the next five years. And Warfield likes your ideas about diversification. He'll finance you until you get it all in place."

"Robert—and Jewel." Sky choked. "I . . . I can't say—"

"Business, Sky!" Robert broke in, raising his hand in protest. "A matter of business, that's all! No need to make a fuss!"

"No, Robert, it's more than that," Sky responded. "You didn't do this for business reasons."

"That's right!" the captain added. "I'm afraid I shall have to tell you what a good son you are, Robert. I've never been so proud of you!"

Robert felt a lump in his throat. His father's approval had always been the desire of his heart, but despite all his achievements he had never been sure of it. Now he looked across at the warm smile on his father's face and *knew* he had it!

Rebekah went to Robert, and with misty eyes, put her arms around him, then embraced Jewel. "Thank you, Robert and Jewel," she said quietly, "for saving our home. God bless you!"

After the meal, Dan sought out Belle. With a troubled look he said, "I—I can't believe I didn't have enough sense to see through the White Knights, Belle. I guess I trusted Beau too much."

Belle hugged him. "Dan, I can give you some good advice—don't let guilt destroy you. I know what that can do! You were misled, and Beau's going to have to find out he's headed in the wrong direction."

"I'm leaving for Texas pretty soon," Dan said. "But I'm glad I got that nonsense out of my head before I left." He smiled, then hugged her until she gasped. "If that preacher gives you any trouble, you just write me, you hear!"

"I'll take care of her," Davis said, coming up behind them.

"You'd better!" Dan laughed as he left.

"Let's take a walk, honey," Davis suggested, snuggling her arm in his. They strolled slowly down the long walk under the canopy of stars overhead.

"I'm so happy, Davis!" she murmured when they paused. "How can we *ever* thank your parents?"

"I think they're getting just as much out of this," Davis commented. "They've changed so much while they've been here, I can't believe it."

As they stood in the warm darkness, thoughts of the past washed over Belle, but she shook them off, as she had learned to do. "Well," she smiled, "tomorrow you'll have a wife—but in two weeks, you may have no church."

He put his arms around her, and his lips touched hers. "I love you so much, my darling!" he whispered, tightening his hold. Time seemed unimportant at the present as they relished the moment.

Finally Davis sighed, "There is only one Belle—but lots of churches!"

"Will you be sad if we have to go?"

"I suppose so," he replied, his finger tracing the line of her face. "But whatever happens, we'll be together."

They remained in warm embrace, letting the April moon pour its golden blessing over them, and then, arms around each other, they turned and walked back toward the house.